"If you never have read a Steve Dahl novel be sure to start with this exciting and adventurous one staged in Eastern Europe, *Onion Dome*. You will think you've guessed what happens next, but don't count on it. Full of adventurous surprises and good fun."

—*Sherry Young, columnist for the* Deseret News, *Salt Lake City, Utah*

ONION DOME

I0542069

A novel by

STEVEN I. DAHL, M.D.

Onion Dome, Published April, 2016

Cover Design: Howard Johnson

Interior Design & Layout: Howard Johnson, Howard Communigrafix, Inc.

Editorial & Proofreading: Eden Rivers Editorial Services and Karen Grennan

Photo Credits:
Kacpura, *Diamond And Gems From Oyster*. Depositphotos.
Stocker, *City Twilight*. Depositphotos.
T. Klassen Photography, *The Pryma Church*. Top Stock Photo.

Author photo courtesy of Steven I. Dahl.

 **SDP Publishing**

Published by SDP Publishing, an imprint of SDP Publishing Solutions, LLC.

The characters, events, institutions, and organizations in this book are strictly fictional. Any apparent resemblance to any person, alive or dead, or to actual events is entirely coincidental.

All rights reserved. No part of the material protected by this copyright notice may be reproduced or utilized in any form or by any means, electronic or mechanical, including photocopying, recording, or by any information storage and retrieval system, without written permission from the copyright owner.

To obtain permission(s) to use material from this work, please submit a written request to:

SDP Publishing
Permissions Department
PO Box 26, East Bridgewater, MA 02333
or email your request to info@SDPPublishing.com.

ISBN-13 (print): 978-0-9968426-1-7

ISBN-13 (ebook): 978-0-9968426-2-4

Library of Congress Control Number: 2016930815

Copyright © 2016, Steven I. Dahl, M.D.

Printed in the United States of America

ACKNOWLEDGMENTS

Many thanks go out to my patient publisher, Lisa Akoury-Ross, and my even more patient editor, Lisa Schleipfer. Special thanks to my designer, Howard Johnson, for his expertise. Many friends and family have given me good ideas. Thanks to all of you including Chuck Stoddard, Sherri Young, and Dennis Tolman.

Good health is a marvelous gift from God that we too often take for granted.

"Brayden? Can you hear me?" hollered his wife, Paula Ballard. Her voice carried as if from a megaphone up the narrow spiraling stone staircase, which led to the balcony of an ancient, Orthodox Church. "You've got to get down off of that ladder right now! It's starting to rain again and everyone else has already gone back to the bus."

She couldn't see her husband, but she knew he had climbed a rickety, wooden ladder that led from the top of the spiral stairs into the building's onion dome. She knew because ten minutes earlier she had led the ascent to the centuries-old, copper-sheeted dome. She had returned quickly to ground level when low clouds had moved in, decreasing the ambient light, and the cannon-like boom of thunder had flushed out raven-size bats. One had flown straight down from the dome's darkness, momentarily tangling itself in her curly, auburn hair. That did it for her. She had scrunched her lithe body to the side of the passage and let Brayden squeeze by on his way upward.

"I'm not coming back up there to get you," she yelled, standing on the stone floor of the ancient church.

"I hate bats!" Paula said to her best friend Julie, who had returned to the church in search of her and Brayden.

"Why were you even up there in that spooky place anyway?"

"Brayden wants to see how the architects constructed the framing and trusses inside the onion dome. He's mentioned it a dozen times as we've driven by all these majestic churches. He must have taken a thousand pictures of them the last couple weeks. I was a hundred percent on board with my goofball husband—checking out the inside structure of the dome seemed like a fun idea—until I was attacked by that bat. You should have seen the thing. It was as big as a pigeon, with beady, red eyes! It gets really dark at the top of the spiral stone staircase, and then there's a ladder that goes straight up. I'm sure he can't see a thing up there."

"I'll go tell Dennis to make sure the bus waits; he's probably out in the cemetery studying some new kind of flowers that grow best above the dead," assured Julie. As she left, she smiled at the withered, little woman sitting beside a table near the heavy, wooden exit door, hoping to sell one last candle or postcard before the church closed for the night.

The bus was waiting in the driving rain, its door closed until the driver saw Julie running toward it. The nearly full bus held an eclectic group of tourists who had spent the last twelve days touring the flatlands of western Russia, beginning the tour in Saint Petersburg and then driving south into the Ukraine before circling northwest into Poland. The final destination was to be Prague. This particular tour was a favorite of people who had seen all the usual sights of the big cities of Europe and wanted to connect with the real people and history of the smaller villages of Eastern Europe. By now some of the group had grown restless—the quaintness of the country farms, tiny brick houses, and communist-style apartment buildings were losing their savor. Tonight in particular, they were tired and hungry. Many resented having to wait for the curious couple and just wanted to get to the hotel for dinner and bed.

Eighty feet above the worn, stone floor of the three-hundred-year-old Russian Orthodox chapel, Brayden Ballard was on his hands and knees—his tiny, Magnalight flashlight stuck firmly in his mouth. Thank goodness he had worn his jeans instead of his usual cargo shorts. He was examining the space between the curved roof close above his head and the trusses, girders, and crosspieces supporting the ceiling of the church beneath his knees. The space was tight for his six-foot, three-inch frame, requiring both of his hands to maneuver. Fortunately he wasn't overweight and had been working out regularly.

In all of his architectural training, he never remembered seeing drawings or photographs of the inner structure that supports the uniquely shaped onion domes adorning the thousands of eastern European churches. It was the end of a long day of mostly driving when their tour guide allowed the group an extra hour to wander around the quaint little Polish town of Chelm. Brayden took one look at the red-and-blue dome with the late afternoon sun glinting off the gold cross on its apex and turned with a glint in his eye. He hadn't even mentioned climbing into the dome when he grabbed Paula's hand and they headed for the chapel, leaving the rest of the group to wander the town to eat gelato and barter for trinkets.

Now saliva drooled from the corners of his lips surrounding the flashlight and ran down his chin. He wasn't about to touch his face and remove the light just to answer the plea echoing from Paula's voice below. His hands were covered with bat guano, rat droppings, and probably a lot of other unmentionables. Scanning the three-foot, narrow space ahead, he could make out what looked like old rags, scraps of wood chips, plaster, and broken dowels left over from the time the dome was erected. The builders hadn't had nails at the time of construction so they had attached all of the beams with hardwood dowels pounded into hand-drilled holes.

"I should have brought a notepad and pencil," he thought, doubting that he would remember some of the unique bracing techniques the ancients had employed.

"Get down here! The driver is insisting that the bus leave now and will leave both of us behind," Paula's voice echoed up the hollow space. "Are you still even alive?"

"Crap!" he muttered, pulling the wet, slippery light out of his mouth. "I'm coming!" he yelled back. "Tell him I'm saying a special prayer for each of the passengers to save us from his reckless driving."

Reluctantly, he started to back his way around the narrow, curved space toward the ladder. He shined the light back toward the opening then wiped the slippery flashlight handle under his armpit and stuck it back into his mouth. "If only I had brought that headlight I use for night bike riding," he mumbled incoherently to himself.

"Ouch!" he yelled out as deep, burning pain shot from

just above his wrist, up his arm, and into his brain. The flashlight fell from his mouth, clattering into a space a couple of feet below. He could see blood pouring from just above his wrist as he grasped unsuccessfully for the flashlight. It rested momentarily on a ledge, then rolled and toppled three feet downward into a narrow crevasse. The pain from the laceration was intense, but the throbbing worried him much more. "It has to be an artery that's been severed," he thought, feeling pulsation under his fingertip. He looked to see what he had cut himself on and noticed a sharp, pointed, metal flashing sticking out from a corner of the beam—probably someone's modern attempt to patch a leaking roof.

The flashlight was still glowing but was definitely out of reach. Feeling his way with his feet and good hand Brayden backed toward the faint light at the top of the ladder's crawl space. He felt the irregular angles of the hand-hewn beams pressing into his already sore knees as he inched his way along. His left hand was slick with blood, but he had to use both hands to balance between the floor trusses. Then his hand slipped and both arms fell, straddling the wooden beam. Gravity jerked his head and chest forward—banging his shoulder and face on the beam between them. In the scramble to right himself he felt something—something definitely out of place.

The crusty, soft object was quite firm inside. It wasn't wood or tile or bat guano. He would never know what compelled him to reach down into the darkness a second time, but he did it anyway. It felt like fabric or maybe leather, but it was encrusted—probably with bat guano. His right hand worked its way around the object, giving it a slight tug to loosen it from the angled space. His chest and face lay on the crossbeam as he raised his arm toward his eyes to get a look, but it was too dark. The object felt like a sack or satchel, but was heavy. Something solid was inside.

"Hey, Brayden. You still up there? You need to come right now. The bus driver is honking the horn!" The firm, male voice was that of Julie's husband, Dennis.

"I'm almost down!" he screamed, wishing it were true.

He struggled to hold on to the object and get back up on all fours and finally managed to wiggle his body around to face the exit. Five minutes later he was able to make it to the top of the ladder where he finally had enough balance and headroom to sit up. With both hands on the ten-by six-inch object he figured out that it was in fact a leather bag of some sort secured at the top with a drawstring. It felt crusty on the outside as well as moist—probably from the blood that still ran freely from above his wrist. He unbuttoned one button above his belt line and tucked the object inside his shirt for safekeeping.

He now had a hand free to probe the burning spot on his arm and became dizzy when he did so. It was a long, deep laceration. At its deepest place he could feel the tendons between his elbow and wrist. He awkwardly reached around and dug a handkerchief out of his hip pocket. This he wrapped around his arm, and with his good hand and his teeth he snugged down a half-hitch knot creating a makeshift bandage. Wiping his bloody hands on his shirt and pant legs, he took a deep breath and began the struggle down the ladder to the spiral staircase, one rung at a time—the last thing he needed right now was to slip and fall the ten or twenty feet to the stone floor. When he finally made it to the ground floor of the building, his head was spinning and a wave of nausea was forcing his afternoon snack of granola bars and Coke up into his throat.

Dennis was waiting at the base of the stairs, patiently stirring the wax in a votive candle. Without a word he turned and led the way through the steady rain to the waiting bus. The dense clouds made the early evening seem like night. The tall tour bus had its engine running and window wipers slapping back and forth, and then the headlights came on as the two approached. The men were just inside the door when the booing and hissing started and continued until Brayden was settled into his seat next to Paula. There were no questions as to why he was late. No one seemed to care.

"I'm really sorry I made you all wait for me," Brayden said in a loud voice, addressing the bus full of fellow travelers, most of whom he now knew by name. He was answered again by hisses and boos—this time more subdued.

The driver turned on the interior lights, but not to help the two men navigate to the seats. Instead he stood and made the pretense of counting heads. That's when Stacey, a legal secretary from Tulsa, looked at Brayden and screamed.

"What's all over you? Oh my gosh! Mr. Ballard, you're covered with blood!"

The bus ride to the hotel was total chaos. The rain was pounding on the windshield obscuring the driver's vision, thus he insisted on turning all the inside lights off. Paula, Dennis, and Julie all were trying to help quell the flow of blood from Brayden's arm, while some of the fellow passengers craned their necks to see exactly what the problem was. Most of them, however, seemed more concerned with being late for the evening's buffet dinner or checking their e-mails when they arrived at the hotel. A couple of the younger men leaned over their bus seats confirming that the Denver architect was in fact seriously injured, and covered in blood and something else that looked a lot like bird droppings. Once Brayden's active bleeding stopped some of them complained about being late, and now the more nosy questions started coming from his curious, fellow travelers.

Luckily, Julie Cannon was a woman of action and preparedness. She had a new bottle of water in her backpack and an extra sweatshirt that she quickly tore into strips for cleansing rags and bandages. Brayden ignored the questions directed at him, burying his face in his good hand—trying to stop his dizziness—while his wife and her best friend ministered to the deep laceration.

"You have got to have at least ten or twelve stitches to pull the edges of the skin together. Hopefully you haven't cut any nerves or tendons," Julie said. "We have stopped the artery from pumping, but there's no guarantee that the slightest bump or movement won't start it going again."

"How do we find a doctor in this little town?" asked Paula, directing her question to no one specifically.

"When we get to the hotel, the people there will have some idea of where to find a good hospital or at least a decent doctor," said Dennis, hoping he was right. Even on the best map he had in his travel bag, the road they were presently on was a tiny squiggle and the names of the towns were in the tiniest print, the spellings looking more like extractions from an eye exam chart than names of towns and cities. His prediction, however, proved correct.

The cheerful female manager at the small Qubus Hotel took one look at the blood-soaked bandage on Brayden's arm and picked up the phone. Twenty minutes later, there was a knock on the Ballards' hotel room door. When Paula answered, standing in the doorway was a very tall, very attractive young woman. In her hand she held a bulky, black leather doctor's bag. She was thin with high cheekbones, dark-green eyes, and natural blond hair that came down over her shoulders in waves.

"Pardon me," said the woman in a heavy, Eastern European accent. "My name is Doctor Andriana Vlonovitski. The hotel manager telephoned to me, requesting that I come to care for a cutting of the arm."

"Yes, of course. Please come in. My husband is in the shower. Please have a seat and I'll get him," said Paula, motioning the woman to the small chair adjacent to the bed.

She knocked on the bathroom door then slipped inside the little room. She had been helping Brayden with his shower, scrubbing the dried blood and dirt while he held pressure on his wounded forearm. Now, she explained who was at the door and then helped him out of the shower. She dried off his shoulders and back then slipped the uni-size, terrycloth robe over his good arm and under and around the other. She tied the sash as best she could, and then whispered instructions for him to be cooperative with the woman doctor. "Cooperative?" he thought. "I'll do well to stay conscious."

As Paula opened the bathroom door the Polish doctor noticed the man push a filthy-looking brown bag into a corner under the sink with his foot. As he did so, several colored rocks tumbled out onto the bathroom floor. He bent down and pushed them back into the bag and tugged on the leather thongs to close it. The sight startled her and she began to ask what the items were, but then saw his blood-soaked arm and jumped to her feet, pushing the bag further under the sink.

"Thank you for coming, nurse," said Brayden.

Paula planted a light elbow jab in his ribs saying at the same time, "This is Doctor Vlonovitski, darling—did I get your name right?"

"That is close enough, but easier to just call me Andriana," the woman said, blushing at the sight of the handsome American man, his hair wet and messy and his muscular body barely half covered by the obviously too-small robe.

"I don't think it's anything serious," Brayden said, sitting down on the edge of the bed and awkwardly pulling the robe over his hairy knees.

"Would you please allow me to examine your injury?" she said in a business-like tone.

She pulled the small chair up close to the bed and carefully lifted the edge of the make-shift bandage on his forearm. Immediately, the blood trickled down onto the towel Paula had luckily slipped under his arm, saving the bedspread from a nasty stain.

"Perhaps you should lie down," the doctor said, holding the bandage tightly against his arm.

Once he was comfortably situated with his arm between them, the woman removed a rectangular object, wrapped in plastic and sterile paper. Inside there were multiple plastic trays holding an array of instruments, medications, and dressings. She slipped exam gloves over her long, thin fingers—her nails were manicured and painted a light pink. Using blunt-edged scissors, she snipped off the bulky sweatshirt dressing.

Julie had done a good job of cleaning the wound, but a long, rubbery, purple clot clung inside the gaping, six-inch-long laceration. Removing the clot revealed bare tendons and the muscle beneath. Brayden looked away, wincing in pain as the doctor probed and cleaned, and then took out a syringe and a vile of analgesic solution to begin numbing the skin in preparation for suturing.

"At home we would go to the emergency room to have this treated," Paula said, trying to make conversation and distract her husband from the intensity of the situation. "We feel very fortunate that you were willing to come here to the hotel."

"Ambulances—as we call the emergency rooms in Europe—are very busy with bad accidents, illnesses, and dying people. It is much better that you don't see that. I can make your man's arm as good as new and do it here. The only problem is that my government requires me to make a report on all knife wounds."

"But this wasn't a knife wound!" Brayden said, surprised that the woman would imply such a thing. He assumed that Paula had explained the accident. "I tore it on a piece of jagged metal at one of the onion-domed churches—Saint Ivanavich Church or something like that. It was in Chelm."

"Then we must fill out a report so that the building can be repaired. We do not want others getting injured," she said as she opened a package of suture with an affixed needle.

Brayden's arm stung when she first injected the xylocaine, but as she began to sew, his arm felt completely numb. His mind started to wander as he remembered the inside of the onion dome, dropping the light, the searing pain and finding the crusty leather bag. *I shouldn't have been up in the dome, and whatever it is that is in the bag lying on the bathroom floor, could it be trouble?*

"Actually it was a little nail and I pounded it out of the way. It won't bother anyone again," he said, rejoining reality with a white lie.

Andriana looked up at him with a curious stare and asked, "Where exactly in the church were you when you injured your arm? Were you not with the rest of your group?"

The young doctor was looking less attractive and more inquisitive by the second. Paula was passing instruments to the young woman and listening. She too was wondering, "Why all the cross-examination?"

When the woman was ready to leave Paula asked about payment. "I can take cash or a credit card, but not American Express," said Vlonovitski. "Actually, Euros are best." Paula found Brayden's wallet and gave the doctor her Visa card.

"I don't have a machine for the card but will just copy the number."

Uncomfortable at the idea, Paula started to go through her purse, sure that the woman would take US dollars, but Brayden looked at her and shook his head no. Moments later Doctor Andriana was gone along with three hundred charged dollars.

"So, how do you rate getting a movie-star-looking doctor to come to your room and sew up your arm?" chided Dennis. "I saw her in the lobby. At first I thought there was a film star or famous model staying among us."

The two couples were sitting at the end of a long dining table having picked through the buffet table leftovers. Arriving at dinner late wasn't a good idea with this tour group. When the food was gone at the buffet, the meal was finished. Dennis and Julie had been kind enough to wait for their friends to complete the medical care and get dressed for dinner. The meal might have been good an hour before, but the congealed beet soup and selection of breaded mystery meat left a lot to be desired. Even the bus driver and the tour guide already had loaded their plates and were sitting and smoking in the far corner.

"She may have been good-looking, although I didn't really notice," Brayden said, winking at Dennis. "But she was ten times as nosy as she was good-looking. She wanted to know exactly where I was and what I was doing when I cut my arm. She even suggested that it was a knife wound and had to be reported to the police like a gunshot wound is in the States. She made me feel guilty for being curious about an onion dome's construction. Actually, I don't know why I got so interested in them in the first place. There are probably dozens of sites on the Internet telling all about their design and history. I think I'll just stick with the history."

"Oh, give us a break," Julie joked. "Tomorrow you'll be finding another cobweb-filled attic to explore, or some other mystery to investigate that we overlooked. I haven't forgotten the time you made us crawl through that Japanese submarine in Hawaii. And I remember that it was after regular hours so we had to evade the guards!"

"Well, we'll see what tomorrow brings," said Brayden. "Andriana said that she would have to come back here in the morning before we leave—that I'll have to sign some official papers. By the time she left she was becoming a real pain in the butt."

"So now it's Andriana?" Dennis asked, chiding his friend.

"We should be grateful that she would come to the hotel to treat that cut," said Paula, cutting off her husband's whining. "Besides, she wouldn't even let us give her a tip above the $300, which I suspect she will have to share with her boss. By the looks of her dress she could use a little extra money."

"You mean because there wasn't enough material?" Dennis asked with a laugh that brought smiles to everyone's faces, thus changing the mood as they picked through the leftovers.

"Well, when she comes by in the morning you can offer her some of your homemade oatmeal cookies that you brought for the trip. By the looks of this meal, that may be the rest of my supper," said Brayden.

They laughed as they finished up their dinner and said good-night, but for the Ballards there was a long list of questions to answer before they would be able to even think about tomorrow.

The first thing the Ballards noticed when they returned to the room was that the mess—the bloody towels and the paper wrappings left on the table by Doctor Vlonovitski—was gone. The bed had been straightened and turned back, and there was a weird-looking candy on the pillow. Brayden went straight into the bathroom and shut the door. The dirty leather bag he had found in the church dome's attic was gone. Immediately he felt a hot flush and then a chill down his spine accompanied by a sense of unease in his gut. The rush of panic would not be calmed. He was sure he had left it on the bathroom floor, but the room was too small to hide anything and the waste basket was empty.

"Did you take anything out of the bathroom?" he asked, flinging the door open and confronting his wife.

"What are you talking about?" she asked in a defensive tone.

Brayden sat down on the edge of the bed and took a much needed deep breath. "When I was up in the onion dome rafters, I dropped my flashlight into a space between the floor timbers. When I reached down to get it I felt something wedged in a corner. I can't remember if it was before I cut my arm or afterward. Anyway, the thing was a small bag or a sack, made out of leather. There was something heavy inside. First you, and then Dennis, were yelling at me, saying that the bus was going to leave, so I stuck it down the front of my shirt until we got back here to the hotel. I didn't ever have time to open it or even get a good feel of it. When we got back to the room I wiped the bat guano off of the outside with a towel and hurried and took a shower. When I heard the doctor come in I put it on the floor in the corner, behind the wet towels. I didn't exactly expect turn-back bed service in this place."

"Could this be what you are looking for?" Paula said, lifting the disgusting-looking brown satchel off of the dresser top and holding it out to him with two fingers, like it was a dirty diaper. "It was in the corner behind the door."

Shaking his head in disbelief he took the mystery find from her and went back into the bathroom, immediately returning with a hand towel. He spread the towel out on the bed between them and carefully began to untie the leather thong at the gathered top. It reminded him of an old bag his father had saved from his childhood to hold his favorite marbles—his cat's eyes, flints, and steelies.

"It looks like some kind of money bag, or maybe a bag for the bullets they used hundreds of years ago," Paula said.

There was a knot in the leather thong securing the neck of the leather pouch so it wouldn't open completely. Struggling with it, Brayden became frustrated and went to find the Swiss Army pocket knife he always carried in his shaving kit. While he was away, Paula picked up the bag, hefting its weight, and then with the towel wrapped around it she squeezed the contents.

"It feels like it has coins or flat stones inside," she said, handing it back to him when he returned.

His sharp knife blade made quick work of loosening the leather thong. He then put two fingers into the bag's tight opening and gently pulled the neck—causing crusted flakes of dried debris to fall onto the towel. Then, to Paula's frustration, he stopped.

"Get me another clean towel, please. I'm going to dump the whole thing out, but I want it to be onto a clean towel."

She started to disagree but realized it was useless, so she stood and went into the bathroom, returning with a full-size, but damp, bath towel. She spread it out on the bedspread where she had been sitting and stood—hands on hips—waiting to finally see what really was inside the filthy, mystery pouch.

With a single motion, Brayden cupped the leather pouch in the palm of his hand and inverted the whole thing. There was the tinkling sound of metal and possibly stone on stone. When he gave the bag a little shake, its entire apparent contents spilled out onto the towel. Afraid to squeeze the bag for fear it might crack and fall apart he laid it aside on the smaller dirty towel. With his index finger extended he slowly began spreading and stirring the contents.

Paula dropped to her knees to get a closer look. "Oh my gosh," she said. The towel was covered with a rainbow of gemstones mixed with dirt, droppings, and flakes of old, dried leather from the pouch.

"There must be twenty or thirty of them," Brayden said. "And they all look like they have been cut and polished." He carefully picked up an almond-size, blood-red stone and held it toward the table lamp. In spite of the detritus that soiled it, it sparkled.

"You know jewels better than I do," he said. "What are they?"

"You know I haven't worked at that jewelry store since college, but these have to be precious stones. They look like rubies, sapphires, emeralds … I think these two are lapis lazuli … and here are several diamonds. Look Brayden, these three look just like yellow diamonds. It's strange how they are cut—no one cuts stones like that anymore. These things could be hundreds of years old."

Silently, with both of their hearts pounding and their fingers shaking, they rolled and turned and trans-illuminated the stones until they were all spread out on the full length of the towel. Paula reached over and lifted the satchel, dumping it upside down once more. To both of their surprise, out tumbled a large, dirt-encrusted, gold ring with a colored stone setting.

"What the heck is that?" Brayden exclaimed, picking it up from the towel.

"It looks like somebody's old college class ring. The thing is filthy," said Paula, taking it from his fingers. "It's got to be washed off."

He followed her into the bathroom and watched as she first put the stopper plug in the drain and then slowly ran warm water over the gold-and-blue, cut glass ring.

Little by little the encrusted dirt and grime dissolved into the water, revealing the true size and appearance of the piece.

"I need a toothbrush. Grab yours from your shave kit."

"No way! Use your own … you don't brush at night anyway," he said, smiling at her and then handing her his toothbrush.

Using small, precise strokes she brushed away the dirt and grime. His wrist began throbbing again and he became slightly dizzy watching her work. Finally, he went back to sit on the bed.

"It's a school ring all right. It must be a college or high school graduation ring? Wait, it's got some Greek letters on it. It looks like an E and an X, and there is a year … 1992. Here, have a look," she said, drying the ring with a washcloth and handing it to Brayden, who by now was lying alongside the bejeweled towel on the bed with his feet still on the wooden floor. "Are you okay?"

"I'm just a little dizzy, but I'll be fine. Any idea where it's from?"

His face was as white as the pillowcase and instead of looking at the ring he was resting it on his golf shirt. She took it back from him and moved the gem-covered towel so he could put his feet up on the bed, then bent down and lifted his legs one at a time onto the bed.

"You look horrible, I'm calling Dennis and Julie," she said.

"I'll be fine. I just lost a little too much blood and the excitement of finding all of my treasures made me lightheaded."

"I'm calling them anyway. What if you die? I don't

want the Polish police to blame me—what with all of your treasures lying around the room," she tried to joke, but got no response.

"So, you're going to tell them both about what I found?" Brayden asked in a whispering voice.

"We still have four days of traveling with them. How are you going to keep it a secret?" she said, gathering the stones, ring, and pouch into the middle of the towel and bunching the ends together. "But maybe we won't tell them tonight. That's up to you, but I'm calling them anyway." She dialed the front desk and with significant language trouble was finally connected to the Cannon's room.

Julie Cannon had been a school nurse for twenty-five years. The trip to Europe and the former Soviet satellites was, in part, to celebrate both her and her husband's retirements. The call to come check on her best friend's husband came more as a relief than a surprise. She hadn't approved of the apparent nonchalant attitude of the young female doctor regarding Brayden's blood loss. She had said as much to Dennis earlier, but he, being the eternal optimist, had insisted that everything would be fine in the morning. They were already in bed when the phone rang.

"We'll be there in one minute," Julie told Paula, and they were.

Julie showed up at the Ballards' door dressed but sans makeup. She checked to be sure the dressing on Brayden's arm was dry, and then slipped her blood pressure cuff— she would never leave home without it—over her friend's good arm and pumped it tight enough so that Brayden squirmed.

"How much blood did you leave in the church?"

His voice was weak, but he was alert enough to answer. "I couldn't put any pressure on the cut until I got down to the ground so I guess it was quite a bit."

Julie felt the pulse in his wrist and again in his ankle then stood, replacing the stethoscope and blood pressure cuff back in her travel bag, and shined a tiny light on his retracted lower eyelid. "It looks like you'll live."

"He needs lots of fluids, protein, and rest. I'll bet by morning he'll do a lot better," she said to Paula. "I can set the alarm and come back and check on him in a couple of hours."

"Thanks, but I'll wake up and make sure he is okay. If there are more problems I'll come and knock on your door," Paula said, giving her friend a hug and opening the door. When she turned back toward the bed, Brayden already was asleep.

4

"Wake up, sleepyhead," Paula whispered in his ear. "The tour bus leaves in less than an hour and you still haven't eaten breakfast. Have a quick shower then I'll change your bandage."

Paula had gotten up twice during the night to awaken Brayden and make him drink a glass of water each time. The second time she had reinforced the slightly soggy dressing on his lower arm. When the alarm went off a few minutes later, he managed to stand on his own and make it to the bathroom. He skipped his usual shower and took extra time eating breakfast. Fifty minutes later he climbed the steps onto the bus with Dennis right behind to steady him and catch him if he fell. They were the last ones onboard.

"We're off to Krakow," announced the heavily-accented tour guide as the bus pulled out of the hotel parking lot.

Brayden stared out the window at the red, tiled rooftops of the village houses. Far in the distance was the brightly-painted onion dome of the Church of Saint

Ivanavich, with its gold cross reflecting the morning sunshine.

"Lean back," Paula said as she focused her telephoto Nikon though the window and snapped five or six quick pictures of the onion dome. "We don't want to forget what the place looks like, do we?" Her husband couldn't agree more.

The breakfast buffet had done wonders for all of them. "It's the best meal of the day," they all had agreed. Nearly every hotel they had stayed at on their trip they could count on a variety of juices, cereal—even Frosted Flakes—and numerous kinds of cheese, eggs, cold meats, fruit, and wonderful breads. Many of their lunches and evening meals had been less appetizing—making them opt out for pizza. That morning had been no different, except the normally indifferent hotel staff today made Brayden feel like every eye was watching him. Maybe it was just the bulky, white dressing on his arm. Or was it the crusty leather satchel hidden away in Paula's trusty travel bag?

The first stop of the new day was a World War II war memorial where the Europeans on the tour had flocked off the bus to smoke and take pictures of one of the few places where the Polish army had put up a fight during the blitzkrieg. The four American friends stayed onboard.

"While we're alone, there's something we have got to tell you," Paula said, leaning across the aisle toward Julie and Dennis. Brayden had his head against the window watching for intruders.

"Let me guess … you're pregnant?" said Dennis.

The comment caught the Ballards off guard and

brought a quick snicker of laughter, which lightened the mood.

"Since her uterus is safely stored in the Denver hospital pathology lab, diced in little pieces, you can bet that that isn't the news," Brayden said, showing the most animation anyone had seen from him all morning.

"You are not going to believe it, but while Marco Polo here was exploring the crawl space in the church's onion dome last night, he found an old leather satchel." She reached into her spacious travel bag and produced the leather relic. "You may not want to touch it—it's filthy." Julie held her hand out anyway.

Dennis—never one to mince words—asked, "So what was in it?"

"One look is worth a thousand words. Be careful not to drop anything," Paula warned, handing them one of her white, anklet socks in which she had placed the heavy stones and hidden it in the satchel.

They sat in silence as Julie stretched the neck of the improvised container. She and Dennis each reached into the bag, felt around inside and then removed a sampling of the stones. Their surprise was evident as they examined a stone and then replaced it and retrieved a new one to see and feel. Dennis looked around to be sure they were still alone and then held one up against the morning sunlight shining through the bus window.

"I'm no gemologist, but I would venture a guess that this emerald is over ten carats," he said, "And it's one of the smaller ones in the bag."

"Someone's coming!" warned Brayden.

Seconds later the sock and satchel were again hidden

away in the zipper compartment of Paula's red travel bag—the elastic scrunchy she used when she wore her long, auburn hair in a ponytail secured the stones in the sock.

"How's the arm feeling today?" had been a frequent question all morning, and continued to be as their fellow travelers re-entered the bus. From their expressions, Brayden could tell that some of them were still upset about having to wait for him the previous night.

As they got underway, rolling through the small towns, and the road widened to two lanes, he leaned his head back against the seat and looked out of the window. A recent-model, black BMW sedan traveling slowly alongside the bus caught his eye. At first he thought he was daydreaming, but a second look confirmed his sighting. Although the car windows were darkly tinted, the rear window was down a couple of inches. He was almost certain that sitting in the backseat was none other than Doctor Andriana Vlonovitski. As the distance widened and narrowed between the moving vehicles due to the other traffic, Brayden could make out two men in the front seats.

"Paula, look! There's the doctor from last night," he said. "What's she doing here? Why are they following the bus?"

Paula leaned across the seat, momentarily crushing his bandaged arm as she pressed her face against the glass. "Are you sure it's her?" she asked, leaning back into her seat.

"Positive. What the heck is she doing here?" he repeated. "Those guys she's with look like hoodlums, with their black, shiny hair and three-day beards. They're probably all part of some kind of Polish Mafia. No wonder she was so nosy."

"Your imagination is running on overtime. Eat that box of raisins I gave you and have another drink of Coke. You need to build up your iron and stay hydrated," said Paula. She was used to him thinking strangers looked like people from their past or celebrities.

"Tell me this. If it's not her and they aren't interested in us, why in the world would a BMW be driving as slow as our bus? The other traffic is going twice as fast."

At the lunch stop, Dennis couldn't wait to get Brayden alone. The dining room was set up to accommodate tour buses arriving on a tight schedule to unload their hungry passengers and then get them back on the road in time to be ready for the next group. Their wives already had taken seats next to a couple of retired school teachers who were extoling the wonders of Polish pottery. They talked loud and were way too nosy for the men. Nodding at Brayden to follow, Dennis led them to a small table set just for two.

"Tell me the whole story about the bag," Dennis insisted after a waitress brought their plates.

"I thought I knew the whole story, but now I'm not sure." Looking over his shoulder and around the room, Brayden proceeded to tell about finding the guano-encrusted, leather bag and then in the stress of getting cut and receiving medical care, how he had forgotten about the satchel until the doctor came into the room. "When we finally dumped out the contents, there were about thirty stones—mixed evenly with rubies, sapphires, emeralds, diamonds, and two dark blue stones Paula says are lapis lazuli. As you saw for yourself, all of them have been cut and shaped, but not like we see precious stones today."

"They have got to be worth a fortune!"

"I don't have any idea about their value or even if they are real, but listen to this, the stones weren't in there alone. There was also a gold ring—"

"Maybe it belonged to some knight or a duke or the Kaiser," Dennis interrupted.

"Not likely. It's some school's class ring or fraternity ring that is stamped with the Greek letters E and X, and the date 1992, and there is a misshapen, gold cross covering the ruby-looking stone. It looks like a shield of some sort," said Brayden.

"I'd have to see it, but it sounds like a fraternity ring—probably Sigma Chi if it's American, but then it could be some kind of family crest. But, why the date 1992 and why would it be in an antique leather bag along with precious stones? And in the onion dome of a Russian Orthodox church in Poland?"

"Your guess is as good as mine," Brayden said—his mouth full of some kind of breaded, mystery meat. "But, that's not the entire story. The doctor from last night is following us in a car with a couple of guys that look like crooks. I've caught a couple of glimpses of her blond hair. I'm sure it's her."

"I swear Ballard; you can get yourself into some weird situations. A blonde in a black sedan could be anyone. Are you even sure it's a BMW and not something else? They all look pretty much the same. Why would the blond doctor be following you anyway? Maybe you are just a little low on hemoglobin. Incidentally, how is the arm doing? I can't believe how much it bled."

"It's going to be fine."

"I would have to see her myself. There are lots of good-looking blondes in Europe," said Dennis, finally digging into his plate of strange-looking food.

Later, as the mixed group of travelers was standing outside of the bus waiting with the last of the smokers to finish their fix and get onboard, Paula came up behind Brayden. She grasped his arm and whispered in his ear. "Do you think that's the car?" Then, without waiting for an answer, she got on the bus.

At first Brayden acted confused, but then he looked toward the far end of the parking lot and saw a full-size, black BMW. During their tour, they had been surprised at how many fancy, new Mercedes, Audis, BMWs, and even occasional Bentleys and Ferraris they had seen in Eastern Europe. But this one seemed to be different. It appeared to ride lower to the ground, had tinted windows, and the license plate had some kind of deflector screen, making it hard to read the letters and numbers. Unlike the hundreds they had seen on the eastern European streets and motorways, this one just looked suspicious to Brayden. It remained parked several spaces away from any other cars in the parking lot and yet closer to the buses than one would need to park. The windows were lowered a couple of inches and cigarette smoke was wafting from the openings. Just when he began to doubt it was the same car, he once again glimpsed a flash of a woman's blond hair.

"Let's get on the bus," he said to Dennis. "I don't

know what's going on, but I sure don't like it." When they got to their seats he asked Julie to trade seats so he could sit beside Dennis—something he seldom did.

"So what's up?" Dennis whispered.

Brayden looked to be sure the people in front of them had their headphones on, and were listening to the recorded tour dialogue, although it didn't matter since the couple was from Japan and could barely speak a word of English.

"It's that same car again. And I saw her blond hair again. I'm sure it's her in that car with those men. They're sitting there in the parking lot right now," he said pointing toward the lot. When they both turned to look, the car was gone.

"And where is the car?" Dennis asked, a doubtful tone to his voice.

"It was just there. Paula saw it too. It must have just left or moved behind us to follow the bus," said Brayden. "It's a black BMW sedan."

Dennis took a close look at Brayden and then across the aisle at the two wives. Paula and Julie were chatting away about some sort of hand-painted baking dishes. When he looked back at Brayden, his eyes appeared wide and anxious.

"Are you sure you're feeling okay?" he asked. "Julie, you need to take a look at Brayden and make sure he's okay."

"I'm fine … well, actually my arm is throbbing and my head hurts. I forgot to take the antibiotic that doctor gave me. I was supposed to take it with lunch."

"Maybe you better take Julie's velvet neck pillow and lean against the window by Paula and get some sleep. Have you got water?" Dennis asked, feeling real concern for his friend.

"Okay," he said, standing to switch seats again, "but keep an eye out for a black BMW sedan with a blond woman in the backseat." Dennis rolled his eyes at his friend and asked the two women to get out of their seats and reposition.

The two couples had known each other for years and had traveled together on numerous occasions. Unlike so many couples, where there was a husband or wife that one of the other husbands or wives didn't necessarily like, all four of the Ballards and Cannons liked to be together. That didn't mean that they overlooked every flaw or idiosyncrasy, for they each had several, but the four always had a fun time together.

Brayden Ballard was a brilliant man who had made a good living as an architect. His tall, muscular build, warm smile, and logical designs had been a magnet for customers. The biggest project of his career had been for the University of Colorado and had brought him national recognition as well as a handsome fee. Deciding he wanted to retire on a high note, he had recently sold his firm to three younger partners. He was now just a part-time consultant and maintained an office in his old building where he was able to work on his own schedule and could come and go as he pleased.

Dennis had never known Brayden to be paranoid, but he could get a little obsessed at times when he got on the scent of something he couldn't readily figure out. Insisting on checking out the darkest corners of the museums and castles was not unusual and had held some interesting surprises. But his recent obsession with the onion domes had become an inside joke between Julie and Dennis. Now, Brayden looking for boogeymen in black BMWs was really out of character; then again those rocks Brayden had shown them looked surprisingly real. Dennis smiled at his friend who was now snuggled into Julie's bean bag neck pillow—fast asleep. *He must have lost more blood than I thought.*

"Another *Great Church* and another *Wonderful Castle*," Paula mocked the tour guide's voice and then she and Julie pulled their rolling suitcases toward the entrance to the five-story, glass and brick hotel. They had finally arrived in Krakow after a long day's bus ride. Knowing that her husband wasn't feeling well had kept her distracted from enjoying the unique sites and the beautiful countryside. Unlike her husband, or Julie and Dennis for that matter, Paula was not a science and math person. She had attended a liberal arts university and had focused on history, art, and geography. She could name most of the major works of the master impressionists and most of their present locations as easily as she could list the birthdates of her children and grandkids. Seeing the places where history was made brought her great joy. Today had been different. She had even stayed in the bus at one of the day's most noteworthy stops, not feeling up to being reminded again of the victims of the holocaust.

"Are you coming right down to dinner?" Julie asked, seeing that both Brayden and Paula looked beat.

"I need to eat and so does Brayden. It's probably best

to eat now and get to bed early. Later you need to come by the room and have a better look at Brayden's special treasure."

The sarcastic tone in Paula's voice was unusual, but Julie knew her friend well enough to read stress in her voice. "We don't need to do that tonight if you are too tired," she said.

Paula looked around to be sure no one was eavesdropping. "Actually, tonight after dinner is good. We need to talk some sense into my husband. He is obsessed with that ring he found. He's even talking about leaving the bus tour and going back to the church in Chelm. He just asked me to check us into the room while he goes to the business center to research the Sigma Chi Fraternity website, if there is such a thing. He wants to see if someone has reported a missing ring. I tried to dissuade him, but it's useless until he gets an answer."

Brayden's mind was still foggy from his nap on the bus. He was having trouble logging on to the hotel's computer. It had a European keyboard so he kept mixing up the letters—something he was not accustomed to at home. Getting online had been a test of patience ever since they arrived in Saint Petersburg. He had never trusted using his own computer when he traveled, for fear of picking up some kind of invasive virus. He always had Paula check their e-mails and send notes to the family using her iPad. Using the hotel's computer seemed to be a safer way to search for information without compromising his personal identification. Now, at the hotel, he had to sit back and wait for the snail-paced system to download what he wanted.

He finally was on the Sigma Chi Fraternity's website. To his surprise he discovered way more information than he ever had imagined. He soon gave up finding anything on lost and found—since there didn't seem to be such a thing. But, he did find the merchandise site. There, clear as day, was a picture of an identical gold signet ring, exactly like the one he had found in the satchel with the jewels. On close inspection he noted that each school had its own tiny initials etched at the bottom of the setting, and of course the date of graduation or becoming an active member changed. He glanced up and saw that Paula was waiting for him by the elevator. Just as he was pressing the button to close out the search, he saw a small notice titled: "Missing Brothers."

The Qubus Hotel was a beautiful place compared to some of the dilapidated hotels they had stayed in while in Russia and Belarus. It appeared brand-new in contrast to the decades-old town surrounding it on the banks of the Vistula River. Their room was small but clean, and when Paula mentioned that the place had a rooftop swimming pool, Brayden was out of his clothes and into swim trunks in seconds. He had Paula wrap a woman's plastic shower cap around the bandage on his arm to keep it dry and begged her to join him. She was a water baby until after the kids came, and then insisted that she would rather watch the kids than swim with them or with him. Just as he expected she said no to the water, but at the last minute agreed to come up and watch him attempt to keep his stitches dry.

He made a good effort. The cool water seemed to wash away the stress of the last twenty-four hours. Though he couldn't swim laps, he could kick his legs and lean his head back into the water just as long as he kept the arm against the pool's dry edge. When he got out to dry off, Paula was surprised to find that his dressing was in fact dry.

"Good job, Flipper. Nonetheless, you should take an extra pain pill once we get back to the room," she said as she dried his back for him. "You do a pretty good job with armless swimming."

"You really should have come in. The water felt awesome," he said, stepping back from the door so that she could insert the magnetic door card.

"Oh my gosh!" screamed Paula as she stepped into their room. One quick glance revealed that the place was a jumble of clothes, bedding, and furniture. Their suitcases and her makeup kit had been dumped out onto the bed; even her goose down pillow from home had been slashed and the feathers strewn around the room.

"What?" he asked, as she pushed him out into the hallway.

"Stay out! They might still be in there. Run and get Dennis and I'll get the manager," Paula said, pulling the door closed and heading down the hall.

Brayden was left standing there—still dripping water—not having a clue what was going on. He didn't know what room his friends were checked into or who it was that Paula said "might still be in the room." He paused for a few seconds then reached for the door handle and pushed—half-expecting it not to open.

Instead, his hand was yanked inward by the handle. He stumbled half a step before he realized that their room—that was just moments before fully lighted—was now dark. A large, rough hand grasped his right wrist pulling him into the room and forcing him onto the floor. The towel he was holding was smashed onto his face by a fist and another strike hit him in the ear. He tried to resist being held down, but what seemed like a second person was holding his legs while his head was twisted to the side and a face pressed up against his right ear.

"Where have you hidden it?" a heavily accented voice bellowed.

Brayden tried to speak but his wadded towel was clumped between his mouth and the hardwood floor. Again the man asked the question. Brayden, finally recovering from the sudden shock of the attack, nudged the towel aside.

"Get off of me" he gasped. "I don't know what you're talking about."

The person behind him made an urgent statement in a garbled, foreign tongue and suddenly the pressure on his legs and face was gone. Before he could turn his head, the door was opened—letting in the hallway light—and then quickly shut again.

Brayden rolled onto his back in the dark room and grasped the side of the bed to try to sit up. A profound wave of dizziness hit him, so he lowered himself back onto the floor. He could feel a new pain in his injured forearm, and touching it revealed a hot wetness on the dressing. Later, he couldn't remember whether he had passed out or not, but when the door opened again and the lights were turned on, he was staring up at the ceiling wondering why the bed was so darn hard.

The Krakow police inspector spoke barely passable English, but between the man and the stylish-looking hotel manager, Paula was able to establish her and

Brayden's side of the hotel break-in story. Dennis had taken the bleeding Brayden to his room to evaluate the injuries. There was no way he would agree to be treated again by a local physician. Paula explained about the black car following them all day and about the cut on her husband's arm and the female doctor who had treated Brayden in Chelm possibly being in the black car. What she of course left out was the leather drawstring bag, the gemstones, and the signet ring.

With Julie and the inspector at her side she searched through all of their belongings to see if any of their ordinary possessions had been taken. The inspector commented about how strange it was that Brayden's gold Omega watch and Paula's iPad were laying on the floor next to his shaving accessories. Paula and Julie's eyes darted toward one another, both having the same thought that this break-in had nothing to do with watches or iPads.

The tour guide showed up and saved Paula and Brayden a trip to the police station in the city, stating that their visa was only good if all of the tour members stayed together at the hotel. The white lie was a lifesaver. Nevertheless, the crime report took hours to complete. It was past ten when Paula and Julie returned to the Cannon's room.

"Doc Dennis here did a great job of sewing my arm back on," Brayden said as the ladies entered the room. The dressing table looked like a war zone. Bloody towels and a wet bathing suit lay on the floor.

"Did the police find anything helpful?" Dennis asked.

"Not a thing, but the maid came while we were there and she and Julie put the room back together. Here's your watch," Paula said. And then seeing his questioning stare she said, "No, Brayden, they didn't find the leather bag. I didn't look inside so I don't know about the ring, but it must be there. I guess they weren't interested in dirty underwear ... that's where I hid the jewels ... inside the socks in the dirty clothes bag."

Brayden laid his swollen face back on the pillow with a sigh.

"By the way, the policeman wanted to know why you refused to go to the hospital to get treated. Did you really sew his arm back together?" Julie asked her husband.

Dennis held up a small hotel courtesy sewing kit smudged with drying blood. "He told me his head hurt so bad that he wouldn't notice any pain in his arm. Don't worry. I sterilized everything with my Old Spice aftershave."

This brought smiles to everyone's faces. Together they helped the injured one back to his room. Close inspection of the jewels was procrastinated. Just before settling onto the bed, Brayden checked a small concealed pocket in his laptop case and felt the oval shape of the Sigma Chi ring. Now he really had to find the original owner.

The American tourists awoke to a bright, sunshiny day. Other than a localized headache, Brayden felt great when he finished breakfast and headed to join the rest of the tour group for the day's activities in Krakow. His arm was tender, but not throbbing like it had been the day before.

As he approached the bus, the Krakow inspector was leaning on his gray Alfa Romeo sedan, holding a clipboard.

"Good morning Mr. and Mrs. Ballard," he said, handing Paula the clipboard. "If you would be so kind as to please autograph my document?" he asked politely.

"Do you have any idea who attacked me?" Brayden asked, but immediately realized that the question was futile. He climbed up the steps into the bus, leaving his wife to deal with the situation. Once seated, he scanned the adjacent parking lot for any sign of the suspicious BMW, but saw nothing of interest.

The bus made it just halfway around the second large traffic circle when Dennis leaned across the aisle and whispered to Paula, "There is, in fact, a large, black BMW sedan following this bus." Dennis excused himself and moved to the far back of the bus—those seats were always empty anyway—and waited for the chance to take a picture of their pursuers. He had barely turned on his camera when the car came into view. He raised the Nikon and clicked off three finely-focused shots when he was thrown forward by the lurching motion of the bus as it came to a noisy halt.

"What happened?" a chorus of protests arose from the fellow travelers, many of whom were jarred back to alertness from their early morning, post-breakfast stupors.

Dennis was the first to smell the mechanical stench of the overheated engine. It wasn't long before the bus driver was off the bus and had the engine cowling open and was diagnosing the cause of the engine's overheating: There was a cleanly severed radiator hose.

"Hooligans!" cried out the banker from Chicago.

"Damn Communists," said the mayor of a small town in Maine.

Brayden climbed down the bus steps and conferred with his traveling partners. "Did you see the car?" he asked.

"I saw it all right, and just like you said, the blond-headed doctor was in the backseat behind the driver," said Dennis. "I snapped off some shots with the telephoto lens on the camera."

"What's going to happen now?" Julie asked.

She didn't have to wait long. The bus driver made a call and shortly received one back. The tour guide reassembled the group onto the bus and with the microphone announced that the bus was damaged and had to be repaired. Due to the busy tourist season there wouldn't be a replacement for at least a day. The good news was that there were enough rooms back at the Qubus hotel for them to check back in. Taxies had been called and would be there shortly. Unfortunately, they would have to spend one less day in Prague; he apologized, but promised to organize a "fun day of special activities in Krakow. You have only seen one-tenth of the marvelous things in this city. Now, you can see the rest of them."

The murmurs and grumbling were met with the ever-present, vocal optimism of the spinster twins from North Dakota, who suggested that they all sing songs while they waited for the taxies. Brayden had another idea. His two Diet Cokes and four Advil finally had kicked in. He dug out his guidebook and opening the map of Poland and Belarus, started calculating the mileage back to the town of the red-and-blue onion dome.

"Paula, I'm going to go back to that little town to find some answers. If Dennis will go with me, fine. But, while you wait for the bus to get repaired I'm going to find out how that ring ended up in that church tower."

"You have got to be kidding!" Paula said in protest, but knew in her heart that he wasn't. "Twenty minutes ago you could barely hold up your head." She watched as he whispered to Dennis, who looked at him with a questioning stare, but then nodded in agreement—a slight smile on his face.

The men made sure that their wives retrieved the luggage from stowage under the bus and were able to check back into their rooms. They also made sure they had enough cash for the day's odd expenses, and then Brayden checked his backpack. He borrowed Paula's extra bottle of water, gave her a kiss, and then started walking away from the group with Dennis just steps behind. When the first taxi came around the corner, he and Dennis were in it before it came to a complete stop. And then they were gone.

From across the nearby parking lot, the events surrounding the bus were observed. Doctor Andriana Vlonovitski leaned forward in the deep, leather seat and appeared to give instructions to the driver. When the burly man in the front passenger seat began to protest, she reached forward and slapped him on the back of the head and scolded him for several minutes. This gave the taxi a two-hundred meter head start. They then followed the black car.

The taxi driver spoke fair English, and after a short give-and-take agreed to give the Americans a flat rate plus his fuel expenses for the day's excursion. They had a lot of kilometers to travel, thus the scruffy-appearing man—with greased-down hair and Coke-bottle-thick glasses—drove like a wild man, or maybe that was how everyone in Poland drove The driver, "Alexandy," was cheerful and curious and in his broken English tried to make conversation with his fares. Before long he quieted for lack of response and concentrated on the road ahead. They were driving against the incoming traffic as they left the city and once on the country highway were able to go even faster. The only slowdown was for the speed trap cameras as they entered each small village.

Dennis pulled a paperback from his backpack and tried to read. Brayden just stared out of the window, often glancing back to look for anyone following them. It would be impossible, he concluded, to keep pace with Alex's rally-car-like driving.

"Let me tell you my plan," Brayden said, leaning

against Dennis, and steadying his injured arm. "I'm certain that in the rush to get out of the church's tower, I overlooked something. The woman and her friends know that I found something in the church, but I don't know what it is or even how high I was when I found it. My guess is that there hasn't been anyone up in the onion dome's loft for years. What I want to do is climb back up there while you keep a lookout. I have a good light and can take my time."

"And just what do you expect to find?" Dennis asked for the third or fourth time.

"Well, if I find some clue to the whereabouts of the owner of the ring, it might give some sort of closure to the guy's family."

"We don't know what we might find. There could even be someone's body up there as well as some kind of clue as to where all this loot came from," said Dennis.

"Why else would someone leave his fraternity ring and a bag of jewels in a church attic unless his life was in danger? And if he isn't dead, why not come back for it?"

"Suppose you actually find something—say a body or skeleton or some other clue? What are you going to do then?" asked Dennis.

"Contact the local police of course," stated Brayden. "What else could we do?"

Dennis turned his head toward the window. His only conclusion to the plan was that the combination of Brayden's obsessive personality and the pain medication was convoluting his thinking. He was beginning to think that the idea was a waste of time and wished he had stayed in Krakow with the women. He gazed out the taxi window at the passing countryside wondering when this wild adventure would end. They entered another wide traffic circle in the middle of nowhere. As they took the third exit toward Chelm he thought—no, he knew—he saw the black BMW. A cold chill shot through his body.

"Say, Brayden, how about we go to the police first and let them help us search for clues? Did you bring the ring and the bag of rocks?"

Brayden thought about the question and was about to launch into what he considered a rational answer when chaos erupted. With the loud roar of an engine and screeching tires, a car flew through the traffic circle's yield sign and crashed into the back of their taxi. All three of the men's heads smashed back into the headrests as the Fiat taxi jolted forward and then lost control. The driver did his best to steer the car, but the momentum transferred by the much heavier sedan forced the Fiat into oncoming traffic. A huge, sixteen-wheel freight truck veered off the road to avoid crushing the taxi and ended its travel in the bushes alongside the narrow road, dumping its load of scrap iron across an adjacent field.

The Fiat taxi clipped the rear bumper of the truck and started spinning like a top. The second or third time around, it too skidded into the three-foot-deep ditch and came to an abrupt halt lying at a thirty-degree angle. Fortunately, the driver and the two passengers had their seat belts fastened. As the dust settled, Dennis was half-suspended by the seat belt and was in danger of falling onto Brayden when and if the belt gave way. The driver wasn't as fortunate. He had been thrown toward the front passenger seat by the car's gyrations and then back under the steering wheel with an abrupt deceleration as the car hit the ditch.

It took what seemed like minutes before the men in the backseat were thinking clearly enough to realize what had just happened. There was the acrid smell of electrical burning and the nauseating odor of diesel fuel mixed with the dust that hung inside the car.

"We've got to get out of here!" shouted Brayden. His shoulder was wedged against the broken window, which was up against the dirt wall of the ditch.

"Help me get some slack in this seat belt so it will release," Dennis said, ignoring the shattered glass. He reached across the car, grabbing the driver's headrest and pulling his body upward. This allowed Brayden to push the release on the belt. The door was stuck, so searching for footing and finding the passenger seat headrest, Dennis was able to push his body up and out of the broken rear window. He could feel crumbled safety glass shards scrape his belly and knees as he tumbled onto the ground.

"Wait a second and let me see if I can pull the door open from out here," he shouted to Brayden.

"Try to get the driver out and I'll come through the window."

By then the truck driver and several passersby were standing beside the car and were organizing themselves to help. The taxi driver was unconscious, but the risk of fire was too great for them to wait for the paramedics to extract the man. A large fellow in motorcycle leathers asked the others to step aside. With a loud groan he pulled the passenger door open, leaned in and grasped the driver by the shoulders, and eased the man out through the door onto the ground. Everyone, it seemed, had cell phones, and within minutes the wail of sirens could be heard.

There was total confusion on Dennis and Brayden's part as they tried to explain to the police and paramedics what had transpired. Everyone spoke at once and none of the conversations were in English. The police examined the rear bumper of the taxi and listened to the truck driver's story. No one seemed interested or understood what the Americans had to say regarding how the accident had occurred. Fortunately, the car had not caught fire and after some first aid, the taxi driver had awakened and was placed in an ambulance and driven away. Over an hour went by before a tow truck arrived and the scene was cleared. The freight truck managed to drive out of the ditch, and using the forklift hanging on the back of the truck, soon had his load back on the truck and was headed down the road.

Brayden and Dennis were shaken, but the paramedics had given them just a cursory exam and then turned their attention back to the taxi driver. The Americans had gathered their backpack and found a shady bus bench near the scene to rest on. Much to their surprise, after the tow truck and the semi left, the police got in their cars, and without further discussion, drove away. Brayden and Dennis were left, right there along the side of the road, to fend for themselves. They could see the church steeple of the nearest village, but could only guess its distance.

"Now what?" Dennis asked, his head leaned back against a cement light pole.

"They could have at least offered us a ride into the town," Brayden said. "As to what now, we need to find another taxi or someplace we can rent a car, or I guess we can wait for the bus and hope it's going in the right direction. I still want to go to the church. We owe it to the man who lost his ring—at least to make sure his body isn't lying up there with the bats."

As it turned out, the police hadn't abandoned them after all, but just didn't know the words to explain their plan. The Americans had started walking toward the village, but had only gone half a mile when a cream-colored Skoda sedan pulled up alongside of them and stopped.

"Police call me. Say you need taxi," the skinny, young driver said. "I take you. Cost fifty Euros to go to next town. If you want to go to Krakow, cost hundred Euros."

Before Brayden could answer, Dennis had his hand on the door handle and was getting into the car. Brayden took a slip of paper out of his pocket with the name of the church in Chelm and handed it to the driver, then walked around to the other side and snuggled into the narrow space in the back.

"Can you give me a little more leg room?" Dennis asked the driver.

"No problem Joe, I got short legs. No good food as boy," the driver said. "My name Nickzilosky Mizkylinzki— just call me Nick. You pay me fifty Euros now?"

Brayden dug into his pocket and withdrew his money clip. He peeled off a twenty and a ten Euro note. "I pay the rest when we get to Chelm."

Without further discussion the driver did a rapid

one-eighty and headed east. At first he had the car radio blaring on a low-fidelity, Polish news station with musical commercials. Dennis tapped him on the shoulder and asked Nick to turn it down, but instead he shut it off and began a non-stop, tour guide speech in English that was so broken neither man could follow exactly what he was saying.

The countryside was beautiful, and in spite of the new aches and pains from the taxi accident, and his arm laceration, Brayden was feeling good. He interrupted Nick with a few questions about life in Poland. Dennis had drifted off to sleep. When they stopped for fuel and a break Brayden let Dennis continue his nap and got in the front seat to visit more easily with Nick, whose English was getting better with each sentence—like he was getting warmed up. In spite of the comfortable feeling he was having Brayden kept looking in the rearview mirror for a black BMW.

It was just after one when the Skoda came to a stop in front of the onion dome church. The sunny day had faded as gray clouds filled the sky. There were a few locals on the main street leading to the churchyard, but the shops had all closed for the midday meal and rest.

"Time to wake up buddy," Brayden said, tapping on Dennis's knee.

Dennis jolted awake with a look of defensive anger on his face. "Get away!" he shouted swinging his arm toward Brayden. In his hand was the pocket knife he always carried with him. The largest of the blades was open.

"Whoa! Dennis wake up! We are here at the church."

Dennis shook his head and looked around, then folded the knife blade and crawled out of the car. That was the first time Brayden saw the matted blood on the back of his friend's head. Neither of them had mentioned any specific injuries after the wreck, but Dennis had obviously hit his head and possibly had a concussion.

"Nick, change of plans, you need to take us to the hospital," Brayden instructed as he looked at the half-inch long laceration at the base of Dennis's hairline.

"Forget it," Dennis said pulling his head away from his friend's inspecting hands. "I'm fine. It's just a scratch. Let's get this dome checked out before it starts to get dark. Those clouds look menacing."

Nick tugged on Brayden's sleeve and held out his hand to be paid.

"You wait here," Brayden said. "In one hour you take us back to Krakow."

"No way, Joe! Krakow is long way. Cost two hundred Euros."

"Fine," said Brayden. "I'll pay you when we get there … but not two hundred. Now you wait."

There was a small café a few doors down from the church. Brayden took Dennis into the surprisingly clean rest room, and using paper towels and some hand sanitizer from his backpack, cleaned up the wound on Dennis's head.

"Why didn't you show this to the ambulance guys?"

"Did you notice their hands? They were filthy," Dennis said. "I'm better off with my own bacteria—American bacteria."

Ten minutes later the men were back at the church

and had hidden their backpacks behind one of the pews. The only person visible in the entire church was an old woman dressed in black who had her head bowed in supplication. The men silently slipped into the alcove leading to the circular stone steps ascending upward toward the dome.

Brayden had purchased a new little flashlight at a shop in the Krakow hotel. He turned it on as they entered the dark stairwell.

"Are you sure your head is feeling good enough to do this?" he asked Dennis.

"I'm fine, but let me go first and you follow with the light."

The spiraling staircase was even narrower than Brayden remembered. The steps were rounded off from centuries of wear. Each step was anchored into a central, stone column—making them ten or twelve inches wide at the outside and less than one inch wide at the pivoting edge. Around and around the men went as they ascended, their feet occasionally slipping off of the narrow part of the stone. There was a small, vertical "loophole" that allowed in light. It gave them new confidence each time they circled to the outside wall.

"These slits look like the ones we've seen in the fortresses and medieval castles we've been visiting," commented Dennis, stopping to peek out and to suck in a breath of fresh air. The rising temperature of their bodies in the narrow stairwell, combined with the mildew smell, made the air difficult to meet the demand of the men's rising heart rates and their increased demand for oxygen. Brayden was getting more anxious with each step. He calculated that they should be nearing the vertical ladder at the base of the dome when he stopped at a loophole and held his wrist up to the narrow beam of light. He took a sigh of relief when he confirmed that the dressing was still dry. It had been throbbing ever since the auto accident.

As he turned away, a flash of the sun's reflection caught his eye. A car was pulling into the church parking lot. It was too far down and far away to be sure about the car itself but the head of a blond woman sitting in the backseat was unmistakable.

"They're here! You know, our buddies in the black Beemer," Brayden said to Dennis's rump as he caught up with his injured friend making the last turn of the staircase.

"That's just great! We're trapped up here in this vertical dungeon with the bad guys below. Too bad we don't have a few hundred gallons of boiling oil and shot put-size rocks to dump down on them. The worst thing is we don't even know what it is they want."

"Get moving and maybe we'll find out," said Brayden, nudging Dennis toward the narrow, wooden ladder.

Brayden needed both hands to climb so he agreed to go first and let Dennis shine the light up the ladder. The old, dry wood creaked with the weight of the two men. True to form, and of their poor luck thus far, just as Brayden wiggled into the opening of the dome, he banged his head on the inner framework, biting his tongue in the process. An unsettled family of beady-eyed bats squeaked in protest, and then with a flurry of wings flashed by Brayden's face.

"What was that noise?" Dennis whispered from two feet behind.

"That was the sound of a skull being fractured and a family of bats having a good laugh," Brayden said, dragging his body onto a flat spot and massaging the goose egg that was forming on his balding pate.

With both men finally inside the actual inner dome, and having a good flashlight, they were able to look at the magnificent arching and bowing of the wood the craftsmen had accomplished.

"Look at those dowels and those perfectly sized wedges that lock the trusses and beams in place. This place is like a hundred-ton, Chinese puzzle box—and to think they did it all without power tools or cranes or good lighting. What a masterpiece!" Brayden concluded.

"There is your other flashlight," Dennis commented, shining the light into a deep niche. He crawled forward and leaned down onto his chest. With outstretched fingers he was able to tease the Magnalight close enough to grasp it. "Got it," he said with satisfaction, groaning as he carefully sat up in the cramped quarters. "I hope you brought extra batteries."

Always a good Boy Scout, Brayden dug into a pocket in his cargo pants and handed Dennis two AA batteries and held the light while they were installed. "You go that way and I'll circle this way. Look for anything—and I mean anything—that looks out of place," said Brayden.

Flashes of light jittered to and fro on the timbers as the men started their search of the thirty-foot diameter crawlspace. More bats screeched and fluttered about, protesting the intrusion, and the men mumbled and groaned, bumping their shins and elbows as they wiggled their way—away from and then toward one another.

Brayden had navigated just ninety degrees of the circle when he stopped. An air vent from inside the church dome blocked his progress, making him climb higher on the convex surface in order to get around it. That's when he saw the dusty, crumpled body.

Krakow appeared to be a very busy and interesting place for the ladies. There were a lot of places in the hotel's guide book, "In Your Pocket," to see—including the old Jewish ghetto. There were numerous interesting places to eat and, of course, shopping of every sort from a daily flea market, to the more famous Paris design houses that had infiltrated every major European city.

They had left the hotel shortly after their husbands departed. The hotel provided a free boat shuttle to the base of the Wawel Royal Castle giving them an overview of the city. They took a tour through the centuries-old castle, and then headed for the center of Old Town and the main market square. They paid the driver of a six-place golf cart to take them on a low-speed, high-information tour that would include the Old Town, the Jewish quarter, a place called Schindler's factory, and the Jewish ghetto. Just as they were pulling away from the curb a Caucasian woman with dyed red hair, dressed in jeans and a red, silk blouse stepped in front of the cart and held out a hand to stop them.

"I'm by myself," she said in accented English to the handsome driver. "Would it be possible for me to join you? I'll pay my share of the tour."

The college student guide turned to Paula and Julie for their approval. They both shrugged their shoulders, having no good reason to deny the woman and a discounted fare. "Sure," they said in unison.

The woman, who looked thirtyish, climbed into the front seat next to the driver. This partially obstructed their view, causing a fleeting disappointment, but they adjusted quickly and were lost in the sights and history.

The driver plugged his iPod into the cart's speakers and soft, Polish music began to play. Dialogue began and the church in front of them was described in detail. Occasionally, the driver would turn to the three women and give his personal description of what they were seeing and answer their questions. The woman in the front didn't actually seem all that interested in the history. When they stopped at a fourteenth-century church and were encouraged to step inside to see the special, hand-carved, wooden encasements around the pillars, she remained behind.

"Something is weird about that woman," Julie whispered as they walked up to the gilded alter.

"She seems anxious," said Paula. "She keeps looking all around and over her shoulder but not really seeing the sights the man points out."

Back in the golf cart, Julie leaned forward and attempted to start a conversation with the woman, but just then the music and dialogue restarted and driving over the rough cobblestones also made conversation difficult. Julie gave up and as the tour proceeded, losing interest in the nervous woman. The tour finished in the main market square near where they had started.

"Thank you for letting me join you," the woman said, taking money from her small Prada bag to pay the driver.

"It was our pleasure," said Julie. "We were just going to find a sidewalk table and have a light lunch. Would you care to join us?"

"That is so kind of you, but I need to check out of my hotel and get to the airport. I'm flying back to America today." She offered her hand to the women but didn't offer her name or any more personal information. Moments later she was lost from view in the market square crowd.

"She seemed really nice," commented Paula, "for a blatant liar that is. I saw her passport when she opened her purse. It was Russian—not US."

"But why would she lie to us? I mean what is the point? Why would we care?' Julie asked.

"Why would a woman with a Russian passport have a fake, midwestern American accent and be wandering around all nervous and spooky acting in a Polish city?" Paula added.

Their questions went unanswered. They found a table at a small Italian tratoria and ordered soft drinks and a pizza Margarita. The stone buildings lining the square still hadn't heated up from the previous night, so the temperature was comfortable. The waiter took his time taking their order, but the food came quickly thereafter. They were trying to decide on what to do during the afternoon when they heard the woman's voice. It wasn't hard to pick out in the babble of foreign languages parading by.

It was for sure the woman with the red blouse from the golf cart. She was walking slowly and talking to a pair of policemen, but she wasn't speaking English. The three of them were scanning the faces of the passersby and the customers at the tables. A small Italian Cyprus tree in a pot partially concealed Paula from their view. Julie, feeling suddenly nervous, removed her yellow sun hat, and her big sunglasses and let her long blond hair down—giving her a somewhat different look. Nevertheless the trio turned toward Julie and Paula and the woman pointed straight at Julie.

"Are they looking for us?" Julie asked.

"Why would they be? We haven't done anything wrong," Paula answered.

The police ignored the pointed finger and passed by the ladies, turning instead toward the restaurant next door. Paula, keeping them in her peripheral vision, stood slowly and walked toward the inside door, past the kitchen and restrooms. When out of sight of the police, she quickly descended the spiral steps into the ladies restroom. Once inside, she pulled a black scarf from the bottom of her purse and wrapped her head. She was pretty sure that she had worn her sunglasses on the golf cart tour, so she put on her reading glasses and headed back up the stairs. She peeked around the corner just in time to witness a scene only the movies could make believable.

Julie was being briskly escorted from the tiny table by the two uniformed policemen. A blue-and-white police car, with it lights flashing, had appeared on the pedestrian-only plaza and stopped in front of the tratoria. Julie was led to the car where she was pushed over its hood. The smaller of the policemen held her arms while the other one did a rough pat down. As she tried to stand up straight a third man—the driver of the car—screamed at her in Polish. The woman in the red blouse was nowhere in sight.

Paula fought her impulse to grab a wine bottle from one of the tables and rush the policemen to free her friend, but she was vastly outnumbered. Survival instincts, which she didn't realize she even had, made her crouch down behind a counter and observe. A mob of spectators had gathered around the car, making it hard for Paula to see exactly what was happening. Julie had her head on the car's hood and was now being handcuffed with her hands behind her back.

Paula's mind raced through the possible causes for the apparent arrest, foremost among them being the probable actions of her idiot husband, Brayden. *What had he done now?*

Two hundred kilometers and five hundred years away from their wives' problems, trapped in the attic of the church tower, Brayden and Dennis had their own concerns. It had taken Dennis nearly ten minutes, numerous wood slivers in his hands, and painful bruises on his shins to circumnavigate the inner structure of the onion dome. He hated the architect who had made the space so narrow, angulated, and rough. When he finally made it to the area by the internal vent, he found Brayden lying flat on his belly shining his light into a space below.

"It's the body of a man," Brayden said in a near whisper. "The body looks mummified, but the clothes are still there. Look, he's wearing a Polo golf shirt and khaki slacks. I can even see his shoes—brown penny loafers with no socks. This guy has got to be an American."

"He's got to be the owner of the ring. Can you reach down far enough to get to his hip pocket? Maybe he's still got a wallet," Dennis suggested.

"I can't do it. It's not that he is so far away, it's just that he is wedged into the angled space between the roof trusses and the ceiling of the dome. It's like he forced himself into the crack to hide and couldn't get out. Lie down here on this beam and I'll move so you can see better."

It took considerable contortions, but with Dennis's smaller frame he could wedge himself down into the space without lying flat. In that position, nearly standing on his head, he could touch the body.

"I think I can get a hold of his belt ... just a second ... I think I can turn him ... hey!" he shouted as a pair of bats flew past his face.

"Can you feel a wallet?" Brayden asked. He was finally sitting in a reasonably comfortable position rubbing the knot on his head.

"I can't breathe down here," Dennis said, turning his head upward toward Brayden. "The ammonia from all of the bat guano is overpowering. That's probably what mummified Ralph Lauren here."

"Do you want me to trade you? My arms are longer," Brayden offered.

"No! If you get stuck down here you'll never get out."

"Then try reaching into his pocket again," encouraged Brayden.

The silence of the inner dome was interrupted by occasional cooing of pigeons on the outside ledges, brief gusts of wind, and the groans of Dennis Cannon as he stretched his arms to the limit.

"Brayden?"

"What?"

"I've got it!"

"Got what?" Brayden asked in frustration, not being able to see anything from his position, with his outstretched arm pointing his flashlight into the crevice filled by Dennis's body.

"I have a leather wallet," he whispered—almost in reverence. "Can you reach my belt and pull me out a little until I can get my left hand free?"

"Don't drop it! Whatever you do, don't drop it," Brayden pleaded.

"That shouldn't be too hard. There is a hole through the middle and I have my little finger hooked in it," said Dennis.

More groans and grunts filled the sun-heated space as the men twisted and turned to maneuver their way out. As an afterthought Brayden leaned back around the corner of the vent chimney and dug deep into his hip pocket. His iPhone didn't have a European SIM card—making it useless for calling—but he supposed the camera would still work. Why he hadn't thought of it earlier made him feel stupid. He pointed the tiny camera's lens toward the deep crevice and touched the exposure button three separate times. There was a flash on the third touch.

Now, he had proof of the body's presence. It wasn't just their imagination.

Dennis's flashlight flickered on and off and then wouldn't come back on. Needing his hands free to grip the wallet and still maneuver his body, Dennis dropped the light, letting it clatter downward until it found a resting place. It flashed back on again, creating a weird showdown of the two men on the far timbers, and then it went off. Brayden's little light was still working, but of little help to Dennis.

"I'm getting lightheaded from these fumes. I think I got some photos of the guy, but I've got to get out of here."

As the men awkwardly inched toward the exit, a dim exterior light became visible.

"We're almost there," whispered Dennis, immediately wondering why he was whispering.

"Please don't drop the wallet," nagged Brayden.

Finally able to stand erect, and clear of the overhead beams, the two men paused at the top of the ladder to catch their breaths. Dennis showed the brown, leather men's wallet to Brayden using the fading glow from his flashlight. Just like Dennis had claimed, there was a half-inch hole punched clear through the middle the wallet.

"Do you want to look inside of it now?" Dennis asked.

Brayden didn't have time to answer. A loud voice echoed up the spiral staircase and ladder tunnel.

"Mr. Ballard? Are you up there?" The voice was familiar, female, foreign-accented, and definitely not wanted.

"Great, just what we need," said Brayden in a disgusted whisper.

"I guess she and her gorilla friends have become tired of just shadowing us," Dennis said. "Any chance there is an alternate way out of here?"

"There are lots of doors on the ground floor but we have to get there first."

"Where's that bucket of boiling oil when we need it?" Dennis said. "Here, you keep the wallet and I'll go down and confront them. Maybe I can give you a chance to get out of one of the side doors. You remember seeing a police station on our way through the village? I think it was just next to a bakery."

"I'll try to get there, but don't you do anything brave. All four of us know that female doc's face. Remind her of that and maybe they'll be a little nicer," said Brayden. "You sure you want to go down there alone?"

"Hello down there!" Dennis yelled as he put his foot on the first rung of the narrow ladder and started a slow descent toward Dr. Vlonovitski and her apparent buddies. He turned toward Brayden. "If we get separated, how about we meet at the police station?"

"It's a date," said Brayden.

He took one last look around the inner dome, searching for something—anything that he could use for a weapon. Just as his light was flickering out he saw it. *It* being the flange of metal flashing that had lacerated his arm thirty-six hours before. Gripping it carefully with his handkerchief, he wrapped around the edge and was able to wiggle it free from its wedged-in corner. It felt like a scrap of modern, galvanized roofing material about ten inches long and two inches wide. *A near-perfect butcher knife.* He stuck the discovered wallet in his front pocket, next to his money clip. He tucked the homemade stiletto in his back pocket. *Now, to get down and not get caught.*

"Hey, how are you folks doing today?" Dennis asked as he emerged from the narrowly arched doorway. "I hope you're not planning on going up that stairwell. It's like a pizza oven up there and the view is terrible. Look at my shirt, it's soaking wet."

Facing him were two hefty-looking men, both with darkly colored, silk shirts—the collars open, revealing gold link necklaces. One of the men had a manicured mustache that turned down at the corners, giving him a Tombstone cowboy's look. The other wore a three-day stubble and a single earring of thin gold. He was leaning against the stone wall, his right arm concealed behind his back.

Standing to the side, but slightly behind the two men was Doctor Andriana Vlonovitski, her silky blond hair aglow in a beam of afternoon sunlight that had found its way through a stained glass window near the church ceiling. When Dennis got close enough to see the three faces he knew none of them were smiling.

Without any hesitation he headed straight for the front door, past the rack of prayer candles and a small "word of honor" postcard stand with its metal canister ready to accept change for the cards and candles. None of the three people spoke to him, but he could hear quick footsteps and then the moustache man planted his muscular body in front of the ancient, wooden door.

"Aren't you going to wait for your colleague to come

down?" the man asked in an accent almost too heavy to be understood.

"My friend is already outside," said Dennis, struggling to come up with a workable lie. "I'm supposed to meet him at the police station. He lost his mobile phone here two days ago. He's checking at the police station to see if anyone turned it in—you know—the lost and found?"

Dennis tried to step around the man, but viselike hands grabbed his arms from behind, pulling him backwards, and wrenching his shoulders.

"Doctor!" Dennis screamed. "Tell your friend here to get his hands off of me."

"You should not—"

As the woman started to speak, Dennis twisted violently to his left, then instantly swung his right elbow upward, breaking the man's grip and smashing his elbow into the cheek of his assailant. Thirty years of summer National Guard training camps with their frequent hand-to-hand combat training hadn't been entirely forgotten. Dennis ducked a thrown fist and grabbed a row of candleholders with their burning candles and hurled the hot wax and flames into the face of the mustached man. As though being chased by a hungry gray wolf, he zigged and zagged in and out and around the massive stone pillars of the pew-less church until he and his pursuers were at the opposite end of the building from the exit. Then, like a racehorse out of the starting gate, he sprinted for the exit. From his peripheral vision he saw the blond doctor watching—but not moving—as Brayden emerged from the shadows just in time to open the massive entrance door. The timing couldn't have been more perfect if it had been rehearsed.

"Slam it!" Dennis commanded Brayden as they both cleared the building's threshold. And he did with a vengeance.

Even from outside the medieval chapel, the thunderous crash of the six-inch thick wooden door was eclipsed by the scream of one of the pursuers as his hand was crushed in the door jam.

Outside the church the only other sound was that of an old, two-stroke tractor motor working in a distant field. The village was quiet. Brayden glanced around the church door hoping he could find something to block it from outside, but there was nothing short of the key for the lock to do so. "Let's just run," he shouted unnecessarily, since Dennis was already ten yards ahead of him. Brayden hadn't forgotten the piece of metal flashing in his hand. As he ran past the black BMW, he bent down and made an angry slash at the side wall of its front tire. Although the metal felt like it made a cut, the tire appeared untouched.

They had just cleared the corner of a line of small houses when they heard the shouts of the men from the front steps of the church. They ran until both were exhausted and completely out of breath, and then they ducked into a small patch of field corn whose tassels were above their heads. Sneaking down the corn rows to the end of the field, they finally collapsed into a knee-high field of pasture grass. They lay there panting and trying to listen. The shouting stopped and was followed by the sound of car doors slamming, then the screeching of tires.

For what seemed like hours they heard the car's high power engine racing up and down the narrow streets of the little village then finally the sound was gone.

"You think we're safe?" Dennis asked. Not waiting for an answer, he stood and then quickly ducked back into the rows of corn.

"Where are you going?" Brayden asked.

"We need our backpacks, and I'll bet a six pack of Mountain Dew that our friendly taxi driver is still waiting for his money."

"What about the dead guy's body?" Brayden asked, his mind turning the clock back an hour.

"I'm all for getting out of here and letting the Polish police in Krakow investigate," said Dennis.

8

"We are truly sorry madam," the police captain—his badge said Akardiski—told Julie as he extended his hand to assist her from the backseat of the sedan. The man's English was word-perfect, with a slight British accent. At his side was the United States consulate's attaché in Krakow, who had introduced himself as Steven Hicks.

Paula was standing on the hotel's curb holding Julie's purse. It had taken all afternoon and numerous phone calls before Paula had made contact with the right people at the US embassy in Warsaw, who had eventually found the location where Julie was being held by the police. The management at the hotel had been lifesavers with the many phone calls. Once the apparent arrangements were confirmed the hotel manager warned Paula to stay in her room until the American authorities arrived with her friend. Paula was finally asked to come down to the lobby. She then was accompanied by the hotel manager to the front door to meet Julie and her police escorts.

Mr. Hicks made a polite bow toward Paula and then explained, "We have still not been able to find your husbands. Their names came up as having been involved in an automobile accident about midday, near the town of Chelm, but no one has seen or heard from them since then."

This was not news to Julie who had heard it all before, but was being re-explained for Paula's benefit. She felt the rekindling anger she had felt since the moment the handcuffs had been removed from her tender wrists and her fear had subsided.

"Please rest assured that the Polish police are very efficient here and will find your husbands soon," the hotel manager offered. "Also, we are compensating you for your room charges."

"The only compensation I want right now is to know why I was arrested and held in the police station all day."

"We can only say that it was a case of mistaken identity," Captain Akardisk said. "Our officers thought you met the description of someone involved in a kidnapping and the theft of part of our country's meager national treasure. More I cannot say. As I told you before, you are free to go about your tour, but we must insist that you not leave the country for the next twenty-four hours. That includes you and Mrs. Ballard."

Paula looked up at the stranger, surprised that he knew her name. The men bid their farewell and the American women were escorted by hotel staff into the hotel.

"Please feel free to enjoy our dining room—again with our compliments," the manager offered, opening the elevator doors for them "Unfortunately, the bus tour guide has made plans to leave early tomorrow morning.

I would suggest that a private van be reserved for you for the day after tomorrow since you will be remaining in our city for another day." He gave them a sly smile as the elevator doors closed.

"Are you okay?" Paula asked as they rode the glass elevator to the seventh floor.

"I'm fine, but I need a long, hot bath and a baseball bat to use on both of our husbands. You know it's because of them that we were watched and followed and then I got arrested. Those jerks! And now we're off the bus," said Julie, stopping to look directly at Paula. "I still don't understand how you lucked out and didn't get arrested."

"I saw what was happening to you so I was on my knees under a dining table hiding until the police car drove away. I figured I could do more good outside of the jail."

As they walked down the hallway to their room, Julie started laughing. "Actually, I didn't ever see the jail. They took off the cuffs as soon as we got to the police station and had me wait in a small office the whole time. It had an overstuffed leather chair and magazines—all of which I read or at least looked at the pictures. I'm now an expert on Polish fashion, by the way. They even brought me a nice lunch and a Coca-Cola Light about two o'clock. That redheaded woman we saw in the red shirt wandered through a couple of times and asked me a bunch of questions about you and our husbands and about the doctor that sewed up Brayden's wrist."

Paula opened the door with the key card and followed Julie into the room. A large bouquet of flowers was on the dresser and a bowl of fresh fruit was on the desk.

"Wow! Somebody is really sorry for their mistake," said Paula, plucking a stem of grapes from the bowl. "Have a nice bath and I'll come by in an hour and we can get something to eat downstairs. Maybe our trouble-making husbands will show up by then."

The ladies had bathed, dressed in their least-wrinkled outfits, and were halfway through their shrimp and filet dinners when an old taxi pulled up to the hotel entrance. Brayden and Dennis emptied the last of their cash into Nickzilosky's—the taxi driver's—hand and then dragged themselves inside. When their wives spotted them through the glass wall of the dining room, they couldn't believe their eyes. Both men looked like homeless vagabonds.

Julie started to get up to go speak to them but Paula put her hand on Julie's arm. "Let's let them worry about us for a few minutes. Besides, my steak might get cold." Julie, still a jumble of nerves, agreed.

They watched the men board the elevator and ascend out of sight. Five minutes later both men were rushing out of the elevator, looking in every direction for their missing wives. A desk clerk nodded toward the dining room and the reunion was achieved. The ladies remained seated as the men approached the table.

"You are not going to believe what all has happened to us today while you ladies went shopping and hung out at the spa," Brayden said, snitching the last bite of his wife's steak with his fingers.

"You were sure gone a long time. You must have

seen lots of interesting sights," said Julie, as she looked at Dennis's blood-matted head and the dust and grass stains on his khaki slacks. "You'll have to tell us all about it, but not at this dinner table. You look like a train wreck."

"Why don't you go get cleaned up and we'll order room service for you. Julie has some nice fruit in her room to complement the meal," said Paula, giving her husband's hand a subtle slap as he tried to get her last shrimp.

"Fine," Brayden said, "I'll have what you just had—steak and shrimp, right?"

"Why are your wrists red?" Dennis asked. "Were the spa rocks too hot?"

"We'll talk about it later, Dear," Julie said, turning her attention to her dessert.

Back in the room, the men's room service dinners were getting cold before the lengthy stories were exchanged and questions asked—not that there were a lot of solid answers. The men listened in awe at Julie's story of arrest, detention, and interrogation, followed by the profuse apology. Neither woman could explain why they were being followed by the woman with the red silk shirt.

"Couldn't you tell anything about the dead man?" Paula asked.

"He was too deteriorated, like he was mummified and covered with dust and bat guano, but his wallet should give us some information, except there seems to be a hole through the middle of it," said Dennis.

"I think we should turn it over to the police in the morning." Brayden said. "I think that we're all too tired tonight to make any rational decisions."

"If you need the police, Julie knows just the man to call," Paula said with a smirk.

The Ballards said good-night and went to their room. Brayden checked his hiding place under the bedroom dresser and found the leather bag, gems, and signet ring to be safe. He started to place the wallet in the plastic laundry sack holding the other treasures, but hesitated. Paula was in the bathroom with the door closed and in spite of his own recommendation of putting aside the mystery for the night he couldn't help himself.

The leather wallet was quite dirty so he took the wastebasket from under the desk and turned it upside down to use as a little table. He put on his plastic reading glasses and gently inspected the well-worn, bi-fold wallet. It was stiff with age and what he now suspected was dried blood. He glanced at the bathroom door, not sure what Paula would say to his contradictory activity. She was singing softly and probably brushing her long, brunette hair.

The alleged bullet appeared to have entered the wallet from the concave side (the side that would have been against his buttocks) because the entry hole was smooth. On the slightly convex side, the bullet had torn the leather, pushing it outward and dragging tiny fragments of the wallet's contents, including something that looked like paper money. Brayden's conclusion thus far was that the bullet had gone through the man and then through the wallet in his hip pocket. Carefully concentrating, he separated the two folds creating a small cascade of tiny confetti and dried blood.

"What do you think you're doing?" said Paula, putting her soft, long fingers on his bare shoulders and filling the room with the fragrance of her soap, shampoo, and perfume.

"I had to have a quick look or I wouldn't have been able to sleep."

"Dennis is going to be disappointed if you solve the mystery without him."

"You're right," he said, closing the wallet and placing it back in the plastic bag with the treasures.

"Please put this back where you hid it last night and go wash your hands."

The next morning, the two couples walked out of their rooms within seconds of one another. The ladies started through the buffet selections while the men found a table and ordered their beverages, and then joined the food line. Few words were exchanged back at the table as they picked at their food. By now they had eaten breakfast from buffets for two straight weeks and it was all starting to taste the same. It was Julie who raised the question on all of their minds.

"Well, what are we going to do now? The tour bus is loading but we have been told not to leave the country."

"I'm tired of the bus and the boring people," said Dennis. "The guys we met yesterday were a lot more interesting."

Glances were exchanged, and raised eyebrows on the ladies were met with shrugged shoulders by the men.

"You guys are a lot of help," said Paula. "First you get

us kicked off the bus tour so we are missing Wroclaw, the best city on the tour, and worse still, we're going to miss the very best shopping place. It's that little town where they make the Polish pottery, Boleslawiec."

"We'll just have to rent a car and catch up with the tour group before they get to Prague. We can make short stops along the way and still make the flight with the rest of the group," Dennis concluded, taking a bite of the tomato and cucumber salad—something he would never in a million years have eaten for breakfast at home.

"What about the police and the wallet and the guys that attacked you yesterday? Do you think all of that is just going to go away?" Brayden asked. "We left a dead man with a bullet hole in his butt stashed in a church attic … what are we going to do about him? Just go off sightseeing and pottery shopping?" The emotion in his voice was attracting the attention of four businessmen sitting nearby.

"We brought an extra suitcase just for Polish pottery. It's supposed to be for the extended family's Christmas gifts. We have got to stop in Boleslawiec or whatever the name of the town is," Julie insisted.

The foursome lowered their voices and agreed on a plan, then finished breakfast and went to their rooms to prepare to leave. Brayden stopped at the tiny Eurocar office and secured a full-size sedan for the trip to Prague. The price was ridiculously high, but he had no good alternative. Thirty minutes later, the car was packed and the two couples were headed out of the hotel parking lot for the expressway to Wroclaw. They didn't get far.

Brayden never had become accustomed to the

warbling sound of European emergency vehicle's sirens. The blue-and-white sedan following the Americans had to turn on its blue flashing lights and finally pass their car and then come to an abrupt stop to get Brayden's attention.

The drivers of the cars behind him were furious and didn't refrain from letting him know with their honking horns. The policeman got out and angrily gestured for the Americans to pull into a small parking lot nearby. When the two policemen approached the rental car they acted nervous as though expecting trouble.

"Well, there goes the pottery shopping," Julie mumbled.

Brayden started to get out of the car, but judging by the expression on the faces of the policemen, knew that it was the wrong thing to do. The gibberish of Polish words from the policemen meant nothing to the Americans until "passport" was repeated several times. At that moment Julie had a startling revelation when she searched her purse and suddenly remembered that the police had never returned it to her after her arrest. Confusion escalated when Dennis got out of the car and insisted that the police stop yelling at his wife.

Things didn't settle down until a young university student who was walking by stepped into the fray, offering his translation skills. The officer explained that he had stopped the car only because there was a radio alert to do so. A flurry of phone calls followed and twenty minutes later two additional police cars arrived. Sitting in the passenger seat of the second car was Captain Akardiski—Julie's new best friend.

"Mrs. Cannon, I apologize for the interruption of your travels," the captain said. "I'm sorry to report that you left your passport in my office. When I called the hotel to see if you were still there as we had requested, they mentioned that you had left in a rental car. When I spoke to the rental agent he happened to mention that your credit card had a warning notice on it."

"I rented the car," Brayden interrupted, not knowing what Julie's passport had to do with his Visa card.

"I see," said the captain. "So you must be Mr. Ballard?"

"That's right," he said, getting out from behind the wheel.

"Well, Mr. Ballard, it seems that your Visa card was used to pay for a doctor's treatment in a small town in eastern Poland. Unfortunately, the credit card number has become associated with the possible theft of a national treasure and a possible kidnapping."

"I have no idea what you are even talking about. How could we have kidnapped anyone?" Brayden demanded to know.

"Pardon me, but your wife and her girlfriend are familiar with the situation. As you well know, Mrs. Cannon was in police custody yesterday. No one is accusing you of committing any crime, but there have been crimes committed and the lady doctor who treated your arm and whom you paid with your credit card is missing and in addition, there is a—"

"I'm not familiar with any situation other that being harassed by you Polish police. How in the world could anything you are talking about have anything to do with us?" interrupted Paula. She had gotten out of the car and was standing at her husband's side. She had lost her patience with the police and the whole situation. She had a wild look in her eyes and stood inches away from the man with her hands on her hips trying to resist slapping the arrogant little twerp.

"Just give my friend her passport and let us get out of your disgusting country! It's been twenty years since the Russians went back home. Haven't you learned anything about manners and human rights since then?"

"Madame Ballard, it would be wise for you to get back in the automobile and allow me and my colleagues to fulfill our responsibilities to the citizens of our disgusting country."

Brayden opened the rear door and guided Paula back into the car. He then turned back to the captain and apologized. The policeman reluctantly accepted the apology and began asking a list of questions about where they had been and why Brayden had needed a doctor. He had not mentioned anything about any national treasure, and Brayden wasn't about to bring up anything regarding being at the onion-domed church—or about the leather pouch and its contents. It was unnerving enough, being interrogated by the police while standing alongside the road with cars honking and drivers and passengers rubbernecking. Even the policemen who had originally pulled them over were getting weary of the captain's redundant questions.

"Just one last question, Mr. Ballard, and then you can be on your way. Let me understand this correctly. You cut your arm and the lady doctor came to your hotel room to sew it up. I presume she did a good job," he said with a smile which Brayden returned with a nod. "Where were you exactly when you cut your arm?"

The hair on the back of Brayden's neck began to stand up. Suddenly, the sworn statement of a former president of the United States of America came to his mind. "I don't remember," he said. He then opened the car door and got in.

9

"I thought I was going to have a heart attack," Brayden finally mumbled, after a long silence.

"Your face turned bright red—a stroke might have been more likely," said Dennis.

"I thought they were going to arrest you, Paula," said Julie as they headed up the ramp to the motorway.

Paula was sitting with her face against the window. She was still trying to calm down. She had been terrified that the policeman was going to search her and her purse. At the bottom, in a plastic, zippered case—the one she usually kept her makeup in—was the leather pouch, the stones, and the fraternity ring. Before they left the hotel Brayden had insisted she take them, knowing that they would have to leave their luggage in the car while they did their sightseeing and shopping for pottery.

She was embarrassed at her outburst to the policeman. She couldn't remember the last time she had yelled at anyone, let alone a policeman.

She finally dabbed at her eyes and turned to the others. "Do you think he was telling the truth about

Doctor Andriana? I thought you guys said that she was with the men in the church and in the car."

"She didn't look like she was being held captive to me," Dennis said. "I must admit though that she wasn't trying to help them."

For the next hour they drove through beautiful, Polish farmland on the best highway they had seen since they left the USA. The ladies had relaxed and were visiting about the kids back home. Brayden was concentrating on keeping the car under the one-hundred-thirty-kilometers-per-hour (ninety-mph) speed limit. Dennis interrupted the wives and began to read a paragraph from the tourist guidebook on Wroclaw when a sedan BMW sped past them, cut in front of them, and then slammed on its brakes.

"Brayden!" Julie screamed.

The big, black sedan had locked up its brakes creating a cloud of gray smoke that obstructed Brayden's view. His reaction was quick and his lighter car was able to slow down just enough so, as the distance between the cars closed, he was able to jerk the wheel to the left and go around the BMW. Once around it he stomped on the accelerator, but the small, four-cylinder engine was no match for the big, German V-8.

"They are catching up again," Paula yelled.

"Keep your seat belts tight and hang on," Brayden warned.

For their entire trip through Russia, Belarus, and Poland, the big transport trucks had been an annoyance. They slowed traffic on the small roads, blocked the tour bus from passing, and belched black, diesel exhaust that smelled like burning garbage. When Brayden saw the lineup of five or six of the trucks a quarter mile ahead of him, instead of annoyance, he felt inspired. The trucks were nearly bumper-to-bumper, drafting on the lead truck as they sped down the highway.

The BMW was right on the rental's bumper, apparently waiting for the traffic to clear enough that it could ram them like it had the little taxi the day before. As Brayden pulled into the passing lane and passed the first of the three large trucks he saw his chance. A gap of less than fifty feet had opened up between a bright-orange, logging semi and a red oil tanker.

"Hang on," he warned again, then jerked the wheel to the right and slipped the rental car into the narrow space between the two trucks.

The air horn of the orange truck vibrated the inside of the rental as the idiot driving the BMW jerked his wheel trying to stay on Brayden's bumper, but instead was hit by the massive steel bumper of the orange truck. The Americans could only imagine the panic on the face of the BMW driver as the black sedan veered away from the truck. The driver overcorrected and then ran back into the second row of tires on the trailer, which was full of logs. The car was out of control as it spun away from the truck, off the pavement, and into the median steel barrier, and then back onto the highway into the path of another truck in the lineup.

At the speed they had been traveling, the rental car was a quarter of a mile down the road before Brayden was safely able to stop. The trucks ahead of them had kept rolling, but all of the traffic behind them had been forced to come to a stop. Brayden pulled off on the shoulder of the highway and was able to look back up the road. At first a cloud of dust was all any of them could see, but then as a light wind cleared the air, the black sedan came into view. It was upside down with its front tires still spinning. A passenger door opened and a man in a black shirt and pants crawled out onto the pavement followed by a woman with long, blond hair.

"Drive, drive, drive!" Dennis yelled.

"Don't you think they need help?" Julie said in a moment of displaced empathy.

"Just get us out of here," said Paula.

Brayden followed his wife's admonition and pulled back on the road and stomped on the gas. Within minutes they had passed the red truck. No one in the car spoke as they distanced themselves from the chaotic scene. Each of them was pondering what exactly had happened. Yes, someone had tried to make them crash—probably trying to kill them. Yes, they were in violation of several Polish and international driving laws including leaving the scene of an accident. And yes, they were in possession of material, the ownership of which was questionable, but most likely stolen and involved with the murder of the onion dome man. The four Americans were most definitely not the owners of the gemstones, but who was?

"We all need to talk," Paula said, breaking the silence in the speeding auto. "We were in mortal danger back there and in danger of being arrested back in the city. What's going to happen when we get to the border? What's going to happen when we catch up with the tour group? And how about when we try to get through immigration and security to board our airplane to go home?"

No one answered her questions. The only sound was the whine of the small diesel engine and the hum of the tires on the pavement.

Finally, Dennis spoke up. "None of us have done anything wrong! We are tourists on a vacation, who found a lost ring that belongs to an American male a few years younger than we are. We are taking it back to return it to his family."

"Good grief! If that isn't a simpleton's explanation," his wife said. "How are you going to explain that little leather satchel full of precious gemstones?"

"And what about the blood-encrusted wallet with a bullet hole through the middle? It's pretty suspicious that the contents are still there and you didn't report it to the police," Paula said, her tone a mixture of derision and fear.

"I didn't report it because I've never looked inside the wallet. Every time I try, somebody or something interrupts me," said Brayden, trying to listen, think, and still keep the car on the road. "I'll figure out what to say, if I have to explain anything."

"Wow! I can't wait to hear that conversation," said Julie in a mimicking tone. "Officer, I didn't have time to look in the dead man's wallet because I was too busy hiding these precious gemstones, which I found near a mummified body. I was also very busy trying to escape from a gang of greasy mobsters and a kidnapped female doctor, all of whom were trying to kill us." She started laughing and within seconds had everyone in the car joining her.

"Well, that's a sad truth, not that I will ever admit it to anyone outside this car," said Brayden as he checked his rearview mirror for the hundredth time.

"I need something cold to drink … and a bathroom," said Paula. The others all agreed.

"There is the sign for the Wroclaw Airport. How about we stop at the rental car place and switch cars to something a different color and with a more powerful engine?" said Dennis. "It would be great to get out of Poland before the doctor and her buddies catch up with us again."

Two hours later the couples had swapped their bright-blue Skoda sedan for a gray VW minivan. They had eaten a delightful lunch at a sidewalk café in the main market square of the town of Wroclaw—hiding in plain sight—surrounded by magnificent eighteenth-century buildings, all of which had undergone major restoration. Finally, they were back on the motorway headed toward the tiny town of Boleslawiec, known worldwide for its handmade, Polish pottery.

Paula dug down into the bottom of her travel-beaten handbag to retrieve the name of the "special" discount store her friends at church told her about. When they found the dusty, warehouse-like store, it was everything she had dreamed of. The hand-painted serving dishes, pitchers, and platters were each so unique and beautiful that she would have loved to buy out the entire inventory, but then Brayden reminded her of their weight limit on luggage for the flight home.

"Don't worry honey, there's always UPS," she warned him back.

He and Dennis loitered near the front door watching the parking lot in anticipation of another suspicious BMW or police cars showing up. In spite of their fears the entire problem they had experienced in Poland appeared to evaporate into the cumulus clouds on the eastern horizon.

By the time they were ready to leave the pottery store, Paula and Julie had purchased and shipped home over a hundred pounds of assorted Polish pottery. At the last minute Brayden picked out a small urn with a matching lid then went to a separate cashier out of the other's view to pay for it.

"Brayden! You've got to be kidding me? You actually paid money for that thing? That is the worst looking piece of pottery in the whole town," Paula said, taking it from his hand and inspecting the urn. "The colors don't match anything we own and the painting is poor. Look, the label on the bottom says that it is grade five. That's the worst quality. You should take it back."

"I'm keeping it anyway. It's mine! Look how tightly the lid fits. A little super glue and it will never come loose. I think I have some in my shaving kit."

Both women shook their heads at the man's stubbornness.

It was an uneventful drive the rest of the afternoon in the noisy minivan. Crossing the border into the Czech Republic went nearly unnoticed as they slowed down to read the direction signs. Numerous large, abandoned buildings and traffic booths stood off to the side—the only mementos of the fallen Communist regime. Two hours later they were at the airport in Prague, reunited with the members of their bus tour group. Everyone was overloaded with packages and their carry-on luggage. Everyone, that is, except Brayden, who carried his scuffed-up backpack and a newly purchased, fabric shopping bag.

Eleven hours later the US customs officer at Denver's Stapleton Airport looked at the luggage cart with its unbalanced stack of suitcases, carry-ons, and personal bags and nodded at the Ballards.

"Welcome home ma'am … sir. Here are your passports. Do you have anything to declare other than the small items you have listed on the customs form?"

"Just what you see," Paula said with a weary smile.

"How about you, sir?"

"I've got a whole suitcase full of dirty laundry. I'm pretty sure the dirt is European, but I doubt it's worth anything."

The agent pretended to laugh at the lame joke that he hadn't heard for at least twenty minutes. Why was it that everybody thought they were comedians?

It took the four weary travelers nearly a week to get over their jet lag. Getting caught up with their kids' lives, the laundry, and the housework had helped Paula avoid the midday siren song of the bed or the couch. Brayden had enough work piled up on his desk at the office that barely gave him time to eat lunch, let alone think about sleeping during the day. He recently had hired a yard man to trim the lawn and keep the sprinklers working; and thank goodness for that. It made him wonder why he hadn't done it years before. Ever since the twins went away to Stanford he had slowly gotten behind with the yard work. That had been their turf to earn their spending money. They always complained that they were the only girls in the neighborhood who had to push a lawn mower and dig out crabgrass on their hands and knees.

The girls were home for a long weekend and it was the first time everyone had time to eat a leisurely breakfast together. The rest of the family: the two married daughters, their husbands, and the three grandkids, were coming for Sunday dinner—so Paula and the girls had a grocery shopping list underway.

Brayden changed the subject when he asked, "Paula, when I get home tonight, would you mind trying to take out the stitches in my arm?"

Paula looked at him over the top of her mug of hot chocolate and made a face. "Why don't you stop by your friend Alan's? It would be a bad idea to take them out before it's healed, and I have no clue when that would be."

"How did you get that cut anyway, Dad?" Hailey asked, looking at his long-sleeve shirt and wondering what he was talking about.

"I'll take the stitches out, Dad," Ashlyn said. "We're doing frog dissections in my Zoology class. The lab assistant thinks I'm pretty good with the scalpel. Taking out stitches will be a no-brainer."

Brayden smiled at his beautiful daughters, to whom he and Paula had told little of the last days of their trip to Eastern Europe. They were the joy of his and Paula's lives. They had been surprise babies after the older kids were both in grade school. He looked at his wife, whose eyes warned him against Ashlyn's offer, but he took it anyway.

"Well, I'm off to the office. You ladies try not to have too much fun at the grocery store and the outlet mall, which I'm sure is also in your plans. If you haven't maxed out the American Express card when I get home I'll take the three of you out for Mexican food."

"But I get to take out the stitches first," he heard as the door closed behind him.

As he drove to his office he thought about the other thing he needed to do over the weekend. The homely, orange, Polish urn had been sitting on a shelf in his clothes closet waiting for him to have the courage to do something about its contents. He needed to do something, but just didn't know where to begin. He had jumped the first few times the phone rang after they returned home, thinking it would be a call related to their experience in the onion dome. He needed to talk to Dennis. Whatever the gemstones were and whatever they were worth was partially his responsibility too. Paula had made it pretty clear that for the time being, she didn't want anything to do with the leather bag and its contents.

Brayden's office was in a beautiful wood frame building that he had designed around the setting of a two-acre pond lined with old, huge cottonwood trees. There were always ducks on the water, and in the winter when the trees were bare he could watch the sunset with its reflection on the icy, mirrored surface. When he pulled his chair up to his desk and opened the lid to his laptop he saw that he had three new, urgent messages. The first two were from junior members of the firm, asking for his advice on a new high school auditorium they were designing. The third was short and just vague enough that it sent a chill up his spine.

HOPE YOUR ARM IS GOOD. I NEED HELP.
WHERE ARE MY JEWELS? AV

Brayden didn't understand the e-mail at first, and the more that he thought about it he understood it even less. He got up and closed the door to his office and picked up the phone.

"How did she get your e-mail address? Read it to me again," Dennis requested.

"I think that when she took care of my arm, Paula must

have jotted down the address. They were talking about pottery and she said she would send Paula the address of a place in Belarus that had unique vases—something like that—I don't really remember. I can forward it to you, but better still is that you meet me at noon. We need to figure this thing out."

"What did you do with the wallet?" Dennis asked. "It didn't fit in the pottery jar, did it?"

"Meet me at Mike's at noon and we can hash this out," Brayden said, too nervous to talk about it on the phone. "If you get there first order me a tuna on rye."

Mike's ice cream and sandwich shop was in an old strip mall. It was the veteran of the strip-mall era, having seen lots of tenants come and go. The men liked it because they used real, homemade bread and extra-tall, Coke glasses with lots of ice The owner was a high school classmate of Dennis's, whose hobby was rock collecting, and the place was cluttered with amethyst diodes, crystals of every size and color, and broken-off stalagmites picked up over the years and traded to him by customers. Mike had never had the money needed to collect his real love— precious gems.

The men sat in a corner booth quietly waiting for their orders to be delivered by the young waitress in the pink plaid dress with the white apron. Mike always had insisted on the uniform for his employees, but none of them nowadays would agree to wear the starched hats he had provided in earlier years.

As they dug into their sandwiches and crunched home-fried potato chips, Dennis asked his question again, "What did you do with the wallet?"

"Like you had inferred, it wouldn't fit in the orange Polish vase, so I put it in a sock in the bag with the rest of our dirty clothes. I barely rescued it when Hailey offered to do a load of laundry," Brayden said with a smile.

Dennis seemed a bit irritated at the nonchalant answers Brayden was giving him. He finally put his hand on Brayden's glass and said, "The four of us need to sit down someplace private, where we will not be interrupted. We need to inspect the wallet and the gems and the ring and do it in such a way that we don't destroy any possible evidence that the police could use. Then we must decide what we are going to do with them before that blond doctor, and her buddies or captors or the Polish police or whoever else was chasing us around Poland, shows up on our doorstep. We don't even have a consistent story to tell."

"I couldn't agree with you more. I'm sorry I haven't been more available," Brayden said, wiping mayo from his mouth.

"I'll make sure my house is available tonight. Would you and Paula please be there at nine?" Before Brayden could ever answer, Dennis stood up, wadded up his unfinished sandwich, pickle, and wrappings then shot a perfect set shot at the garbage can across the room. "Nothing but net," he said, ignoring Brayden as he walked out the door.

"I didn't realize he would be so upset," Brayden explained to Paula as they cleared the dinner dishes.

"What did you expect? You have kept everyone in the dark since the whole thing started with your climbing up into the onion dome. He hasn't even had a good look at the gemstones and none of us have inspected the wallet. Our lives have been threatened, Julie was arrested, and Dennis took the brunt of a car crash, and yet we aren't even sure why. It's high time you do precisely what he asked. I'll bake my German chocolate cake that he loves and take it with us. You get your stash together, and don't forget the wallet."

Dennis and Julie's house was in a narrow canyon on the fringe of the city. It backed up to a steep hill that was covered with small trees and brush. Their yard was a showplace of greenery and the long, wide, front porch had a fantastic view of the valley beyond. Since his retirement Dennis had spent a lot of time and money on the yard. The inside of the house was spotless as usual, and a fresh bouquet of colorful, fall leaves was in a large vase on the dining room table. The ladies began chatting about where Julie would place her new pottery when it arrived and the men looked at the tracks of a mountain lion that Dennis had discovered in his freshly spaded garden.

"Time for cake," Paula called out to the men.

"I don't want anything until we've settled the other matter," Dennis said, moving the plates and forks off to the side of the dining room table before he would even sit down. He turned up the brightness of the chandelier and spread a white dish towel out in front of Brayden. "Show us what you've got."

From a small shopping bag, Brayden removed the orange vase and a small tack hammer. Next, he unfolded a small hand towel and removed the wallet, which scattered bits of dried matter on the white cloth. As he picked up the hammer, Julie interrupted.

"Can we start with the wallet?"

Brayden handed the crusty wallet to Julie who was sitting across the table from Paula. Paula helped—their hands gently working together to open the leather folds and to remove the paper and plastic contents without doing any damage.

"I don't think I've ever seen anything like this in my life," Julie said. She held up an American Express debit card with a neatly-outlined, half-inch hole through the lower fourth—exactly where part of the owner's name should have been. There were three other pieces of paper. Each had the bullet hole through the left lower third, obliterating the letters of the owner's last name. The first name, however, was intact.

"Wilson, whatever your last name is, at least we're making some progress," Paula said, wiping the first card with a damp cloth.

"Don't do that!" Brayden warned. "There are probably fingerprints on the cards that the police can collect and match."

"Oh sure!" said Paula in a defensive tone. "Like we're going to march into the Denver Police station and ask the officer in charge to run fingerprints we found on a dead guy's credit card?"

Then Dennis got into the fray. "Maybe we'll get desperate."

"It seems to me we are already there," said Julie, picking up the wallet and turning to a clear plastic window. "My, my, look at what I found."

She got up and went to a drawer in the hall and returned with a pair of tweezers. She also brought a small magnifying glass. Carefully, she teased a discolored piece of paper out of the confines of the tattered, plastic window.

"Oh my gosh!" said Paula, looking first at the badly stained front of the paper and then the back. "It's a driver's license."

With the aid of the magnifying glass the four friends examined every millimeter of the document. It was in fact a driver's license, issued by the State of Michigan. It was for a male driver, born April 6, 1964, and was valid until 1992. The owner's eyes were blue, his hair light brown, and he required corrective eyewear to drive.

"Well, that certainly narrows it down to less than four or five million possibilities," Paula said.

Just like the credit cards, the bullet hole had gone right through the owner's printed name, and with the lamination disrupted, the blood and body fluids had fouled the rest of the document enough that the signature was unreadable.

"Julie, get a piece of paper and write down this number. I can read the last several digits," said Dennis, straining his eyes and then repeating the seven numbers.

"Those could be part of his Social Security number. My driver's license number back then was the same as my S.S. number," Brayden said. "Is there anything else in there?"

There was no other identification, but there was a wrinkled photo of a young woman, which had been folded over, and a corner was torn by whatever had made the hole in the wallet. In addition, there were several large-denomination British pound and Swiss franc notes—all having sustained considerable damage. No Polish money was present, which they all commented on. Tucked deep in the corner, maybe pushed there by the force of the bullet, was a silver coin.

"Can you read where it's from?" Julie asked her husband.

"It's written in Cyrillic. It looks like a five-hundred ruble coin, maybe Russian?"

Brayden stood up and paced the room to burn off some pent-up anxiety. "How are we ever going to find out who this guy was?"

"Enough with the wallet," said Paula. "Let's see the gemstones and the ring."

The wallet and its contents were slid into a business-size envelope. Attention was focused on the homely, orange vase. It only took a couple of sharp taps with the little hammer and a fine-line crack appeared in the vase's neck. Brayden gripped the bottom and lifted off the top. One by one the precious stones tumbled out of the vase onto the towel, adding a glitter to the Cannon's dining room it had never before experienced. Just like with the leather pouch, the last item out of the vase was the class ring.

"How about we wash these marbles," Dennis said, getting up from the table and returning moments later with a large, plastic salad bowl half-full of soapy, warm water.

"If we get caught with these by the Polish police all of our friends and families will know that we lost our marbles," Brayden said as they started to scrub and dry the stones.

Ten minutes later the thirty gems and the ring were

laid out on yet another clean dishtowel under the light of the dining room chandelier. Tiffany of New York couldn't have come up with anything more spectacular. Even the generic college fraternity ring sparkled as it sat curiously at the end of a row of six- to eight-carat sapphires.

Paula picked up the ring from the display and the magnifying glass from the end of the table. Amid the others' excited chatter, she inspected every millimeter of the ring on the outer portion and then inside the infinite circle.

"Brayden, did you see this engraving?" she asked excitedly. "Look on the ridge near the inside of the stone. There is a name!"

While the ring and magnifying glass made the rounds among the other three, she booted up her smartphone and Googled the name. "Just like I thought," she said. "It's the name of a manufacturing company … and they make signet rings among other memorabilia. Maybe there's some way for them to trace who bought it."

"You have got to be dreaming," said Dennis.

"He's right. A company like that probably makes tens of thousands of rings and even if they have records of sales it probably was too long ago for them to have it on a computer," Brayden murmured.

Julie retrieved her laptop from the kitchen and opened it. "It's at least worth a try. Read the name of the company and the address please."

Brayden took Julie's chair at mid-table and began playing with the stones, putting them in different order and mixing up the colors "Maybe we should forget about the ring and figure out something to do with these gems.

Just for fun, let's say that each stone is worth—what do you think—$10 thousand. Say we can sell them for eighty cents on the dollar, that's $240 thousand. That would be $120 thousand per couple. Not bad for a vacation souvenir."

"That's hardly enough money to change our lifestyle, but maybe it would buy some nursing home insurance. When those Polish guys catch up with you two and beat you to a pulp you're going to need the money for a nursing home," Julie joked.

"Or a funeral home," said Paula.

The room was silent for several moments and then Julie read aloud the ring company's website information and contact numbers as Paula wrote them down. Julie then snapped the lid on her computer closed. "Well, that has certainly awakened my appetite for silence and keeping my nose in my own business. How about some cake?"

As the ladies adjourned to the kitchen, Brayden turned to Dennis. "There is no way that I can just let this thing go. I feel a moral obligation to that poor, dead man in the church. His family needs to know where he is and what happened to him. These jewels may not make a huge difference to you or me—just more things to pick up or pack up—but to his family they might make a world of difference. I have got to keep searching."

"Hey, I didn't see the guy, but I think you're absolutely correct. These rocks mean nothing more to me than something to perk my family's curiosity and someday a great story to tell the grandkids. A hundred and twenty grand won't be enough to change either of our retirement plans, but we'll both get a lot of mileage out of the story once we put a happy and safe ending on it by bringing some sort of closure to the dead man's family."

"Then you're in on the hunt?" Brayden asked.

"I have been since the skirmish at the church and will be until the end. Show me the e-mail from the doctor one more time."

The sun was now setting earlier every afternoon, making it dark enough in Brayden's office that he had to turn on the lights early to finish up his project for the day. When he finally looked up from the drawing of a university administration building on his drafting table and out the window toward the view of the western mountain peaks, he noticed that the office parking lot was nearly empty. He didn't have a clock in his office because the ticking annoyed him. He dug his grandfather's pocket watch out of his pocket and noted the time. Paula would be calling any second, wondering why he wasn't there to cook the ribs on his fancy outdoor grill.

"I'll be home in ten minutes," he said when the phone rang, pressing the hands-free button and not looking at the caller ID.

The person on the other end of the line was silent at first and then spoke in a faint, broken-English voice. "Do you remember me?" asked the female.

Brayden dropped his pencil and stared at the phone. His was the only button of the multi-line phone that was alight.

"Who is calling?"

"How is your arm healing, Mr. Brayden?" asked the woman.

"It's doing fine," he said, his throat tightening when a wave of recognition swept over him. His voice sounded abnormal, but hers was crystal clear. "Where are you calling from?"

"That is not important, Mr. Brayden," her tongue rolling the "r" like a vibrator. "Please listen to me carefully. The men you saw me with the last time we met are dangerous people. You misjudged the situation if you thought they were my friends. They are not my friends and certainly not yours. I had never met them until the night that I treated your arm. These men know that you have something special and they think it belongs to them. Whatever you do Mr. Brayden, do not ever come back to Poland and do not contact the Polish police. I wish you a happy life with whatever you might have brought back from Poland. Remember, however, that the Weznitski brothers are smart in ways you can't imagine. I do not think you will be able to enjoy whatever it is that you have. In fact you and your family's lives could even be in danger. Take care, Mr. Brayden."

"Don't hang up! I have some questions that I need to ask you about…," but he heard the disconnect click before he could get out another word. This time he did look at his caller ID, and to his astonishment saw that the area code for the number was 949. He jotted the full number down, then quickly dug through one of the bottom desk drawers and pulled out a dusty Denver Area telephone book that he hadn't used for eons. It took him a minute before he found the correct reference page and then the area code listed on the caller ID. Nine-four-nine was the area code for Irvine, California. *What was Doctor Vlonovitski doing in California? How had she obtained his phone number? Why would she call and warn him not to return to Poland? And why not involve the police?*

As Brayden cleaned off his work area and headed out the door, he tried to recall the name she had used—the Wez-something-unpronounceable brothers. As hard as he tried, the name wouldn't come back to his memory. Once inside his car, he felt a cold chill far in excess of the low, ambient temperature. As he approached his car, his hands were shaking the keys as he searched the parking lot for any sign of a stranger's vehicle. He even went so far as to turn on the dome light and look into the backseat to be sure he was alone. He started the engine to get some heat in the car, but before he put it into gear, he hit the speed dial on the bluetooth car phone. He needed to speak to Dennis.

"I can't keep bringing more things home to worry Paula," Brayden said, looking across at his friend. They were in the Cannon's driveway. "But I can't just forget about the gems or the dead guy. I've got to find his name and where he lived and why he had the gems."

"If they were even his; I doubt that he bought them or was given them by some long lost uncle," Dennis added. "How do you think the doctor found you?"

"I've no idea, but if she could find me, those two hoodlums can too!"

"I'm sorry I dropped the ball. I got busy and sort of forgot to follow up on the ring manufacturer. I've got a light day tomorrow and can spend some time on it," said Dennis.

"You know that if you tell the girls about the phone call, they will insist that we call the police or FBI," Brayden warned.

"I'll make you a deal. You get the stones appraised and I'll track down whatever I can find out about the ring," Dennis offered.

Their eyes met in the dim light and they both nodded in agreement.

Denver is the geological capital of the world. The city's website lists an eye-numbing array of geological engineers, mineral assay companies, oil exploration and drilling firms, plus a lot of plain old rock shops. Early Saturday morning, Brayden set out to find someone who would give him an honest appraisal of the thirty mysterious gemstones. There was no way he was going to take all of them to one single place or to have a pawn shop or local jewelry store owner get a glimpse of them. He had a better idea. Playing dumb wasn't his strong suit—so he dressed in his business casual togs and drove into downtown. The name plate at the entrance to the twenty-story office building listed hundreds of businesses, including a Hakes Gemologist and Mineralogist. He had called ahead to be sure the place would be open for business and it was. The building's security guard was on his toes, asking for identification before Brayden could enter the elevator.

The 18th floor elevator door opened silently onto an expanse of marble and glass that took Brayden off guard. He was expecting some steel desks and prefab workstations instead of an office layout that put Wall Street attorneys to shame.

"You must be Mr. Ballard," came a friendly voice from Brayden's left. He turned to see a six-foot-plus, gray-headed man with bright blue eyes, a rosy complexion, and a smile that brought a feeling of confidence and trust. The outstretched hand and the firm grip were followed by a nod toward an inner office.

"I'm Glade," said the man, waving Brayden toward a chocolate-colored, leather couch. Brayden paused along his way there, to take in the view through the vast expanse of tinted glass. The glass-walled, corner office looked toward the west at the towering Rocky Mountains. The fiery-red scrub oak at their base gave just the right amount of contrast to the greens and grays of the mountains to make Brayden instantly jealous of Mr. Hakes's office view.

"Those mountains are quite a creation. Don't you agree?" Glade said. "Some days it's hard to get any work done around this place. Everyone just wants to stand and stare out at the mountains."

"Sorry, and here I am taking up your time, staring at the mountains," Brayden said with a laugh.

"Not a problem my friend, but why don't you have a seat and tell me what it is that I can do for you. Your phone call left me with a feeling of impending intrigue."

Brayden sat down and then reached into his jacket pocket and retrieved a small plastic medicine bottle. The label said Advil, but when he removed the lid and poured the contents onto the large, driftwood coffee table, no little brown pills or blue capsules spilled out. Instead, tumbling out—almost as though in slow motion—were three gems, the largest of which was a diamond the size of a Bing cherry. Next to it lay a bright blue sapphire and a bluish-red ruby; both nearly as big as the diamond.

Mr. Hakes was standing over the low-lying table—at first standing erect studying the three stones. The morning light from the opposite side of the building wasn't direct enough to make the stones sparkle, but instead gave them a transilluminated appearance, casting a colored shadow onto the desk. Hakes retrieved a jeweler's magnifying loupe from a drawer and took a seat beside Brayden.

"What have we here?" he asked softly, picking up the ruby and studying it with his loupe.

Brayden started to lean back into the comforting couch, but could instantly feel that his back was soaked with nervous sweat. He straightened his posture and waited for the expert to speak.

"This stone is definitely a real ruby," Hakes exclaimed. "And by my guess I would say ten to twelve carats, maybe more. It's not often one has the chance to heft a gem this size. When I was a boy my father ran a jewelry store right here in Denver. I used to help him when I was growing up. We had a saying that 'anything over two carats is cut glass.' I can assure you that this stone is the exception. It's the real deal."

He set the ruby aside and picked up the slightly larger, blue stone, hefting it several times in the palm of his hand. He then put the loupe on the stone and gave a slow deep whistle. "Oh, my, my, my! Another exception to the rule," he said.

The largest stone was left for last—whether by intention or default Brayden could only guess—but when Mr. Hakes picked up the yellow-white diamond and held it between his thumb and index finger, he seemed to do so with an air of reverence. Hakes couldn't sit still, but stood and walked to the window, using the outside light to examine the diamond. He took several minutes, rotating it to and fro, letting the natural light from outside set the stone aglow. Then he walked back to the couch and sat, gently placing the diamond next to the other stones.

"Well Mr. Ballard, that little plastic bottle certainly held some surprises."

"I appreciate you taking the time to look at my pills," Brayden said, making a slight jest to ease his tension. "Could you give me a shoot-from-the-hip evaluation?"

"Well, I know what they are, as I'm sure you do too. I know about how old these gems are by the working on the facets ... this kind of cutting and polishing hasn't been used since the turn of the last century. The weight is close to twelve carats for the ruby and I would guess about the same for the sapphire. As for the diamond, that is an exceptionally rare yellow color and the quality is as good as I have ever seen. The monetary value of stones of this size is relative to clarity, the number of flaws, and of course the ever changing market. I'm pretty sure that this stone is nearly flawless and the clarity is as good as it can be until further polishing is performed. I'm guessing when I say the weight is close to fifteen carats."

"I guess I really don't need to know their dollar value,

I just needed to know that they were real," Brayden said, almost apologetically.

"If they were in my possession I would want to know their value," Hakes said with a jolly laugh. "And I would want to be sure that a three-hundred-pound, gorilla-like bodyguard wasn't ever more than ten feet behind me."

"Okay, that's something I need to think about," said Brayden. "What is your best guess as to their realistic value?"

Rather than doing the math in his head, Glade surprised Brayden by returning to his desk and bringing out a thirty-year-old Texas Instrument calculator with a roll paper printout. He tapped away on the machine for a couple of minutes, and then tore off the paper and wadded it up. He hit a button once again, and when the paper had stopped printing carefully tore away the three-inch printout.

He handed it to Brayden, looking him in the eyes and raising his eyebrows to await the response. Brayden looked at the three subtotals, took a deep breath and then looked at the bottom number.

Brayden looked up over the top of the cheater glasses he had just slipped on. "I'll accept cash," Brayden said with a grin.

"I don't own a money tree or a printing press, but if you're really interested I might be able to find you a buyer in New York," Mr. Hakes replied. There was no levity in his tone.

"If only they were mine to sell, then I would ask for your help," Brayden apologized, knowing that such a referral would include a commission to Hakes. "I still need to find the rightful owner, if that's even possible. I am a good judge of people and feel I can trust you. What would you say if I told you that there are more stones where these came from?"

"I would say that you should first hire Wells Fargo to guard them and then not wait too long to make a disposition with the stones. The precious gem world is smaller than you think and word travels quickly. I don't know how many others you have shown that diamond to, but multiply $300 thousand times the number of gemstones you have, not to mention that beauty of a diamond. That amount of money will raise the eyebrows of a lot of people."

"I appreciate the time and the expertise. You have my card, please send me a bill for your time," Brayden said, offering his hand. The three stones were already safely back in the pill bottle and sitting deeply in his pocket.

"You won't be getting a bill. Incidentally, did I say that I doubt anyone has cut or polished gems in that manner for over two hundred years? The enchantment of holding such rare gems far outweighs any value I could put on my time card. However, I would love to let you buy me lunch some day and tell me the story of the gems, both the past story as you know it and the story yet to come. You pick the restaurant."

Hakes walked Brayden to the elevator door where they shook hands and said farewell. As the elevator doors closed Brayden caught a reflection in the corner of his eye and glanced toward the small security camera—its red light on. *How many other cameras have I been scrutinized by, and why did I give him my address?*

"Two hundred years?" Dennis repeated into the cell phone, causing some of the heads in the waiting room to turn toward him. "That would put them back in the late eighteenth century. There was a lot of wealth and the spoils of numerous wars floating around Europe at that time." He turned away from the passing throngs of people in the massive student union hall. He was looking out of the windows at rows of stately, old brick buildings. The lawns were scattered with the fallen leaves from the giant oak and sycamore trees that seemed to shade the entire Michigan State University campus.

He glanced at the "take a number" tab in his hand and realized that his turn was next. "Brayden, I'll have to call you back after I meet with these people. I've found someone who can give me information. I'm running out of leads to follow, but the ring manufacturer is pretty sure that this is the place where the ring ended up."

Brayden knew Dennis had flown to Lansing, Michigan and had agreed to split the expense. His gut feeling was that the trip would come to naught, but it was worth a try. He was anxious to share the mind-boggling numbers with Dennis, but it would just have to wait.

"What can I do for you Mr. Cannon?" a white-haired woman asked, looking at his name on the sign-in sheet. He had been sent by the cute, young coed at the information booth to an old building several hundred yards away. The elderly woman didn't stand up to greet him—she didn't look like she could. Her aluminum walker with the yellow Penn tennis balls on its legs confirmed the conclusion that she was as feeble as she appeared. Her skin was draped like fine pastry crust over the veins and tendons of her manicured hands. "We've just a few minutes before our alumni office closes. We're only open on Saturday because of the football game. I've had tickets now for sixty years and haven't ever missed a home game."

"Thank you Ms. Wild," Dennis said, reading her name from the brass placard on her desk, trying to imagine what she looked like in her truly wild days. "I am trying to trace the location of a person who I believe went to school here in the early nineties. He was apparently a member of the Sigma Chi Fraternity and wore a signet ring with the fraternity emblem. I spoke to the ring's manufacturer who said that the ring had a special code and was sent here to Michigan State. Unfortunately, no one at the fraternity house knew anything helpful."

Ms. Wild coughed into her crocheted hankie and looked over the top of her frameless bifocals. "So far you have narrowed it down to two or three thousand men, however, I think in those days a lot of the brothers also ordered rings for their sweethearts." As she wiped spittle from the corners of her lips, Dennis saw the gold ring on her boney finger. It looked very familiar.

"They told me that this particular ring was different, that they only send one a year with a real ruby stone. The others are apparently all a light-colored garnet," Dennis offered the ring to her to inspect. "I was told that only the fraternity president was awarded a real ruby stone."

The woman's face wrinkled further as she delicately picked the ring out of the palm of Dennis's hand. She brought her desk lamp closer and took her time examining the ring. When she leaned back and looked up at him a tear beaded in the corner of her right eye, magnified by her thick glasses.

He started to form a word then stopped. It was apparent that the ring had struck a chord. He waited several moments, allowing her to dab at her eyes. She held the ring out to him and asked, "What is your intention, should you find the owner of the ring?"

"I want to return it to his family."

The instant he completed the sentence, he knew he had worded the answer incorrectly. He felt a tension envelop the room like an invisible cloud of poisonous gas.

"What makes you think he has a family or that he wouldn't want the ring himself?" Ms. Wild asked, her voice having grown a bit husky.

"I'm not sure of the answer to either of your questions, but please rest assured that it is for his welfare or that of his family that I have gone to considerable trouble to find the man," Dennis said. He placed the ring in a velvet-lined box and tucked it into the pocket of his navy blue blazer. "What can you tell me?"

With considerable difficulty, the woman stood and shuffled a few feet to an oak-trimmed file cabinet. She didn't appear to have to search, but went straight to the second drawer and opened it. About midway into the drawer she pushed apart several files making room for her to remove a blue manila folder. Methodically, she closed the drawer and returned to her desk. She didn't sit this time but opened the folder and removed a three-by-five-inch photograph. To Dennis's surprise it was in color and appeared to be undamaged by age or wear. Hesitating a moment to study the photo herself, she then held it out to him.

"His name is Wilson Arbon. He was the Sigma Chi president from 1991 until 1992." She was reading the information from a standard index card. "He then became the student representative to the State Board of Regents. He was engaged to be married shortly after graduation, but that didn't happen. He went to work for the State Department and never returned from his training course. There exists no status update on him with the exception of a postcard, actually a reunion information card. It was for the five-year class reunion. That was in the spring of 1997."

"Do you happen to remember him Ms. Wild?" Dennis asked.

"Oh, I remember him all right!" the woman said, sinking into the chair at her desk as if conceding that her secret wasn't worth keeping any longer. "He was my youngest daughter's fiancé, but thank goodness he showed his true colors. A couple of months after they broke up we heard that he was in Europe. One of my daughter's

friends saw him a year or two later with a young woman
... a blond woman. I don't even remember which country
they were in. Thank goodness, it happened before he
could destroy my Emi's life. Since he disappeared he
returned only the one annual update card, and has never
shown up again at any of the class or fraternity reunions,
not that I would have heard for sure, but some campus
gossip does seem to filter through these walls," she said
with a shrug. "Luckily, my daughter was able to move on
with her life. She is married and has twin daughters of
her own."

"I'm sorry that your daughter was disappointed by
the man," was all Dennis could think to say. "Would it be
possible for me to get a copy of the photo and that most
recent address card ... the one from 1997?"

"Do you have some kind of credentials you could
show me?"

"I showed you the ring. I didn't come to steal it,
but to return it to the rightful owner. That should be
credential enough."

Ms. Wild bowed her head in a sort of apology and
shuffled toward a large copy machine. Moments later, she
handed Dennis a color copy of the photo and a copy of an
information card that Arbon apparently had submitted at
graduation as well as the 1997 reunion response card. The
address on both cards was a post office box in McLean,
Virginia.

"Just one last question Ms. Wild: Could you tell
me anything about the so-called blond woman that Mr.
Arbon was seen with? What did she look like? Where
was she from?"

Ms. Wild looked like she had exhausted herself with the interview. She ignored Dennis's last questions and sat silently until he had thanked her and turned to leave.

"Mr. Cannon. Would you please take one of my cards? They are there in the dish on the counter. If you find Wilson, would you be so kind as to drop me a short e-mail? Old minds don't handle loose ends very well."

"That won't be a problem," said Dennis.

"Mr. Cannon, I just remembered something that might help. The woman he supposedly fell for was a foreign girl. Someone told Emi that she was studying to be a doctor and that she was quite pretty ... a pretty blonde."

"Did she say which country she was from?"

"I'm pretty sure that she told them she was Hungarian or Romanian; or maybe she was Polish."

Marie Felstein was sitting at her work counter when she felt her cell phone vibrate. She was wearing a green-shaded gambler's visor and her bifocal magnifying loupes. She was searching the small mound of diamond scrabble for a stone that would fit the white-gold setting the senior jeweler was working on. She was trying to keep the look of the piece uptown but the price downtown. If the price of the ring was right she might buy it, with her discount, for her girlfriend Kristen Peterson—one of her few friends on earth.

She brushed her silky, brown bangs away from her hazel eyes. Her long, painted nails were covered with gloves. Marie always wore wafer-thin, linen gloves when she handled gemstones. It made it easier for her to pick up the tweezers and other instruments, and even the stones. It also kept her hands from getting too clammy on those muggy, summer days. She was about to decide on a diamond when her phone vibrated again. She removed the gloves and whispered into the phone for the caller to hang on a minute. Once she was in the women's restroom she checked the stalls to be sure she was alone and then spoke to the man.

"Go ahead," she said, keeping her voice down.

"I told you I would call if I ran across anything interesting," he said, "I didn't see the stone myself, but have been told that it is at least twelve carats, flawless, and a faint amber-yellow color. I promised you a break and this could be it. The owner of the stone is not talking sale yet, but I understand he was given an estimate in excess of three hundred grand for the diamond, and he has more than just the one."

Marie was listening intently and picturing the stone in her mind. "If it is anything like you say it is, the wholesale price on it is probably closer to a million—maybe more. Is there any way to get a look at it or even a good digital photo?"

"It is going to take a little time. First comes the trust and then comes the bust," he said, bringing a smile to her face. "One thing my contact said, however, is that the cutting on the stones is old ... like ancient. Probably rules out Liberia or Sierra Leone as the source. Maybe the boss in DC won't want us to do anything about it."

Marie heard the bathroom door open, so whispered, "I've gotta go right now, I'll call you back tonight."

"A big bust would be good. It had been quite a while since the last blood diamond sweep," she thought, closing her phone and flushing the toilet. She went to the mirror, straightening her blouse and skirt as she smiled at one of the other gemologists. She checked her hair and makeup then returned to her workstation.

Mr. Freiberg was a grouch to most of the people he

employed, but seemed to have taken a liking to Marie since she came to work for him two months before. There was little doubt that she was the prettiest woman in the shop, but that wasn't the reason. He had been her uncle's friend and knew him from family get-togethers. When she finished college and left town for two years, no one thought she would ever return to the Big Apple. But suddenly there she was, asking for a job in the gem business, whining about how she hated living in the boring "other world," which she defined as anywhere but Manhattan. Freiberg had taken a look at her delicate hands—and probably her figure—then had given her an employment form to fill out. He hired her the next morning. She was proving to be a good hire, he assured himself. She knew diamonds and could grade the average stone in less than sixty seconds.

Marie had been anything but a novice when she arrived on West 47th Street. She had just finished an immersion course in diamond appraisal with an agency operative in Tel Aviv. Previously she had been assigned to counterfeit investigation, but the newest digital scanners were so good at picking out bogus treasury notes that the trained eye had become obsolete, thus making her year of study and on-the-job training start to look like a dead end. The funding of the drug and terrorist trade with diamonds and other precious gems was increasing daily and positions were open. In her mentor's opinion no computer or digital camera would ever pick up the nuances of a three-carat diamond as well as the human eye.

Like any red-blooded American girl, she was enamored with any precious stones, and diamonds were her favorite.

Getting to work with them every day had sounded like a blast—the next best thing to arresting bad guys.

Living back in New York had been a fun change from DC and the endless travel to the various federal deposit banks where she was usually sequestered alone in some cubbyhole, straining her eyes to pick out bogus banknotes. Occasionally, she had been allowed to travel to Europe, but was seldom given the time to do any sightseeing. She was sick and tired of scratchy sheets, smelly, cheap pillows, and chicken salad sandwiches. She was glad to be back in the land of bagels and pizza.

She had yet to be involved in the actual arrest of any of the big-time forgers she had helped ferret out. All that extreme training at Quantico: the running, pushups, obstacle courses, and firearms scenarios had thus far gone to waste. She was still required to put in time on the target range and to pass the physical fitness test, but for what she didn't know.

She took her lunch break at a local deli and was just sinking her teeth into a pastrami on rye when her phone vibrated again. The caller ID was a Denver area code and the number looked like one of the guys she had worked with in counterfeit.

"What's up?" she asked in her best Bronx accent.

"Hey Marie, how's the diamond dust business?" said Alan Lee.

"Dazzling. I have to wear sunglasses all day," she joked.

"Well, listen to this story. When I heard it I couldn't help thinking of you. I just finished a workout at my new fitness center. It took some luck, but I found a machine at the right time in the right place. The two women on the elliptical next to me had a very interesting conversation. They were sure that I was tuned into the TV with my ear buds firmly in place. It's amazing how loud women's voices are when they think they are alone. It seems that they and their husbands just returned from a tour of Europe. Anyways, the story rang a bell in my brain regarding a note that came across my desk from airport security. It turns out that the scanners at the Denver International are every bit as good as we were told. The scanner had picked up a bag of some kind of stones that came in on an international flight a few days back. It was seen after the fact and they couldn't identify the owner. Anyway, the ladies couldn't help chatting about the one's husband just getting back from Lansing, Michigan, where he learned— to quote the woman—'a lot about the ring's murdered owner.' I don't know what their husbands have gotten themselves into, but the women look like everybody's young grandmas. In any event I did some snooping, got their names and checked them out."

"What do their backgrounds look like?"

"I could barely stay awake reading what little there was available. They are four of the most boring people on the planet. Middle America, college graduates with grown kids already out of the house. Both the men are retired. I'll e-mail you the specifics if you're interested."

"Sure, Alan. That would be great. I'll see what I can dig up from my end. Let me know if the stones turn up. I've got to get back to the sweatshop," she said, closing her phone.

Marie liked the sound of the agent's voice. He had

a casual way about him. Maybe if things went right they would actually get to meet face-to-face someday. The secure Skype connections they had used in the past didn't do justice to one's real looks—making everyone's face look out of proportion. She wished she still had her high-tech iPhone so she could at least do FaceTime with Alan—if that was really his name. The boss had warned her about looking too "techy" on the new job, so she was back to an old Motorola clamshell. If he had his way she would have had to use the pay phones.

She finished her sandwich and was back at her workbench in time for Mr. Freiberg to confirm that she wasn't late. He could be a real jerk if anyone wasted a second on his clock. With any luck her probation period would end soon and she could get a bench near the front of the shop, where she could keep a closer eye on The Grump—her silent name for him. The boss in Washington suspected that Freiberg was dirty, but no one had ever been able to prove it.

It was Monday night before Dennis was able to come by the Ballards' for a report on his weekend trip and to score a plate of Paula's always wonderful peach crisp. Julie was babysitting their grandkids, so he planned on making a quick report, filling his stomach, and then catching the second half of the Broncos/Cardinals game. The timing couldn't have been better. He was telling them about the elderly woman's mention of a Polish connection to the dead ring owner, Wilson Arbon, when Brayden received a phone call from the Denver gemologist.

"I'll have to think about the offer and get back to you," Brayden told the voice on the other end of the call. "I need an appraisal from a certified expert before we can move forward—there's no one in L.A.? I understand. Call me back in 48 hours. I'll try to have an answer."

"Who was that?" Paula asked.

Brayden turned to Dennis and Paula and started to answer, but then took a deep breath and slid another slice of peach crisp on his plate, leaving them in suspense until he sat down at the table.

"That was a Mr. Hakes—the guy I took the stones to last week. He says that if we are willing to take a quick trip to New York, that there is a diamond dealer there who is willing to buy the yellow diamond. Just based on Hakes's assessment—the man will pay us $400 thousand."

The silence in the room was absolute, except for the sound of three hearts pounding and periodic deep breaths followed by sighs. Finally, Paula stood up from the table gathering the plates and forks. She placed them in the sink and then turned, wiping her hands on her apron. She leaned against the sink and with hands on her hips said, "If someone's willing to pay that much money, sight unseen, then that diamond has to be worth a whole lot more than $400 thousand. That's the kind of jewel they sell at Sotheby's in London and New York."

"The problem, according to Hakes, is that the stones have no history attached. He called it 'provenance.' If it were proven that the stones were stolen and belonged to a museum or a government, then they could insist that they all be returned. We would get nothing and might come under suspicion as thieves. After all, we did take them out of a foreign country and bring them into the US without declaring them. We could all end up in jail."

"Surely you didn't admit to the guy how you got the stones," Paula said, exasperated at the thought.

"No, no, no. He didn't ask and I didn't say," Brayden said defensively.

"Well, we need to know who the dead guy is—if it really is this Wilson Arbon. So far we know there was a dead man in the onion dome and we know that there was a leather satchel with gemstones and a ring, but we don't know that the man had the stones before he was shot and we don't know why he was there in the first place," Dennis reminded them.

"Hello!" Paula said. "The ring was in the bag, with the stones and the man's clothing, and the age fit the description of your Mr. Arbon from Michigan. And he had a blond girlfriend from Poland. It doesn't take a Sherlock Holmes or a Miss Marple to make the connection. Why the man died, we might never know, but one thing is for sure: I am not going to prison for a bag of rocks and a dead stranger, even if the rocks are worth millions. I'm perfectly happy with my boring, middle-class lifestyle."

Brayden's and Dennis's eyes were staring at the emotional woman as she spoke. When she finished her diatribe she calmly took off her apron, hung it on a wooden, toll-painted rack on the kitchen wall, and excused herself.

Neither man spoke for several minutes, their minds contemplating the past and projecting into their potential future.

Finally, Dennis cleared his throat and stood up. "I

better get home. I've got to bring Julie up to speed. We need to do some heart searching. Give me a call and I'll meet you for lunch."

Marie couldn't believe her luck. She was standing at Freiberg's desk waiting for him to sign off on a grouping of diamonds for a dinner ring when the call came. The boss turned away from her and after the first few words must have forgotten that she was even there.

A garbage truck on the street below was dumping it's load and then backing up with its annoying beeping noise—so she missed the first of his responses, but then it became quiet enough for her to get the gist of the conversation.

"Yeah," the old man said in his heavy accent to whoever was on the other end of the line. "Get me a picture of the stone and I can make a rough guess. It's better than nothing if you can't send me the real thing. Remember, you have got to put something in the photo for comparison like a quarter or a nickel. M&Ms work pretty good because their size is pretty consistent. Plain or peanut, it doesn't matter."

He listened for a minute and then said, "Yeah, sure, if I give you a price, I can back it up with the cash ... what do you mean you want two opinions? You go showing that yellow diamond all over town and the only opinion you'll get yourself is from some judge, deciding whether you should do twenty or twenty-five years. Post it on the Internet as usual and ask for a hundred bucks. Call it 'amber cut glass.' I'll give it a look."

Marie watched the boss write down something on his work pad and then hang up the phone.

"You still here Felstein?" he said, giving her his usual scowl. "What do you want?"

He looked over her selection of small diamonds and nodded his approval. As she turned away, she let one of the smaller stones fall out of the envelope onto his desk, where it landed and then rolled over the edge and onto the floor.

"What the hell!" he said. "How can anyone look so good and be so clumsy?"

"I'm sorry, I'm sorry," she said, moving around to get down on the floor.

"I'll get it!" he replied, groaning as he stood from his chair. "Just don't drop the rest of them."

As he bent down to search for the rice-size stone, Marie leaned across the desk and read the note he had just written. She was quick, had excellent eyesight, and a near photographic memory.

"I found it," he growled, handing her the tiny stone. "Now go make something beautiful with it."

She didn't need a second invitation to leave. As soon as she was back in her niche she jotted down the note, as she remembered it.

9-12 ct y f-1 www:craigslist/denver/jewels.

"How stupid is that?" she thought. "Put a ten-carat diamond on Craigslist and sell it for a hundred bucks?" Then the more she thought about it the more she respected whoever was on the other end of the conversation.

It wasn't until after work that Marie had the chance

to report in to the agency. She picked up Thai takeout and walked up the three flights to her studio apartment in Queens. The place gave her the creeps, but as long as she was assigned to the New York office she doubted she would be able to afford anything better. Her dinner got cold as she looked online for the supposed stone, but it hadn't been posted yet. When she explained the situation to her boss at DEA, he sounded enthused.

"Keep checking the list," he said. "This is the best lead we've had on any of these dirtbags in months. When you get a picture and find out who has the stone, we'll set up a sting on the whole greedy bunch of them. Until then there isn't much anyone can do but watch and wait."

Marie nuked her cold dinner and turned on the TV to distract her mind while she ate what now was a tasteless glob of noodles and what used to be fresh vegetables. "I can't just keep waiting," she said out loud to the made up face on the TV. "I've got to make my own plan."

Brayden noticed the strange-looking envelope before the stack of mail was even sorted. He was standing at the reception desk of his architectural firm, chatting with one of the younger partners about a new skating rink the firm was designing. Why it caught his eye was the color and odd size of the envelope—sickly yellow and a full inch larger in width and length than a standard American mailer. He waited until the partner had departed and then leaned over the counter and gave the envelopes on top of it a little nudge. They slid off to the side leaving the oddball's address and stamp exposed. It was definitely a European stamp, and there in the middle of the envelope was his name, written in cramped block letters and numbers. The ones and sevens were the giveaway—they were written by a European.

Trying not to look curious in front of the receptionist, he browsed through the mail picking out a few third-class advertisement cards and then the envelope.

"Here Amelia, you can throw these away," he said,

handing her the junk mail and turning away with the yellow envelope.

He almost ran to his office, avoiding visiting with others as he passed them in the hall. He shut the door and pulled his chair in close to the desk. For some unknown reason he became cautious about touching more of the envelope's surface than necessary as he slit the seal with a sharp letter opener. He pried the paper leaves apart and teased out a single, folded sheet of stationary. As he did so, a weird vision of white anthrax powder or some other dastardly dangerous poison flashed through his head. Carefully, using a pencil and the letter opener, he pried the folded paper open and flattened it enough to read the typed message.

```
MR B.,
I KNOW YOU HAVE SOMETHING THAT IS MY
COLLEGUES'.
YOU MUST RETURN IT TO THE CHURCH IN CHELM
IN TEN DAYS.
IF YOU DO NOT RETURN IT YOU WILL NOT BE
SAFE.
YOUR FRIENDS WILL NOT BE SAFE.
YOUR WIFE AND CHILDREN WILL NOT BE SAFE.
PUT IT BACK EXACTLY WHERE YOU FOUND IT.
THEN ALL WILL BE FORGOTTEN.
PLEASE DO THIS FOR ALL OF US.
A.V.
```

"We just should have given everything to the police investigators in Poland, then we would not have to worry about all of this mess," Paula said as she cleared the dinner table. Most of the food had gone uneaten.

"Well, what we could have done and what we should have done are completely irrelevant, because we didn't do it and what we did do now needs to be addressed," Brayden said, trying to defend his actions.

"Well, you can't just hop on a plane and go back to Poland. You think those hoodlums will let you crawl back up into the church dome and drop the bag and leave? Fat chance for that! They'll have your throat slit and dump you in a ditch twenty minutes after your plane lands. And what about Dennis and Julie? It isn't like they are out of the picture either."

"I don't need to involve them anymore. I'll just take care of it myself."

"Oh that would be real smart," she said, tossing the dish towel into the sink. "What about all the money Dennis spent to go to Michigan? Julie already has hinted that she plans on redoing her kitchen, when all that money you have been bragging about starts pouring in from selling the gemstones."

"We haven't ever spoken seriously about selling the stones. We need to find out who they belong to. If it was that guy's—Wilson Arbon's—body in the onion dome then they most likely belonged to him. Thus, they now belong to his estate."

"And where did he get them—win them in a poker game?" she said sarcastically.

Brayden stared out of the window at a drift of new snow. It wasn't like he and Paula to fight about anything. He took a deep breath and let his mind take another track.

"What if we just ignore the letter and sell the whole bag of stones. There has to be some kind of loophole in the import laws so we can sell them and pay whatever taxes are due. That's all our government will care about ... getting their share of the money. Then we can ask the police to protect us from those Polish Mafia guys. We'll split the money with Dennis and Julie and live happily ever after."

"I swear Brayden, you are getting senile. Don't you think that the second anybody in the government hears that you brought millions of dollars worth of precious gems into the country without declaring them and without a reasonable explanation as to where you got them that they will have us all locked up? You watch enough TV to know that some federal prosecutor will read about us and think we are his or her ticket to the governor's office."

He took a minute to process her complicated question and suggestion. "What if we take them out of the US and sell them someplace where the money can't be traced?"

"Oh great! Now you're Mr. International Gem Smuggler. And how's that going to work for us? Do Julie and I each get a big, buff bodyguard to part the crowds in front of us and do we both get to pack pistols? Or maybe we move all of the family to our own tropical island and have our own little army to protect us from the Polish Mafia, Interpol, and the FBI?"

Brayden hadn't seen his wife so worked up in years. She wasn't one to cry or raise her voice, but her body language told him that he better come up with something good and he better do it quickly. At that moment, he was saved by the bell—the doorbell. A few of her friends were due to arrive for a meeting.

"I'll finish the dishes. You go visit with your book club committee. As for the gemstones, just give me a couple of days and I'll figure out something to keep us safe and out of jail," he said, pulling her in close to give her a kiss. At the last second she turned her head away so his lips pressed against her ear—an old trick of hers when she was upset with him.

"Is this Mr. Cannon?" asked the female voice on the phone.

"The last time I looked in a mirror it was," Dennis answered. The call had awakened him from an afternoon nap. He was still getting over his trip to Michigan. Although the time change was only an hour, his flight times and a layover in Chicago had messed up his normal sleep patterns.

"This is Helga Wild, remember me? I'm the secretary at the Michigan State alumni office?"

"Of course I remember you, Ms. Wild," he said, swinging his stiff legs off the couch.

"Well, I hope I'm not bothering you, but after you left the other day it started me thinking about Wilson, you know, the man who we think owned the ring that you found? I told you that my Emi was engaged to him at one time. Do you remember? That was before she met her husband Gerald—he's a patent attorney."

"Yes. I mean no, you're not bothering me at all and I do remember. What else can you tell me?" he asked.

"When we talked I didn't tell you some of the story about him. Didn't I mention that he went to work for the State Department in Washington?" she said. "Well, my

Emi received a postcard from him several months after he left town. She was so excited, thinking it meant that he still loved her and would eventually return. Then he called her once. He said he was in Switzerland and that he missed her. Next, there was a card from him, postmarked in Turkey. He said something to her about the countryside near the northern border of Iraq being green. She showed me the card and it was very strange because everything was brown and dry. It didn't look the least bit green in the picture. He apologized to her for leaving suddenly and he even mentioned a honeymoon ... in Tahiti ... and a new Corvette for a wedding present.

"I for one thought it was ridiculous of him because he had been flat broke all through college. Then Emi pointed out something at the bottom of the card. He wrote it in tiny printing; that the country was green like the color of money. Only, he used a dollar sign instead of the word money. Two days later she received another postcard. It was a picture of some Sultan's palace. I think the place is famous for the king keeping harems and fantastic treasures. That was the last time he ever wrote. It broke her heart. It still seems quite strange to describe Iraq as being green."

Dennis tried to get more information, but the Wild woman had taken off on a tangent about how good a husband Gerald was and how the grandkids all looked just like her. He hung up the phone confused until he thought it through.

"So here's my theory," said Dennis. The two men were in the elevator riding up to the office of Mr. Hakes. He and Julie had counseled with the Ballards and decided it was time to find out for sure just how valuable the stones really were. "These gems I found, and maybe many more like them, could have come from a cache of some Ottoman treasure that this guy Arbon somehow found. He was apparently somewhere in Turkey near the Iraq border when he was on assignment, serving for the State Department. Back in the nineties Saddam was still in power in Iraq and we had hundreds of spies up on the border where the Kurds lived. He must have come across the stones there."

"But how do we explain him ending up in Poland? You think my lady doctor could be the same woman the old lady in Lansing told you about? If so maybe the gems have nothing to do with Iraq or Turkey and are part of some Polish or even Russian royal treasury—you know, like the crown jewels in England?" Brayden asked.

"The stones could explain a lot of things, but not the age difference of the women. The woman Ms. Wild talked about would have to be about forty by now. The woman that sewed up your arm looked more like twenty-five or thirty. Something's missing in this story. They have got to be different people; or maybe all women younger than me look like they are twenty-five. It would be nice to know who really owns the jewels."

"Possession trumps everything else; if the real owners can't be found or proven, as far as I'm concerned, they are ours," said Brayden.

"Nearly all high-value diamonds cut in the last forty years have a microscopic laser inscription." The statement came from Mr. Hakes in answer to Brayden's question about how one might trace the ownership of a diamond. They were sitting across the desk from Hakes as he re-examined the large, yellow-hued diamond with a magnifying loupe.

"Do you mind if I take a picture of this beauty?" he asked in his always polite and gentle voice.

"As long as you don't post it on the Internet," Dennis said with a smile. "We aren't officially offering it for sale. We do want to pay you for your appraisal though."

Hakes took his time using an expensive Nikon camera with a macro lens, taking shots of the stone from numerous angles and with varying light. Next, he used a small scale to re-verify the stone's weight. Finally, he took out his magnifying loupe and studied the stone from every possible angle.

"It weighs very close to fourteen carats. This gemstone belongs in an exhibit or museum, not in the vault of some wealthy woman's jewelry drawer," he said, handing it back to Dennis along with the loupe. "Look at the bottom of the facets. There are the marks of the clamp which held the stone while cutting it. No one has used a clamp of that sort for hundreds of years—maybe longer. My guess is the stone was cut and an attempt made to polish it sometime in the Middle Ages, and certainly before the Renaissance era."

"So does the cutting and mark help pin down the place it came from?" asked Brayden.

"And does that add to or diminish the value?" Dennis added.

"Gentlemen, you are asking me things that are far beyond my expertise," said Hakes. "If this were my diamond, I think I would take it to London and have the experts at the Tower of London look at it. The men there, who watch after the Royal Jewels, spend their entire careers looking at irreplaceable gems. Not everything there is behind glass cases, and there is a constant upgrading and adjusting of the collection. The people in New York do a good job of setting and marketing; then there is Antwerp, where lots of large stones are processed, but most are newly found stones. I still think London would be your best chance of learning the provenance and thus the real value of this," he concluded, lightly touching the yellow diamond resting in Dennis's palm.

"If this was your diamond and you were inclined to sell it, what is the least you would take for it?" Brayden asked, reluctant to leave without a better dollar value in his head.

"That would depend on how desperate I was for money, but assuming I wasn't on the verge of starvation, I wouldn't accept less than $600 or $700 thousand dollars. By the way, Mr. Ballard, the ruby you showed me the first time you came by ... it might be worth more than I originally quoted. Let me make this suggestion. Why don't we set a time and you bring in all of your stones. I'll invite one of my acquaintances from New York to be here and look at them, unless that is, you decide to take them to London or the Netherlands for appraisal. I might warn you though; when you go through customs you must be very careful. The DEA people are always on the lookout for precious diamonds that aren't laser marked. You know ... because of the blood diamond business in West Africa and its relationship to supporting terrorism."

Brayden looked at Dennis and then at the diamond. "I think we need to ponder our situation a little longer. Thank you for your time Mr Hakes. Please, send me a bill for the appraisal."

"Don't mention it, and call me Glade. There won't be a bill. It's very rare for someone in my field to ever see, let alone hold a gem like that one. Just stay in touch."

The home security alarm went off at the same time Brayden heard the shattered glass tinkle to the floor. He could feel Paula lift her head abruptly off of the pillow and as he tried to listen beyond the screech of the alarm system's speaker, he realized he was getting dizzy from holding his breath.

"Call 911!" Paula said out loud.

"There is no need. I had the alarm company upgrade our service this week. They will have called already and have one of their cars on the way as well," Brayden said as he slid out of bed and slipped on a pair of jogging pants. His old US Army-issue, Colt 45 automatic was out of the nightstand drawer and weighing heavily in his hand.

"And what do I do while you play hero: crawl under the covers and hope the bullets won't go through Pima cotton?" Joking always had been Paula's pressure release valve.

It took sixty long seconds for the alarm to stop its one-hundred-decibel screeching. When it stopped the house was silent. No more breaking glass, no footsteps or creaking floorboards. Just silence. Brayden had taken a post in a hallway niche near the master bedroom, hoping that there was no one in the house with them, but ready to protect Paula at any cost.

The next substantial sound he heard was a siren. Within fifteen minutes of the house alarm going off and the breaking of glass, two armed officers had searched the house with every light in the place ablaze. The glass was from a back patio French door. A single eight-by-ten-inch panel had been broken. There was a baseball-size rock lying on the ground next to the door. There was also a streak of wet blood on the door handle and several fresh drops of blood making a trail toward the back gate.

"Looks like your intruder changed his mind after he sliced his arm on the glass and heard the alarm siren," the officer said as he pulled a notepad out of his pocket and began making notes. "We'll get some swabs of the blood for DNA and send them in to the Feds. Do you keep anything here worth breaking in for—I mean, it's a nice house and all, but anything out of the ordinary?"

"Just my wife, she's way beyond the ordinary," Brayden joked, trying to diffuse the officer's question.

Going back to sleep wasn't going to happen, thus at 7:00 a.m. the Ballards were sitting at the Cannon's kitchen table, drinking hot chocolate and trying to make a major life decision.

"We could sell the yellow diamond and donate the rest to the Smithsonian to cover the taxes. It might put a quarter million in each of our pockets," Dennis said, breaking the silence that had dominated the room after Paula told the story of the attempted break-in and answered the flurry of questions that followed.

"Or we could sell all thirty of the stones and pay the

taxes and put $5 million in each of our bank accounts," Paula said. "I could do a lot of damage at Nordstrom and Niemen Marcus, or take a Mediterranean cruise with that kind of money."

"Wearing designer prison gowns wouldn't replace freedom and that's what we'll all lose if we don't do the right thing," said Brayden.

"And just what might that be, oh Great White Leader?" Paula mocked. "As I understand it, the minute you crawled into the onion come you started breaking laws and haven't stopped since, including lying to the police three hours ago. I'm sure that falsifying your customs declaration alone would be good for a dozen years in jail."

Julie and Dennis were staring at the weary Ballards, hoping an all-out fight wouldn't erupt in front of them.

"I'll take full responsibility for the criminality," Brayden said in an exasperated tone. "You three can spend the money while I'm writing my memoirs in prison, but first I need to find out who murdered Wilson Arbon and why."

15

"Retirement is such a nice thing," Dennis said as he reclined the seat in the British Airways business class compartment. He was sitting next to Julie. Brayden and Paula were across the aisle. In the overhead compartment was a new, polished aluminum briefcase with a combination lock. They were taking Mr. Hakes's advice.

Although neither of the couples were flush with vacation funds—their last American Express card bills were still due—the ladies insisted that if they were going to do another ten-hour flight, they weren't going to do it at the "back of the bus." Brayden had cashed in an old IRA he had carried over from his very first employer and paid for the four tickets. Dennis agreed to pay for the rest of the trip's expenses. The goal was to visit the jewel experts in London and then to return to the town of Chelm, Poland and the little church. There they planned to revisit the dome and if the body of Mr. Arbon was still there, they would report it to the local police. To cover themselves with the authorities, they already had notified the US embassy in Warsaw that they were searching for the missing man and would contact the embassy if they found him. Both men had purchased new iPhones and Paula had leased the latest model satellite phone for a month. All the necessary numbers—embassy, police, hotel, rental car, and each other—were already on the speed dials. The night the decision was made to return to Poland, they had called a friend who sold life insurance and each had taken out a new million-dollar policy, making the other three equal beneficiaries. Dennis said it was like taking an umbrella on a picnic, "If you take it with you it for sure won't rain." Just in case it did rain, Paula had picked up a couple of small canisters of pepper spray that she packed deep in her checked luggage.

Marie Felstein was walking down Third Avenue on her way to get a pastrami on rye at her favorite deli when she got the page. Her handler had insisted that she not communicate with him on a regular cell phone, thus he had given her a tiny, vibrating pager the size of a Fig Newton cookie. She had beeped him and now he returned her call-back beep. She found the closest working pay phone and dropped in a quarter.

"What ya'll got?" answered the voice in a smooth, southern accent.

"I have a very pretty picture of a yellow rock that has to be almost fourteen carats," she said, looking over her shoulder as she spoke. It came in about noon and was just lying by the fax machine. I made a quick copy and left the original. Where can I meet you?"

"Who has the stone now?"

"I have no idea, but the fax came from a server in Denver, so the stone is out West somewhere," Marie said. "There is something odd about the gem though. It doesn't look like it is newly cut. The photo is good quality and whoever took it used a perfect light and background. I really need to see the actual stone, but my guess is that it isn't the kind of diamond we're looking for. This one's probably not a new stone from Sierra Leon or Namibia, unless someone has found a way to make them look old."

"That's not for you to decide," said the man. "Your job is to get your hands on the stone or at least pinpoint who has it; then our tough guys can move in with the federal prosecutor and make the arrests."

"And if it has nothing to do with our blood diamond arms dealers, what happens to the poor sap with the stone?"

"That's his problem. There ought to be a law against being rich enough to have a diamond like that anyway," the handler said followed by a soft laugh.

Marie hung up the phone and walked back toward her employer's sweat shop. It was getting harder each day for her to face the mundane tasks she was assigned. Even some of the nicer settings were starting to look like the junk found at the strip malls. In her mind, it would be like sorting chickens all year just to find one baby peacock. She was ready to move on to an action role. She could be one of the tough guys too.

The stop in London proved to be a bust. The city was closed down for some long dead queen or king's birthday and so they made a quick change in plans and headed back to the airport. Their connection at Heathrow was late, giving the four weary travelers time to feel the jet lag of the nine hour flight. Paula tried to interest the others in a game of gin rummy, but the others all just wanted to sit and stare out the window at the arriving and departing airplanes.

Paula took a walk down the corridor to look in some of the shops—although she had no intention of buying any of the $1,000 purses or $500-an-ounce perfumes. She was in the Prada store when she saw the man who she was sure was on their flight from Denver. He was a handsome guy with a deep tan and a fit physique. Somewhere in the back of her mind he looked familiar. "Maybe he's an actor," she thought.

Ten minutes later she had visited the ladies room and was in a Burberry store looking at a scarf when she caught another glimpse of the man. When he suddenly turned away a cold chill ran down her spine. She took the scarf to a three-way mirror and tried a couple different ways of tying it, and as she did so she looked for him. There he was again, pretending to look at a window display. "Maybe he needs a raincoat," her mind told her—always giving others the benefit of the doubt.

She returned the scarf with a slight regret that she wasn't comfortable spending $300 on a scarf—*maybe after the gems are sold that won't seem like such an outrageous price*. As she passed the display window where she had last seen the familiar-looking stranger, she looked at the display. It was for little girls' clothes. When she got back to the waiting area the others were asleep.

It wasn't until they were off the ground on their way

to Dresden that she saw the man again. He was in an aisle seat near the front of the Airbus 310. She was sure that he must have boarded at the very last moment. Once the seatbelt light went off, she crawled over Brayden's lap and walked to the front of the plane. She wanted a close look at the man and wanted him to know that she had seen him. She picked a magazine out of the back of an empty seat and laid it on the man's drink tray.

"Did you drop this, sir?" she asked, giving him her best smile.

"Why thank you ma'am," he said in Southern Carolina accent. "If you say I did then it must be so."

She studied his face then looked him in the eyes long enough to leave no doubt that she knew he had been watching her.

"What was that all about?" Brayden asked. "Are you feeling okay?"

"Much better now, thanks."

"Pack your bag," said the deep, southern, male voice. "We have a problem. The stone is on the move in Europe. I received a call yesterday from the guy in Denver who was persuaded to give us the name of the owner of the diamond. He and his wife and another couple boarded a flight to London yesterday. Now the four of them left London this morning for Dresden. I'll try to stay close but you need to take over as soon as you arrive. They must be on their way to market the stones. There is a flight to Berlin leaving Newark in four hours. Your tickets will be at the check-in desk. A rental car will be at the Hertz desk with instructions where to go and how to reach me. I'll follow them as long as I can, but one of the wives is already suspicious. Now is your big chance to show off your skills."

"What do I tell the Grinch here at work?" Marie asked, trying to suppress her excitement.

"Use that female thing ... it works every time ... right?"

She started to chastise the man, but decided to save it for future fuel against her boss and hung up on him instead. She finished up the setting she was working on—an engagement ring of white gold in the shape of a heart with numerous scrabble stones around a princess-cut diamond the size of an M&M. When she took it to be inspected the old man looked it over carefully—then nodded his approval without so much as making eye contact. It would be a pleasure leaving this job.

"I'm not feeling well," she told him. "I need to see my doctor this afternoon, so I probably won't be back until Monday."

He looked up at her over the top of his glasses and growled something in Yiddish then went back to his paperwork.

Marie caught a cab to her apartment and quickly filled her carry-on with several interchangeable outfits, trading her spiked heels for a pair of Clarks flats that were comfortable and quiet. She could buy more clothes in Europe if she needed them. She checked her purse for her passport and the Visa card the agency had issued her. She pulled the false bottom out of the kitchen utensil drawer and slipped the stack of hundred dollar bills into her wallet. She poured the milk down the drain and set the garbage out in the hallway. She was almost out the door when she remembered the charger for her iPhone and then remembered the knife. It was a spring-blade folding knife made of carbon fiber with a millimeter-thin, Solingen steel edge running along the blade like a finely painted line of mercury. It was the sharpest thing she had ever touched. The agency had given it to her for just such a trip.

"It doesn't show up on airport screening and is small enough to hide in your bra," her Quantico trainer had explained.

To date she had never taken the knife out of its case. She felt a slight chill run down her spine when she slipped it into the zipper pouch of her bag and put a couple of metal lipstick pencils on top of it.

The tickets were waiting for her at the counter where the smiling male ticket agent showed her the selection of remaining seats: a back row, one beside the restroom door, or a non-reclining exit aisle seat.

"What about an upgrade to business class?" Marie asked as though she had done this before.

"Sorry sweetheart, but that would cost you over a thousand extra dollars, and it's full," the man smirked.

"Then what about first class? Any available seats there?" Marie asked with a sweet smile.

"We do have an open seat ... 6-C, but sweetheart, that little luxury will cost you about $3,000 extra," the man said, abruptly looking up at the line getting longer behind Marie then glaring at her.

"I'll take the closest one to the front—in coach," she said.

When the agent handed her the ticket she slipped her hand over his right pinky and with a quick twist, dislocated the finger.

"What the hell," he yelped, yanking his hand away from her and turning his back to the counter as he hopped around shaking his hand and cursing the woman and the pain.

Marie grabbed a blue marking pen from his station and quickly crossed out her seat assignment on her ticket—writing in 6-C in its place.

"I'm not your sweetheart; you're lucky I don't turn you in for sexual assault," she said over her shoulder as she walked away toward security.

She didn't even think about the knife in her purse as she held her arms up for the total body scanner, was given the all-clear wave, and grabbed her purse and carry-on from the conveyor belt.

She was settled into her new seat—6-C—enjoying a glass of champagne and a bowl of warm cashews when a perky flight attendant stooped next to her and asked, "I'm so sorry, but the computer made a mistake on our manifest and didn't include your name on our list of customers. What is your name, madam?"

"It's Bond ... Jane Bond," she said softly, raising one eyebrow at the woman.

The Ballards and the Cannons had spent a short night at a hotel next to the Dresden airport and eaten brötchen and cheese for breakfast. Now they were headed back to Chelm and the unknown. They were jet-lagged and very nervous as their rental car crossed the Germany-Poland border on the expressway at Görlitz. Every black BMW that they even came close to drew nervous stares. But, when a tiny, white Opel hatchback drew close to their rear bumper and then passed them they didn't notice it. It stayed right in front of them for five kilometers—then slowed, letting them pass. For another fifty kilometers it stayed within vision, but they still didn't even notice it was there. The female driver was gabbing on her cell phone—her hand covering most of her face each time she was alongside of them. They hadn't realized how easy it was to see their orange Skoda sedan from a distance.

"I want to stop at the pottery place again when we leave," Paula said as they sped past the exit to Boleslawiec.

"Me too," said Julie. "I can do the rest of my Christmas shopping at the one store and carry it home on the plane for free."

Brayden and Dennis gave each other an eye roll, but withheld any comments. The goal was to get to Krakow where they would catch up on badly needed sleep and get a decent meal or two. The next morning, they planned to drive to the little town of Chelm, and with their cell phones and cameras ready, the men would crawl up the ladder into the onion dome and "rediscover" the dead man's body. After making a thorough search of the dome attic space for any other treasures, they would call the local police and then document the removal of Mr. Arbon's body with sound and pictures.

Brayden had hidden twenty-nine of the gemstones at a location back in Colorado that all four agreed only he would know—they had all seen too many torture movies. He had left a sealed document with his attorney disclosing the location of the stones, just in case something "really bad" happened. The gold-and-ruby, Sigma Chi ring was in Paula's coin purse, wrapped in foil. The intention was to have it returned to the family with the body once complete identification was made. How they would pull that off remained to be seen.

That just left the yellow diamond to account for. Paula had been in favor of leaving it home. Julie was all for selling it and splitting the money. Dennis wanted to see the look on the Polish hoodlums' faces when they were in handcuffs and he gave them a secreted glance at the stone they had probably killed for, but would never enjoy. As for Brayden, he wanted to find the provenance of the stone, and if necessary return it and the others to the rightful owners. If a small reward—or a large reward—was given in appreciation, that would be all the better. For now it was hidden in Paula's make-up case in her carry-on, where no one would think to look.

Marie had received photos of Brayden taken by the surveillance cameras at Mr. Hakes's office. The DEA bloodhounds had found the photos and had a long, serious discussion with Glade Hakes. They promised a reward if the jewels were recovered and a prison sentence if he didn't cooperate. As for the other three Americans, Marie had only government passport photos and general descriptions.

The flight to Dresden had been heavenly. By the time the airline crew realized that she was a first class stowaway, she had become best chatting friends with her next chair companion—a junior vice-president of Lufthansa. The flight attendant supervisor had recommended that they let the situation evolve on its own; and it had. The man invited Marie to have dinner with him in Berlin the next time she passed through town.

She was handed an envelope at immigration, which contained car keys, a Garmin GPS, more photos, and the arrival time of the Ballard and Cannon parties. She was a bit frazzled and seriously jet-lagged when her handler called and gave her an update. Finding and following the Americans had apparently been easy for him, and soon she was sitting outside an airport hotel looking at their rental car—a garish, orange Skoda sedan. Her only problems thus far were that she had no local currency and had overdone it with the drinks on the flight. When the couples—she now knew their names—finally pulled off the expressway and stopped for fuel and a pit stop, she sighed in relief. She stopped at the ATM for money and made it into the restroom just as the woman named Paula began washing her hands.

Marie ducked into a stall and tried to listen as the other woman joined Paula.

"I still can't believe that we are back here so soon," said Paula.

"Well, I just hope we can get some rest tonight in Krakow and then get to Chelm early and find that poor man's body and whatever else those Polish Mafia guys are looking for," Julie's voice trailed off as the hand dryers drowned out their voices.

"Hey boss, I just got to overhear the American wives in a gas station restroom," Marie said into her iPhone. "They are spending the night in Krakow and then are off to some place called Chum or Phlegm or something like that. It sounded like it wasn't very far from Krakow."

"Give me a few minutes and I'll have you a reservation for tonight and see if we can figure out where they are going in the morning," the slow, southern voice drawled. She couldn't believe how clear the connection was.

Marie turned off her phone and concentrated on her driving. She was trying to keep a consistent half mile behind the orange sedan. They had passed the major intersection into Wroclaw when her phone rang again.

"My computer assistant needs a raise. Can you believe she was able to get into the hotel booking sites of Poland and find their reservation? Would y'all believe it, it's a Holiday Inn Express?"

Marie just listened to the man. She was trying to not lose the Skoda while not getting too close in the traffic.

"Are you still there?" he asked

"Yeah, yeah. Just get me a room," she said. The jet lag was starting to dominate her thought process and the man's slow-talking voice wasn't helping. Also, she had leg cramps from sitting in the airplane too long and from now being wedged into the tiny little car the agency had reserved for her.

"Done," he said. "Don't let them lose you in the morning. It sounds like the place they are going is called Chelm. That's the only town with a name anywhere close to what you heard. It's about an hour from Krakow. Why they are headed to that place is anybody's guess, but the good news is that we've retrieved the x-ray scans from the airport in Denver and it looks like they are carrying a rock in one of their carry-ons."

A smile spread across Marie's face. This was getting more exciting by the minute. Now, she just needed sleep.

The hotel bed was worse than sleeping on the floor—hard as a rock with occasional lumps. There was no way a person could spend more than a couple of nights on those beds without getting bed sores. Brayden woke up four or five times to shift the weight on his hips and shoulders. Each time he had to force himself not to think about what lay ahead the next day. When the alarm went off at 7:00 a.m. he felt more exhausted than when he went to bed.

He rushed the others through the buffet breakfast line and insisted Paula take some extra cheese and rolls to stash in her purse. "Who knows when we'll have time to eat again."

Once in the car, Brayden was anxious to leave and was revving the engine and had it in gear before Dennis could even close the trunk lid.

"Why the big rush?" Paula asked. "It's not like the dead guy is going anywhere this morning."

"We need to solve the mystery and get on with our lives," said Brayden, steering the Skoda onto the expressway.

"I'm all for that," said Julie, still trying to get her seatbelt fastened.

The thought of finding the dead man, and simply turning the gemstones over to the authorities or a government-owned museum had been the subject of a late-night discussion in the Cannon's hotel room. Dennis was a team player and always had been so. From his early days at high school where he was on the state champion football team, to the academy at West Point where he and his fellow cadets had led the rest of their classmates in nearly every competition, to the swamps of Panama and the desert sands of Kuwait and Baghdad, he always had been loyal to those under his command. He wasn't even capable of thinking otherwise and he now looked on Brayden as a commanding officer of sorts. Julie, however, was putting the pressure on Dennis to think beyond the framework of his normal personality.

"This is the one time in our entire lives that a very real opportunity is staring us in the face that can make us wealthy," Julie whispered.

They were snuggled together in bed trying to get

warm after Dennis had left the window open a little too long against the late fall breeze. He hated the smell of the commercial cleaning products used to clean the hotel room.

"But our life is fine without a windfall from stolen treasure," Dennis said, rubbing her shoulder and neck. "My retirement is more than most people make at a good, full-time job and the consulting fees I've been getting are frosting on the cake."

"I realize all of that, but can you imagine having $1 or $2 or $3 million in an offshore account with a platinum credit card to use at will? We could take the kids on exotic cruises and send the grandkids to the best universities and you could join the country club and play golf every day. And how about me never having to do any house cleaning or yard work?"

"But on the other hand," he whispered, "imagine coming to visit me once a month at the federal prison where if we ever got to snuggle like this, it would be for a one-hour, conjugal visit on a stained mattress with cameras watching."

That had ended the conversation with Julie leaving the bed and taking a long, hot bath with the bathroom door shut.

Marie didn't have a bed partner to keep her warm or make her frustrated. She had slept like a cadaver until the alarm went off at six. She had rushed to shower and get dressed and then sat at a table in the corner of the hotel's breakfast room waiting for a sighting of her jewel thieves. She had watched them arrive and rush through breakfast—the wives filling their purses with rolls and unpeeled fruit, obviously for a later snack. The man, who ended up being the driver, appeared very nervous and the other man looked weary and cautious, glancing over his shoulder at times and following the actions of arriving and departing hotel guests as they came and ate and left the room.

Her bags were in the car and her bill was paid. She had thought about trying to move to a table closer to where the couples were eating, but didn't want them to get a clear look at her face. She might have to be a lot more visible later. As they got up to leave the dining area, she made a quick trip back to her room. She hadn't taken five minutes, but the elevator was full when she back down to the lobby. She peeked out of the window from her fifth floor room and watched the four Americans get into their orange car.

She dashed down the emergency stairwell—down and around, down and around—for five flights with double landings—and then the door didn't even open into the lobby, but to the outside, opposite from the main entrance. By the time she rushed back through the lobby, the Skoda was gone. She jumped in her car, which fortunately was right out on the street and ready to go, but it was too late. The orange Skoda was not just gone, but completely out of sight. The street signs in front of her were in Polish and might as well have been in Martian. *Why have I been so stupid?*

The car behind her honked several times to prod her to get moving. The red light had changed to yellow and then green. As she accelerated away a dark-colored, BMW sedan honked again and quickly pulled around her, cutting her off. The passenger gave her an angry gesture as the car took a last-second turn onto the expressway heading east. Marie, already committed by the surrounding traffic took the same turn. Hopefully, the jewel thieves were going in the same direction. She drove for several kilometers and was starting to panic when she saw the sign stating, "Chelm 86 km."

Sunlight was glaring through the bug-splattered windshield of the Skoda, making it difficult for Brayden to see what was ahead. The others weren't even trying to look toward the sun in the east, which may have saved them a lot of problems—in more ways than one. Brayden was having trouble finding any road signs indicating the turnoff to the village of Chelm. The GPS was acting weird, showing them off-road when on motorways and then "recalculating" and giving them contradicting directions. The further east they drove, the fewer and more poorly the signs were marked. It was Julie, staring off to the north, who first saw what could possibly be the church they were looking for, with its unique bell tower, dome, and cross.

"Brayden, I think that's it! Look to the left," she said. She was sitting behind him, but as she began to point the church out to the others, and Brayden put on the brakes, slowing the car to a crawl, a small car with a woman driver nearly rear-ended them.

"Watch out!" screamed Paula and Dennis in chorus, bracing themselves for an impact. They all had heard the screech of the brakes. Dennis turned just in time to see the car veer around them, avoiding the collision from behind, but the car then crossed the median strip, nearly hitting an oncoming lumber truck whose blaring horn added to the startling effect. Brayden's quick reactions saved them: He slammed on the brakes and jerked his car onto the shoulder of the road allowing room for the sedan to come back into their lane, thus missing the truck.

"We're fine," announced Brayden, as much to himself as to the others.

The small car had straightened out on the road ahead and continued to widen the gap as Brayden brought the Skoda nearly to a stop, pulling off of the two-lane highway onto a graveled, farm road. His heart was pounding as he got out of the car and shaded his eyes to see the car fade into the sunlight.

"I can't believe how close that car came to killing all of us," Paula said, taking her shaken husband's arm.

"That was great driving back there, partner," said Dennis, giving his friend a pat on the shoulder.

Brayden turned to Julie. "You said you saw the church? I don't see it from here, maybe because of all of the trees?"

"It's off to the north a couple of miles. But Brayden, the woman driving that little car...."

"What about her?"

"I think I saw that woman at the hotel this morning. She was sitting in the back of the restaurant when we ate breakfast. I noticed her because she looked like an American and I remembered wondering why she was alone."

"I think you're right," said Paula, slipping her arm

around Brayden's waist. "I saw a woman at the restaurant wearing the exact sweater that I almost bought from a Nordstrom's Internet ad. It looked great on her."

"Enough with the fashion review. We need to find the road and get to the church. Back in the car everyone," Dennis said.

As they pulled back onto the paved road, none of them noticed a black sedan stopped alongside it, three hundred yards back. The occupants had been watching the Americans through binoculars and had now confirmed their identity.

Marie was so mad at herself that she could barely think. The crappy little car the rental agency gave her didn't have a drink holder, so she had wedged her twelve-ounce coffee cup between the parking brake and the passenger seat. When the idiot she was following stopped suddenly, she had been taking a swallow of the tepid brew. She now had eight or ten ounces of creamy, sweet coffee down the front of her sweater and in her lap. She could feel the liquid squishing between her thighs and working its way under her seat. She was so uncomfortable that she had to stop and change clothes.

She obviously couldn't change while standing alongside the highway, and if she went too far ahead of the Skoda to pull into a gas station or rest stop, they were likely to pass her by. *After all, it was purely by accident that I caught up with them in the first place.*

She continued driving slowly hoping they would catch up to her again, and then it occurred to her that they had reached their destination and had slowed down to turn off the highway. Nevertheless, she had to do something about her sopping-wet slacks.

Marie took the next exit from the main road where a tiny sign indicated that the road led toward Chelm. Maybe she was luckier than she gave herself credit. She drove about a hundred yards along the forested road and then pulled into a narrow, gravel lane obscured by small pines and bushes. Not a soul was in sight. She carefully slid out of the car, feeling the sticky—now cool—liquid running down the inside of her pant legs. "This is disgusting," she said out loud, startling a crow out of the branches of a nearby oak tree that had long since lost its foliage. She looked around at the damp, leaf-covered ground and smelled the rich loam of the forest. It gave her a momentary sense of peace. Then she heard the motor of a car coming in her direction.

Quickly popping open the car's hatchback, she dug a clean pair of slacks out of her suitcase and peeled off her soaking pants, struggling to get the cuffs over her tennis shoes. The light breeze against her moist, bare legs sent a chill up her spine and goose bumps down to her ankles. Hopping up and down to get the tight, dry pants over her still-damp ankles, she stumbled and fell to the ground.

"Damn, damn, damn," she screamed, looking at her bleeding right hand. She had landed on a shard of glass from a broken bottle.

"What are you laughing about?" Julie queried her husband.

"Did you see that car back in the trees? There is some

half naked-woman hopping around it, trying to pull up her pants. I guess she missed the last rest stop. I think it's that same car that nearly rear-ended us and then almost creamed the truck," said Dennis.

The others hadn't seen Marie or her car and quickly dismissed Dennis's comment as they came to a fork in the road and had to decide to turn left or right.

Julie made the decision since she had claimed to have seen the church dome. She guessed wrong. They followed the paved road out of the splotch of forest onto an open plain of harvested cornfields

"Look behind us," said Paula.

Far off to their left and back in the direction from which they had come, was the little town of Chelm. Prominent on its limited skyline was the beautiful onion dome of the basilica. Ten minutes later Brayden pulled the car to a stop in front of an old house a few hundred yards away from the church. Some of the neighborhood had a familiar look to Dennis and Brayden.

They sat in the car, looking out at the church, each having different feelings about being there. Although they had all been inside the building—the men twice—the place just didn't seem the same. Their memories of other churches and villages, plus all the talking about it over the past few weeks had somehow altered their memories.

An occasional car drove past, but when a tractor pulling a load of sugar beets turned the blind corner and almost ran over them, Brayden took his foot off the brake and pulled into the far end of the parking lot.

"You can't park here," insisted Paula. "We're going to the church anyway so we might as well park right in front and get done with your searching. Then we can leave in a hurry."

"Paula and I will wait right here, hiding in the car, just in case you need us to scream or go find the police," said Julie, bringing a moment of comic relief to the foursome.

The church was cold inside—cold and silent. There was no sign of a priest, worshippers, or even a caretaker. About a dozen or so candles were lit and burning in the nave adjacent to the stairwell. The men moved inside toward the curving stairwell. They were prepared for a thorough search this time; both wore high-intensity head lamps whose beams could be focused or spread out with a twist of the lenses. Both men wore thin, leather gloves, sweaters, and kneepads. They looked more like tile setters than crime investigators, but their looks didn't affect their mood. They were deadly serious as the memory of their previous violent encounter at this exact spot came strongly to mind. Neither mentioned it, but nodded in unison toward the onion dome above.

The men were out of breath by the time they reached the steep ladder at the top of the circular stairwell. Since their last visit, a handmade, wooden sign had been placed on the first two rungs of the ladder. The black, plain writing was in Polish, but left no doubt as to its meaning. "Nie Wchodzić" was hand printed above a skull and crossbones, making it clear that this should be the end of the line for nosy tourists.

Brayden pushed the sign aside to get a handhold on the cold, metal ladder, and then ascended into the pitch-dark onion dome. Dennis took the time to unwind the wire holding the twelve-by-eighteen-inch board and laid it quietly on the ground. Then he followed his best friend up the ladder.

They waited until their eyes had adapted to the dark before they switched on their headlamps. At the top of the ladder Brayden began watching out for the sharp, metal flashing that had injured him previously. He crawled onto an adjacent truss and began working his way around a thirty-some-foot diameter space. With the beams, trusses, and floor joists coming together at odd angles and the convexity of the floor beneath them—the ceiling of the chapel thirty feet below—Brayden was already out of Dennis's line of sight when he emerged from the narrow ladder's opening.

"Have you found anything?" Dennis asked in a firm but subdued voice.

At first there was no answer, then he heard Brayden say, "Oh crap! The body is gone! I'm certain that it was right here."

"Hold on, I'll be right there."

The two men, both on their hands and knees, focused their lights on the space beneath them where the body of Wilson Arbon had rested just a few weeks prior. There was nothing. No body, no remnants of clothing, and even the area beneath the site of the body looked undisturbed compared to the area around it.

"This can't be! We saw a body right there less than a month ago. How could those gangsters have removed it and not even left a trace?"

The arching beams supporting the onion dome spread from a central point in the middle like the radius of a wagon wheel. Dennis moved to the men's left—to the next deep place—and shined his light downward. Arbon's body was not there either, but down in an angled crevasse Dennis's light reflected off of something shiny.

"Come look over here, Brayden; somebody has dropped their car keys down there."

Brayden hadn't forgotten the long reach he'd had getting the leather bag with the gemstones on his first excursion here. Out of his backpack, he withdrew a telescoping rod just twelve inches long, which extended out five feet. There was a curved hook on the end.

"This should work," he said. "There's also a strong magnet that one can attach to the end if we need to retrieve something with iron in it."

"That should work great," Dennis whispered, amazed at the ingenuity of his friend—then wondered why he had just whispered. There was no one around to hear their conversation or see what they were up to.

The little device Brayden picked up at a store for the disabled worked perfectly. Thirty seconds later, Brayden and Dennis were examining a dusty, guano-encrusted set of four keys. They were on a plain, metal ring, dangling on the end of the nifty hook. Two of them looked like ordinary house keys. Another one was an obvious key to a car—an Audi logo of four interconnected rings was stamped into the base. The fourth however, was different.

"That isn't any ordinary key that I've ever seen," Dennis said, reaching for the ring. "It looks a little like the key to the safety deposit box at the bank where my dad used to keep important documents." He held the key up to the light to get a better look. "After Dad died, my older sister opened the thing and all she found were old love letters from my mom to dad and a TWA stock certificate worth almost nothing."

"Don't touch it with your fingers. I have a Ziploc bag. The police can probably get fingerprints off of it if we handle it carefully. Let's see what else we can find."

Dennis took the plastic bag and holding the retriever in one hand, dropped the ring of keys into the clear bag, zipped it closed, and put it in his jacket pocket. Brayden was already several feet away scanning the crawl space with the powerful headlamp. Millimeter by millimeter he searched, ignoring the filthy timbers and the occasional angry bat that he flushed out. Dennis began moving in the opposite direction. The men had a plan in place, to circle in opposite directions, meeting halfway around the dome's attic space. Once there, they crossed over one another in order to cover the inspected areas with a new set of eyes. This time, they didn't want to leave anything behind. They were almost finished. Both men's knees and hands ached from crawling on the rough surfaces. Then Brayden saw the writing scrawled on a flat, smooth, surface of the wooden beam. It was in a cramped print written on an angle that could only have been done with someone's left hand. The words were printed in English. *Banc Constantinople. Help me.*

Lying in a narrow crack below the writing was a stubby pencil with a broken lead point and no eraser. Brayden reached down and retrieved the pencil and studied it, and then dropped it into the plastic bag with the keys. Stamped clearly on the side of the little pencil was yet another clue: *Lansing Country Club.*

✦ ✦ ✦

In spite of the bright sunshine, the inside of the Skoda was getting freezing cold. The wind had picked up, sucking the heat out of the engine and car body. Julie was reading a travel guide, trying to find Chelm on the map and trying to figure out exactly why any tour guide in their right mind would bring a busload of seniors here to this particular village. The hotel they stayed at that night was in a nearby town, but the old part of that city had been devastated by the Nazis in 1939 and again in 1944 by the Russians. The only thing of visible interest in this place was the unique, ancient church and its immaculate dome.

Paula had developed a migraine so she took three Advil and was sipping on a tepid Coca-Cola Light for some relief. She was resting her head against the window with her eyes closed listening to the gusts of wind.

A man in a gray uniform hammered on her window. Paula screamed. Julie, unsurprised because she had seen him coming, jumped at the loud pounding and harsh voice. He shouted something, but neither Julie nor Paula understood a word of it. Julie's first thought was that he was the police, ready to arrest her again. Then they both heard the revving of an engine and turned to see a huge truck idling just a few feet behind the Skoda. The man was already climbing back into the truck.

"Oh my gosh! It's just a garbage truck," Julie said, relief flooding her thoughts.

"No wonder the man looks mad. Look where we're parked. My idiot husband parked in the access way to the dumpster," Paula concluded. She didn't hesitate, but got out from the backseat and walked around the car to the driver's seat. She could plainly see the garbage man watch her with a lusty gaze as she nodded her understanding of what he expected. With some difficulty, she backed the car out of the truck's way and parked it in a spot near a row of green hedges adjacent to the tiny church's graveyard.

The garbage man waited as though he was hoping for another close look at her walking, but she stayed in the car. The driver maneuvered the rust-spotted truck into position and the hydraulic arms lifted the dumpster up over the front of the truck and rotated the bin, creating a cascade of paper and black plastic bags, many of which were caught by the gusting wind. Within moments the truck was gone and the only sound was the wind whistling around the car.

"What a creepy-looking guy," Paula said, getting a nod of agreement from Julie. "But that fresh cold air felt good. Maybe it will help my headache. I think I'll take a walk and see what's taking the boys so long. Want to come with me?"

"No thanks, I'll just wait here," said Julie, turning her attention back to the travel guide.

Inside the dome, Brayden and Dennis put away their gear and made their way to the top of the ladder. Brayden had taken several photos of the scrawled writing. The keys, the pencil, and the writing were the sum total of their findings. Inch by painful inch they backed down the steep ladder until they reached the landing near the top of the stairs. There was a small, pane-less window at the top of the spiral staircase and a low, curved doorway that led to the organ loft.

"I can't wait to get out of this place," Brayden said, coughing to clear his throat. "My lungs may never recover from that dust and bat crap."

Dennis put his hand to his ear, at first making Brayden think he hadn't heard his complaint, but then he also heard the sound. It was a motor—of what they couldn't tell.

Three minutes later they were on terra firma where they both took a second to get a drink of water from the bottles in the backpack. Brayden snapped a picture of the entrance to the spiral staircase just as he had done while in the attic space. Both men stretched and rubbed their knees and the sore palms of their hands. Dennis checked his jacket pocket for the Ziploc bag, brushed off the dust and grime, and then headed for the six-inch-thick, carved wooden door, fresh air, and the bright sunshine outside.

The first thing Brayden noticed was that the car had been moved. It was behind a stand of shrubs but appeared fine. There was a WC sign on a small nearby building that caught both men's eyes. Dennis nodded toward the restrooms and Brayden followed. Freshening up and washing their hands sounded like a splendid idea. When they finally approached their car, Julie's head was against the back window and her eyes were closed. Seeing the other backseat empty gave Brayden an instant abdominal cramp.

"Where is Paula?" he asked Julie, opening the door and awakening her.

Julie shook her head, not believing that she had

nodded off. "Ah … she went for a little walk in the fresh air."

"How long has she been gone?" Brayden asked, trying to stay calm.

"She left right after she moved the car for the garbage truck," she said, feeling defensive at Brayden's interrogation.

In the meantime Dennis had thrown the backpack in with the luggage and secured the plastic bag with the Audi car keys in the glove box. "Would you mind checking the ladies' restroom for her?" he asked his wife. "Brayden and I will walk around the church in opposite directions."

"If you find her please come right back to the car and lock the doors. We need to get going as soon as possible," added Brayden.

Dennis went left and Brayden right. In spite of the church being small, the church grounds including the cemetery extended over several hundred square meters. A well maintained path circled out wide from the building, weaving in and out around headstones—some with dates as old as the fifteen hundreds.

Rushing along and periodically calling out her name, Brayden was getting more and more angry with Paula as his anxiety level increased. He met up with Dennis and they doubled back on Dennis's path.

"This is ridiculous. Why she would leave the car I'll never understand."

"There's probably a simple explanation," Dennis said, trying to calm his friend's frazzled nerves. "Maybe she headed toward the village."

"You mean like we did when we were being chased by the Polish gangsters?" Turning to Julie, who was holding out her hands indicating her failure to find Paula, he said, "Julie, will you please wait here in the car while we look for her? If she shows up honk the horn three times."

"And keep the cars doors locked," Dennis admonished, pressing the lock button and firmly shutting the door.

Marie had driven in the wrong direction at the fork in the road. It had taken her five or six minutes to realize that the Skoda must have turned the other way. By the time she got back to the outskirts of the little village of Chelm, she had almost given up hope of finding her new best friends. The village was small and quiet. There was a one-pump gas station with no customers, a few shops that looked open, and there was only an occasional pedestrian. She passed an old woman riding a rusty bicycle with a wicker basket on the front and was tempted to stop and ask the woman if she had seen the Skoda, but then remembered where she was and that they didn't speak a common language. A big, faded-yellow garbage truck passed her, taking up more than its share of the narrow street, and then she saw the bakery.

It was a newer building set back thirty feet from the main street. It was well lit and had a car in the parking space in front. She rolled down her window to get a closer look and could see some dark-haired men sitting at one of the few small tables inside. There was a clerk

173

behind the counter and a woman talking to the clerk. Marie could smell the fantastic aroma of baking bread, which brought a sudden pang of hunger.

She was tempted to pull into a parking spot and pick up a sweet roll to eat in the car, but the fear of not finding the American couples made her drive on past the bakery toward the end of town, where above the roofline of the small houses and shops she could see a brightly-colored onion dome. *Must be the town's church.*

When she pulled around the corner of a row of very old, attached houses, she gasped in surprise. There, less than a hundred yards ahead, was a small parking lot, and at the far end sat the elusive, orange Skoda. She turned her car around and went back up the street two blocks and parked facing away from the church. *The Skoda will have to pass me as it leaves the church parking lot.* Just as she put the car into park, she was distracted by a black sedan that had stopped abruptly alongside a pedestrian. Two men appeared to be forcing the woman into the car. When the woman threw her head to the side in an attempt to resist, Marie suddenly recognized the woman. It was Brayden Ballard's wife.

Paula had gone into the church and could hear faint voices echoing down from the direction of the choir loft above. The men were obviously still looking for their clues to the treasure and Mr. Arbon. She turned and headed out the door. She was walking back toward the car when she smelled the fresh, baking bread. Her stomach growled in response to the olfactory stimulus—so she looked toward the center of the town and back at the church and her car. Julie was sitting in the same place Paula had left her, her head resting against the window. Another waft of the baking bread and her feet were already moving. Everyone would enjoy a late morning snack—maybe they would have apple pastries or raisin cinnamon rolls.

She followed the aroma, passing several quaint houses, a few open shops, and two side streets. An occasional car would pass and she could hear a baby cry and a TV or radio playing. There were no glitzy signs to guide her way, but just as she was about to turn back she saw a woman walk out toward the street and place a long baguette into a wicker bicycle basket. Paula turned down the street and in a matter of seconds was walking into a brightly lit bakery. This was definitely the place from which the fresh bread smell was coming.

A woman in a car slowed as she drove by, but then headed up the street. The woman's appearance caught Paula's attention for some reason, but she quickly dismissed the thought as she turned toward the glass showcase full of enticing, bakery goodies.

The dark-haired clerk behind the counter smiled at Paula and said something in Polish, apparently asking if she could help. She was wearing an embroidered apron over a gray, snug-fitting knit shirt. Her hair was piled on her head and held in place with a hair net. Paula tried to order two croissants and two raisin buns, but even pointing wasn't getting the message across.

"She doesn't speak English and can't see what you are pointing at," came a gruff voice from a small table in the corner of the room.

Startled at the intrusion, Paula turned to face the source of the voice and saw two men sitting at a table in the corner, smoking and drinking coffee. They could have been brothers; their appearance was so similar with their black hair and week-old growth of whiskers. Both were dressed in dark jeans, pointed-toe shoes, and dark, turtleneck sweaters. Both had dark, leather jackets strung over the backs of their chairs.

She didn't know quite how to react, but the speaker's English was quite good so she asked him to order the pastries for her. Without getting up, he gave the order in a commanding voice that made the clerk mumble a complaint as she picked out the items. The clerk handed over a paper sack and Paula held out a bill that she thought would cover the costs. Again there was a flurry of words in Polish.

One of the men in the corner laughed, followed by a hacking smokers cough. "You're giving her a large note that she doesn't have change for. Do you have one with a five on it?" the man asked.

Paula knew that she had just the one bill, and it was a fifty zloty note and some Euro coins. "I don't have anything smaller," she apologized to the woman. "Please tell her to just forget it."

Paula turned to leave when the man stood and said something to the clerk and took the sack off the counter. "We can't have you going hungry," he said with a chuckle, "especially when it is because you have too much money instead of not enough." He handed the sack to Paula and mumbled something to the woman. Paula thanked him and tried to give him the Euro coins but he refused.

She was so embarrassed she had lost her appetite and the only smell she could now sense was that of stale tobacco on the breath of the grizzly man. She started back down the street toward the church and was nearly at the corner of the main road when she heard the car behind her. She stepped closer to the house she was passing on the narrow sidewalk as the car pulled up beside her and stopped. The passenger side door opened wide, literally blocking her way. Startled, she recognized the man from the bakery and started to turn to walk behind the car when the driver appeared at the back of the car. The first man opened the sedan's back door and the driver pointed for her to get in.

"What are you doing?" she protested, as he grasped her arm and shoved her into the black BMW and got in beside her.

She scrambled across the seat and started to open the opposite door, but the second man was now standing there and slammed it shut, nearly smashing her hand. He got in the driver's seat and the car accelerated away throwing Paula back into the deep, leather seat.

"Are you out of you minds?" she screamed, jerking her arm out of the grasp of her former Good Samaritan.

"Your husband and his friend are the ones who are crazy, returning to my country after stealing our precious antiquities. What are they doing, trying to find more treasure?"

A cold chill shot through her body as she finally put the pieces of her memory of the first trip, and the stories Brayden and Dennis had told of the brutal men, the assault in the church, the attack and wreck they had caused with their black car.

"What do you want?" she blurted in the nastiest voice she could muster.

"It's very simple. We want what your husband and friend stole from us. And since you are here, maybe we'll take anything else we want."

The car was moving rapidly through the narrow streets. At one intersection she caught a glimpse of the church dome, but it seemed further away than before. The driver spoke and the other man gave a brisk command. The car made a sharp, right turn throwing Paula against the door. Moments later they were away from the town, heading into a dense stand of trees. They didn't go far when they turned off onto a dirt lane and just a few hundred feet from the road pulled up in front of an ancient brick house. The driver stopped the car and got out, ordering Paula out of the car. He tried to grasp her arm but she pulled away, scowling at him. She saw smoke coming out of the chimney and someone open the front door.

"You are making a big mistake," she said. "You need to take me back to my husband immediately or this place will be crawling with police. You must be an idiot, thinking you can just kidnap an American and get away with it."

"Get in the house," he commanded and grabbed her upper arm with a strong grip.

Paula once again jerked her arm away from the man. Reluctantly, she walked toward the house as her mind raced to come up with a plan. Brayden would at first be angry that she had gone off on her own and then be frantic when he couldn't find her. He would be clueless as to where she had gone or how to even begin to find her. As for calling the police, that would never happen. *I'm going to have to figure this situation out on my own.*

She followed the first man into the front room where she was pushed into a ghastly brown, over-stuffed chair with a broken spring that immediately poked her in the thigh.

"What's your name?" she asked the younger of the two men after the other went into another room that looked like a kitchen.

"Call me Alexander," he said in a calm and almost refined voice. "My brother is named Tito."

"Why are you doing this to me? You don't even know me!" Paula pleaded, trying to hold back the emotion in her voice and the tears that she knew could well up in her eyes at any moment.

"Oh, but we do know you, and we know your husband or boyfriend or whoever he is. We also know your other friend. They stuck their noses into a place they didn't belong and they stole something from us—or maybe you did it!" said Tito as he stood in the doorway to the other room. "What is your name?"

The question actually gave Paula her first glimmer of hope. If they didn't know her name, then they probably didn't know Brayden's or Dennis's or Julie's names. Most likely they didn't know what was found by the men and why they were back in Poland again.

"I don't understand why you kidnapped me and what you want me to do."

"Now, now! We didn't kidnap you," Alexander said. "We bought you some lunch and you wanted to come with us for a … how do you say it? A picnic. In just a little while your husband will come looking for you. It is actually quite fortuitous that you came to us. We were just talking about you this morning … hoping that you would come back to our little town for a visit. Where is your husband…? No, let me guess. He's up in the church loft trying to steal something else. Right?"

Paula didn't answer, but instead asked to use the bathroom and was shown a primitive add-on to the cottage that had just a toilet with a water bowl mounted high on the wall. A chain with a wooden handle went up to the bowl to flush the toilet. The sink was the size of a soup bowl and a shower with a handheld sprinkler head was attached to the sink faucet. A hole in the floor of the shower through which she could see the ground appeared to be the only drain. There was a window that would probably be large enough for her to crawl through. *But then what would I do? Run into the forest and be chased down like an animal?*

She dried her hands on her slacks, afraid to touch the threadbare, brown towel draped over the back of the toilet. She straightened her hair in the tiny vanity mirror that someone had fastened to the wall with roofing nails. She took a deep breath and opened the door. The room smelled of wood smoke and newly brewed coffee, which was a relief from the musty bathroom smell. The two men were standing outside by the car arguing, apparently in Polish. Paula took a chance to look around the little house. There was a kitchen with a wood-burning stove, a near-empty pantry cupboard, and a small table with three chairs. There was no refrigerator in sight. A small bedroom off the kitchen had two beds—neither one with sheets, just rumpled blankets and pillows without pillow cases. *Either these brothers were camping here or lived the life of pigs.*

"Come outside Mrs. Ballard," yelled one of the brothers through the open door.

The command made Paula panic. She had left her purse back in the car with Julie and had just the banknote and a few Euro coins in her pocket. *How did they figure out my name?* As she walked past the kitchen table she noticed a three-pronged, metal fork. In a single motion she deftly snatched it and in the same motion slipped it into the waist band of her slacks.

"Get in the car please," Tito said, opening the front passenger door for her.

Alexander disappeared around the corner of the house and reappeared straddling a yellow motorcycle. When he kick-started the engine the noise was startling. With just a nod to his brother he rode off down the dirt lane toward the highway. Tito started the BMW and they headed down the dirt lane, eating the dust of the motorcycle.

"What is it you think my husband took from you?"

Tito laughed. "You are a very funny lady. You know how to act so dumb but I sense that you are very smart. You know exactly what we want and that we also want you out of our country. How would you like it if we came to your town and started crawling around your church or house and stealing things that are dear to you?"

She didn't answer. The fork was digging into her skin and the bumping from the rough road was making it worse. She decided to play the silent role and wiggled sideways in the seat to relieve the pressure from the fork. Hopefully, it would be worth the discomfort.

Marie was in a major quandary. She knew that the orange Skoda, the two men, and probably the other American woman were at the church, but she felt a strong empathy for the Ballard woman who had obviously gotten herself in way over her head. She was definitely being abducted against her will. There was no predicting where the men were taking her or what they might do to her, but Marie was guessing that it had to have something to do with the diamond.

She doubted Ballard would leave town without his wife so she put the car in gear, and staying several hundred meters back, followed the black car. When it turned down the dirt road, she had passed the entrance and stopped along the shoulder of the highway. She left her flasher lights on and started walking. She had followed the dirt road for a quarter of a mile before she saw the tiny house. Using her phone camera she took a picture of the house and the car, zooming in on the license plate.

Marie ducked down as two men came out of the house arguing. When they appeared to be leaving she made a dash back to her car and barely made it there when a motorcycle with one of the men passed her on the highway. She whipped her car around just as she saw the BMW pull off of the dirt road and head back toward the village. She wasn't positive, but thought she saw a woman's head in the front seat of the car. She opened the glove box and retrieved her Glock, tucking it into her floppy, leather handbag.

The black sedan was driving slowly along the highway, so she stayed back far enough that only the roofline of the car was visible. It took the turn toward the village and a few kilometers later it turned, heading toward the church. The sedan then pulled off to the side of the road and stopped as though waiting for something.

There was just enough curve in the road that Marie felt her car was not visible to the man in the black sedan. Moments later, she heard the sound of a motorcycle. Now there were two people onboard the cycle: a scruffy-looking guy in a black leather jacket and an attractive-looking woman with long, blond hair. The motorcycle pulled up alongside the sedan and there appeared to be a heated argument, and then the motorcycle rode off toward the church.

Marie got out of her car and walked around a small building to get a better look. She strongly considered approaching the car—gun in hand—and ordering the release of the woman, but then it occurred to her that the woman might not even agree to come with her. Those at the car appeared to be arguing, with the man gesturing like an Italian symphony conductor. Just as she had made up her mind to intervene, she saw the car's back-up lights come on and the car reversed into a driveway. She barely had time to duck behind some bushes when the car's tires screeched and it accelerated past her. *And what about the husbands and the other woman at the church?*

She ran to her car, put the car in gear and headed for the church's parking lot. From the looks of things she had arrived just in time. She stopped in the first space of the parking lot and watched in shock as the motorcycle rider and the blond woman confronted the two American men. She rolled down her window trying to listen to the verbal exchange. She kept her car's engine running in order for the heater to offset the cool, country air. Lucky for everyone.

19

Brayden was sick with fear. He and Dennis had jogged around most of the village and couldn't find Paula. Dennis had stopped in several of the shops finding them empty of customers for the most part, but still no sign of Paula. Brayden had stuck his head in the bakery and asked if a tall American woman had been there, but had received a stare of incomprehension and a shrug of the shoulders from the woman clerk. Before he left he noticed a smoldering cigarette on a pastry plate on a small, round table. There were cups and service for two. He ran out the door and was nearing the corner of the street leading to the church when he noticed a fluffy Kleenex on the ground. It couldn't have been there long, it still looked clean.

Under normal circumstances he never would have considered touching the Kleenex, but for some inspired reason he reached down and not only picked it up but immediately brought it to his nose and sniffed it. There was not the slightest doubt in his mind that it belonged to his wife. Poison, by Dior, was her perfume, and nothing else in the world smelled like it.

He broke into a run toward the church, sure that he would find her safely returned, but as his feet were landing cobblestone to cobblestone, he was nearly struck from behind by a speeding motorcycle. It also was headed in the direction of the church—with two people on board. As he rounded the last corner, to his astonishment, the motorcycle had pulled up alongside the Skoda and stopped. A blond woman got off of the back as the man put down the kickstand and approached the driver's side back window, motioning for the person inside to lower it. As he ran closer, Brayden could see Julie lower the window and begin to converse with the man and the blond woman.

Within seconds, Brayden was also beside the car, flaring with anger. From another direction Dennis approached at a run.

"Open the door!" the man in the black turtleneck yelled at Julie, pounding his fist on the roof of the car—oblivious to the two approaching men.

"What do you want?" Brayden yelled, shoving the shoulder of the man away from the car and Julie's window.

When the man drew back his arm making a tight fist, prepared to hit Brayden, Dennis grabbed the collar of the man's leather jacket and in the same motion kicked the back of the man's knee and yanked the jacket collar downward. The man crashed to the ground with a moan, dropping something from his left hand that made a metallic sound on the stone, and then slid under the car.

As Julie stared out of the car window in shock, the blond woman, dressed from head to toe in black leather, took control of the situation. She stood on the opposite side of the bike, both feet firmly planted, and softly began speaking—and at the same time cocking the hammer of a small revolver.

"Hello, Mr. Ballard. It looks as though your arm is well healed," said Dr. Andriana Vlonovitski.

The gun in her hand wasn't pointed at Brayden or Dennis, but was eight inches from the partially open car window framing the face of Julie Cannon. Everyone froze in their places except the hoodlum Alexander, who, grimacing from the pain in his knee, stood and with a hammer-like swing, slugged Brayden in the right flank immediately above his kidney. The pain was immobilizing—causing his knees to buckle and the full content of his lungs to expel in one burst.

Alexander instantly had an eight-inch switchblade knife in his hand, and with his fist grasping Dennis's collar, slammed him against the side of the Skoda and pushed the knife up under his chin. Andriana held her position with the gun inches from Julie's face.

"Where the gemstones are?" the hoodlum growled in a lead-heavy accent and an obvious grammatical error.

Brayden was now on his knees and elbows slowly catching his breath, and trying to keep from vomiting from the pain. He was of no help to Dennis or Julie. "Where is Paula? Where is Paula?" his mind kept repeating over and over—then he saw the gun under the car.

"Get up!" the man commanded Brayden, still holding the knife under Dennis's chin. A tiny trickle of blood began working its way down his neck onto his shirt collar.

How Brayden instantly came up with his plan, he would never be able to answer. He let out a loud gagging sound as though on the verge of vomiting and threw his body flat on the ground, extending his right arm deep under the car and blindly grasped the 38 cal. automatic pistol, which fit firmly in his grip. It had been thirty years since his small arms training in the National Guard, but like riding a bicycle the imprint on his mind was still there. He found the safety switch, flicked it off, and then rolled to his side, shoving the gun against the Pole's calf. Without so much as a warning threat, Brayden pulled the trigger. He had given no thought to the direction of the bullet after it went through the muscle, but fortunately it was toward the distant cornfield and not Dennis.

Between the explosive sound of the gun and the ear-shattering scream of the hoodlum, Andriana lost her concentration and turned her gun away from Julie. Dennis saw the opportunity and wrenched the gun from her wrist.

In the blink of an eye, Brayden was on his feet with the automatic pointed at the head of the Polish mobster who was now on the ground, moaning and rolling back and forth as blood streamed from below his knee. Dennis had a handful of the doctor's blond hair and was pressing her face against the hood of the car. His right hand held the doctor's menacing little revolver, which he would later learn held no bullets. The switchblade had made a substantial knick in his chin and his daily ibuprofen intake made the bleeding worse. In spite of the blood dripping on the woman's white sweater he didn't loosen his grip.

"Where is my wife?" Brayden yelled at the two assailants.

When the man didn't answer, Brayden kicked at the wounded leg eliciting another scream.

Julie finally had stopped screaming and exited the car on the opposite side from the mêlée. She picked the bloody knife up off of the ground and in an action that astonished her husband and his best friend, she pushed the knife against the woman's cheek and in a voice of desperation screamed, "Where is my friend?"

"I don't know. Ask him," said Andriana, seemingly resolved to accept whatever fate lay ahead. "I honestly don't know where they have taken her. I'm sorry."

The apology surprised the Americans, but there was no time to ponder her real meaning. The loud screeching of tires attracted everyone's attention as a big, black BMW sedan sped through the parking lot entrance, apparently traveling too fast to avoid a collision. Just as the car's tires crossed the curb onto the cobbled stones of the parking lot, the driver seemed to recognize that something was drastically wrong. He slammed on the brakes and spun the steering wheel—causing the sedan to fishtail into a waist-high, cement parking median, crushing the rear quarter panel of the car. He was ignoring everything except his goal to get out of the parking lot when Marie saw her chance and acted.

Marie Felstein couldn't believe her eyes or her ears as she witnessed the screaming and assault taking place two hundred feet away. From her car she watched and listened, trying to fathom what the heck was happening at the side of the Americans' car. She heard the gunshot and the scream echo off of the church walls and then she heard the roaring of a black sedan enter the parking lot. It made a panicky skid sideways and crashed into a cement divider.

Marie thought briefly about getting out of the car and interrupting the fight, but everything happened so fast all she could do was watch. She was parked with her motor running less than a hundred feet from the BMW when it all broke loose. She could see the demonic look on the face of the burly BMW driver as the car skidded past, and then she got a glimpse of Mrs. Ballard belted in the front seat with a piece of silver tape across her face. Marie was the only person within a mile who had a legitimate reason to possess a gun and she had it right beside her. There was, however, no time to even consider using it. The black sedan with it's hostage was going to leave the parking lot, and a gun wouldn't stop it. Jamming the gear shift lever into reverse, Marie stomped on the accelerator and forcibly pushed her head into the headrest.

Brayden, Dennis, Julie, and the two Poles watched in awe as first they were showered in flying car parts and glass from the shattered parking lot divider, and then the black sedan engine screamed to life again and the car began moving toward the parking lot exit. Suddenly, a small, gray car that no one had noticed before bolted backward, tires squealing, on a collision course with the escaping BMW.

As metal met metal both cars spun away from one another and their engines stalled. Marie had failed to refasten her seat belt and was tossed like a wet rag into the passenger side of the car. Her car's left, rear bumper had solidly struck the left, front fender of the sedan, inflating its driver's side airbag and shattering the windshield and driver's window. As the driver pushed the deflating nylon bag away from his bloody face, he tried to restart the black sedan's engine. Paula saw her opportunity, yanked the door open and fled from the car.

Unsure what to do in the confused situation, Brayden continued to point the automatic pistol at his attackers. Everyone watched Paula exit the smoking sedan, tearing silver tape from her mouth and screaming a warning to her husband. "He's got a gun," she yelled, not knowing that the battle was over.

At the same time sirens were heard, far off in the distance.

"Let us go!" pleaded Andriana, "and these men will never bother you again. If the police get here they will arrest all of us and we will all rot in prison, including you and your wives. You are thieves! We just want what is ours!"

"Paula, are you okay?" screamed Julie, tossing the bloody knife into a nearby hedge as she ran toward Paula.

Dennis looked at Brayden who rolled his eyes in relief and nodded toward the blond doctor. Dennis released the woman's hair and instead grabbed the collar of the wounded hoodlum, dragging him to his feet. He nodded to the woman and shoved the man toward the stalled BMW—Alexander's leg leaving a thin trail of blood. Brayden gave his wife a welcome peck, but was still holding the automatic so she quickly backed away.

"You ladies go get in the car," he said to Julie and Paula.

Dennis continued to follow Tito making sure he wouldn't collapse again. Brayden looked in the driver's window of the small, gray sedan, but only saw a large purse with the contents scattered on the seat and the passenger door partially open. He nudged Andriana toward the BMW keeping the gun in plain sight for the dazed driver to see. They were all aware that the sirens were getting closer.

Marie watched from behind a stand of shrubs where she was hiding. Cannon shoved the wounded man into the backseat of the black sedan and motioned for the blond woman to get on the motorcycle. Seconds later, the BMW was gone, dragging part of its exhaust pipe along the pavement. Cannon helped the self-declared doctor pick up the heavy bike, which she mounted, started, and then exited the parking lot in a jerky, unstable motion. Dennis started the Skoda and drove it toward the gray sedan with its crumpled, rear bumper.

"Who are you and why did you do that insane crash act?" came a voice from behind Marie. She turned to see Brayden Ballard standing six or eight feet away holding the pistol, but pointing it toward the ground.

"Be careful with that gun," she said. "You don't want to hurt someone else."

Her confident, New York-accented voice wasn't what he expected from the petite, attractive woman who looked vaguely familiar. The sirens were getting closer and Dennis had given a short beep of the horn. It was time to go.

"Are you okay?" he asked.

"I'm fine, but we really need to get away from here. Polish jails are no place to spend the holidays. Maybe we could continue this conversation another time? Please get rid of the gun. Someplace where no one will find it with your fingerprints."

Without another word she took off running toward her car and dove through the passenger door, slamming it shut. Within seconds her car's engine was running and the tires were crunching over broken glass and plastic car parts. Brayden could have sworn that she had also been gripping a gun in her hand as she ran away.

He ran toward the Skoda that Dennis already had turned toward the exit. Brayden jumped in, pulling the door closed as the car accelerated toward the street leading to the highway. Several people were poking their heads out of the doorways of the small houses, wondering what was happening in their peaceful, little town. The Skoda's passengers were less than a kilometer from the church when they passed the first of several police cars, all with their lights flashing and sirens whining. They would arrive to find an empty parking lot littered with shattered car parts and a trail of blood.

From the backseat Brayden began hearing muffled sobs. It was unlike Paula to cry. When he turned toward the back he saw that it was Julie who was crying and being comforted by his wife.

"I was sure the woman was going to shoot me and then kill all of the rest of you," Julie said between sobs. "That's what she said. If we didn't give Tito the gems—I'm sure she called him Tito—that he would kill all of us. He said that the dead man you found earlier—Arbon—had promised that he would give them the location of the gems, but then he disappeared."

Dennis stretched his hand back over the seat and

patted his wife's knee, then focused on the road ahead. In the rush to leave the parking lot he hadn't paid attention to the directional road signs and had gone through two traffic circles before Brayden asked him if he knew where he was going.

"No I don't know where we're going! I'm just driving as far away from that church, as fast as this car will go. I don't ever want to see it again," he said.

Brayden took the Garmin GPS off of the car's windshield and programmed it for Prague. When it calculated and told them to turn south at the next interchange, Dennis questioned the decision. "I thought we were spending the night in Krakow."

"Krakow is the last place I want to be seen," Brayden said. "We need to get out of Poland—the sooner the better! And when you see the first big river, stop the car. I need to get rid of this gun."

No one disagreed.

Two days later, Marie Felsten was back in New York City. She had reported in to her boss before getting on her flight in Berlin. The regional director had left word for her to return to her work at the diamond dealer as soon as she could get a few hours of sleep. She was to file a report by e-mail. He would call her, if he had any questions.

He'll have an arm's length list of questions, especially when he sees the bill from Hertz for the car repair. She was doing a load of wash after being unable to sleep. In her own mind she kept ruminating over the bizarre altercation in the parking lot of that little onion dome church. As hard as she tried, she still couldn't piece together the various events that had taken place in Poland. There were too many players and too little hard information. And where were the gemstones?

Later that day, she left her apartment for work, but felt strongly that the diamond shop would be the last place she was going to be able to glean together the facts she desperately needed. Chances of finding the mysterious diamond she was supposed to be chasing seemed infinitesimal as this point. She needed to catch up with the Ballards and Cannons to put them in a setting where she could ask some hard questions.

Dressed in pink leggings, purple leg warmers, a black leather coat and a gray knit hat, she punched in her time card and went straight to the break room where she drank three cups of unsweetened coffee. Her plan was more than just to help her stay awake. Ten minutes later the coffee and her over-stimulated stomach acid came back up. She had been loitering near Grumpy's desk when it happened. He was in the middle of giving her a lecture on missing work and on dressing more conservatively when she threw up into his wastebasket and then drooled brown saliva down the front of her fluffy, white sweater. He was about to scream at her, but she looked so pathetic that he took sympathy on her and told her to go home for the rest of the day.

She called her handler and told him—not asked him—that she was leaving for Denver and wouldn't be back until she found the elusive diamond, or at least the real story behind it and her weird experience in Poland. She had no real plan in mind, except to investigate the Ballards and the Cannons, assuming that they had returned. As she packed her bag she put in two extra clips of bullets for her pistol. She had developed a strange attraction for the Colorado couples and didn't want any harm to come to them. She went through the photos she had taken with her little Nikon. None were great, but they fixed a better image in her mind of the four Americans and of their Polish assailants. The one person she had never been able to get a clear picture of was the blond woman on the motorcycle. The blonde always had been in the wrong place, turning the wrong direction, and at the wrong time.

By five that afternoon, Marie was sitting toward the back of a Jet Blue 737 headed for Denver Stapleton Airport. With any luck, she would get in with time to eat a piece of the famous Colorado beef and get a good night's sleep before she set out on another crazy excursion. She doubted that the diamond was going anywhere soon—if in fact it was back in the USA—but trying to anticipate the Ballards' next move left her wondering just how wrong she might be.

The domestic scenes at the Cannon and the Ballard households had played out quite similarly. The jet lag of eight hours flying from east to west along with several hours of layovers and flight delays had left both couples totally exhausted. Finally back home, Brayden had taken the phones off the hook, left his cell phone in the car, and placed a note on the door that everyone inside was ill and to please not ring or knock. Paula had texted her kids to assure them that they were safely back home and that all was well. Then they had crashed into the soft, cool sheets for a long winter's nap.

Exhausted and angry, Julie hadn't let Dennis off quite so easily. He was just turning out the nightstand light when she gave him her ultimatum.

"I can't stand either of us being involved with this insane onion dome mystery another minute. I want to go to sleep for two days and then wake up and not hear another word about the gems or the fraternity ring or the car keys Brayden found or the dead and missing Mr. Arbon—ever again. Do you understand me? Never, ever again! I'm even considering deleting all of my pictures of Poland just so I don't ever have to be reminded of it. Ever again! Do you understand what I'm saying? Never again!" With that said, she pulled the duvet over her head.

Dennis rolled over to face her and leaned up on one elbow and teased the bedcover away from her face. She wouldn't make eye contact with him but he could see the tears welled up in her eyes. He reached over to stroke her cheek but she moved her face away.

"You are just tired," he said. "We are all tired. Let's get a good night's sleep tonight and some exercise when we get up in the morning. Tomorrow we will both feel better."

"Speak for yourself. You didn't have a pistol shoved in your face by a crazy woman who promised to shoot out your brains if you so much as moved. You didn't have to sit in a Krakow jail or be body searched by that smelly, Polish policewoman with sandpaper-rough hands and bad breath. We've spent most of next year's vacation money on your stupid trip to Michigan and our useless trip back to Poland where all four of us could have been killed. I want out!" she insisted, no longer lying down but now sitting on the edge of the bed with her back toward her husband.

"We just have to get a little more information and then—"

"And then what?" she interrupted. "The gangsters show up and shoot all of us and take back their gemstones. Or maybe the police will show up and arrest all of us and we can spend the next ten years in court and prison for smuggling stolen antiquities into the country."

Her voice broke and she started to sob. Dennis got out of bed and came around to stand in front of her, then knelt and held her hands. At first she pulled away from him, but finally let him take her in his arms.

"Everything is going to be okay," he promised, not knowing or really believing that it was true. The one thing he did know was that he would never ever put his wife in harm's way again.

It took another hour of talking and consoling and promising, but she finally succumbed to exhaustion and slept for the next fourteen hours. When he awoke there was eighteen inches of new snow in their backyard. Winter had arrived in the Rockies.

Marie wasn't in much better shape than the Ballards or Cannons. When her flight touched down at Denver's Stapleton International Airport the snow was so deep that the plane sat on the tarmac for three hours before it could move to a gate. Luckily, she only had brought carry-on luggage so she was one of the first off her flight to get in line at Hertz. She had flashed her federal identification to get her gun through security, which had raised lots of eyebrows but no objections.

The Hertz counter representative was very cheerful until he brought up her rental profile. "I'm sorry miss, but there seems to be a problem Someone must have mixed up the records. Certainly you weren't in Poland this week … were you?"

She gave him a look like he must be nuts, shook her head, and asked, "Why in the world would you say that? Has someone stolen my identity? Where is Poland anyway?"

The clerk gave her a worried look and apologized. He quickly processed her car order and without mentioning it snuck in an upgrade to a four-wheel drive, Outback SUV.

The road conditions were pretty bad and she was exhausted, having added another two hours of jet lag to her week. Marie made it to the Hyatt with only a few skids, checked into her room, and texted her handler for any new instructions.

"JUST SIT TIGHT," was all that the return message said.

She could do that. She ordered room service to be delivered in an hour and a pay-per-view movie for later, and then turned up the room heat. She was just stepping into the large Jacuzzi tub of steaming water when there was a knock at the door.

"Great!" she said in disgust. She put on the generic, white, terry-cloth robe and slopped bubbles toward the door. "Who is it?" she asked, not feigning her irritation.

When there was no response she became even more irritated. She went to her purse on the computer table and slipped it over her shoulder with her wet right hand inside, gripping her automatic.

"I said, 'Who is it?'" she repeated in a louder voice. She had been trained at Quantico never to look through the peephole since it would allow a nemesis an easy guess where to put a bullet through a door. Marie stood to the side of the door and asked one more time. When there was no response, she shrugged off the interruption as a mistaken room number and returned to the comfort of the steaming water—this time with her purse within easy reach.

Forty minutes later she was warm and dry and dressed in new, pink flannel pajamas. When room service knocked delivering her dinner she let them in without hesitation. She was starving. The bellman set up the service on a small table and accepted his tip with a smile.

"Oh, I almost forgot," he said. "There was a note taped on the outside of your door." He went back to the door and handed her the folded paper, then he left the room, quietly closing the door.

She tossed the note on the bed and turned on the TV. The movie came on and she settled down to enjoy her meal and the canned entertainment. Later, she found herself falling asleep while sitting at the table; she got up and placed the food tray in the hall and turned off the TV. As she turned back the covers, the folded piece of paper fluttered to the floor. She saw it and remembered the bellman leaving it, but was too tired to read it or have to deal with anything but sleep.

Brayden Ballard's feet sank so deep in the snow that he thought his penny-loafers were going to be pulled off. It was their second day back home. He was walking toward his office building from his car. He was anxious to pick up the mail and catch up on whatever work had piled up since his recent trip abroad. He had awakened early, still with a serious case of time disorientation and his rooting around the house had awakened Paula. She sensed his restlessness, thus suggested he find something to occupy his time while she got started on her Christmas decorating. Then she rolled over and went back to sleep.

The lights were out at his office building except for the interior security lights and the sodium vapor lights in the parking area. He was paying so much attention to walking in the deep snow that he didn't notice the person approach him from behind. Brayden slid his key in the lock and turned the handle. The warning beep of the alarm system sounded the beginning of its thirty-second delay as he punched in the code. Turning to close the door behind him the body of a large-framed man filled the doorway.

Brayden recoiled as if he'd been struck. "What are you doing here?"

Glade Hakes pushed past Brayden, pulling the door closed behind him. "You don't answer your phone. How's a body supposed to deal in precious stones if he doesn't answer his phone?"

"Wow! You startled me. Come on in and warm up," Brayden said to the gemologist, then glanced at the clock on the wall noting that it was not even seven o'clock. No one else would show up for at least an hour. He started the coffee machine and they then settled into Brayden's office.

"What's on your mind?" he asked Hakes.

"I have a cash buyer for your diamond."

"I don't recall ever saying that it was for sale," Brayden hedged, not wanting to offend Hakes, but at the same time not wanting to give up the present location of the stones or any information about them.

"In the world where I live, everything is for sale. That's how the world works. We buy and sell and eat and work and play."

"I'm all for the eating and playing. I've done the work part all my life. As far as the selling goes, I'm not sure the stone is mine to sell."

"Well, just so you know, the buyers of high-end stones in New York aren't stupid and won't wait around for a deal, when the next good one is just a hundred yards down the street. If we act fast, I think I can get you half a million dollars for your diamond. But of course, the buyer will need to see the stone before they will pay for it or even set a firm offer. As for the other stones you showed me and the several you implied that you have, now would be a good time to unload them as well."

Brayden looked across the desk at the man, trying to figure out what he was up to and who he was really working for. He was most curious as to why the man had chosen this time of the morning to suggest a purchase. *Has he been stalking me?*

"I'm not very good at playing cat and mouse games," said Brayden. "I told you before that I was in the middle of some research about the provenance of the stones and when and if I decided to sell it I would let you know."

"Well, I shouldn't be telling you this, but the word on the street is that there are some foreign buyers—maybe 'collectors' is a better word—who want the stones and don't think they need to pay the price others pay. If they were to find out where the stone, or even better, where all the stones were, they might be tempted to just take them. Some of these types of men can be very violent."

"I appreciate the heads up," said Brayden.

"Trust me when I say that you do not want to have dealings with anyone but legitimate dealers," Hakes said as he stood and walked toward the door. "The smartest thing you can do is sell the stones to a dealer as soon as possible. I can help you do just that. Then you and your friends should take the money and run. Run from the bad guys and the IRS and any nosy neighbors or friends."

"Like I said, I appreciate the advice. Just one question before you go? Supposing there are several more stones than the three I showed you … stones of similar quality and size to the diamond. What is a realistic price I should be asking?"

"The diamond is not necessarily the most valuable of the lot, but let's just presume that it is. Did you say you have more than the three stones?"

Brayden reflexively nodded a confirmation, then wished he hadn't.

"And they are all about the same size," Hakes reiterated, obviously doing the math in his head.

"My eye is not trained like yours."

"I'd guess that none of them are newly cut. They probably all came from the same source, maybe a regal staff or crown and have been hidden away for years. Knowing the history of Eastern Europe, they could have come from any number of sources including the Hapsburgs, any of the Saxon kings, or part of the Suleiman era in Persia and Turkey. Oh yes, and then there are the Russians."

"We were talking about the price?" Brayden hinted, sensing that Hakes was enjoying the speculation and could have gone on for quite some time.

"I could most likely find a buyer for around $6 or $8 million for the lot."

At first Brayden was speechless. Then he did his own quick math and realized how "low-ball" Hakes's estimate was. "How can you get me a more exact figure?"

"Probably the best way would be for you and me and a guard to fly to New York with the stones in hand. The buyers there think nothing of making a big-dollar decision on the spot and cutting you a cashier's check while you look at their inventory," Hakes said, still standing in the doorway. "Maybe they'll throw in a nice set of earrings for your wife."

"I'll have to think about it," was the best answer Brayden could dream up at the moment.

"Selling them before they're stolen from you and before you or your wife get hurt is solid advice. Rumors like the one going around right now won't give you a lot of time to ponder the shoulds and should nots. There are plenty of people out there who would kill for a lot less money than the value of your gemstones. Call me tomorrow at the latest."

A blast of freezing air filled the room when Hakes left, leaving Brayden with a cold chill. He hadn't realized how much he had been perspiring. He started to lift the phone to call Paula, but put it back thinking she had fallen back to sleep. He speed dialed Dennis but only got a recording. "Maybe it's just as well," he thought. "How can I make a decision by talking with Paula,

Dennis, and Julie when I don't have a clue what is going to be best for me?"

Marie sat in the Subaru, trying to keep the windows un-fogged enough to see what was going on in Ballard's office. She didn't recognize the bundled-up man going into, and later, out of the office building. *If only my anonymous New York handler would offer up a little more information. That would be nice.*

She was getting too stiff to keep sitting in the car so she decided to take a walk. She planned to keep the parking area where Ballard's car was parked in plain view. The wind was picking up so she headed in the leeward direction of the building. As she got closer she came to a spot where she was looking straight into Ballard's office. Her only cover was a wooden pillar in a darkened area of the building that luckily was close to his window. As she peeked through it, a gust of snowy wind and a little good fortune blew her way.

Ballard was sitting at his desk wearing glasses, which she had never seen him wear. In front of him was a small, metal briefcase with the lid open. He reached into the case and took out a fist-size, beat-up-looking, leather pouch. Suddenly, to her amazement, Ballard tipped it carefully upside down onto what looked like an ordinary hand towel. Out of the pouch poured a rainbow of sparkling gemstones, which, when he spread them out, covered a large portion of the towel. From among the stones, he picked up a large sparkling diamond and held it up against the bulb of a desk lamp. As he rolled the stone in his fingers he smiled. Next, he put down the diamond and picked up a blood-red ruby, examining it the same way.

Marie forgot about the cold wind and everything else around her as she watched him evaluate dozens of the stones, stopping after each one to make a note on a yellow legal pad. She found herself inching closer to the window, slowly losing her concealment to her curiosity. She watched him put the stones back into the leather pouch and then place them in the metal case and set the combination lock. He then picked up what looked like a set of car keys and began inspecting them. Suddenly, without warning, he jerked his head in the direction of the window and picked up the ringing telephone.

Ballard leaned back in his tall, leather office chair and spoke into the phone as he began twirling the key ring around his finger. Any hint of worry or anxiety was absent, but then he looked straight at the window— straight at her—and abruptly sat up in his chair. He stood up, still speaking into the phone and then hung it up. Before Marie could make a move toward her car he was gone from the room.

She tugged the hood around her head as she ran across the parking lot, struggling not to slip and fall on the icy surface or get blown off of her feet by the wind. "I'm an idiot," she told herself as she ran.

"Stop!" screamed a voice from behind her. Instinctively she looked back and saw Ballard running toward her— gaining on her. Her intention was to go to her rental car, but she was running out of time to get there, get inside, and get the car started before he caught up with her. A freshly-shoveled path led off to her right through a stand

208 STEVEN I. DAHL, M.D.

of quaking aspens and then into the nearby residential neighborhood. At the last possible second she veered off onto the path, away from her car.

"Stop!" she heard again, followed by a loud curse. She glanced back to see Ballard's feet shoot out from under him and his muscular frame crash to the snow-covered pavement—his cold, leather-soled street shoes obviously not intended for hot pursuits.

She ran about two blocks and then hid on the steps of a house with no lights on inside. She waited what seemed like forever before she ventured back toward the office building and her parked car. When she arrived at the forested edge of the parking lot she could see that Ballards' Tahoe was gone. She slipped into her car and with the headlights off drove quietly out of the area. She hadn't noticed the tromped footprints around the vehicle. Especially the area around the rear bumper.

"Can you hear me?" Brayden said into his cell phone. "You won't believe what happened since I last spoke to you."

"Can it wait a minute? I've got my arms full of laundry," said Paula, a touch of aggravation in her tone. "Did you forget you were supposed to go to the mall with me to pick out things for the little boys?"

He waited for her to continue as he walked toward his car. Now he wished he had waited until he got home instead of calling. She always was patient and understanding with him—except on the phone. She didn't particularly like talking on the phone to anyone, especially strangers, and would often procrastinate or even forego opportunities just to avoid a phone call.

"I'm back. You're not going to like it when you see the shopping list I've made up. I am skipping buying anything for you by the way, since you were such a bad boy and left home without leaving me a note. Santa's going to hear about it too!" she said, with a wicked chuckle.

Meanwhile Brayden had made it to the car and had settled into the heated seat of his SUV. "Listen to me for a minute and cut the guilt slinging. I've been working, trying to catch up. I was walking out the door when I had unexpected visitors."

"And what was her name?" she said, refusing to give up the fun she was having playing the verbal picador with little jabs.

"Nice—you know that I can't reveal confidential client information," he said, finally giving in to her game and yet trying to sound serious—which he was. "Actually, there were two visitors. The first one—all male—is Mr. Hakes. I'll tell you all about what he said when I get home. By the way, what's for breakfast?"

"And the other visitor?" she asked, not letting him off of the hook.

"Definitely female, and someone I think we have all seen before—in Poland."

"You've got to be kidding. Are you talking about that blond doctor?" she asked. "What the heck is she doing in Denver?"

"It wasn't her. I'm pretty sure it was that woman who followed us around in Poland—the one driving that gray car that saved our hides—but it was still dark and she took off before I could get a good look," Brayden said.

"What in the world was she doing calling on you at your office?"

"Spying on me at my office is more like it," he said. "I'll tell you all about it when I get home. Right now I'm freezing cold and the back of my pants are wet and probably shredded. Call Dennis and tell him we need to meet tonight and don't take no for an answer. All four of us need to meet."

"But Julie said—"

"Tell them it is life or death. On second thought you'd better not say the 'D' word. Just tell them it's vital to our well-being."

It was nearly ten o'clock that night when the Cannons rang the Ballards' doorbell. They had reluctantly agreed to the meeting. As they came into the kitchen, the look on Julie's face was less than pleasant.

"How about something hot to drink?" Paula asked the couple as they took off their down jackets.

"No thanks," Julie said, trying to sound angry, but unable to really be that way to her best friend.

"Dennis? I have hot brownies and cold milk."

"I wouldn't want to be impolite—so yes," he said with a warm smile.

When they had all settled around the kitchen table, Brayden filled them in on the unsolicited meeting and the spying of the woman they first saw in Poland.

"This Hakes guy thinks that if we sell the stones, we can get rid of the criminals and move on. That's what you wanted to do isn't it?" he asked, looking directly at Julie.

"Duh!" she said sarcastically, and then continued, "Let's see. We can go to the police and get arrested for smuggling; or we can throw the stones into the river and have the Polish mobsters kill us after they torture us long enough to be sure that we aren't holding out on them; or we can sell the stones and put the money in an offshore account with debit card access and live happy and rich for the rest of our lives. What a difficult decision! I'd better think about that for about a nano-second. Okay, I've finally decided. I'll vote for option three!" Her cute smile and heartfelt sarcasm brought a laugh from the others.

"But what about the dead guy ... Arbon? What about his ring and the car keys?" Brayden asked.

It was Paula's turn to jump into the standoff. She reached across the table and took her husband's hand, appearing to give him support, but then said, "I'm with Julie. This bizarre life we have had the last few months is damaging all of us."

The room became silent for several minutes—four bright minds working at high speed. The ladies sat quietly watching Dennis and Brayden finish off their brownies and milk. Then Paula spoke up again. "What about a fourth option? We go to the authorities and agree to tell them everything in exchange for immunity. We can help whoever the stones belong to ... you know, to get them back? Maybe we could even receive a modest reward. Then we can help the police find out who murdered Arbon. When that's all settled, we can forget about the whole thing and enjoy the holidays," she concluded with a big, cheerful smile.

"Wow!" said Dennis. "Maybe we could all go into the witness protection program and have the U.S. Marshals put us up in a two-bedroom condo in Lubbock, Texas or Ajo, Arizona?" His sarcasm clearly offended both of the women, who leaned back into their chairs as if to distance themselves. Brayden stood and began pacing the room, wringing his hands and running his fingers through his hair.

"I'm sorry," Dennis said to Paula and then to Julie. "But I think you have both been watching way too much television. My guess is that if we say anything to the FBI or police or IRS, they will make an example of us regardless of how much we help them. I think we need to hide the gems and let the thing cool off for a while. In a couple of years we can start getting rid of the stones, one at a time."

"All of your ideas are good," said Brayden. "But, we don't know who this mystery woman is that showed up tonight. Either she is with the mobsters or one of their competitors or she is with the federal government. Either way, she is not going to just let this thing go away and neither is Mr. Hakes and his contacts in New York. He stands to make a healthy profit if he brokers the sale of the stones."

"And don't forget about our Polish friends," Dennis said. "Just because we ditched them twice, doesn't mean that they've given up. Tracing our car rental or hotel room gives them lots of ways to track us down."

Julie had had enough. She stood up and turned to Brayden with her hands on her hips. "I want my share of the stones and I want them right now!"

"Julie, you don't know what—" Dennis's protest was cut short. "Right now!" she screamed, startling the other three.

Dennis stood and tried to put his arm around her, but she shoved it away. She glared at Brayden, holding out her hand.

Brayden looked at her in disbelief and then slowly stood up. Without a word he walked into his study near the front door. In the deathly stillness of the house, file cabinets and drawers could be heard opening and closing. Moments later he returned with the brown leather pouch and laid it on the table.

"They are all there," Brayden said. "Take all of them. There is also the card with Hakes's name on it if you want to sell them to him. They are all yours, just take them and leave."

He then turned and walked out of the kitchen and out the door into the garage. No one moved from the table until they heard the car's engine start and the garage door opener grind.

Paula shook her head as though suddenly brought back from a confusing dream or nightmare and then jumped to her feet and dashed toward the garage. She was too late. The Tahoe's tires whined on the icy road as Brayden drove off down the street. She called out to him knowing full well that it was futile. Then she saw the headlights of the parked car across the street, about a hundred yards away. Its engine came to life, and then it moved in the direction of the Tahoe. As it passed the street light, Paula glimpsed the profile of a familiar looking woman—the woman from Poland—the woman who had crashed the little gray car into her kidnappers' black BMW.

"Dennis!" Paula screamed, running into the house. "You've got to do something. Dennis?"

The lights in the kitchen were blazing compared to the dim light in the garage, but the room was empty. She called out again adding their names to her plea but the rest of the house was silent. She turned back to the kitchen. The brown leather pouch was gone. She ran toward the front door and yanked it open just in time to see the tail lights of the Cannon's Toyota Sequoia reach the corner and turn toward the main road.

Her first thought was that they had gone after her husband to bring him back—back to his senses, but then the reality of the chaos sunk in. Brayden was gone in a fit of rage; the Cannons were gone, obviously angry, and with them the gemstones with their mystery of Arbon. Paula was in shock. She went back to the garage as if Brayden would suddenly pull the Tahoe back into its normal parking place, but it wasn't there. Next, she went through the house turning the lights on in each room as though looking for something she had forgotten. Finally, she returned to the family room and sat in front of the fireplace and stared at the dying embers of what had once been a friendly, crackling fire.

"What in the world is happening to us?" she mumbled.

Brayden came quietly into the house about two hours later. At first he was annoyed that Paula had left on what appeared to be every light in the house—and then the situation sent a chill down his spine. He went straight to the master bedroom looking for her, only to find the bed still made, and the lights burning brightly.

He called out her name, but received no answer. Searching the rest of the house took less than a couple of minutes, but it was long enough that he was bathed in sweat by the time he found her curled up on the couch with a lap robe pulled over her body, including her head. She was sound asleep.

"Paula," he whispered, gently putting his hand on her shoulder and nudging her. "Come on, let's get you to bed."

She didn't move. Her arm was warm to his touch and he could see her breasts rise and fall with steady respirations, but she still didn't move or even blink when he brushed the fallen hair away from her face. He shook her shoulder and spoke to her in a full voice, "Paula, wake up."

Then he saw the bottle on the floor next to a spilled water glass. He grabbed the brown bottle and rushed to the brighter light in the kitchen. It was his prescription bottle for Ambien—the one he had his doctor fill prior to their first trip to Eastern Europe. He racked his brain to remember how many pills could have been left after their four long flights and extended episodes of jet lag. It couldn't have been more than fifteen. That number caused an instant, intense cramping in his lower abdomen.

He rushed back to his wife's side where, as he kneeled on the carpet, to his relief he felt something crunch under his foot. There, scattered in the deep carpet were over a dozen of the tiny white pills. He knelt over Paula and shook her shoulders again. This time she groaned and pulled an arm away from him. Her beautiful blue eyes opened halfway and she wrinkled her forehead.

"Where have you been?" she slurred in a completely uncharacteristic tone.

He didn't even try to explain, but swept her into his arms and lifted her from the floor. Gently he carried her into the bedroom where he laid her on his side of the bed. He turned back the covers and scooted her over onto the cool, soft sheets. He tucked the comforter under her chin saying a little prayer of gratitude as he did so. Her breathing was regular as she followed his motions with her eyes. *At least she didn't take the whole bottle.* He bent down and placed a tender kiss on her lips and turned toward his walk-in closet. He was unbuttoning his shirt when he heard the bed covers rustle, then the bathroom door close. Next, he heard her violent retching, and relief swept over him.

The sun had been up for hours and the office had called him twice by the time Paula came into the kitchen. She was dressed in a robe and had combed her hair. Brayden sat at the table in front of his laptop. He was shaved and dressed in his usual winter wardrobe of chino slacks and a flannel button-down shirt, but the bags under his eyes looked like he had just awakened. He smiled at her and to his relief, she smiled back—the first one he had seen for several days. For what had seemed like hours during the night, he had held her head, wiped her mouth and brought her sips of water and juice until he was convinced that her stomach was rid of the chemicals. He knew it could take hours before the effect of the medication might wear off. When fatigue overpowered them both, he allowed her to sleep and he had collapsed into bed beside her.

"Can I fix you something to eat?" he offered.

"I can get it," she said, opening the fridge, pouring herself a glass of orange juice.

They sat quietly at the table looking at the sun shining off of the icicles and small snow drifts in the backyard. Both felt a need to talk, but neither one wanted to breach the peaceful silence of the morning.

Then the phone rang again.

"Brayden? It's Julie. Can you please help us?" she said in a soft frightened voice. "We've been arrested."

It was the first time in his life that Brayden had been inside the county's jail facility—or any jail. Dave Colton, his good friend from church and a prominent Denver litigator, was called and had made the necessary arrangements for the Cannon's bail. The weary couple was sitting in a small holding area when Brayden showed up to take them home. He had insisted that Paula stay at home, but instead she had made him drop her off at Julie's house so she could have a snack ready for them when they arrived.

Julie saw him first and rushed to the barred door. "Thank you, Brayden. Thank you, thank you," she said as the officer opened the door allowing her to melt into her friend's arms.

Dennis signed the paperwork and they walked to the Tahoe in silence. When they were out of the parking lot Dennis turned to Brayden. "Our car is at the impound lot. We have got to go there right now. They won't let us take the car, but your friend Dave promised that we could take our things out of it. The gemstones are still in the car."

"I thought that they would have taken the stones when they arrested you," Brayden said. "Isn't that why you were in jail?"

"No. We were in a wreck. Little Miss NASCAR here was driving," he pointed his thumb over the backseat toward Julie. "She was going seventy-five in a thirty-mile-per-hour zone and ran a red light. We hit a police car that was following some drug gang. We screwed up the whole DEA, FBI, and local police operation in addition to wiping out a police car. Luckily, the driver and his partner didn't appear seriously injured."

"Didn't they take you to the hospital?" Brayden asked, prepared to be astonished.

"We're just lucky the operation commander didn't shoot us when he found out that their whole task force's plan was a bust."

"I'm so sorry," Julie said, beginning to sob for the hundredth time. "I was so afraid and so mad that we had the possibility of being rich and you only cared about some dead stranger."

Brayden looked at her in the rearview mirror and realized how devastated she must feel. He looked at Dennis in the seat next to him and realized that their ordeal was far from over, and that if he didn't do something and do it soon, they might all be in jail or worse.

"I'm taking you two home, then in the morning I'll go by the impound yard. Paula is at your house fixing you a snack ... then you need to crash ... sorry, perhaps that's not the best choice of words. Anyway, you need to get some sleep. I'll make some calls and see if I can't do something to resolve the problem with the ring and the car keys and even the stores. I want you to not worry about it for now. Everything will work out for the best."

Dennis and Julie looked at him with a combination of gratitude and disbelief. *Has he gone nuts?*

Marie Felstein couldn't believe that anyone had survived the car crash. When she arrived at the crash scene, the police cruiser was missing its entire rear end—fenders, bumper, trunk lid, and gas tank. The rest of the car appeared intact except for the shattered windows. As for the Cannon's Toyota Sequoia, it looked like it had been put through a blender. The front end was crushed where it hit the police car, but then it had spun out of control and hit a light pole in a glancing blow that took off the rear quarter panel and bumper. All four tires were blown and the roof rack was dangling over the right side. The deflated front and side curtain airbags were flapping in the mountain breeze like trash bags caught on a barbed-wire fence.

Earlier, she had been about to give up her surveillance of the Ballards' when the other couple had arrived. Half an hour later, Ballard's Tahoe had left in a rush and she had started to follow him when the front door opened and the Cannon woman ran out of the house. Marie stopped her car at the corner and waited. The woman was carrying something in addition to her purse and that triggered a hint of suspicion in Marie. A late night meeting with a confusing rushed departure was too good to ignore. She gave the Cannon's car a couple hundred yards lead and then followed them. It was all she could do to keep up with the speeding SUV.

She missed a green light by seconds and so she was forced to stop for the light. She was nearly a quarter mile behind the Toyota when the collision occurred. Even that far away she had heard the violent crash and saw car parts flying as the Cannon's Toyota smashed into the side of a black-and-white police car, which obviously had run a red light on the deserted street. The spinning SUV then smashed into the power pole and seemed to disintegrate before her eyes.

Marie was certain that the light was green for the Cannon's. Her call to 911 had been redundant since two other squad cars were on the scene within seconds. Surely she didn't want to be interviewed as a witness, so she pulled off to the side of the street and ducked down to observe the chaos.

She felt an enormous wave of relief when to her surprise, she saw the Cannon's both walk away from their destroyed car. A single driver emerged from the Ford cruiser. Through her binoculars, she didn't miss the fact that neither the woman nor the man was carrying anything when they left the car. Always suspicious, she couldn't help thinking that they must have left something of great importance behind. *That, I have got to find out.*

By the time all the emergency vehicles finished their tasks and a couple of tow trucks showed up, Marie was nearly frozen and far beyond exhaustion. Once she got back to the hotel she stood in a hot shower for twenty minutes and then crashed into the bed.

Marie woke up the next morning when the laser-bright sunshine from between the hotel curtains crept onto her face. It was after ten when she sat at the edge of the bed trying to wake up and trying to remember the name of the tow truck company from the night before. She needed to search that wrecked vehicle. On the bedside stand was a note that she vaguely remembered having received the night before, but then had forgotten. She grabbed it and put it in her purse—she would read it later.

Dressed in her warmest jeans and a down ski jacket, she sucked on the plastic lid of a venti-size black coffee as she drove across the city to the industrial side of town. There a chain-link fence circled an expansive snow-covered salvage yard. At first glance, it appeared to be her lucky day. Not only had the friendly dispatcher at the towing company freely given her the address where the wrecked cars had been towed, but just fifty feet inside an open gate sat the crumpled Toyota SUV and there wasn't a soul in site. Alongside the SUV was the black-and-white police cruiser. Neither car looked like it would ever grace the streets of Denver again.

She parked her rental outside the gate and wandered inside. Still seeing no one, she adopted her usual attitude of asking for forgiveness—should that be necessary—rather than permission. The passenger door of the Toyota was hanging from just one hinge, but still wouldn't move. The rear door was closed but opened easily. She slipped inside the vehicle, brushing the fragments of glass off of the leather seats, and then quietly pulled the door closed. So far the car lot seemed deserted. Leaning over the seatback she pushed the deflated air bags away and easily found Mrs. Cannon's purse wedged under the passenger seat with a crushed box of Kleenex hiding it from view.

She tugged the purse out and shook the broken glass off of it. She was tempted to go through it right then, but tucked it beside her and continued her search. She probed every niche and crevasse between and under the seats. Debris from the glove box littered the floor in front, but otherwise the car was nearly empty. She glanced in the far back area, but could see only a set of snow tire chains and a pair of jumper cables that were tangled like spaghetti. The entire carpeted floor was covered with glass fragments and pieces of broken plastic. The storage slots on all four doors appeared empty. There was no sign of the leather pouch she had seen on Ballard's desk or whatever it was the Cannon woman had carried out of the house the night before. *Time to go; I'll search the purse when I get to my car and if nothing is there, then I'll return it.*

She opened the rear door, being careful not to cut her hands on the broken glass. Then she started to back out of the tall vehicle. Her legs were nearly to the ground when vice-like hands grasped her waist on each side of her belt line, holding her firmly in place against the cold car seat. Too shocked to think, she froze for just a second. *Darn it! My gun's in my purse in the Subaru.*

"My, but you certainly get around, young lady," the man's deep voice said, increasing his grip on her hips—forcing her pelvis harder against the cold leather seat.

"Let go of me!" she said in an urgent demand, trying to squirm away from her unknown assailant. "I'll scream if you don't let go."

"That will be fine. I can continue to hold you in place and won't have to get out my phone to call the police. When you scream, would you please scream for the police?

They don't like thieves pilfering victims' property … and how about the police car? Did you rob it too?"

"Let go of me, you pervert!" Marie demanded again, but was afraid to try to move.

"I don't think so," said Brayden, adjusting his grip. "Didn't your mother ever tell you that you shouldn't go through other people's cars and steal purses?"

"Didn't your mother tell you not to put your grimy hands on strange women's bodies," she retorted so quickly that Brayden started to laugh and nearly lost his grip.

She continued, "There is a perfectly legal explanation for my being here. If you'll let go of me I'll tell you."

"I'd rather you just scream and we wait for the police," he said.

Twisting her head she caught a glimpse of Brayden and relaxed a bit. Then in a sarcastic voice she said, "And when the cops get here are you going to tell them how you stole gemstones from a poor little church in Poland and smuggled them into the country to sell to the Mafia? Or is it al-Qaida to fund their next bombing?"

"So you are the little fly on the wall that's been following us all over the world? We weren't sure whether you were trying to help us in Poland or kill us before the Polish mobsters had their chance."

"You are hurting me. Please let me stand on the ground and I'll explain. Some broken glass is cutting through my shirt," she said.

"Just leave the purse on the car seat and do not try to run away," Brayden said. The morning sun wasn't the least bit warming and his hands were almost numb. He imagined the woman was every bit as cold. He released his grip and stepped back from the open door just enough to allow Marie to get a footing and turn to face him inches away.

"Thank you," she said, brushing cubes of safety glass from the front of her jacket and her jeans.

Brayden was stunned at how beautiful this woman was who stood face-to-face with him. "Did you watch this car wreck last night or were you following me when I left home? I know you were in a car across the street from my house."

"I have no idea what you are talking about. Now, step back so I can leave," she said trying to nudge him aside.

"Not so fast," he said. "You promised me an explanation. Why are you following us and who do you work for?"

"You know perfectly well why I'm following you and your friend. Who I work for is none of your business. For now, you and Mr. Cannon should count yourselves fortunate not to be in a morgue or a dungeon in Poland or in federal prison here in the United States. You probably deserve both. You should have considered the consequences—"

She was stopped in mid-sentence by the sound of a loud diesel engine approaching the storage yard. She and Brayden turned toward a large tow truck pulling the tractor of an eighteen-wheeler. Together they quickly ducked down behind the Sequoia's open door.

"We need to leave," she said. "Neither of us wants to explain to a tow truck driver why we're here. I'll come to your office at four this afternoon."

He stared at her for a second then nodded in

agreement. "I'd give you directions, but I suspect that you know the address. You go first, I need to get my friend's purse and the car registration."

They separated and she dodged around the junked cars until she came to the gate. Moments later Brayden was at her side, woman's purse in hand. The tow truck had taken its newest fare to the far back of the yard allowing Brayden and Marie to walk to their separate vehicles. Marie got to hers first, and once inside started the engine and made a sharp turn stopping alongside the Tahoe. She rolled down her window and looked Brayden in the eyes.

"Why don't you just bring me the stones this afternoon and we'll put an end to what has to be your family's nightmare, while you and your friends are still alive?"

"I have no idea what you're talking about," Brayden said, "I just came to get the lady's purse."

"I'll see you at four o'clock at your office. As you aptly said, I can find the place. Maybe I can help you remember something the jet lag made you forget." She rolled up her window and with an air of being in full control of the situation, drove away.

"I don't know whether this guy is brave or stupid," Marie said into the phone moments later. "I get the idea that there is more to the puzzling story than just selling the single diamond or even a handful of stones. He had a large diamond and maybe several other stones when he returned to the states the first time. So why did they all go back to Poland? And why did the hoodlums in Poland try to rob them? Surely, they wouldn't have taken the gemstones back into Poland. That would have meant going through U.S. Customs twice. None of it makes any sense. This guy seems like an ordinary Joe. There has to be more to the story than gemstones."

"I don't care if you solve the puzzle or not. I just want you to find out who he plans on selling the stones to so we can make some arrests. We'll look like idiots if a couple of ordinary Joes, as you call them, are dealing in stolen gemstones and we can't figure out where they came from and where they are disposing of them," the voice on the other end of the phone said.

Marie was sitting in the driver's seat of her little Subaru, letting the sunshine radiate through the window to warm her frozen arms. She had told her handler a lot of the story, but had conveniently skipped the part where she was caught and physically held by her prime suspect. The stars must have been lined up just right for her to have gotten away from the man without more complications. Now, her next move was to try to find out who had the stones and then stay with them. *Ballard had the Cannon woman's purse, but were the stones in the purse, or had he returned to the wrecked car just as a favor to the couple like he said?* She couldn't decide where to start first. Never short on courage, she thought, "Maybe I'll try the direct approach."

Alexander and Tito Weznitski had encountered numerous problems getting to Denver; not the least of which was trying to travel with a recent bullet hole in the calf of Tito's leg. They had used up a lot of favors with fellow hoodlums and family members. First, they had to find out who the American couples really were and where they lived. Next, there were the logistical problems: money, passports, and language—neither of them spoke more than passable English and neither could read well enough to translate anything into English. The one thing going for them was that they were exceptionally greedy and nearly fearless.

They began their search of the Americans' identities using the license plate on the rental car—the orange Skoda. A cousin who worked at the airport ticket counter in Krakow obtained the flight information of all Americans using that particular car rental company and the date and location where they turned in the car in Prague. Getting the American's names and flight destination cost a lot more. Then there were the passports. Alexander had a current passport, but Tito had lost his in a card game the year before so he had to pay a thousand Euro to get a forgery that named him as a German, with an address in the border town of Görlitz. To raise the money for the passport they sold the wrecked, black BMW—which they had stolen in the first place. Since its engine and front end were essentially ruined, they barely got enough out of it to pay for the passport.

Getting money for the flight and other travel costs was easier. They went to Krakow and hung out in Old Town where they stole purses and wallets from the wandering tourists who didn't give a second thought to hanging their coats and purses on the common coatracks in restaurants. The other lucrative activity involved golf carts. Tourists wanting to see the Jewish ghetto and the old city would take golf cart-like rides that would make frequent stops. The tourists always were getting in and out of the carts at the various churches and vista points. As they shifted their wallets, purses, and cameras around getting in and out of the carts, they became easy marks for any pickpocket, and Tito had become an expert at "spotting and lifting." He had been caught several times in the past, but the marks were always too busy or rushed making their next bus or plane to stick around as witnesses in the quagmire of the Polish judicial system, thus the crooks usually walked away with a warning. Selling the stolen credit cards and passports was the easiest part. But, since learning about the possibility of the Americans having taken the long-missing gems from the onion dome, petty crime was only a short-term necessity.

The two men talked constantly about getting their

hands on the rumored gems and becoming filthy rich. One by one the obstacles fell by the wayside, and within days they were on a flight to the "Mile High" American city of Denver.

Unfortunately for the Polish brothers, they hadn't been prepared for the penetrating cold of Colorado. Sure, it was getting cold in Poland, but all the movies about America showed long-legged girls in tank tops and short shorts. The men at the stupid American football games wore no shirts and their team's logos painted on their bare chests and backs. When it came time to pack they had left their winter coats at home, bringing just the wool sweaters their grandmother had knitted for them when they turned eighteen.

The brother's new partner in crime, Dr. Vlonovitski, had assured them that the American couples were in possession of treasure with a value beyond their greediest dreams. She had first come to the brothers with her story after having seen an old leather pouch on the bathroom floor at the hotel—the same night she had come to the local tourists' hotel room to sew up the arm of a man, whom the hotel manager claimed had cut it at a local church. The sight of that old, worn, leather pouch had given her a profound flashback of memories. It had been twenty years earlier that she had seen something just like the pouch. At that time it also had been in a hotel room near Krakow, but the room had been registered in her name.

She and Marta, her sister, had met their new acquaintance Wil, at a dingy pizza café. He was an obvious American who was handsome, lean, and broke. He had approached their table near the end of their meal and politely asked for the last two slices of the pizza that they had pushed aside. He was ravenous. Andriana bought him a soft drink to go along with the leftovers, and they had visited the best they could with her limited English. He spoke no Polish so the girls had laughed and flirted and giggled at his jokes. They were especially entertained at his accent as they tried to teach him a few Polish words.

When the café owner started turning out the lights the girls were both smitten. They walked into the plaza with him and then reluctantly said good night, but as he walked away, Andriana turned back, and overcoming her normal shyness, asked him where he was spending the night. He shrugged and admitted that the train station was his destination. The sisters looked at each other, giggled and then invited him to sleep on the floor at their hotel. He would have to leave early they explained, because their aunt was coming to meet them for breakfast and to take Andriana to register at the university.

His only possession seemed to be a blue, canvas backpack which he guarded carefully. It was when the girls offered to let him use the shower—which he dearly needed—that Marta snuck a peak into the backpack and pulled out the brown, leather pouch. Just as quickly she put it back in place and moved to the other side of the room. He was a perfect gentleman to the young ladies, making no advances and gratefully accepting a sleeping spot near the open window. By the time the girls awoke the next morning, he and his backpack were long gone.

It was some time later in the fall when Andriana saw a small poster on a kiosk wall with what she was sure was a photo of Wil. His family was trying to find him and offered a reward of 5,000 American dollars. Just a few days later she saw an article in the student newspaper about a theft of jewels from a museum in Istanbul. It interested her because the journalist claimed that the jewels were originally part of the treasury of the last Russian Tsar— jewels that had originally belonged to the Crown Princess of Poland. Andriana had one last clue that cemented the story in her mind. The stolen jewels had been taken from a showcase that also held a priceless, leather money pouch. A pouch made from the scrotum of a camel and allegedly once belonging to Genghis Khan.

She and Marta had laughed at the story together until their grandmother told them that the story of the lost gemstones had been making its rounds in her village for hundreds of years. They had allegedly been the royal jewels of the Crown Princess Alexandra Feodorovna and had been stolen by the Russian communists, and then traded to Turkey for some forgotten political favor.

A later angle of the story Andriana heard was that a Russian army major stationed at the barracks outside of Chelm had bragged to drinking buddies about taking a leather pouch full of gemstones from an American college student. One of the town elders claimed the stones came from the crown of one of the Kings of Saxony, captured during the invasion by the diminutive French general Napoleon. That story ended with them in the hands of a local monk. However vague, the rumors at the time were like magic in the imagination of the poor, blond medical student studying at the University of Krakow.

When Andriana had seen the pouch in the Ballards' hotel room she had mentioned it to her sister Marta who worked at the local tavern. When Marta told the interesting story to the Weznitski brothers, it resulted in the doctor's short-term abduction and ultimately her teaming up with the hoodlum brothers—out of no choice of her own. They had left her back in Poland with the promise that if they were to find the gems, they would send for her and her sister, then they would all live happily ever after, lying on some tropical beach sipping exotic alcoholic drinks with little, pink umbrellas.

"I coulda use that tropical beach with a lots of a hot girls in bikinis right now," Tito said to his shivering brother. They were sitting in a tiny Nissan that they rented from a company which should have been called Rent-a-Dog. The car heater was trying to keep up with the fifteen-degree morning chill, but the car had been sitting in the cold all night and was frozen from the tires up.

"Just keep yous eyes on da house," said Alexander. "These man has got to work some time and the woman will have to go to market for foods. When the house empty we get in anda search the place."

It was unclear to the Weznitski brothers which of the couples had the treasure—so they had picked the ones with the easiest address to type into their Garmin GPS.

Julie looked out of her kitchen window to see if the paper had been delivered. She had slept poorly, thus she had ended up taking a sleeping pill at three in the morning and was still a bit groggy. Presently, she was having an attack of guilt over her poor behavior at the Ballards' the night before and was still shaken from the car wreck. She had no visible injuries, but every joint of her body ached. Mostly, she was nervous about the police. Maybe the newspaper would have something about the wreck, or if her purse had been found and searched.

Brayden had called Dennis, who lived closer to the towing lot, and he had offered to go find the purse. That was fine with Dennis who was still upset with his wife about her reaction. He had never thought of her as being greedy, but recognized how tight he had always been with their money. Their non-military friends, like the Ballards, had pursued careers that had built a wealth base. Dennis had only his military retirement and the little savings they had stashed away. They had bought and sold homes as they served in various parts of the country and at one time their house had represented a substantial nest egg, but with the national housing debacle they felt like poor cousins again.

He had let Julie sleep in and had gone to the basement to work on a family history PowerPoint presentation he was preparing for a family reunion after Christmas. He could hear her stirring upstairs and considered going up to check on her. Then the phone rang.

"Dennis. It's Brayden. I found Julie's purse in the Sequoia. The car is totaled. You'll never guess what else I found!"

"Maybe you better hang on to it and I'll come by and get it. I know she has a lunch and shopping date with one of the girls, but I'm not sure she'll feel up to it."

Brayden had a sudden feeling of guilt, feeling that

in a way he was responsible for their wreck. "Listen, I'm really sorry about last night. How are you doing?"

"I'm fine, other than the seat belt bruise across my chest. Julie has the same red stripe across her chest. But thank goodness for seat belts or our heads would have gone through the windshield. Her shoulder was hurting when we finally got to bed, but she wouldn't agree to see a doctor last night and she probably won't today either."

"Like I said, I'm really sorry about—"

"Would you mind coming by later and taking me to the Toyota dealer? I need to pick up a rental until the insurance adjuster looks at the wreck and okays the repair or whatever. Maybe I'll just buy something new."

"I just looked at your car and trust me. They won't be able to repair it. I'll be by in half an hour. Remember, I've got Julie's purse and something important to tell you," Brayden said, thinking that Dennis was sounding a bit confused. Perhaps he was still in a bit of shock.

"By the way, you didn't happen to decide what to do with the stones? Is there something else important about the stones? Or ... it doesn't matter anyway."

"What do you mean?" Brayden asked.

"Well I'm pretty sure that the police have them."

Brayden was driving down the interstate as they talked. With Dennis's comment he nearly ran off of the road. Drivers on both sides of him honked and the car beside him waved a crude gesture and sped away.

"What are you talking about? I have Julie's purse right here on the seat beside me. I didn't want to look in it without her present. I just assumed that the pouch was in her purse," Brayden said, as he signaled to get over to the next exit. He needed to find a place to stop and look in the purse.

"I never saw her put anything in her purse," insisted Dennis. "The last I saw the leather pouch, she had it in her lap, and then we collided with the cop car."

He glanced at the bag and wondered why a woman needed a handbag so big it could hold a watermelon. He would never understand, and this one of Julie's was floppy and felt full.

"I need to pay attention to my driving. I'll see you in a few minutes."

He pulled into a gas station parking lot and found a painted space far from any pump or the entrance. Looking around to make sure no one was watching he put the car in park and set the purse on his lap. It had multiple compartments, some with zippers and others with magnetic snaps. The accident had obviously taken its toll. There was a broken bottle of clear fingernail polish coating everything in the first compartment he searched. Makeup and lip gloss were smeared throughout the largest area—making him hesitate putting his hand deep into the bag. He angled the opening so the sunlight could shine in and *voila*—there was the pouch. It was a lot different than the first time he had uncovered it in the attic of the onion dome church. The bat guano, dust and cobwebs were gone. The multiple handlings, openings, and closings had made the leather more supple. Carefully, he withdrew the pouch, trying not to smear the makeup on his slacks or the car seat. He placed it on the Tahoe's wide, center console armrest and slid Julie's monster bag onto the passenger floor. Just as he started to tug at the strings of the bag, there was a loud rap on the passenger's window.

"Sorry buddy, but you got to move your car," shouted a grizzly-looking man dressed in bib overalls and a red-and-black plaid, wool jacket. The man pointed over his shoulder at an eighteen-wheeler Peterbilt truck with a shiny tanker trailer and "Chevron" painted on the side.

Brayden put his hand over the pouch as he spread his legs, letting the bag settle between them onto the floor and pressing the button to roll down the window.

"What did you say?" asked Brayden, his temples throbbing from being startled.

"You need to move your vehicle," the man explained in the tone of an educated scholar. "You are parked on top of the filler lid for the gasoline and diesel storage tanks. Sorry, buddy."

"No problem," said Brayden. He bent down and slid the pouch under the seat and backed his SUV out of the parking spot. He thought about leaving the area, but spotted a dirt access road back behind the station. Again he parked, rolled up the window and turned up the heater. He bent down to grab the pouch and as he picked it up one of the draw strings caught on the seat adjustment lever and the bag spilled its contents onto the floor mat.

"Crap," he swore. *Why do the simplest things have to be so hard?*

There was snow on the ground outside, so he opened the door very slowly, being careful where he put his feet. He slid out of the seat, and with the door wide open and both feet on the frozen ground he began to gather up the gemstones. He counted as he did so, placing them back into the pouch one by one. The eighth item he picked up was the signet ring. Weeks before he had wrapped it in a thin layer of plastic wrap and taped it closed. He continued to gather the stones that—according to Murphy's Law—had found hiding places in the least accessible spots.

"What did you lose?" said Grizzly, leaning over Brayden's shoulder.

Brayden's startled reflex was to stand straight up, throw his head back into the top of the door frame, and bang the nose of his intruder.

A flurry of apologies followed from both men. As Brayden turned to face the man, who by now had backed off a couple of steps, the man looked at Brayden's fingers, which clinched a grape-size ruby. The sun struck the stone at the perfect angle to make the antique jewel come alive.

"My goodness!" exclaimed the man. "Is that what I think it is?"

Before Brayden could react further the man steadied Brayden's hand with his huge glove covered hand and examined the stone. Brayden had no choice but to let the man continue his study until he looked up at Brayden.

"Good gracious man! That is a real ruby and not a carat less than fourteen. I believe it is of an ancient cut—probably out of the Ottoman era. I don't suppose you have any more of those?"

The gesture and question left Brayden dumbfounded. This man was no ordinary truck driver. His accent was British or maybe Scottish. Slowly, Brayden closed his hand over the stone and tried to come up with a way to end the conversation and make the man go away.

"Your accent sounds English," Brayden said.

"Scottish, actually," said the man with a friendly smile. "The little lady and I moved across the pond when our only daughter married a blimy Yank and came with him to the land of fast food and pre-fab houses. Naturally, the little lady couldn't survive without seeing the grandbabies every day, so here I am driving a smelly fuel truck. Used to be a guard at the palace in Edinburgh. That's how I recognized the ruby."

Brayden was sweating in the freezing air. He had to get rid of this friendly guy and do it soon.

"No!" said Brayden, immediately realizing how inappropriate the answer was.

"No what?" asked the man.

"No, I don't have any more gemstones," Brayden said. "Sorry to be rude but I have an appointment to get to."

"Well, don't be in such a hurry that you forget this," Scotty said, bending down and after removing a glove, picking an electric-green emerald—larger than the ruby—out of a frozen footprint. He held it up toward the sun and rolled it around in his fingers, then held it out for Brayden.

"Thanks," said Brayden—still at a loss for appropriate words.

"Got yourself into a bit of a bind, do you," the man stated more than questioned.

The icy sweat rolling down Brayden's spine couldn't be ignored. "Listen, sir, I really need to get out of the cold and my wife is waiting for me. Welcome to America." He started to extend his hand to shake the man's ungloved right hand but realized that he held a ruby in one hand and the emerald in the other. "I'll bet your tanker is about empty by now."

"No, sir. That will take at least an hour at these temperatures," the truck driver said. "If I may be so forthright, I can't help wondering if you realize what it is that you are holding in your hands."

Brayden opened his hands. Again, the sunlight exploded radiance into the red and green gems. Both men stared at them but didn't speak until Brayden turned his back on the man to enter his vehicle.

"You might want to get those into a vault until you can decide what to do with them. I would guess that in your hands right now you are holding over a million British pounds," the man said in a sincere voice. "I truly hope that they bring you happiness instead of sorrow. You have a good day now."

Brayden settled into the driver's seat, temporarily ignoring the rest of the gems scattered under his feet. He dropped the two stones—the ruby and the emerald into the leather pouch and started the Tahoe. He pulled away slowly onto the highway, glancing into the rearview mirror as he made the turn. The truck driver was holding a notepad and a pen, writing something. It immediately struck Brayden that it had to be the Tahoe's license number that he was writing. Life was not getting any easier.

Tito and Alexander were growing restless waiting in the freezing morning air for the Ballards to leave the house. They were certain that the couple had the gems with them. The men were pretty brazen, but not completely stupid. They weren't about to enter the house until the occupants left. Breaking in while it was daylight, however, didn't seem to be of any concern.

"Why don't I go knock on the door? They might have already left and we didn't notice it," Tito said.

Alexander looked at his younger brother and laughed. "And if they come to the door? What will you say? Hi, I'm the guy who tried to beat you up when you were in Poland. You stole some treasure from our church and maybe you saw a body that you shouldn't have. Can we have the jewels back?"

Tito was annoyed at his brother's chiding and realized how dumb the idea was. He reached over and turned the car radio on and fiddled with the tuning knob until he found a station with hip-hop music. "Heh, that's Lady Gaga singing. I didn't know they have Polish music in America."

Alexander looked at him and almost cried. Instead he just wiped the fog from the inside of the window, took a deep breath, and waited. He could be a patient man—especially when the reward would be enormous.

Marie also was waiting impatiently. She was once again sitting in her rental car on a slightly elevated street a block away from the Cannons. She had been back and forth on the phone with her handler ever since her encounter with Brayden Ballard at the impound lot. From there she had driven back to the hotel and taken a hot shower to warm up. Next, she had picked up something to eat and driven to the neighborhood. When she found a perfect place to park and observe, she had called her handler again.

"Just give them a couple of days for things to settle down. Don't call in a SWAT team as if they are some kind of terrorists," she said. "These people have been to hell and back. They are not exactly spring chickens and all the travel and involvement with the police and these Polish mobster guys, not to mention the huge car wreck last night, has got to be wearing on them. Once they have a day or two to relax they might be talked into cooperating."

"Maybe a couple of weeks sitting in a federal prison cell at Leavenworth will loosen their tongues quicker," the well-educated and very grumpy voice of the man she had yet to meet face-to-face said. With luck maybe she wouldn't ever have to look at the creep.

"Listen, Christmas is almost here and these people have families to visit and parties to attend." *Matter of fact, so do I.* "Can I just back off for a few days and let things settle down? Then I will approach the men myself and try to reason with them. I am getting to know these two families better every day. They are not the bad guys!"

"I don't care if they are Andrew Carnegie and Mother Teresa; I want to know if they have diamonds to sell and who they are planning to sell them to. Then I want them arrested for the grocery list of laws they have broken, laws that our forefathers enacted to protect us from just such people."

"Can I just go home for a day or two and get a change of clothes and do some laundry? These people aren't going anywhere," Marie said in more of a demanding tone than she had intended.

"Fine," the man said, shocking her with his sudden friendliness. "You can't go home, but I'm authorizing you to spend the cost of a plane ticket on some new clothes. I realize that you got out of New York in a hurry. Change your hotel to a more comfortable place, but stay close to the suspect's neighborhood. Next, I want you to get into their houses and plant bugs—you did learn how at Quantico right?"

Oh my gosh, she rolled her eyes and hesitated answering—wondering if she could get by with lying.

"Excuse me, I didn't hear an answer. You do know how to bug a house—right?"

"Yeah, sure. But I'm not familiar enough with Denver to go out and buy the equipment I'll need."

"Call me when you get to your new hotel and I'll have everything you need for both of their houses and cars waiting for you. I'll have it delivered to the hotel.

And Marie, stop falling in love with these people. The women aren't going to become your bridge buddies and the men won't want you for a lover after they learn that you are trying to put them in jail. Just get the information and make sure you know where those stones are headed. Once they have sold or traded or given them away—whatever it is they are going to do with them—arrest all four of them on federal smuggling charges. We'll add the rest of the charges later. The more we can charge them with the better it will look on your file."

As he drove back to the house, Brayden was counting his lucky stars. He hadn't taken time to look inside the handbag again but had stopped at a big box store parking lot and gathered up the gemstones from the floor. A quick count seemed to account for all thirty of them. The troublesome ring was also still there. He put them back in the leather bag noting that it had no visible seams. "Strange," he thought.

When he turned the corner half a block from his house he saw the flashing red lights of a police car parked in his driveway. He slammed on the brakes, skidding to a stop on the icy street. His heart was pounding again—surging blood into his temples. He inched the car down the street not knowing whether he should pass by the house or stop, but then taking a closer look, he saw that the police car was in the driveway of his next door neighbor whose garage entrance ran parallel to his. He still decided to make a pass by the houses and go around the block. He needed to speak to Paula.

"What's going on? There is a police car in front of Carl's house."

"I know. I almost had a heart attack when I saw the flashing lights in the window. They lit up the whole house. I called Debbie and she said she had called them because there was a suspicious car out in front of the house for the last couple of hours. Carl went out to get the paper and thought he saw two men looking at one of the houses with binoculars. He watched them for a minute then got nervous and called the police. I guess they are still over there. Where the heck are you?" Paula asked.

"I just passed by the house, but was afraid to stop. I have Julie's purse."

"Well, don't come home right now. The car that upset Carl is long gone, but who knows what the police will want to ask the neighbors."

"What am I going to do? Drive around all morning? I'm cold and starving," he said.

"I'm dressed and almost done with my hair. I'll meet you at that bistro you like at the mall. They open at nine. Order us both some breakfast and I'll be there in fifteen minutes," Paula said. "While we are there you can help me decide on a present I've been thinking about for the twins."

Brayden drove out of his neighborhood toward the main road. He hadn't gone three hundred yards when he passed a parked gray Ford sedan with Florida plates—a dead giveaway for a rental car—with a stream of exhaust curling out of the tailpipe. The windows were fogged so he couldn't make out the driver, but it didn't take much imagination to figure out who it could be. That annoying government woman just wouldn't leave him alone.

As he gained speed he saw the car pull out onto the road and begin to follow him. The intersection ahead was four lanes wide, with a countdown pedestrian light visible to Brayden. He sped up just enough to make it through the yellow light—forcing his pursuer to stop. Then he saw the police cruiser coming toward him. He stomped on the brakes bringing the Tahoe to a halt right on the crosswalk. The gray sedan also had sped up to clear the light, but was forced to make the rapid stop as well behind the pickup next to Brayden. When Brayden looked to the side and back, he was expecting to see the foxy investigator woman—instead he was looking through the frosty windshield at the bearded face of the man he and Dennis had fought it out with in the musty church foyer in Chelm, Poland. Sitting beside him, glaring back at Brayden, was the other hoodlum. The one Brayden had shot in the leg

Brayden wasn't sure whether he was more surprised or angry. He already was furious at Julie for snatching the gemstones and creaming a police cruiser. He really didn't like that female investigator, either. Now, there was this new threat of the two relentless thieves in the gray Ford staring him in the face. When the light changed he made a conscious decision. He reached out and turned off the ignition key.

The police car across the intersection began to roll forward as did the pickup and the gray Ford beside him, but Brayden just sat there. The Ford slammed on its brakes when he saw Brayden not moving. The now backed-up, morning traffic immediately started honking. This caught the eye of the policeman who slowed as he passed the Tahoe, and the flashing lights on the cruiser sprang to life. The cop made a U-turn and stopped next to Brayden. Just as Brayden had frantically planned, the cop rolled down his window and waved for Brayden to do the same. The gray Ford hadn't moved, but now had no choice and accelerated across the intersection and out of sight.

"You got a problem, mister?" the officer yelled, a jet of steam shooting toward Brayden with the words.

"My engine stalled, officer. It happens when it's so cold. I'll get it going in a second. But officer, I'm glad you stopped. I don't mean to be nosy or minding other people's business, but there is a problem with that gray car that was beside me. It's been weaving and driving very erratically for the last few blocks and I think I saw them throw a brown bottle—you know like a beer or liquor bottle—out of the window. I'd hate for them to cause an accident. It was a Ford with Florida license plates."

"I'll talk to them," the officer said. He rolled up his window as the Tahoe came to life and Brayden pulled into the intersection.

At first the officer made a U-turn, and then again on came the flashing lights as the squad car sped in the direction of the rental. Brayden drove a quarter mile when he saw the police cruiser's flashing lights behind the gray Ford, and then heard the siren begin its wailing when the Poles didn't pull over. It was a good half of a mile before the brothers caught on to the fact that they were now the subject of police interest and pulled off to the side of the road. Brayden drove slower as he passed the Ford and smiled at the two burly men in the rental. The one in the passenger seat shook his fist at Brayden, mouthing what couldn't have been compliments.

His shirt was soaking with sweat beneath his down coat when he pulled into the Cannon's driveway. Just to be certain he wasn't being followed he had taken two or three extra turns. He let out a huge sigh as he killed the engine. He glanced at Julie's handbag lying on the passenger floor and another chill went up his spine. *Is all this worth it?*

Before he could open the door, Dennis was standing by the car, waiting.

"What took you so long?" he asked as Brayden got out and handed him the heavy handbag.

Brayden didn't answer the question but rolled his eyes instead and whispered, "We are in this fiasco way over our heads. I think it's time we get ourselves an attorney."

Another kitchen table meeting took place that afternoon. The snowstorm was becoming heavier and a stiff wind had kicked up, creating a natural irritation to everyone's nerves. Also kicking up was another round of flared tempers by Julie and Paula that threatened to derail the logic of the conversation—if there ever was any. In their many years of friendship the men had never quarreled, but the necessity of defending their wives was beginning to endanger that record. The big question kept coming up in the pleas from both women.

"If we have the gems in our possession and they are worth millions, why give them up without trying to at least get something, like a reward?" asked Julie. Paula smiled at her and nodded her head in agreement.

Brayden was sticking to his original goal: that was to find out who murdered Wilson Arbon and how he had obtained possession of the gemstones in the first place. As for Dennis, he just wanted the whole thing over with. He was satisfied with his retirement assets and military pension. He loved the free time, and as for seeing anymore of the world—especially Poland—he could pass. Fishing the mountain streams and maybe some scuba diving in the bathtub temperature water of the Gulf of Mexico was as far from home as he ever wanted to travel again.

"Why don't you call that man Hakes and see what he can get for the whole bag?" asked Paula. "We can use some of the money to work out a settlement with the IRS and you can let the FBI or whoever investigates any Americans dying abroad figure out how and why he died."

"And let them find out who the Polish gangsters with the scruffy faces are and get them out of our lives," said Julie.

"What about the woman you encountered this morning?" Dennis asked Brayden. "She isn't just some concerned citizen. She's some kind of government agent. Maybe we should confide in her and can get her to help us."

Just as the resolves of the men were beginning to weaken to the argument their wives presented, there was a loud knock at the door.

Whoever was knocking on the Cannons' door wasn't patient enough to wait for Dennis or Julie to answer. The ear-shattering crash of the front door's glass jolted the four troubled adults to their feet. Before Dennis could even rush to the entry way, Tito and Alexander burst into the family room waving pistols and screaming orders to the couples to get down on the floor. Their English was poor and in the heat of the moment lots of words were mispronounced, but the meaning was clear. These guys were done with just following the Americans around waiting for something to happen.

"Give to us the jewels," Tito commanded over and over again saying what sounded more like *geeve tu us da gools*. He was walking with a significant limp and every couple of seconds glared directly at Brayden.

Alexander had sliced his hand on the broken pane of glass in the front door and was dripping blood on the light, tan carpet. Julie saw the problem and stood up—in spite of the intruder's increased screaming—and handed him a dish towel, insisting he wrap it around his hand.

"Thank you. Now give us the jewels," Alexander said. This time his voice was a bit more polite, but none the less intimidating with the steel-gray, automatic pistol pointing in the women's direction.

To Brayden's surprise, no one answered the intruders, but merely stared up at them from their recumbent positions. Julie had settled back down on the floor between Paula and Brayden. Dennis was on the other side of the table against the sliding doors leading to the backyard. The cold draft from the shattered front door window already could be felt, and the howl of the wind gave a ghostly sound once the intruders stopped screaming.

Brayden felt Julie rubbing his hand, which he at first thought was her trying to hold his hand to calm her fear, but then he felt the butcher knife as she slid the handle into his palm. In the confusion of her standing and giving the towel to the bleeding man she obviously had snagged a knife from the counter top.

"Great!" thought Brayden. "What am I going to do with this knife besides get us all shot and killed?"

He glanced at Julie who darted her eyes at the burly intruders and then back at him, like he was just supposed to jump up and stab both of them. Instead, he slid the knife under his thigh, out of possible view.

Dennis was the first to answer the plea to hand over the gems, speaking slowly and enunciating each word as though he was speaking to little children. "What are you talking about? We do not know what you want. Do you speak English?"

The question confused both of the Poles and insulted Tito, who, for several days, had been studying his newly purchased Berlitz English learning CDs. "Of course we speaka the English. What language do you think we are talking ... China talk?"

"We do not know what it is you want. We do not have much money," Dennis continued, still speaking in an elementary tone and cadence. "But you can have my watch ... here?"

Alexander made a face and pushed Dennis's wrist away like it was a piece of rotted meat. "You know what we want. We want the jewels you robbed from our church. Do not act so stupid."

"Do you want me to shoot this lady like you shot me?" Tito screamed. He then made a most serious mistake. He reached down and held the gun against Paula's head. Brayden wasn't going to wait and see how desperate the Pole was.

He gripped the butcher knife and like the strike of a snake, he rolled sideways, freeing his arm and driving the knife blade into the top of Tito's forearm. The eight-inch long, steel blade bisected the fascia between Tito's radius and ulna, instantly re-directing the gun away from Paula's head. The heavy pistol flew across the room and slammed against the sliding glass door next to Dennis.

Alexander had been reapplying the dishcloth to the laceration on his wrist when the knifing went down. Though he still held his gun he was too slow and distracted by Tito's scream of pain to prevent Dennis from firing the gun.

The pistol was an old army Colt 45 that fit into Dennis's hand like his old pair of loafers fit his feet—comfortable and familiar. Without needing to extend his arm to aim, and correctly assuming that there already was a chambered round in firing position, he aimed for Alexander's upper leg—less than eight feet of distance away—and fired a single round. The bullet was a soft-point, lead slug that after penetrating skin and thick muscle, struck the bone, fragmenting it into several pieces. Alexander was fortunate in that the rounds were old leftovers from World War II, as was the gun. Had the powder not lost a large percentage of its power the leg would have been nearly amputated by the single shot, but instead the slug left the femur partially fractured, but non-displaced. The surrounding muscle contained the lead fragments, leaving only an entry wound. Nonetheless the pain and debilitation was maximal.

There was the strong smell of cordite in the room. The explosion of the gunshot in such a confined space was followed by a wounded-animal scream that left everyone temporarily deafened. Dennis instantly jumped to his feet and began dragging the wounded intruder toward the entryway. Brayden ignored the whining of Tito, who was hopping around trying to pull the butcher knife out of his arm. Seeing the second pistol lying under the kitchen table, Brayden picked it up and began waving it toward the front door, leaving the wounded intruders no doubt that he would shoot them both if they resisted leaving. Seconds later, both men were literally thrown into the gray Ford sedan with Tito behind the wheel—the butcher knife retrieved by Dennis—and Alexander in the backseat. Dennis screamed instructions to find the nearest hospital. The car's engine sprang to life and the car sped away from the pointed guns of the infuriated

Americans. As they walked back to the house Brayden couldn't help but notice the trail of crimson contrasting with the white snow.

Back in the house there was silence. Paula and Julie stood by the kitchen counter with arms around one another, their shoulders heaving slightly. Both held blood-stained towels, but had abandoned their cleanup tasks as the trauma of the past twenty minutes settled in.

Marie Felstein had missed the entire scene at the Cannons' house, including watching the mild-mannered architect literally herd the injured and bleeding Polish thugs to their car. She had become so cold earlier in the day at the auto tow yard searching the Cannons' car that she was sure her toes had frostbite and would never thaw out. When she left New York City to follow the trail of the supposed "super diamond," the weather had been unusually mild. She hadn't even thought about taking severe weather clothes. She hadn't had time to pack her silk long johns or her knitted wool ski socks, even if she had thought about it.

Now, her toes were killing her. The moisture on her tennis shoes had frozen solid, and when she took them off she practically expected to see white blocks of ice on toes that looked like frozen scallops. Fortunately, her toes still looked like toes, but as she rubbed them they became beet red and began to sting. She ran a couple inches of water in the tub and put them in to warm up, but instead of that soothing comfort she expected, it felt like someone had poured gasoline on them and thrown in a match. Ten minutes later she was under the hotel bed covers, still shivering and cursing her handler, the Ballards, the Cannons, and all jewelers the world over. She was especially angry at the jerk she worked for in New York. She even was trying to convince herself that she hated diamonds, although deep down in her heart she knew that they were the light of her life.

When she finally warmed up enough to stop shivering, she began to think rationally. Still sitting in bed, she opened her laptop and reviewed her file on the missing diamond and its possible accompanying gemstones. *Why had the Cannon guy taken a trip to Lansing, Michigan? What was that all about?* And there was the mystery gemologist Hakes who may have started the whole fiasco with a call to her boss at the diamond dealer's. Then there was another person who kept showing up in reports by the Polish police captain, Akardiski: A woman doctor whom he called "Vlonovitski" was somehow involved.

Rather than running around on the frozen tundra like some sled dog following a bloody bone, she decided to follow up with her HP laptop and the Internet. Within an hour she was getting a headache from all the things she had learned, one of which was the phone number of a woman in Lansing named Wild. She was listed as the caretaker of the school's alumni library and had been paid a visit by Mr. Cannon. Marie made the call.

"Hello, is this Ms. Helga Wild?" she asked in her sweetest tone of voice.

"Yes," the woman answered.

"I'm with the DEA—the drug enforcement agency of

the government. My name is Agent Felstein. I am looking into the activities of two men named a Mr. Ballard and a Mr. Cannon. Our records indicate that one of these men visited your office a while ago. We need to know the nature of his visit."

"Deary—you do sound like a young lady, but we do not allow any drugs in our little alumni museum. Your agency won't have any work to do here, but we do get numerous visitors in here every day. If I'm to help you I'm afraid you would need to be more specific."

"I'm really not suspecting you of involvement with drugs. Sorry I didn't make that more clear. The person I'm referring to had just returned from Poland and might have been asking about someone from Poland or something to do with diamonds or antique jewelry."

"Well, let me think."

For a moment, Marie thought that the line had gone dead, but then the woman's shaky voice was back.

"The only visitor that comes to my mind right now was not asking about jewels or drugs. I wonder if you could be talking about a very kind gentleman who visited us here earlier in the fall. He was inquiring about the disappearance of one of our alumni. I don't remember the visitor's name but the missing man's name is Wilson Arbon. He was a wonderfully talented young man who went on a trip to Europe years ago and no one has ever seen or heard of him since."

Ms. Wild went on to give a few more details, stopping several times to snivel and sniff and also to re-ask Marie if she was in fact a federal agent. By the time the conversation was over, Marie was completely warmed up, especially her brain. Now, she had to decide what to do with the information: Take it to her boss or solve the mystery on her own?

Glade Hakes wasn't a man who was used to being manipulated. He was a knowledgeable geologist who had made a good living from the oil exploration and mining business in the Rocky Mountains; however, he was fascinated by the geology of gemstones. He had seen other's fortunes come and go with the rise and fall of economies, but had been fortunate with his hobby as a buffer against hard times. Ever since his youth he had enjoyed gemology. The extra money he earned was tucked away for retirement, and what he told his wife was to be their "fun money." The visit from the architect months before hadn't produced anything but a good cocktail party story—until the phone call Saturday afternoon. Now, the man, Ballard—the guy with the plum-size diamond—wanted a meeting and he wanted it immediately.

Hakes had tickets to a Denver Nuggets game that night. "I don't want to miss it," he told his wife. "But honey, you won't believe the size of the rock this guy has. Why don't you go ahead to the game with the neighbors and I'll meet you there by tip-off?"

She rolled her eyes at him and picked up the phone. The next-door neighbors wouldn't be her first choice to spend the evening with, but her alternative of staying home waiting for him would be torture. They agreed that he would not miss the introduction of the players and off he went to his office.

Except for the area around the arena with its sports bars and high-end restaurants, downtown Denver was a ghost town. Hakes parked his car in a handicap spot, knowing that at that time of night with the weather being so lousy, no one would care. He hadn't even opened the door when Ballard was pounding on his window. He didn't hesitate, but opened the passenger door and restarted the engine to keep the heater's welcome air flowing into the Cadillac.

"Thanks for meeting me," Ballard said, holding his hands over the dash's air vent. "I'll try not to waste your time. I wasn't very honest the first time I showed you the diamond and told you about it."

"I barely remember the story; however, I seldom forget a stone's face," Hakes laughed at his lame joke as he lied. "Let me have another look at it. I could care less about the story."

This surprised Brayden, since the story had, in his mind, become much more important than the diamond. He unzipped an inside pocket of his down coat, and pulled out a small jewelry box he had taken from Paula's dresser drawer (leaving her pearl earrings lying on the dresser). Hakes turned on the dome light in his sedan and slipped on a pair of reading glasses before accepting the box. He opened it carefully, and then paused, handing the box back to Brayden. He slipped off his lambskin driving gloves and took back the open box. This time he tipped the box, allowing the diamond to roll into the palm of his hand. Once again, with the motions of one practiced in the inspection process, he looked at what seemed like every facet of the gem. The basketball game was quickly losing its importance on his priority list.

"So, what is it that you want me to do for you Mr. Ballard?" he asked, continuing to admire the diamond.

"We—I have decided to sell it."

"What have the other appraisers said it's worth?" Hakes asked.

"There haven't been any other appraisers," Brayden admitted, suddenly feeling foolish and very vulnerable.

"And the other stones? Where are they?" Hakes asked, putting the stone in the box, closing the lid, but not handing it back.

"They aren't important right now. It's the diamond that I need to sell. We'll work on one thing at a time."

"I'm fairly sure that I can broker the diamond for you, but it obviously can't be done without making some calls and probably will take a couple of days—working days."

"So how much do you believe I can get for it on today's market?" Brayden asked, suddenly becoming more anxious and even looking over his shoulder into the backseat of the sedan as though there might be someone hiding in it.

"You might regret selling it without getting several appraisals, but then the liability of walking around with such a valuable diamond does carry risks too."

"Please stop playing with my mind and give me a figure that you can make real as soon as possible," Brayden said, letting a slight tone of anger leak into his voice.

Hakes looked at his watch and then slipped his cell phone out of his breast pocket. He stroked it a few times until he had the correct application and then tapped in some numbers.

The car's windows were fogging over in spite of the heater and defroster running. Brayden was getting claustrophobic and beginning to wish he hadn't ever called Hakes. What had seemed like an acceptable compromise with Paula and the Cannons was beginning to feel like a trap. Finally, Hakes turned off his phone and put it back in his pocket. He picked up a pen and a business card from the car's console and slowly wrote numbers on the back of the card. He handed the card to Brayden.

Brayden had to fish in his shirt pocket for his reading glasses to see the numbers that were written in a small, tight script. He held the card close to the light and looked, gasping as the amount registered.

"Well?" said Hakes. "Do we have a deal?"

Brayden divided the amount by two and couldn't believe the figure. "How do we handle the money?"

"You can have it any way you would like. A check or even cash, but I would consider you to be downright stupid not to have it wired to an offshore account in the Caymans or Luxembourg or some other sheltered place."

"Won't the government know immediately about it if we do it offshore?" Brayden asked, surprised at the suggestion.

"That's typical IRS intimidation. They put out news releases that there are no more secret accounts and that all of the governments are cooperating with the US, but the reality is that unless your name is Abdul or Ishmael, or you're carrying a Venezuelan passport, they could care less. Have you ever heard of anyone whose foreign bank accounts have been audited?"

"But once the money is there how do we get our

hands on it?" Brayden was sounding like a freshman coed in a high school introduction to business class.

"All it takes is an ATM card from the bank and you can spend it anywhere in the world, including right here in Denver. Listen, I need to meet my wife at the Nuggets game in twenty minutes. Do you want me to sell this or not?"

"Is $600 thousand the best you can do?" Brayden asked, not believing that he was actually asking for more money than he had ever seen in one place at one time.

"I'll tell you what. You be at my office on Monday morning at nine and bring all of the gemstones with you. If I can sell them as a lot, I might get more for the diamond. I need to know how many stones you actually have."

Brayden already was feeling like he had said too much, but was feeling trapped and the massive figures swirling in his head made him want to bring the meeting to a close. "We have thirty stones. I think they are all either rubies and sapphires and emeralds except for a few diamonds a little bit smaller than this one." As he said the words he realized that his jewelry box was no longer in Hakes's hand or on the console of the Lincoln. His heart raced for a second, then he saw Hakes pick the box up from the dashboard and hand it over.

"It's your decision, but I can't do much without seeing all of the stones."

"I can probably be there on Monday," Brayden said, taking a quick peek in the box and then clenching it tightly in his fist.

Hakes laughed and looked sideways at him. "Until

I see the other stones, it could be even less than the four hundred each. As for the diamond, the offer I just made is only good until you get out of the car. I will not get into a bidding war with you or anyone else."

Hakes's voice suddenly sounded angry. Brayden asked a few more logistical questions then nodded in agreement and got out of the car. A gust of wind almost blew him off of his feet and as he reached out for the car fender to steady himself, the Cadillac already was moving away toward the parking lot exit. He realized immediately how sweaty he was from the stress of the meeting with the gemologist, whom, twenty minutes prior, he had considered an honest man. Now he wasn't so sure.

The announcer's voice was rocking the walls as Hakes walked into the Nuggets' arena. With the football season over, and short days with long, cold nights, the city was now in love with the basketball team. Before he could get to his seat, the national anthem was being butchered by a female soul singer whose idea of patriotism was to drag out the end of every refrain with a warbling screech. Hakes wiggled his way to his upper-level seat just in time to sit down and then stand up again for the introduction of the players.

"You made it here on time," his wife, Patty, said with a smile. She was his anchor in the crazy world of modern technology. "I sent you a text, to pick me up a hot dog—guess you didn't get it," she said, looking at his empty hands. It was a long way to the refreshment stand.

"With luck this will be the last game that we're sitting

up here in the nosebleed section," he said, reaching over and giving his wife a squeeze.

"You find a pot of gold—did you?"

"If the guy I met with doesn't flake out on me it could be worth a lot more than any pot of gold I've ever imagined," he yelled over the noise.

Like most wives she had heard the stories of possible wealth just around the corner, but for the most part didn't really care all that much about changing their lifestyle.

His attitude was far different. Locking the office door a final time was a dream he had imagined for years. *This could be it. Really, truly it!*

26

Marie spent an hour and a month's paycheck at J.Crew and Eddie Bauer buying warm clothes, and it was paying off. Her toes and hands were finally thawing out. She had been sitting in front of the Ballards' house for more than an hour when she saw Brayden drive off in his Tahoe. Traffic was slow on the icy, slick streets, so following him had been a cinch. When she watched him meet the gemologist in a parking lot, her heart began to race, and the feeling of closing the case was inching to the reality part of her brain.

Warm and confident, she watched the two men— who seemed to be arguing as they fogged up the windows of the sedan. She watched Ballard leave the car carrying a small box in his gloved hand and lay it on the hood of the vehicle as he fumbled for his keys to get in his SUV. It wasn't until he was inside and about to shut the door that he appeared to remember the box and jumped out to retrieve it. Something was making him very nervous. When he turned the vehicle in the direction of his home, Marie decided that tonight she would follow the other guy.

Buying a scalper's ticket to the Nuggets game had been easy, but not knowing where Hakes was sitting presented a problem. There were guards at every tunnel leading into their respective sections, except the upper arena where apparently one was on his own to keep poachers out of one's reserved seats. By pure dumb luck, she located Hakes in the crowd and followed him up the stairs until she was out of breath. When she finally settled into a seat just two rows behind Hakes she was completely winded from climbing the three flights of stairs. She watched him give an attractive woman a perfunctory kiss. Looking down at the playing court, it seemed like it was a mile below. She wondered why anyone would pay for such crappy seats.

"You're in my seat, lady," said a skinny, middle-aged man with wire-framed glasses and an overfilled, plastic beer cup.

Flustered, at first she thought about moving; then on the spur of the moment had another idea.

"I have a ticket for a seat on the main floor level. Would you consider letting me stay here for just tonight? I'm meeting a guy for the first time that I met online. I'll even buy you a 'Nugget Dog' to go with your beer."

The man took her ticket and after serious perusal, smiled, and disappeared.

The Hakes couple was intent on watching the game, but also had a back and forth conversation going on that didn't appear to have anything to do with basketball. When the man in front of Marie stood up during a time-out and then left his seat, she crawled over the row and settled momentarily immediately behind Hakes.

Leaning forward, it didn't take long to pick up the gist of the conversation. They were talking money—big money. When Marie heard Monday's meeting mentioned several times in the same context as the gemstones, she had all she needed to know. Before the time-in buzzer sounded, she was up and moving out of the row and toward the exit.

"It is going down on Monday," she said into her phone. "I traced the plates to be sure and they belong to the guy Hakes who called my diamond store boss in New York. I've got his office address. I'm assuming it will be at Hakes's office, but I won't know for sure until it happens. Are you going to be here?" She had waited until the next morning to call her handler, being considerate of the two-hour time zone difference.

"I'll have your backup in place by Sunday night. I'm going to monitor the situation, but won't be physically present. Did you move to a comfortable place like I suggested?"

"Yes, I'm at the Hyatt. Are we using any of the local cops?" she asked, wondering why he hadn't mentioned them.

"Our guys can handle it without involving the locals. You could probably do the whole takedown by yourself. Right?"

"Right!" she said, trying not to let her lack of confidence show in her voice.

"Your first big confrontation?" he asked.

"Yeah, sort of, but that won't matter. I'll be there and I'll be ready."

This is all sounding way too simple! The thought kept playing over and over in Brayden's mind. *There has to be a catch somewhere in this grandiose plan of trading the gems for cash—or maybe a trap.* In the back of his mind there was also the recurring worry about the dead guy, Arbon, who somehow he suspected wasn't done playing a role in the whole fiasco. The *catch* was just two miles down the street at Dennis and Julie Cannon's house. The *trap* was even closer to home.

The Denver police department wasn't the quickest mousetrap ever built, but it wasn't staffed by the mentally challenged either. By 5:00 p.m. the report on the Cannon's auto accident from the night before, and the complaint phoned in by the neighbors reporting gunshots being fired in their normally sedate neighborhood, made it to the duty officer's desk. Sergeant Preston Rosen didn't believe in coincidences. That a serious auto accident and a shooting would involve the same mild-mannered family in a twenty-four hour period just didn't compute. On an otherwise slow Saturday night it would be worth his time to check it out.

The knock at the door interrupted a late supper for the Cannons, which they were eating on TV trays, wearing their bathrobes and fur-lined slippers. Frankly, Dennis had been surprised that someone hadn't come around sooner, but had accepted his good luck and was relaxing in front of the TV. Officer Rosen was polite and asked for just a few minutes of the Cannons' time, but the canine unit's Doberman took less than sixty seconds to smell the blood out at the street and then tried to barge into the house following the blood-trail of the Polish hoodlum. Rosen was considerate enough to allow the Cannons to get dressed and grab their coats before he escorted them into the squad car while he awaited a search warrant. Fortunately, he had forgone the usual pat-down search of the couple. Dennis had slipped his cell phone into the pocket of his jeans, and once in the car, he called Brayden.

"You won't believe where we are sitting right now," he began.

"I give up," Brayden said. "But I have some major news for us to ponder regarding the gemstones. We might have them sold by Monday morning."

"Well, unless you have them safely hidden in fifteen minutes they will be in the possession of the Denver Police. We are sitting in a squad car right now while a search of our house is going on. It won't take them long to be knocking on your door and going through your drawers as well."

"What the heck happened?"

Dennis gave a brief explanation then made a suggestion. "You, Paula, and the gemstones need to leave town! And do it soon!"

"We can't just pack up and leave. Christmas is just a few days away. There is no way my wife will leave and not be here for the holidays," Brayden said.

"If we're all in jail, there won't be a holiday for any of us for years. They will search your house and if they find the stones or the ring or even that old leather bag they will start digging until the whole story comes out," said Dennis, trying to prevail on the logic that was usually Brayden's strong suit.

"I'll just hide the stones," Brayden said.

"Don't kid yourself; these guys brought a sniffer dog who looks like he eats criminals for breakfast. You've seen enough movies and TV to know that they will look everywhere that you might possibly think to hide something. If they have the slightest hint you are hiding something they will interrogate you until one of you breaks and tells them everything. The best thing would be if you just aren't there, and in a week the whole thing will be old news and the police will have ten other crimes to investigate."

"And what about you and Julie? You're going to be able to keep a straight face when then find the ticket receipts for your two trips to Poland and your trip to Michigan? And what about the blood and the bullet they find in the Pole's leg at the ER—assuming he didn't die from blood loss and they find a body instead? You know they'll put it all together. They are trained to get people to confess. How will you resist?"

Brayden was pacing back and forth in his den, talking in a loud enough voice that Paula came in to find out what was going on. The look on his face was enough to give her cold chills and a queasy stomach. When she heard the word confess, she collapsed into his desk chair and put her head in her hands.

"You forget that we were in the military and have been well trained at covering up mistakes. Neither of us are going to ever mention the gemstones. We don't know the men who broke into our house, and the trips were for pleasure and genealogy—to research my grandmother's home village," Dennis said, sounding convincing. "But,

I know that they will come to your house, so get out of town, if just for tonight. Go stay with one of your married kids or go to Vail. Go somewhere! Do it for all of us. I've got to hang up; the sergeant is coming."

Paula couldn't remember ever being so angry at her husband. He wouldn't tell her anything about the conversation with Dennis until he had burst into the bedroom lugging her carry-on bag and insisting that she immediately pack enough clothes and essentials for three days.

"Something important has come up. We have got to get out of our house. We're going to Scottsdale for a few days and soak up some sunshine. It's too cold and dreary here anyway," was all he would say.

"You can go to the moon for all I care! I've still got Christmas shopping and decorating and baking to do. The last thing in the world I'm going to do is traipse off on another one of your secret adventures," she said, in a tone that didn't leave room for any discussion— reasonable or otherwise.

"Maybe you'd like to spend Christmas in jail? That call was from Dennis. The police are searching his house as we speak. He thinks that ours will be next. If they find any evidence of the gemstones or our trips to Poland, we are in big trouble. He wants us to get away for a couple of days. He thinks if we're not here, they won't even bother to return to serve a warrant."

"Did he tell them anything about the jewels?" she asked.

"No. The search is about the shooting at his house

and the Polish hoods. He had to give our names because the neighbor who called the police about the gunfire had written down our license plate number."

"Terrific! Well, I'm still not going to Scottsdale—running from the police like some modern day Bonnie and Clyde. No thank you! We can go to the Westin Hotel near the mall in Parker and spend the night. That's as far as I'm going. You can hope they won't bother searching the house while we're gone and it will all blow over in a couple of days."

That she would leave at all was good enough for Brayden. He went to the garage and studied his shelf of hand tools. *Perfect.* He emptied the plastic clamshell holding his power drill case. He took out the extra battery and the container for the spare bits and placed the leather pouch in the empty space, leaving just the drill. *Too visible.* He took the rows of drill bits out of their separate container and though it was a tight squeeze, he was able to replace the bits with the pouch of gems, close the drill bit case and then place it inside the much larger power drill container. It snapped shut and when reopened looked like a normal drill and extra supply of bits. Just to add credibility he fitted a 3/8-inch bit into a crack and reclosed the case. He put the other pieces of the set in a drawer and placed the power drill behind the driver's seat of the Tahoe.

Back at the Cannon's home, the police had finished a cursory search of the house and garage, but much to Dennis's surprise, hadn't asked to see any credit card records or other evidence of travel. Sergeant Rosen had been called away in the middle of the search to investigate the scene of another violent crime—a knife fight at a bar—and the other men had quickly lost interest in the Cannon's rather orderly domestic abode. They did ask for and obtained the name of the other party present at the time of the home invasion—the Ballards—but that had been the end of their inquiries. Dennis went to a nearby convenience store and used the pay phone to call Brayden, worried that his home phone might now be tapped and his cell phone traced. He planned to tell Brayden not to worry about the police for the time being. But, he was too late.

"They'll be too late," Brayden said in a distracted voice, "we are already on our way, but don't ask where. What did the police find?"

"Other than a couple swabs of blood from the hall carpet which Julie already had cleaned, and the door sill, they didn't take or confiscate a thing. They were upset that they didn't find a bullet, so I presume the man still has it in his leg. They have a call out to all the emergency rooms in the state. The head guy did reconfirm your address and phone number. I only gave him your landline, not either of your cell numbers. Hopefully, they'll get called about more interesting cases over the weekend and leave you two alone. Is there still a plan for Monday?"

"That's the last I heard," Brayden said, anxious to hang up and concentrate on the icy road. "I'll give you a call tomorrow night."

"I will be glad to get it all behind us," said Dennis. "Won't you?"

Brayden didn't answer but pressed the off button instead. He was tired of talking about it, listening to everyone else's opinions. And most of all, he was tired of the stress. Yes, he would be elated to get it all behind them, but he couldn't see an end in sight any time soon. There would be too many loose ends to snug up.

When they arrived at the Westin Hotel, Brayden was exhausted. Fortunately, they had a room available, so he handed his American Express card to the night clerk without giving it a thought and received two plastic pass cards.

He was in the beautifully appointed bathroom putting his shaving kit on the marble counter when the room phone rang. Paula picked it up and out of habit answered, "Hello. Yes, this is Paula."

The Weznitski brothers' actions may have seemed like the "Dumb and Dumber" of Poland to those following in their wake, but a lot of their problems were due to poor timing. They were highly motivated, and often their enthusiasm to get their hands on the gemstones—which they had never actually seen, but just heard of in local legend—made them act in haste. No one who knew them well, however, could fault their tenacity, but their methods had gotten them into a desperate situation.

"What's going on, Alex?" Doctor Andriana Vlonovitski said in a dreamy voice, speaking in Polish and trying to wake up. It was four in the morning in Chelm and the outside temperature made Denver seem like Palm Springs.

"Tito has been shot in the leg and is losing a lot of blood. My hand is deeply cut and won't stop bleeding. We need a doctor. Why didn't you come here with us?" Alex demanded.

Rather than argue with the man, she gleaned as much information as was possible over the phone, learning that the bone in Tito's leg was likely to have been shattered, but that the bleeding seemed to be venous, not arterial. They hadn't applied enough pressure to stop the bleeding, so that was one place to start. And they needed to start Tito on antibiotics. She had given them a small bottle of a broad spectrum cephalosporin before they left for Denver, so she insisted that they start on it immediately. When she finally got Alex calmed down a little she asked about the gems, and more specifically, about the missing ring. It bothered Alex that she was always more worried about the American guy's ring than she was about the million's worth of jewels.

"If he isn't doing better in the morning, you better take him to a doctor, but do not go to a hospital. Just tell them it was a hunting accident. I've heard that everyone in the American West have guns and shoot the wild animals every time they see one," said Andriana. "Where are the Americans now and where are the jewels and the ring?"

"How should we know?" Alex continued in Polish, screaming into the phone. "They shot Tito and would have killed us both if we hadn't have escaped and now the police are looking for us. How should we know what those American thieves are doing or where they are? I think we should go to the airport and come home. You can come and find your boyfriend's ring yourself."

"You take care of Tito's leg like I told you and stay where you are. If he isn't any better do as I told you. Have you seen any animal hospitals close to you? You could take him to a veterinarian; they probably don't have to report gunshot wounds to the police. I saw on the television that normal doctors have to call the police whenever someone gets shot."

Tito grabbed the phone away from his brother. "We're done looking for jewels. They probably don't even exist anyway. We're coming home before I die. I do not want to die in America!"

"Stop your whining. You're not going to die. Now give the phone back to Alex," the woman demanded.

"Where are you staying right now?" she asked Alex when he was back on the phone. He told her the name of the motel and then gave the other information he had assembled including the addresses of the Ballards and Cannons. (He had gone through their garbage and had found some old receipts with partial credit card numbers.) She hung up the phone dismissing the brothers from her mind. She washed her face with cold water to try to wake up and then put on her heavy, cotton robe. She turned up the heat in her apartment and booted up her computer. With what Alex had found in the garbage and the information she already had from the American's stay in Poland, she went to work. She would track them herself. Her first Google search was for airline tickets, and then she hacked onto the credit card's internal website. It was still like magic to her what she could learn and how easily the American's personal information was available with her little computer. It was a strange mix of extreme intelligence and mindless stupidity how one's personal records were so readily available.

Marie awoke to a winter wonderland of snow-covered trees and buildings. As she lay in the hotel's warm bed, a wave of homesickness crept into her head and heart. *What am I doing here in Denver?* The question kept playing over and over in her mind, like a bad advertising jingle that wouldn't go away. Already, she had missed two Christmas parties and was sure to miss her grandmother's traditional dinner with all of her family if she couldn't wrap up the Hakes/Ballard case in the next two days. *And who in the world—other than my boss and a couple of federal attorneys—even cares if a diamond is sold or not and who gets what from it.*

She abandoned her ruminations and took a hot shower and got dressed. She was on her way down the hall to the breakfast buffet when her cell phone rang.

"Your Polish boyfriends are at the airport. They both hold tickets to Krakow. We have nothing on them to detain them. Looks like they either found what they were looking for or have given up trying. We're probably better off with them out of the picture," her handler said. "Are you sure Hakes and your architect didn't have a meeting with the Poles without you?"

"Everyone was tucked in their homes last night when I came back to the hotel," she said.

"Well, that's very interesting. Our inside source at the DPD claims that after they investigated the shooting at the Cannon's house, they dropped by to ask the Ballards a question or two and found that the couple had left town. Who do you think has the diamond now?"

"That I just don't know, nor do I believe that the Ballards are on the run," she said. "Maybe they had a family event to attend."

"Perhaps you could tear yourself away from your fancy Sunday brunch long enough to drop by their house and double check," he said with more than a little sarcasm. "When you find the architect, why don't you cut a deal with him—give him the chance to fess up and help you build a solid case against Hakes and whoever he works for. Who knows? Maybe you could wrap this thing up with a confession and a deal." He went on to bring her up-to-date on the information the Denver Police Department had gleaned and then challenged her to close up the case by midweek.

"By the way, did I mention that one of the Polish brothers has a cast on his leg?"

Before she could respond the line went dead. This man was so infuriating! Ever since she went to work for the DEA she had been bossed around by men—men with bigger egos than brains. The idea of just walking up to the Ballards' door—if they were home—and asking them to confess to the possession of stolen property and the rest of the grocery list of crimes they may have committed, in exchange for some type of clemency, was a joke. Besides, from what she learned they weren't even the bad guys. Mr. Hakes was another matter. In spite of looking like a legitimate businessman, he had connections with someone on the inside of the illegal diamond trade. Then there were the mystery men with the scruffy beards and Polish passports who apparently had tried to kill everyone with their car when she was in Poland, and yesterday tried to rob the Cannons. Marie always had enjoyed working alone, but today felt the need for a partner. Once again the irrelevance of the whole thing was playing on her mind. There were crimes and incidents all over the country a great deal more important than the sale of a diamond or two. There had to be more to this story than she was aware of.

Her phone gave a little train whistle sound indicating a text message. Her tech guy had just sent her word that the Ballards had used a American Express card at the Westin hotel in Parker and at the Chico's in the mall next door. *Now, what were they doing in a hotel so close to home?*

Paula had called her daughters to meet her at the mall for lunch. Normally, she wasn't a Sunday shopper, but this was not a normal day in her life. While she and the twins were wearing out the Visa card, Brayden was back at the hotel surfing the Internet. In all the past weeks since he found the leather satchel in the onion dome of the Chelm church, he had never tried to research the actual gemstones. Dennis had looked a few times and reported finding little of importance, but Brayden decided to put his mind to an extensive search.

Brayden had retrieved the stones from their hiding place before he and Paula left home. Now, he laid them out on a bath towel and took a close up photo of them with his iPhone and sent it to his web address. With the stones safely hidden away he brought up the photo and studied each stone, then went to a site with the famous gemstones of the world.

He easily found an extensive list: the British Crown Jewels, the Vatican treasury's hoard of precious gems, the Hermitage in Saint Petersburg's collection including the fabulous Fabergé eggs, the spoils of war collected by the sultans of the Persian empires, and enough other collections to make one wonder if any of them were really that rare. Then he noticed a small print link to "missing gemstones."

He brought up the site and was less than eight or ten lines into it when his eye caught the number thirty. He clicked on the page and suddenly there in front of his eyes were the exact antique-cut gemstones he had just photographed in his room. He went to photos and brought up the picture of the diamond. He shuffled back and forth a dozen times. He was sure that the large diamond was the same as the one in the article—the same in every way that he could judge without actually having the stones in his hand.

The original history was vague, but a collection of antique stones—possibly as old as being the spoils of early pillages of Genghis Khan—were thought to have been included in the personal collection of the Russian Tsar

Nicholas II and his family. The jewels had disappeared during the First World War; and then with the abduction and assassination of the Tsar's entire family, they disappeared never to be seen again. Rumors circulated that Lenin and later Stalin had them in a private stash, but nothing was ever substantiated. Soon after the famous meeting of Stalin, Winston Churchill, and Roosevelt in the port city of Yalta, rumors again surfaced that they were seen in the Crimea. On rare occasions they would show up on lists of missing treasure. Perhaps the Nazis or the Polish reformists or even the Allies had come across the stones. Somehow, some place, someone had gathered them into that strange leather pouch and hidden them.

Brayden got up from the computer and walked in circles trying to decide what to make of the finding. *Clearly, they were not the property of the Polish government; nor were they his, or Paula's, or the Cannons'. They were most likely a family heirloom that belonged to the descendants of Tsar Nicholas, but those people were all dead—or were they?*

"How did Wilson Arbon come to be in possession of the bag of jewels? Were they his? Did they now belong to his estate? And why was he murdered? And why in the onion dome of a tiny Polish church?" Brayden asked out loud, surprising himself at his audible brainstorming.

His head was throbbing when Paula called requesting that he meet her for lunch. "The girls don't usually stop for lunch so they went on to Macy's, but I need to eat something."

By the time he was dressed and walked through the hotel lobby, he had firmly resolved not to sell the diamond or any of the stones, but to find the rightful owners and return them. Moreover, he felt a profound sense of a personal mission to find the murderer of Wilson Arbon. The task would be formidable. Convincing the Cannons of his resolve would be a challenge of its own.

Walking the two chilly blocks to the outlet mall, Brayden suddenly felt the least anxious he had felt in months. He had surprised himself by truly joining the tech-generation. *Imagine being able to glean the information about the stones without leaving the comfort of my hotel room.* It seemed that a gray cloud had been lifted from his shoulders. Even the aching in the scar on his wrist was gone. He was anxious to share his elation with Paula—he just knew that she would understand.

"You have got to be crazy! So here we go 'round again!" Paula exclaimed after hearing his decision. Her outcry was drawing attention from the customers at the nearby luncheon tables.

"Dennis and Julie are going to murder you and if they don't, those Polish gangsters will. We need to get rid of the jewels, but not by giving them away. What about the money? You as much as promised the Cannons millions of dollars."

"Please lower your voice," he said, leaning across the table, trying not to make eye contact with anyone nearby. "It is the right thing to do. Imagine if there was a family heirloom belonging to your grandparents or great grandparents; wouldn't you want to get it back?"

"Yes, I'm all for heirlooms. My grandchildren will love to get the heirloom in the form of cash. We found it and it is rightfully ours. They will enjoy being spoiled by the many things their grandmother can buy for them with their heirloom. Get real Brayden! You are never, ever, ever, going to find the true heirs to the Imperial Russian throne even if any of them are still living. And just suppose you did find them. Wow! I can picture it now. Dinner in a grand, gilded ballroom in Saint Petersburg and you in a tux and tails—maybe with a silk stovetop hat—bowing in front of the regal lady and handing over your guano-encrusted bag of gemstones. And them rewarding you with what? A shiny ribbon to pin on your puffed-out chest. More likely, will be that one of their bodyguards will lead us to the bottom of an abandoned salt mine and handcuff us to a rusted mine cart. Just think honey, we can starve to death in each other's arms. Trust me sweetheart, I'm not going to like it."

Brayden looked away and then back at her starting to respond, but she immediately continued.

"Don't just take my word for it though, darling, ask your best friend Dennis how he is going to like you relieving him and Julie of their heirloom," Paula said, pushing her chair away from the table. "Excuse me, but I need to meet our daughters at the Coach store and finish buying Christmas presents for the kids and for the rest of the family before you max out the credit cards on airline tickets and private investigators. After all, it will probably be our last Christmas alive—or at least out of prison."

If Paula's eloquent monologue hadn't been expected, Brayden might have been angry, but he knew his wife. He felt sure that his honesty and expressed desire to do the right thing would wear on her conscience until she came around to seeing things his way. She was allowed to blow of a little steam. While she was talking he had seen the familiar looking woman enter the restaurant. She looked an awful lot like the woman at the wrecking yard—"the federal agent." The longer he looked, the more he was sure of it. Then she glanced at him and quickly diverted her eyes away. What in the world was she doing here in Parker?

His attention was distracted by the waitress with his check and a dozen questions about how he liked the meal and was there something wrong with his wife's meal since she had left so suddenly. By the time he looked up again he saw the woman pointing her phone camera at him and then walking quickly away. *Great! So much for my plans.*

Marie couldn't believe her good luck. She had struck out at the hotel trying to find information about the Ballards. Disappointed, she had wandered into the adjacent mall to buy something warm to drink. All of a sudden she saw the Ballards sitting sixty feet in front of her. She stood across the room and observed the wife delivering a long lecture to her husband—the way her mom used to talk to her about dating boys with long hair and tattoos. Then abruptly, the woman stood up and left. The husband remained at the table picking at his food.

Faking taking a picture of the giant Christmas tree in the corner, Marie turned her phone camera toward Ballard. "Crap," she couldn't help saying when she saw his reaction and knew he had seen her. Two minutes later she was walking briskly down the mall, trying to catch up with Mrs. Ballard when she felt a crushing grip on her arm.

"Aren't you a long way from home?" Ballard said,

reducing the pressure on her arm but still not letting go of the sleeve of her coat.

She didn't answer, but met his gaze as he nudged her toward a small service alcove. "Would you please let go of me?" she demanded, trying to pull away without creating a scene.

"Who are you really?" Brayden asked, looking her in the eyes with a determination fired by a combination of anger and fear.

Marie was so overwhelmed that she was unable to come up with a feasible story. "Whoever you think I am, I'm going to become your worst nightmare."

"So why were you in Poland?" he said, giving her coat sleeve a brisk shake. Her face gave him the answer he already was certain of.

Glaring at him she hissed, "You are making some big mistakes. You first need to let go of my coat and then you and your buddy need to stop whatever game you are playing in Denver or Poland or Lansing."

She immediately regretted mentioning Lansing, but it was too late.

"Who are you?" Brayden demanded.

Marie hesitated, her mind racing, wishing for some past experience to guide her words and actions, so made a snap decision that she instantly regretted.

"I'm a federal agent, Mr Ballard. I know all about you and your accomplice, Mr. Cannon. I know all about the big diamond. And I know you have plans to sell it. You have two choices: let go of my arm and sit down with me to talk, or I'll arrest you and you can explain your actions of the last four months to a judge and jury."

"What is going on?" demanded Paula. Brayden turned his head and saw his wife standing five feet away—her hands on her hips.

He was no longer in the surrender mood. The sudden appearance of the woman and her accusations brought back all of the anger and fear he had felt both times they were in Poland and the night of the shooting at the Cannon's house.

"Paula, please go and wait in my hotel room, I need to speak to this woman," he said, loosening his grip on Marie's arm and handing Paula his room key. "It's room 409. I'll meet you there as soon as I'm done."

"Wait just a minute! I know your face, lady," Paula said to Marie. "What is she doing here, Brayden?"

The question was never answered. Two security guards pushed their way between Paula and her husband grabbing Brayden by the shoulders, pulling him away from Marie. Everything happened so fast that even Marie was bewildered.

"Is this guy attacking you?" the older of the men asked as he twisted Brayden's arm into a hammer lock and pushed his face up against the wall. "We got a report this man was trying to rob you."

"What are you doing?" screamed Paula into the man's ear. "He's my husband. Let him go or I'll call the real police!"

At the same time Marie was trying to decide what to say. A small crowd was gathering to gawk at the scene so she saw her chance to end the debacle.

"It's just a little lover's spat," she said to the guards. "He didn't do anything. You better let him go before you're at the wrong end of an expensive lawsuit."

Then she surprised everyone—including herself—by reaching up on her tiptoes and giving Brayden a kiss on the cheek and whispered into his ear, "You will be hearing from me." Before he could react or respond she had disappeared into the crowd.

The guard released Brayden's arm and instead of apologizing asked for his ID. It took ten agonizing minutes for the guards to get all the information for their report. Paula snuck away and was sitting at a table in the far end of the food court when Brayden was finally allowed to leave. He was given strict warnings to keep his romantic frays at home. By the time he got to Paula's table she already was on her feet—headed toward the hotel end of the mall.

"What do you mean you've changed your mind?" Paula asked. "You're now going to go through with selling the gems instead of just giving them back?"

"That woman said she is a federal agent, but she's never shown me a badge or ID. I'll bet anything that she is part of that Polish gangster mob or maybe some competing bunch of crooks. Why should I let her get her hands on them?"

Soon they were in the car, leaving the hotel garage. They had checked out quickly, not bothering to look at the bill. Paula had phoned her daughters to cancel the shopping for the rest of the day. Both girls were upset with her. Hailey even asked if she and Brayden were having some kind of marital problem. Paula assured them that it was a sudden, work-related emergency, glaring at her husband as she was forced into the little white lie. There was a problem all right. The problem was that they had no plan. Brayden admitted as much as he steered the car toward the freeway heading south.

"No plan. That's the problem with this whole adventure, Brayden," Paula said. "First you hide the gems from everyone and then you include me and the Cannons making big promises of millions. Next, you come up with some Jonny-Do-Gooder idea to give the gems back—to whom I haven't a clue. And now without consulting any one of us including me, your wife, you are going to sell them. In the meantime we are being chased, assaulted, manhandled, and now you get a kiss from a federal agent who is probably building a case to put all of us in prison for the rest of our lives."

The huge overhead freeway signs were indicating lots of options: west toward the Eisenhower tunnel, south toward Colorado Springs, east toward towns Paula had never heard of, or a bailout exit that would head them back north toward Denver and what had been the security of their home. Paula held her breath and her tongue waiting for Brayden to choose one. When he did, she flopped her head back into the headrest in a state of complete exasperation.

"You've always said that you wanted to spend the holidays in Hawaii. They might even have a holiday sale on their flights," he said, having picked the one freeway exit she had failed to see—the one toward the airport.

"Brayden! Listen to me! You are cracking up. We need to go back home and call an attorney and then we need to get you a shrink. Your thinking is not just off the wall—it is completely out of touch with reality."

Marie was starting to feel like she could anticipate the Ballards' next move. There was no need in her mind to do anything else that day, except follow them home from a safe distance. She would give the couple some time to mill over the words she had whispered in the architect's ear, and then in the morning she would show up at their front door. She expected that by then she would receive nothing less than full cooperation.

She always had made it a practice to call her mother on Sunday afternoon while the football games were still being decided and before the prime time TV shows started. *Why not call now, as I tag along behind the white Tahoe and my cornered prey?* She dug her cell out of her hip pocket and punched in the number. Just as her dad answered the phone, extending her a cheerful greeting, Mr. Ballard—without so much as a turn signal—wheeled his car out of the main traffic lanes of the freeway toward the exit for the airport.

Panic hit her brain sooner than the reflex to turn the wheel. That was a blessing. She was in the wrong lane and an eighteen wheeler had crept up along her right side. The gigantic truck was filling every foot of the lane she desperately needed to make the turnoff. With the truck's giant tires humming along on the wet road surface mere inches from her right rearview mirror, she had three choices: floor the accelerator and hope the little Japanese rental had enough power to get ahead of the truck, slam on the brake and swing in behind the truck (the timing would have to be perfect), or stay where she was and risk losing the Ballards and possibly the gems.

Her dad had no inkling of her dilemma saying, "Hey there sweetheart, are you still there? Your mom's out on the porch talking to a neighbor. I'll go get her. How have you been? And where the heck have you been? We drove by ..."

The rest of the one-way conversation went unheard as Marie tossed the phone onto the passenger seat and smashed the brake pedal to the floor. She might have had enough time to make the turn off, if only a red Mini Cooper—sitting so low that it was nearly invisible in her rearview mirror—hadn't been tailgating too close behind. What little screech of brakes there might have been was concealed by the sound of plastic and metal colliding. Her head was thrown back into the padded headrest, and then for a moment everything in her mind went blank. Since both of the cars' major momentums were still traveling forward at the time of the collision, the crushing was minimal, but they did lock bumpers. When they finally came to rest, they were wedged against the concrete side railing. The massive semi with its trailer was long gone— as was Ballard. The cars that had been following Marie and the Mini were able to come to a stop or swing out around the wounded autos, but none bothering to stop to render assistance.

Marie sat still trying to let her head clear, but then she was brought back to reality by her mom's voice coming from the floorboard of the Subaru where her phone rested.

"Can you hear me? Marie, can you hear me?"

Glade Hakes and his wife Patty were enjoying watching snowflakes falling onto their backyard grill. The Denver Broncos were putting a final blade into the heart of the rival Dallas Cowboys when the house phone rang. Patty was dressed in her favorite pink velour jogging suit and had her bleached-blond hair in a casual ponytail when she answered. She was sure it was one of her three sons, asking if she would be available to do his dirty laundry. Even though the boys had graduated from college, they still thought Mom was the washer woman; and of course there were always tasty leftovers in the fridge when they dropped off the overflowing laundry bags. At first she was relieved to hear a stranger's voice.

"Glade, it's some man who insists on speaking with you," she said putting her hand over the mouthpiece. "I can barely understand the poor thing. He must have a speech impediment."

Reluctantly Hakes put the TV on pause and walked over to take the phone. He rolled his eyes at her as if to tell her she should not have answered it.

"Hello. Whom am I speaking with?" he asked in a tone of voice that left no doubt he didn't appreciate the interruption. His body went rigid as he recognized the accent—definitely Eastern Europe—and listened to the message.

"Mr. Hakes," the stranger said. "My colleagues have given me reason to believe that you are about to come into possession of something very rare and very valuable, which may actually belong to my country. We feel it would be a great service to my country if you were to allow us to examine the merchandise once you obtain it. Then, perhaps we can come to some sort of an arrangement to compensate you once we have it back. Call it a reward. We strongly recommend that you not pay a great deal of money for the item, since we are such a very poor country. It mainly has sentimental value anyway," he added. "Just let us know when the exchange is taking place and we'll be there to help. You can send a text message to this number."

Glade began to formulate a verbal denial, but was cut off before he could say word one.

"Don't think you can deceive us by exchanging the item for something different. We have been watching you and your foolish friends for some time now. Trust me, Mr. Hakes—we know what you are doing. We are not fools."

Glade stood staring at the phone, hearing only the dial tone as the caller hung up. *Perhaps these men were not fools, but were just poorly informed. The man had specifically spoken of a single item.*

"What was it, dear?" Patty asked, clicking the TV's sound back on.

"Just a new client—one that I probably can't satisfy no matter how hard I try. Everyone expects perfection these days," Glade said, returning to his leather recliner. After the game ended and Patty had turned her attention to a Hallmark movie, he slipped away into his office. He booted up his computer and went to his office contact list. He found the cell phone number for Brayden Ballard and dialed.

"Mr. Ballard? This is Glade Hakes. Sorry to bother you on a Sunday evening. By the way did you see that game? That's too bad. Manning had his usual problems, but earned his fat paycheck in the last quarter. Listen, something has come up with my schedule for the next couple of weeks and I was wondering if it wouldn't be possible to conclude our exchange of the stone tomorrow? You name the time."

"Now what?" Paula asked as the Tahoe pulled into the garage and Brayden pushed the close button on the rolling door before he even put the SUV in park. He had been on the phone—primarily listening—for the last mile of their ride home. As he listened, his face had become redder and small beads of perspiration had popped out on his forehead. Paula's question were the first words they had spoken in nearly an hour. The first words since she had threatened to call her nephew on the Boulder police department and tell him the whole story of the gemstones if Brayden didn't turn the car around and return home.

They sat silently in the darkened garage as the

294 STEVEN I. DAHL, M.D.

motor cooled, making a ticking sound, and the light on the door opener finally clicked off—leaving them in total darkness. She could hear Brayden breathing, but wasn't going to be the first to open the car door—not until he answered her question.

"That was Mr. Hakes. He wants to buy the diamond and he wants to do it tomorrow at ten. He insists that it be tomorrow. The problem is that he didn't really say the 'stones', or, 'the gems,' he just said 'the diamond' as though he didn't want to discuss the other stones. In spite of my having shown him a ruby and a sapphire. Maybe I am losing it," he said, letting out an enormous sigh. "In any event, this thing is going to come to an end soon."

"It better," Paula said. "None of us can take the pressure any longer. Julie started crying when I talked to her. She is petrified that those Polish men are going to come back to the house and kill Dennis. She thinks that they know he is the one trying to solve the murder of that man you found in the onion dome, since he was the one who went to Michigan. As for me I just want the whole thing over with. Maybe you better call your cute little girlfriend from the mall and just give her the cursed stones."

Paula had the kind of deep, beautiful eyes that immediately translated her words into her real meaning, but Brayden couldn't see his wife's eyes in the pitch black of the garage. As it was, he couldn't believe the words he was hearing. He reached out for her hand, but couldn't find it in the dark. He did however, feel her recoil as he touched her knee.

"I've been thinking about this for awhile. You and

the Cannons deserve more from all that I've put you through. What if we give up that big diamond since Hakes and the woman seem to be focused on it? Later I'll find someone else to buy the other gemstones. We can give Dennis and Julie their share of the money from the single diamond, turn Hakes over to that federal agent woman—if that's really what she is—and then let things settle down for a while. I can take the other stones to New York in a few months and get the rest of the money."

He could hear her breathing, but she didn't give any response. Finally she opened her door, lighting up the cabin of the Tahoe. He looked for any kind of expression—consent or derision—but could see only the back of her head. He stayed in the car a while longer working out the details of his confusing plan. He finally got out of the car, and taking the gems out of their hiding place near the spare tire cover, he heard Paula's screaming followed by the siren of the home security panic alarm.

He slammed the tailgate on the Tahoe and dashed into the house just in time to see the figure of a midsize person dressed in black running pants, a black sweatshirt, and a black, knit ski cap escape through the back patio door. He wasn't sure whether it was a man or a woman. Paula was standing by the kitchen sink holding the biggest butcher knife they owned. She was staring at the back door as if standing guard in case the intruder was to return at any second.

"Did you see his face?"

"It was a woman," Paula said in a subdued tone, "but not your friend from the mall. She was in our bedroom going through my closet. My gosh, Brayden! These people are invading our home. They're shooting guns at us. They are threatening to send us to jail. Don't you get it? They ... whoever they are, are not going to stop until they have what they want. Every day we keep the gems we are committing more crimes and exposing ourselves to more intrusions into our life. It's not fair! I just want our life back the way it's supposed to be. I'm so tired I can't even think."

Brayden closed the patio door, stopping the freezing draft just as the house phone rang. It was the security company verifying that there was a real emergency. He told them that it was an accidental push of the button, but they insisted on coming by the house anyway. He gently and carefully lifted the knife out of Paula's hand, laid it on the counter, took her in his arms, and felt her seldomly shed tears drip onto his neck. He guided her into the bedroom and turned back the covers while she washed her face and put on her nightgown. When the bell rang, he went to the door to assure the security guard that all was well, and then he returned to Paula. Their conversation was minimal as he tucked her in bed and turned out the light on her nightstand. He sat on the edge of the bed until he heard her breathing transition into the restful pace, indicating sleep.

Dennis took the call from Brayden in the quiet of his study. The snow was still falling outside—dampening the sounds in the neighborhood. The only thing he could hear was the screeching of a city snow plow on a nearby street. He had been looking at the year-end financial plan his accountant Mike Gallagher had given him. His retirement pension from the army and the income he received from his consulting with several of the local highway construction companies had grown into a substantial income for the year. In spite of the increased discretionary income, he hadn't managed to save much. He was going through his credit card records trying to dream up excuses to deduct some of the charges from his tax bill when the phone rang.

"I'm glad you called. I m working on tax strategies before the year end. I don't suppose you could back up my claim that the trip to Poland and the flight and car rental in Lansing were deductible expenses could you? And how about the carpet cleaning we had to pay for after the shooting?" He laughed at his wishful thinking, but didn't get the usual good-humored response from Brayden.

"Sorry I can't help you on that one—better talk to Mike. But listen up! Our day—Paula's and mine—has been far from uneventful." He explained the encounter with the "woman from Poland" and the break-in at their home by yet another mystery woman.

Dennis listened patiently as Brayden rambled through his own thought processes of the day, including finding the rightful owners of the gems and giving the whole lot of them back. He concluded by telling about the call from Hakes, the mineralogist, with his offer to buy the diamond the following morning.

"Did Hakes give you any new indication of how much the gems are worth?" asked Dennis.

"That's just it. At the time I saw him last he seemed infatuated with that stone. I know he thought I was an idiot for walking around with it in my pocket. He thought I should hire Brinks or Wells Fargo to guard me. Maybe he was closer to reality than we thought."

"Well, did he say he was willing to pay for it tomorrow?" asked Dennis. Brayden's answer had the potential of a life altering windfall.

"That what I'm hoping for," said Brayden.

"So what are you going to do now? You can't just drive up to his office in the morning with the diamond in your pocket and walk out with more than half a million in cash. Our guardian angel lady—the one who crashed her car for us in Poland—will be waiting with a battalion of U.S. Marshals to haul you off to Fort Leavenworth."

"Well, that bag of rocks is half yours and Julie's. Why don't you come up with a plan? Right now I'm so exhausted that throwing the whole satchel, including the fraternity ring, into the deepest channel in Lake Powell sounds like a great idea."

"Well don't do that. That really would be stupid. There seem to be a lot of people who know that we have something, but no one that really knows the extent of what we have. Why don't we just disappear for a while and let everything cool down?" said Dennis.

"And what are you going to do about Christmas and New Year's Eve? Between work and the family we probably have a dozen events of some kind or another scheduled, not the least of which is my firm's office party, which we are having at our home next Friday," Brayden said.

"A lot can happen in five days," said Dennis. "We could be arrested and arraigned by then."

The frankness of the statement left a blanket of doom on the conversation. Brayden could hear Paula calling his name and said he had to conclude the conversation.

"Whatever we do, we need to do it together," Dennis continued. "Two heads are better than one and whatever we do we need to leave the wives out of it completely from now on. If we get arrested or shot, so be it but the wives need to be removed from harm's way immediately."

"I agree one hundred percent," said Brayden.

Having the critical conversation on the phone seemed like the wrong thing to do from the start, but in fact, they were getting somewhere and seemed united with their desire to keep their wives safe and to resolve the problem.

"So make a suggestion," Brayden said.

"How about trying to find someone new to deal with the stones? I have been racking my brain to think of somebody and then it came to me. I had a guy that served as an assistant to me when I was at Fort Polk, Grant Peterson. He was the son of a big time jewelry dealer in Las Vegas. I think he got out of the service last year and was talking about going back to work for his dad. What do you think of me giving him a call?"

Brayden was silent for a moment. The idea of complicating the situation with yet another person seemed idiotic at first, but then his frustration and weakening resolve gave in to his fatigue.

"Yeah! Sure. Give him a call and see if he could help us. We are already on a sinking ship. One more person on board won't make it sink any faster."

Marie Felstein was pacing the floor of her hotel room. Her plan to kick back and enjoy the rest of the day had evaporated with the ringing of her cell phone. She had just received another call from her handler. *Was the man obsessed?* He was now insisting that some other agency was invading their diamond sting operation. He had received a tip from a listener at Homeland Security that someone had broken into the Ballards' home. He called Marie to find out if she knew anything about it or "have you ignored my orders" and was she the intruder.

"I told you to wait until he meets with that mineralogy guy, Hakes, to make the arrest—not go breakin' into houses! I knew it was a mistake sending you out into the field by yourself," her handler admonished.

Marie hadn't even given him the satisfaction of denying the accusation. After all, he had admitted that he was worried about someone else infringing on their turf—so she hung up on the jerk. *Let them fire me—I'll just get my hands on the diamond and keep it for myself.*

Finally, she stopped pacing the room. In her mind she had come up with a workable plan. She ordered a meal from room service. The French onion soup and a salad sounded good. While she waited she found a movie from the in-house TV menu and punched in her selection. It was already dark outside so there was nothing in the world she could do about the diamond tonight. Everything would have to wait until the morning when she just knew that her long hours of snooping and planning would come together.

29

The morning's first flight to Las Vegas left Denver International Airport at eight thirty. It was still dark when Brayden kissed Paula good-bye and drove out onto the icy street. She had promised to spend the day at one of the kid's houses—anything to keep her mind off the catastrophic corner Brayden and his friend Dennis had backed the families into. She even stood at the front window as he drove away to make sure no one was following him. She went back to bed after locking the door and setting the alarm. The broken kitchen door's windowpane was covered with a piece of cardboard and strips of duct tape to cut off the draft. It would have to wait until later to be properly repaired. Her next thought was to call Julie. She started to dial the number, but hesitated. There was no telling what Brayden had cooked up and not shared with her. Julie had been so upset the last time they were together that Paula was afraid to share what little information she knew.

Brayden's plan was simple. He was going to drop in cold on three or four of the fanciest, privately-owned jewelry stores along the strip in Vegas. He would see what kind of offers he could get and then call Dennis. He hoped Dennis would agree to accept the best price for the diamond. Just in case he struck big pay dirt, he had also brought along a trio of other precious gems—a ruby, an emerald, and an indigo-blue sapphire that was quickly becoming his favorite of the gems. The other twenty-six stones were safely hidden away in a mason jar that he had planted under a large tomato plant on the sunporch. Even Paula didn't know where to find them.

When the plane landed in Vegas he walked out through the terminal past rows of ringing and dinging slot machines with automaton-looking travelers feeding money into the insatiable slots. Once outside, he was forced to stand in line at the taxi stand for nearly half an hour. Finally, he was loaded into a ten-year-old Dodge minivan with two blue-haired spinsters from a farming town in Iowa. By the time they were dropped off at the circular drive of Caesar's Palace he had heard unsolicited versions of both of their life stories and had a standing offer to "join us for dinner."

The long, glittering arcade of shops at Caesar's Palace was deserted except for a few wandering souls—perhaps recent arrivals from an eastern time zone or big losers at the tables the night before who were too shocked to go back to their rooms. Brayden tried the door of the first jewelry store he encountered, not sure if it was even open. He heard the jingle of a tiny bell and within seconds a head popped up from behind one of the long, brightly polished beveled glass showcases.

"May I help you?" said the woman as she stood

erect. She was an attractive, fortyish blonde with her hair pulled into a braid on one side and a whiff of bangs and ear locks surrounding her narrow face. Her makeup seemed extreme for the early morning hour, but her smile displayed a sincere, warm welcome.

"Good morning," Brayden replied. "Is the owner or manager in yet?"

"Goodness no," said the woman. "I can give you the same excellent deals that the manager has authorized. The owner is a corporation in Brussels. What exactly is it you are looking for?"

"Actually, I have something to sell," Brayden said, realizing too late as he looked around, that this was the wrong kind of jewelry store. The prices on the displayed rings and necklaces were all printed on large placards and were all less than five hundred dollars. The word *cubic zirconium* came rather slowly but clearly to his mind.

"Sorry," the woman apologized. "We only buy items from our wholesale partners."

Without so much as an excuse, Brayden was out the door and headed toward the galleria's exit, fifty yards away. His powerful intentions and cheerful attitude about selling the diamond were rather quickly abandoning him. Next door to the Rocky Mountain Chocolate Factory was a rather narrow-fronted store with a handsome display of high-end watches. Before he could make up his mind whether to try another jewelry store, the aroma of roasted almonds and fudge prompted him to at least stop by the chocolate store. Unable to resist the temptation, he had soon bought a pound of milk chocolate fudge— the creamy kind with roasted almonds. He had paused in front of the window with the watch display to put his money back into his wallet and break off a piece of the fudge when he noticed an elderly man adjusting the display of Cartier watches. The man smiled at him and motioned for Brayden to come in. That's all it took.

"Das is ein very interesting diamond," the man said with his German accent, looking up at Brayden through his monocle. His other brown, speckled eye squinted. His forehead was more than wrinkled—garden furrows would be a more realistic analogy. "Where did you say you obtained these a stone?"

Brayden cleared his throat hoping to tell the lie in a convincing tone. "My dear mother ... bless her soul, was given it as a wedding present from my grandfather, who supposedly got it from his grandmother. She was born in western Poland. They called the country Konigstein in my grandfather's day. She, my mother, kept it to give to my sister when she got married, but she died of infantile paralysis ... you know polio?"

The jeweler nodded in supposed understanding. He was still studying Brayden and the diamond with up and down glances. "You may go on with your story," he said. His accent was diminishing with each sentence.

"I had been told about the diamond but never really held it until recently. I had a neighbor look at it. He is a gemologist," Brayden added just to let the man know that he wasn't entirely clueless.

"So, if it's such a family heirloom, why would you want to sell it?"

The unexpected question brought tiny beads of sweat to the surface of Brayden's brow. This whole ordeal was getting more complicated by the minute. His next thought was to grab the diamond and bolt from the store. His grandmother explanation hinted of some degree of estate tax fraud. Maybe the old guy knew someone at the IRS and would blow the whistle on him before he could get away.

"I am very interested in your diamond, mister. Vas did you say your name is?"

"Wilson ... Wilson Arbon." Brayden said. *Oh Crap! Why did that name come to my lips?*

"Now that doesn't sound too Polish to me. Maybe you Grandfather received the name at Ellis Island like my Papa. My name is Smith. Johnny Smith. My real name looks like an eye examination chart. Now, honestly Mr. Arbon, do I look like a Smith, or a fool?"

"You look like a very intelligent man who owns a very nice business and are hopefully in the market for a very special diamond," Brayden said, finally getting his brain and his mouth working on the same wavelength.

"Fine," Mr. Smith said, leaning back in his chair. He held the diamond in the palm of his hand like it was a baby chick. He rolled it from side to side letting the light it collected send tiny intense beams to the surrounding walls. He leaned forward and placed it on a miniature scale then slid on a pair of thick, smudged reading glasses. He wrote down some numbers on a notepad and then tapped numbers into a small, seventies-era calculator. He also typed something into his desktop computer's keyboard, but didn't appear to even look at the hidden monitor screen. The adding machine went through its mechanical grinding, the sound masking Brayden's rumbling stomach.

"Would there be anything else that your grandmother left for you to sell?" Smith said, wrinkling his brow again and glancing at the small travel bag sitting beside Brayden's foot.

"Let's just stick with the diamond," said Brayden, shifting weight from one leg to the other.

"Well, Mr. Wilson Arbon, I like your diamond and will pay you $310 thousand. On sales of that amount I will have to call my banker to have her prepare the cashier's check. She in turn is most likely obligated to report the large transaction to the US government. You understand that we don't keep large sums of cash lying around the shop?"

The reality of the business deal hit Brayden like a stinky, wet mop. He didn't have to speak. His expression was enough. This was all too much to take—possible IRS reports? He coughed and turned looking for someplace to sit down. He was getting dizzy and nauseated. *Maybe too much fudge on an empty stomach.*

"There is one other possibility," said Smith. "If by chance you have more gemstones … perhaps enough to make up a package deal of sorts, I have an acquaintance in California who is able to do cash transactions. He really doesn't like to be bothered with the smaller deals. If your grandmother happened to leave you any other stones he might be even more interested?" Smith was obviously good at reading body language. He nodded toward a small folding chair in a nook by the vault door. "You look tired, Mr. Arbon. Why don't you have a seat?"

Brayden's head cleared slightly. Smith stood up and fetched a bottle of cool water from an under-sink refrigerator, handed it to Brayden, and then went back to his chair. There was a long, silent pause as Brayden drank water and tried to focus on the task at hand.

"What exactly do you mean by a package ... package deal?" he said, having to pause to cough and clear his throat.

"Simply stated, it would mean that if you could assemble several gemstones of similar quality and size then a less public exchange could take place," Smith said.

Brayden started to answer with the affirmative; that he had other stones, but then thought better of it. "I don't have other stones," he lied.

"That's a shame. If only you could come up with say, twenty or thirty, nice-quality precious gems, my friends would most likely pay something like $5 to $10 million ... depending on the stones of course. Obviously, with such a large transaction there would have to be a lot of discretion exercised by both parties. There wouldn't be any banker or government agents involved."

"Like I said, I have only the one diamond ..."

"I believe you, Mr. Arbon. I believe you. But who knows what the future holds. Maybe tomorrow or even later today your grandmother's attorney shows up with a surprise package. One never knows what the future holds, now does it, Mr. Arbon?"

Although extremely nervous, Brayden wasn't stupid and the sudden implication of thirty gemstones put his senses on maximum alert.

"So let me get this straight. Your maximum price for my diamond is what, three-hundred-something-thousand, and you have to pay it with a check from the bank? Wouldn't it be possible to wire the funds?" asked Brayden.

"That would depend. Where exactly is your bank?" asked Smith—still maintaining his placid but wrinkled face and demeanor.

"I would prefer to use a numbered account—an offshore account."

"I'll tell you what, Mr. Arbon. You go back to your room and think about it for a few hours. I have a ring fitting soon ... you understand these spur of the moment Las Vegas weddings? My other employees are due in any minute. Why don't I meet you at the store, tonight at ... shall we say seven? I'll see if I can tweak out a few more dollars for your diamond and you think about the possibility of there being more gemstones back at your grandmother's house. And as you say, wiring funds is very nice. Perhaps you could bring your bank information and we could complete the transaction during dinner?"

Any hint of Smith's previous Germanic language roots was gone from his accent. He was looking intently at Brayden, probably reading him like a map. This man had heard something about the stones and that probably meant that lots of others knew about them as well. He nodded his agreement to meet Smith that evening. His legs felt like rubber at first, but he was soon out the jewelry store door and was standing in the polished marble arcade.

He felt a bit dizzy and confused. What to do next. *Try more stores or wait?*

He had walked aimlessly down the strip from Caesar's Palace, not sure where to go. There were lots of new hotels built since he and Paula had spent their honeymoon at the Dunes eons ago. The Bellagio's spraying fountains with their accompanying music caught his attention, ultimately attracting him into the hotel's lobby like a mouse to cheese. Once inside, he stood and stared like a kid at his first carnival. The registration area of the Bellagio Hotel held a wide spectrum of contrasting visual effects. First to catch his eye were the fabulous handblown Murano glass chandeliers with their beautiful flowers in a kaleidoscope of colors. Most of the guests in the lobby were well dressed and mild mannered, but standing beneath the center chandelier was a cluster of poorly dressed, overly tattooed, disheveled appearing teens carrying beer bottles and arguing with the security personnel. That, in a way, proved to be good for Brayden. The desk clerk was so annoyed by the teens that she gave Brayden an upgraded room at a discount price and apologized for the ruckus.

With only a small carry-on bag it didn't take him long to settle into the room and fill the deep tub with steaming water. The last article of clothing he removed was the waistband type of money belt which he had purchased years ago for a trip to Central America. He had used it only once—to hide his cash from the banditos who were alleged to be in every nook and cranny of the four countries they visited. He hadn't seen a soul who looked more dangerous than his own neighborhood paperboy.

This time it was different. The four jewels were hidden safely in the pockets of the money belt. He folded it carefully and placed it in the hotel room's safe—first trying the locking mechanism several times to be sure he could get it open. He used his usual password which he and Paula used on everything: "DOGBITE." He was so tired he couldn't even remember which one of the kids came up with it or why.

He could hear the musical fountains outside his window and peeked out a time or two. Once in the tub, he carefully placed a call to home using the bathroom extension of the room phone. There was no answer. Next he tried Paula's cell phone, hoping to catch her in her car with no one else around. When she finally answered the first background sounds he heard were the voices of kids laughing.

"Where are you?" he asked, as though it made a difference.

"I just picked the grandkids up at preschool and we're going to stop by the mall to see Santa," Paula said with a cheerful laugh. "How has your day gone so far?"

He knew that it wasn't the right time to explain everything so he just said he was fine and the work he was doing was still in progress. He didn't even tell her where he was staying—slightly embarrassed at the opulence of his room and surroundings.

"I've got a meeting tonight and will call you back when I know more. Hopefully I'll be able to fly home tomorrow."

"You better give Dennis a call and bring him up to speed. He has called twice to ask about you. Did you shut off your phone?"

"It's not working. I took the battery out so no one could track me," Brayden said.

"You did what?"

He could tell that that piece of information didn't enhance his wife's confidence in his plan. Luckily, the grandkids in the background were drowning out the conversation so he said good-bye and hung up the phone. Next, he dialed Dennis's phone number, letting it ring just three times before he put the tub-side phone back on its hook. An update would just have to wait. He turned the jets on in the tub and let his mind go blank. Twenty minutes later he was in bed asleep.

Brayden thought he heard a phone ring, but pulled the pillow over his head and went back to his dream world. His "quick nap" after his bath had turned into a three hour crash of much needed REM sleep. When he did finally awaken, it was the boom of the Bellagio's cannon-like fountains outside his window that brought him back to the real world—a world that for Brayden Ballard was going to get more intense than he could have ever imagined.

Marie Felstein had intended to sleep in that Monday morning, but was awakened by the booming sound of the bellman pounding on her door.

"Sorry to bother you, Madam, but there was a phone call for you and your telephone seems to not be working. May I please come in and check it?"

She didn't answer but stood back away from the door allowing the man in.

"Look here," he said, picking up the phone cord which was no longer plugged into the wall jack. "It must have come loose." He plugged the clear plastic end into the wall and then picked up the phone. "Voila!" he said. "It is working again. Here is the number of the man who called. He said that it was very important."

She dug her cell phone out from between two thick towels where she had placed it in order that she would not hear the noise of its vibration let alone its ring tone. The call history told her that she had eight missed calls. Seven of them were from the boss. The last one was from an unknown caller. At first a wave of fear went through her body worrying that she might have missed a call from Ballard turning himself in, along with the diamond. But, the call had an out-of-state area code which she didn't recognize—*probably just some solicitor.*

Marie took a quick shower and got dressed, paying more attention than usual to her hair and makeup. Today could be a special day. She pulled back the curtains to check the weather, which she found to be clear and sunny with a dusting of new snow on the trees. She found her cell phone and then made her call.

"It's Marie," she said when the gruff voice answered.

"Well it's about time," the man said. "When you didn't answer right away, I figured that you were already on the plane to Vegas."

"And just why would I want to go to Vegas?" Marie asked in a sarcastic tone of voice. She was sick and tired of the man's brow-beating attitude.

"You mean you didn't know that your 'Diamond Boy' was checked into the Bellagio?"

"That's impossible. I just saw him late yesterday evening."

"Well, look out the window, bright eyes. It's daytime and he's been in Las Vegas for two hours. He just used his American Express card to guarantee a room at the Bellagio. And why aren't you standing watch outside his door?"

She thought of several excuses and then momentarily even considered resigning her position right then and there. Instead she listened to his demands and hung up the phone. She looked again at the recent calls on her phone and was about to cancel all of them, and then—out of curiosity—dialed the last number. There was a pause before it rang and then there was an unusual ring tone, not like any conventional American phone.

"Pronto," said the female voice. The word was Italian, but the accent was more Eastern European.

Marie almost hung up, but instead said, "Someone from this number called me?"

"I think we have a common enemy," said the stranger. "The man has something of mine and I would like to get it back. I believe that you know how to help me."

The woman's accent was definitely foreign, yet her English pronunciation was excellent. Marie didn't respond to the statement, but listened carefully as the woman continued.

"I know that you have been watching our friend ever since you were in Poland. I know that you know he has my family's antique gemstones. They are not his and they are not yours, but belong to me and my family. I will pay you if I must or I will hurt you and Mr. Ballard if I must, but I will get them back. It would be a lot easier and safer for you if we work together. The man Ballard and his friend are fools, but very lucky fools or they would have died in the little town of Chelm three months ago."

Marie waited for her to continue, but there was silence so she finally responded. "I have no idea what you are even talking about. How did you get my phone number?"

"Of course you know what I'm talking about Ms. Marie Felstein of New York City. Miss CIA agent or whatever it is that you are. You know all about Mr. Ballard and his friends the Cannons. If you do not help me I am going to go to the newspapers and tell them how you and your government helped Mr. Ballard steal a national treasure from my family and my country."

"And just what country would that be?" Marie asked in a tone more rude than she had intended.

"If you do not know by now, then maybe you are not as smart as I thought you were. In any event the jewels are not his and not yours and definitely not your country's. The jewels belong to my family and have for centuries. They were lost for over eighty years and just when we found them, my friend was murdered trying to protect them. And then they were lost again. I know that Mr. Ballard has them and I need you to help me get them back," the foreign woman said.

Marie hesitated before speaking, making sure the words were correct. "Your story is very interesting, but I still have no idea what you are talking about. In any event it is against the law to threaten a United States federal law enforcement officer. I could arrest you right now and have you deported. Once again I ask: How did you get my number?" In her mind, pieces of an enormous jigsaw puzzle were starting to fit together, and at the same time forming a picture of curiosity.

More jewels—ancient jewels—lost for eighty years in Eastern Europe—they belonged to a family that is desperate to get them back—a man who came to the rescue of the jewels is dead?

"Are you still there?" the stranger asked, bringing Marie out of her ruminations.

"I am listening."

"Would you please meet with me? I am a desperate

person. For decades we thought that the jewels would never be found—that they might not even exist and then one night I saw them with my own eyes. Please help me," she said in a soft emotional tone of voice. "I'm sorry about the threats." The pleading in her voice touched a chord in Marie's soul.

"When do you want to meet with me? I have to leave for Las Vegas immediately and I don't know if I will be coming back to Denver," said Marie, realizing that she was giving more information than was necessary.

"So that is where Mr. Ballard is now," the voice said. It was not a question.

"Think whatever you like. I'm leaving my hotel in less than an hour. Assuming I would meet with you, how soon can you be here?"

"I am sitting in the parking lot of your hotel right now. I will take you to the airport. We can talk on the way there."

Just after breakfast, Dennis received the call from Paula. He had been cleaning his carpet with a carpet scrubber he rented from Home Depot and didn't hear the phone at first. He shut off the awkward machine to add more water and cleanser when the phone made its last note of the ring tone.

"Hello," he said, sounding somewhat irritated.

"Dennis? It's Paula. I need to talk to you."

He listened, swore under his breath at the stupidity of his ordinarily very smart friend, and then made a promise to Paula that he didn't know he could keep. Twenty minutes later, listening to warnings and advice from Julie as he got in his car, he headed for the airport.

It was the usual Monday morning traffic nightmare and the wet, icy roads weren't helping. By the time he parked, took the shuttle to the terminal and arrived at the ticket counter, Julie had made arrangements and had called Dennis with the flight information and a confirmation number. He only had to print his boarding pass. He took the shortest line only to find that the people in front of him were from the Marshall Islands and hadn't a clue how to use the boarding pass machine. When he finally made it to the security line he had less than five minutes until takeoff. Just as he was collecting his shoes, travel case, and slipping on his belt, he heard his name announced. It was his last call.

The flight attendant was scowling at him as he dashed down the ramp and onto the Boeing 737. He heard the plane's door close behind him and was told to take the first available seat. It was clear at the back of the plane, next to a woman who had to pick up her toddler to free up the middle seat. He apologized and the only response was, "Jerk."

His head was pushed into the headrest as the plane accelerated and then rotated getting the hundred-some-odd tons of metal and flesh airborne. That's when he remembered seeing two familiar faces sitting toward the front of the plane. He hadn't had time to say hello or to even look closely at their faces, but he knew that he knew them—but from where?

Dennis kept looking at his watch wondering what Brayden was doing and why he hadn't confided in him before he left town. He tried to organize some sort of plan, but at the moment didn't even know where to find Brayden once he got on the ground. He was distracted for most of the two-hour flight by the little girl sitting on her angry mother's lap. Each time Dennis would begin to read a magazine the little girl would reach over and grab at the pages, often tearing them and then chewing on them. The mother seemed oblivious to the intrusion. When they made their bumpy landing the little girl promptly spit up her pretzels and apple juice on Dennis's lap.

He was halfway down the terminal heading toward the taxi stand when he saw one of the women again. She had stopped at a magazine stand and was looking at a map. As he walked past he glanced backward, catching the blond woman's stare. It was her all right—the good-looking blond doctor from Poland. The other woman with her he then recognized. She was the one from the little, gray car that probably saved his life by colliding with the black BMW. *Oh crap! What has Brayden done now?*

Julie called as he was getting into a cab. It was perfect timing since he had no clue where to tell the cabbie to take him. "He's got a room at the Bellagio Hotel. I just hung up talking with Paula. Apparently, he has been trying to find a jeweler to look at the stones."

"The Bellagio Hotel," he told the taxi driver. He looked out the back window to see if he could see the two women, but had lost them in the throngs of people.

Las Vegas wasn't new to Dennis. He was a military man and had often laid over there on transfers and temporary duty assignments. For three years he had been a liaison officer for the army to the air force and had spent weeks at a time at Nellis Air Force Base meeting with his counterparts. The Bellagio would not have been his first choice of hotels—too expensive, and the Four Seasons had a better view of the strip and there wasn't a noisy casino in its lobby.

When he arrived at the hotel, Dennis went to the house phone and tried to call Brayden's room. It was busy. He tried to bribe one of the bellmen with a twenty to get the room number, but the guy turned up his nose at the paltry amount—apparently inflation had arrived in Vegas.

He was starving so he found one of the restaurants in the center of the casino that had a table with a view of the walkway between the lobby and the bank of elevators to the rooms. The waitress brought him a menu that nearly gave him a heart attack. A cheeseburger with fries and a side salad was twenty-two bucks. He ordered it anyway and got a double chocolate shake to go with it. *Who knows, this could be my last meal. Brayden's probably going to get us all killed or imprisoned.* No sooner had his meal arrived and he had the burger doctored just right—catsup, mustard, mayo, and plenty of pepper— than he looked out across the constant stream of people and saw the two women. It was the doctor from Poland alright. She was tall, blonde, with shoulder-length hair tied up in a ponytail—and she was every bit as gorgeous as he remembered her at the tiny hotel in Chelm. Her cheekbones were prominent and she walked with an elegance that he seldom saw in Denver or any other US city for that matter. He was beginning to doubt whether the other woman was who he thought she was. She looked quite different now from the person he had seen in the small car in Poland. She was definitely the right size and complexion, and there was a determination on her expression that fit, but she was rather cute. The woman in Poland looked downright mean.

"Is everything all right?" asked the waitress, staring at Dennis with his burger in both hands and yet no bite taken.

"Yeah. Sure. Everything's fine. I was just looking for a friend and thought I saw him. Could you bring me the check as soon as possible? Matter of fact, I'm not feeling well and probably shouldn't eat. What do I owe?"

"I'll go ring it up."

"I don't have time. Here," he said, handing her two twenty dollar bills. "Keep the change." He took a longing look at the chocolate shake in its tall, frosted, silver container. Even the whipped cream and cherry on top looked perfect, but the women were disappearing from sight.

By the time he saw the blond ponytail again the two women had rounded the corner from the casino floor and were waiting in front of the elevators. He saw the short brunette show something to a security guard who then pressed the button for them. When he tried to board the next elevator, the same guard asked him for his room key.

"My wife has it. She just got on that previous car. She was the blonde with the ponytail. I stopped to play that stupid wheel of fortune game and lost twenty bucks in twenty seconds," Dennis said. He had no idea where in his brain the spontaneous lie had come from, but it seemed to work. The guard smiled and pressed the up button.

The next problem was what floor button to press.

There were twelve choices. He was trying to make some logical guess when a plump woman with too much make up, too much perfume, and too short of a skirt slipped into the car and pushed number seven.

"Do you always stay on floor seven too?" she asked.

Dennis smiled and nodded.

"Ever since I saw that movie about those darling casino burglars, I always stay on floor seven and I always win at the slots," she said with a little giggle.

As the elevator door opened, to Dennis's amazement, he caught a glimpse of the two mystery women as they passed into the corridor to his right. He allowed his co-passenger to leave and was lucky again—maybe seven was a lucky number—the woman headed the same way. He gave her a fifteen foot head start, keeping the duo in sight, but essentially hiding behind the plump gal.

The two were approaching the middle of the very long hallway when they hesitated in front of one of the rooms. Neither of them seemed to have room cards. They stepped aside for Dennis's new friend to pass and then looked suspiciously up and down the corridor. Dennis quickly turned to face a room and as he did so reached for his wallet, giving the appearance of retrieving his room key card. The women didn't even notice him as the brunette knocked on door number 7314 and shouted, "room service!" When there was no immediate answer she pounded her fist in what looked like suppressed rage.

Dennis was dumbfounded. He didn't want to miss the outcome of the "room service visit," but couldn't just stand in the doorway gawking at the two women either.

Like a guardian angel coming down from on high, a

maid in a starched, blue-and-white striped dress opened a door from inside, just two doors down from Dennis. As she pushed her linen cart into the hallway and turned toward the two women, the door behind her began to slowly swing closed. Like an elusive mouse, Dennis slipped into the service room, keeping the door open just enough to peek around its frame. The brunette was knocking again, but not so angrily. The women then had a short conversation and turned toward Dennis and the elevators. He held his breath as they passed, but held the door open the tiniest crack. The risk paid off.

"He must be out trying to hustle the diamond to the locals," the brunette said as they passed the service door. "Let's go eat and then when he comes back I'll call for some backup and we can arrest him."

The blonde started to protest the plan, but they had moved too far away for Dennis to hear the rest of the conversation. He closed the service door and to his delight saw a hotel telephone hanging on the wall just inches away. He picked it up and remembering that the operator could see the number he was calling from, he winged it. "Hi, I'm doing maintenance up on seven and need to know if the guest in room 7314 is still in the room."

"Just one moment and I'll put you through," she said with a smiley voice.

The phone rang and rang and then just as Dennis was moving the phone back to its cradle he heard Brayden's voice. "Who's calling?"

Dennis peeked out the door to be sure the women were back on the elevator and then dashed down the hallway to Brayden's room.

"Let me in," he mumbled into the door, leaving his face just far enough away from the door so that Brayden could see who it was through the peephole.

"What in the world are you doing here?" Brayden asked, pulling Dennis into the darkened room and quickly shutting the door.

"I should be asking you the same thing."

The two friends stared at one another for several seconds, then Brayden walked to the window and drew open the curtains letting in the afternoon sunlight.

"A lot has happened in the last forty-eight hours," said Brayden.

"You can say that again. I just watched two women try to pound down your door and we know them both. Your blond doctor friend from Poland," he said pointing to the fleshy scar on Brayden's wrist. "And a brunette who looks a lot like the woman in that gray car that saved our butts in Chelm."

"She claims to be some kind of federal agent. Maybe customs or DEA, I don't know for sure," said Brayden.

"So that's how they got your room number," Dennis said. "The dang hotel people wouldn't even take a bribe to give me the number. What do the women want?"

"They want what everyone wants, the big diamond and the rest of the jewels, if they even know about them. Everyone wants the diamond. They couldn't have shown up at a worse time. What time is it?"

Dennis looked at his watch and said, "Four twenty."

"At seven I have an appointment—to sell the diamond." The statement was met with a hard and not very friendly stare from Dennis.

"The buyer is a crusty old jeweler who owns a shop over at Caesar's Palace Galleria. I expect to get about three hundred thousand just for the diamond, and the guy wants to buy anything else I have as well. I intended to call you for approval once the offer was solid."

There was a silence in the room as the fountains began another display of musical waters. The men watched silently until Dennis finally commented. "So are we still partners in this deal or are you on your own? I thought we were going to talk about this and work out a plan together to resolve the thing."

"Too much has happened. First the shooting at your place, then someone tried to crash into Paula and me on the freeway and then they broke into our house. I decided that it was too risky for us to drag this thing out. Somebody already died—Arbon. I don't want one of us to be the next body. We need to cut our losses, sell the cursed jewels, and get on with our lives."

"But now the federal authorities are after us? And what's the blond doctor doing buddying up with the federal authorities? I don't get it," Dennis said pacing back and forth in front of the window.

"This is the first I've heard anything about her," said Brayden. "Are you sure it's her?"

"I'm as certain as I can be. I'm sure she and her new friend will be back and you can see for yourself."

"I have no idea why she would be here unless she is working with the Polish government or with those gangsters. The last time we saw her it looked like they were holding her hostage."

"Face it, Brayden. We are in trouble. Selling the

diamond will only compound the problem. What are you going to do with the money? It's not like we can suddenly go out on a spending spree. If the government knows we smuggled the gems into the country and we sell them, we will get arrested. Then they'll implicate Paula and Julie as well. The way I look at it ... we are toast."

"But by selling the stones we will at least be rich toast," Brayden said trying to add a touch of levity. "At least we will have money to pay the attorneys."

"What about an alternative plan? I had a thought that came to me on the flight here ..."

Before he could finish his statement there was pounding on the door.

Like most hotel single rooms, the luxury rooms at the Bellagio have only one door—one way in and one way out. Brayden looked through the magnifying peephole in the door and saw the two women. They looked exactly as Dennis had described them. It was, in fact, the Polish doctor Andriana Vlonovitski, and the self-proclaimed "federal" woman. They both looked angry and determined. Just as Brayden reached for the door handle to let them in Dennis had a sudden idea.

"Wait! Don't let them in just yet."

He picked up the telephone and in a frantic but quiet voice said, "I think that the room down the hall is on fire. When I walked by I could smell smoke and thought I heard flames crackling."

Less than thirty seconds later the fire alarm in all of the seventh floor rooms and hallways began flashing and an annoying squawking sound pierced the entire hotel. Brayden looked at Dennis and just shook his head in disbelief. He looked out of the peephole again and saw several people rushing past the room.

"Clear the hallway," shouted a demanding voice. The men could hear loud knocking on the room doors as security men attempted to alert any sleeping guests.

Brayden jammed his scattered clothes into his travel bag and he and Dennis made their escape. Felstein and the Polish doctor were nowhere in sight.

"Go to the right please," a pleasant woman in the hallway instructed. "The elevators are not working for the moment. Go calmly please. Proceed to the stairwells and go down to the lobby."

When the two men entered the stairwell Dennis grabbed Brayden's arm and tugged him toward the stairs leading up. "This whole thing will be over in ten minutes. Let's just go up to the lounge on the top floor."

"How do you know there is even a lounge there?" Brayden asked.

"Just follow me," Dennis said, offering no further explanation.

The men ascended the stairwell taking two steps at a time, passing those rushing down the stairs. On each floor's landing they paused to catch their breath and peek out the tiny glass window at the respective hallway. It appeared that only from the tenth floor down people were being evacuated. By the time they were on the twelfth floor, the alarm had stopped flashing and making its annoying squawks. Out in the hallway there were a few people milling around but no sign of security. Brayden followed Dennis who seemed to know where he was going.

They entered an elaborate lounge through the emergency door into an area where the lights were

328 STEVEN I. DAHL, M.D.

dimmed almost to the point of darkness. They found an empty booth as far from the main doorway as possible and ordered Perrier. Neither man was interested in anything stronger. There they remained, huddled, while they waited for the appointed time of the meeting with Smith the jeweler.

An elderly couple took seats in the booth next to the men. When the waiter came they complained how they had been rousted from their room on the seventh floor because some idiot had fallen asleep while smoking in bed. Brayden had left his shaving kit as well as other items in the room and was pondering when to go by to get them when two policemen in Las Vegas uniforms showed up at the lounge's door. They walked slowly through the lounge, taking a close look at each of the customers and giving Brayden a closer look than most. He was saved when the woman seated in the next booth began asking questions about the fire and demanding answers. The officers were immediately annoyed with the woman's relentless questions and moved on through the area to the exit.

"I need to go back to the room," Brayden said. "I forgot something."

"Unless it was the diamond I suggest that you leave it there."

"We're going to need someplace to sleep tonight. We might as well go there and if the two women come back, we just won't answer the door," said Brayden. "Actually, the gemstones are in the hotel room safe," he admitted.

"Well, so much for that decision being carefully

weighed. How are we going to get in there? The hotel security and those women are looking for us."

"You stand watch and I'll sneak in, grab my things and then we'll head for the meeting with Smith."

Five minutes later they were back on the seventh floor where everything seemed to be back to normal. There were two couples arriving with their small rolling bags and a room service waiter pushing a large cart draped with a white tablecloth. He stopped to knock at a door two doors from Brayden's room as the men slipped by. Brayden slid his room card into the locking mechanism expecting a green light and a click but a red light blinked and remained red. In a panic Brayden tried again. No green light appeared. He mumbled a curse under his breath and tried a third time. Still there wasn't a green light.

Two doors down the door opened and a woman's voice invited the waiter and his cart of food inside. As he turned to push the cart Dennis saw the master key card dangling on a lanyard around his neck. Sixty seconds later he was back out in the hall with Dennis standing in front of him.

"Pardon me. Could you help me?" Dennis confronted the young waiter. "My room key isn't working and my friend is deathly ill. Could you try our key? Maybe we're not doing it right."

"I'll be happy to," the man said with a smile, which grew bigger when he saw a folded fifty dollar bill in Brayden's hand and a look of anguish on his face. He tried it three times, but to no avail. "If I could just see some identification, I can check my computer and have another key sent up."

"Here," Brayden said, practically shoving his open wallet with the exposed driver's license in the man's face. The waiter took a quick look at it and then turned to a small tablet computer on his cart and moved the iPad out of the men's sight. Moments later he turned back to Brayden. "The computer says you have checked out Mr. Ballard, but it wouldn't be the first time the thing has screwed up. I'll get the door, and then you can work it out with the front desk. I've got more meals to deliver."

He swiped his master card in the door and a green light immediately appeared. "Next time you go down to the lobby just have them re-boot your card." He reached out for the tip offered by Dennis, which had changed instantly to a ten dollar bill.

Inside the room, Brayden could see that the maid had been there. The bed was made and none of his personal items were visible. Anxiously, he opened the closet and was relieved that his shaving kit and a pair of socks were sitting on the shelf. The safe was winking its red light—the door safely closed. Carefully, he entered the family password into the safe's keyboard and heard a reassuring grinding sound as the locking mechanism opened. Inside the darkened cavern lay the money belt with its pricey content.

He loosened his shirt and pants and then strapped the belt around his waist, feeling the reassuring bulge from the gemstones. Brayden stuffed the shaving kit and socks into his carry-on suitcase then surveyed the room for anything else he might have forgotten.

"Did you bring any clothes?" he asked Dennis, not remembering having seen a bag.

"Nothing but my coat and wallet," Dennis said. "I didn't think it would take that long to claim your body from the police and fly you back home."

Both men smiled and then Brayden peeked through a crack in the door and waved for Dennis to follow him into the hallway.

Paula's telephone rang just as she was coming back home from her daughter's. "Is this the home of Brayden Ballard?" the pleasant voice asked.

Paula's defensive antenna went up immediately before she answered. "Who is calling?"

"My name is James Busch. I'm the assistant manager at the Bellagio Hotel in Las Vegas, Nevada. A Mr. Ballard, first name Brayden, is registered in one of our rooms. He called in a fire alarm this afternoon, regarding a nearby room, but it appeared to be a false alarm. Since the fire alarm, Mr. Ballard has not returned to his room and we have been unable to find him. Is it possible that he has checked in with you at home? We just want to be sure that he is safe and in good health."

"How did you get this phone number?" Paula asked in a not-too-friendly tone.

"This is the contact number the credit card company gave the police investigator," the man said looking over his shoulder at Marie Felstein.

"I have no idea where he is," she said and promptly hung up the phone. Her hands were trembling as she picked up her cell phone and punched in Brayden's number. *Has the man gone completely crazy?*

She had barely left a voice mail on Brayden's unanswered cell phone when her home phone rang again. The caller ID listed the caller as Cannon, D.

"Have you heard from Brayden yet?" Julie asked.

"What are you talking about?" said Paula in a voice that hinted more irritation than confusion. "He doesn't answer his phone. Why? What's going on?"

"Dennis is in Las Vegas with Brayden. He left just after you called him," Julie said. "He just texted me that he is okay and he has an important meeting tonight. I presume they are together. I just thought that you would want to know."

"I didn't expect Dennis to go with him. I had hoped he would when we talked, but he sounded mad at everyone—especially Brayden."

"Well it's not surprising," said Julie. "When Dennis found out Brayden had gone to Las Vegas, he tried to call, but got no answer so he just grabbed his coat and left. I tried to talk him out of it, which was useless as usual. He did say that he would be back at home tonight, but it's getting late enough that I doubt it."

Paula looked at the clock on the family room wall and tried to force the tears back into their ducts. *Why, oh why, did we dig ourselves into such a hole?*

Marie and Andriana had slowly become accepting of one another. Each figured that the other one had some knowledge and skill that would assist in achieving the goal—getting possession of the gemstones. For Marie the goal was really all about the diamond. For Andriana it was all or nothing. If she returned to Poland without the full complement of stones, she and her entire family would consider the trip a failure.

In her small clutch purse Andriana carried a dog-eared photocopy of an old, family photo. Unlike most family pictures taken with a small inexpensive camera, this particular photo was taken in front of the elaborate bath house at the Russian Tsar's summer palace referred to as Peterhof. It was taken by a team of photographers whose very lives depended on a perfect outcome. The medium-framed woman, standing erect beside his royal highness, was wearing a necklace of hazelnut-size rubies, emeralds, sapphires, and at the apex of the necklace, weighing down the material between her breasts, was a diamond of much greater size. On each of the woman's ears hung a trio of diamonds at least as large as the colored stones in the necklace. In spite of the photograph's original black-and-white format, color enhancement had demonstrated the differences of the colored stones.

Andriana's glimpse of the rumored pouch holding the gems was the first sighting in decades. The rainbow of sparkling stones spilling out of the guano-encrusted satchel at the small hotel in Chelm had at first made her question her vision, and out of fear, she told no one. It was not only the first time she had ever seen the legendary gems, but the first anyone had heard of them since her young American friend had reportedly found the stones in an abandoned dacha somewhere south of Saint Petersburg. That had been nearly twenty years ago. His story conflicted with the news report of the theft of a large number of rare gemstones from the Topkapi Palace in Istanbul. Shortly thereafter her friend had vanished, and so had the jewels.

When word spread that those same American tourists were returning to Chelm she called her colleagues, Alexander and Tito, with the news. She soon realized that was a huge mistake. They became greedy and decided that if there had in fact been precious jewels in the onion dome of the little church, they wanted the proceeds for themselves. She had tried to intervene, but had been treated like a hostage instead. Now, thank goodness, they had given up their quest in Colorado and it was up to her to find the gems. She and the American federal agent sat at a table keeping a close eye on the corridor passing through the Bellagio's casino. The men from Denver had given them the slip and the only hope of seeing them again in Las Vegas was to watch the place where they had last been seen.

Marie and Andriana were a total mismatch as investigators. Each time Marie made a suggestion where to wait, how to wait, and what to do should Ballard show up, Andriana would suggest something entirely different and then insist on doing it her way, leaving Marie shaking her head. They finally agreed to sit in the lounge area along the main casino breezeway, although sitting in clear view of the throngs walking through the casino was in direct conflict with everything Marie had ever been taught about surveillance. Andriana however, made the point that if they sat any further away from the walkway, the men could walk briskly by and disappear again before the women could catch up with them. So they sat and they waited, bickering from time to time about what to do when they cornered Ballard and Cannon.

Glade Hakes paced back and forth in his office. It was a stormy day in Denver, and the glass wall looking out toward the towering mountain peaks was obscured with blowing snowflakes. He pressed the intercom button on his phone and for the third time in an hour quizzed his secretary, Stacey, "I've expected a Mr. Ballard to arrive by now. Are you certain that he hasn't called or left a voice mail?"

"No, Mr. Hakes. I could call down to the security desk and see if they have heard anything or if there is any mail that has arrived. Sometimes the FedEx guy just dumps stuff on the counter if Chuck isn't standing right there."

"Why don't you take the elevator down and see for yourself. Maybe Mr. Ballard is just sitting there waiting for permission to come up. He's pretty shy," Hakes said in a hopeful tone, his stomach continuing to churn.

He had spent the weekend making calls and studying the price of diamonds on the various world markets. Prices fluctuated just like gold or oil, depending on supply and demand. The DeBeers syndicate had owned the market for decades, but the opening of the former Russian states and rogue mines in Africa, South America, and in the northern provinces of Canada had begun to skew the predictability of the prices. The newest generation of synthetic stones also had caused palpitations in the hearts of the diamond traders since the introduction of intentional microscopic flaws in the synthetic stones. A trained eye could still detect the real diamonds from the synthetic because of the sharpness of the cut edges—diamonds were still significantly harder, thus the edges didn't round off as did the best of the synthetics. Hakes had found one diamond of similar size and clarity to the Ballard stone. It was available for $850 thousand dollars, but there was still the age factor of the mystery stone that could make it worth much more.

By Monday morning Hakes was convinced that Ballard had a genuine, antique diamond and was prepared to give him a cashier's check for $500 thousand. He would take the stone to New York himself to get the best price—hopefully with a tidy three- to four-hundred-grand profit. But, now there was no Ballard and no diamond. His stomach churned as he stood by his office door waiting for Stacey to return.

Marie was the first to see the men. They had come from the opposite direction and walked right by the women. They were both wearing baseball caps; it was a lucky bump of a cocktail waitress's elbow into Dennis's arm that made him pause, turning his head toward the waitress to apologize.

"There they are!" she whispered, taking a quick swallow of her drink to cover her face.

"Where?" asked Andriana, starting to stand.

"They are walking the other way. They are wearing blue baseball caps."

"Where?" demanded the Pole in a loud voice. "I don't see any baseballs."

Marie grabbed Andriana's arm and pulled her back into her chair. "We need to wait for a minute or they are going to see us."

"I don't see them. I think you are mistaken."

Marie put some cash under her glass and nodded for them both to get up and walk. The ball caps bobbed up and down in the crowded walkway. Once past the turn to the elevators, the men took a right into a massive, arched breezeway lined with shops and restaurants. There the crowd thinned out and the women were forced to drop back.

"Walk on the other side," suggested Marie. "We'll be less likely to be recognized."

Andriana started to protest, but then got the idea of them not being side by side. She took her role as a casual tourist further by walking alongside a young, college-age man and starting a conversation. Up ahead, Brayden took a moment to look over his shoulder. His eyes scanned the group of people behind him skimming over both of the women then coming back to Andriana's blond hair just as she turned her head to converse with the young man. Nothing suspicious registered.

The corridor was coming to an elevated intersection with bridges going over the main avenues. The men took the bridge to the left. They were headed for Caesar's Palace. At the base of the bridge over Tropicana Avenue a large group of tourists were gathered around a guide who was waving a small purple flag. Brayden and Dennis had to separate to get around the group and walk toward the hotel's shops. Mr. Smith would be waiting—hopefully with a fat checkbook.

Just as the two female sleuths' feet hit the street level sidewalk there was a shout from one of the tourists. "Doctor Vlonovitski!" a woman shouted. "Over here. It is I, Olga Polanski, your favorite patient. What are you doing in America?" the woman said in strongly-accented English and then repeated her greeting in Polish.

Andriana tried to duck into the crowd, but it was too late. Both Dennis and Brayden heard her name called out loud and clear. Both did an abrupt glance behind and saw the doctor.

"Crap!" said Brayden, pulling Dennis's coat sleeve to duck behind one of the large columns nearby. The men looked at one another as if the other had an answer to the obvious question: *What do we do now?*

"We can't go straight to meet with your jeweler," Dennis said. "I'll tell you what. You go on ahead and I will go back and confront the two women. There is nothing they can do to me and I'm sure I can divert them long enough that they won't know where you have gone. We can meet up at the Bellagio's pool area."

Brayden merely nodded and walked around the column and dashed toward the circular drive leading to the hotel's entrance. Dennis turned toward the women and removing his cap, stared straight into the eyes of Marie Felstein. She stopped her fast walk and grabbed Andriana's purse strap.

"What?" asked the Polish doctor, still irritated by the delay caused by her former patient. The woman had insisted on them posing together for a picture in front of the hotel. She was forced into being rude to the woman to get away from her and catch up with Marie who was waving impatiently from behind a statue of some unknown Greek goddess.

"We've been busted," said Marie. She peeked around the corner toward the direction of the men when Dennis stepped into her line of view—six feet away.

"Pardon me, but you look real familiar," Dennis said to the Polish doctor, expressing a big smile. "Who is your friend?"

Both women stammered to find words to answer the question, and then Marie spoke up. "My friend doesn't speak English. She is from Russia. Now leave us alone before I call the police." She tried to step around Dennis who moved his wide shoulders to the left, blocking Marie's view of the hotel and its entrance.

"Are you insane? You have till the count of three to move before I scream rape and have you arrested for assault."

"Well, you are not very friendly. I'll bet your blond friend here would be more inclined to let a lonely American buy her a drink," said Dennis trying to fake a southern accent.

Meanwhile Andriana had walked away from the pair and headed toward the hotel entrance. After fifteen or twenty paces, however, she stopped. Brayden was gone from view. She turned back toward Dennis, coming up to him from behind. Now, it was her turn to be aggressive. She had learned a trick or two growing up in a male-dominated culture, where attractive young females were often taken advantage of. With an extended thumb placed strategically into the nerve bundle in the side of Dennis's neck, she pushed his whole body up against the base of the Grecian nude. The pain immediately brought tears to his eyes and a sense of paralysis to his left arm.

"Cut it out!" he yelled, trying to twist away from the beautiful and obviously motivated woman.

"You and your friend have a sacred family heirloom that belongs to my family. I want it back," the woman said in her heavy accent, negating the claim of her lack of English.

Dennis finally caught his breath and grabbed

the woman's wrist, twisting it away from his neck and holding it firmly. She tried to pull her hand away, but he held it tight and in his strongest military voice said, "*That* was assault, lady. I'm the one who is going to be filing police charges against both of you," he said, still gripping Andriana's wrist, but directing his glaring anger at Marie. "But you need to leave me alone. If you follow me or touch me again, I'll have you thrown in jail."

It was all Marie could do to not pull out her credentials and arrest the man, but she was too close to some kind of closure on the diamond case to risk it. Up close Dennis was much more handsome and way more fit than she had taken the time to notice. His commanding military presence gave her a flashback to her trainer at Quantico—a man she truly feared, yet admired.

"Let's get out of here," Marie said to Andriana, tugging her sleeve and nodding back toward the bridge to the Bellagio.

Andriana glared at both of them and then looked down at her wrist as Dennis released it. It was beet-red, especially around her metal watchband, which had dug painfully into her skin.

"I want my family's gemstones. I will not stop until I have them. Do you understand?" she said, making unbroken eye contact with Dennis. Tiny tears were beginning to track down her cheeks.

Dennis looked around behind him where a few curious passersby had paused to stare at the threesome. When he looked back the two women were gone.

Brayden had found the octogenarian-appearing Smith, standing behind the counter of his Rolex and Cartier watch display. A woman wearing a gold-embossed sari and very petite man dressed in an expensive, silk suit were standing in front of Smith holding a watch that looked more like a diamond-encrusted broach. Smith made eye contact, but continued his explanation of the features of the watch that Brayden immediately guessed would cost more than a new Mercedes. He milled about, checking out the necklaces and engagement rings on the opposite side of the store, ever vigilant for the arrival of Dennis and possibly the women—and even more possibly the police.

Ten minutes later Smith shook hands with the couple and handed over a glossy gift bag holding the watch and their receipt. Smith then turned toward Brayden and nodded for him to follow him into the back office. They hadn't closed the door when Dennis showed up at Brayden's side, slightly out of breath.

"Allow me to introduce my friend and partner, Dennis. My name is Brayden just in case you didn't remember," said Brayden to Smith.

"I must insist on seeing both of your identification papers. A driver's license will suffice," Smith said in a humorless voice.

The two men exchanged glances and reached for their wallets. Smith placed the IDs face down on a photocopy machine much like Brayden had at his home. He pressed the copy button and the three men waited for the machine to make its numerous wake-up noises and finally grind out a sheet of white paper with the color images of the two licenses. Smith handed the originals back to the men and led them to the corner of the room where he finally turned on a little charm. He offered them coffee from a small at-home brewing machine. Both declined.

"Well then," said Smith. "Let's have another look at your stone. While you are at it why don't you show me everything else you brought with you."

Brayden turned his back away from the man and unfastened his money belt. He removed a small felt satchel with the name of a jeweler embossed on the brown container.

"You bought these from Ganem's in Scottsdale?" Smith asked in surprise.

"No, no. The bag is from an old gift I bought for my wife when we were on vacation. It has nothing to do with the diamond."

The three men settled into leather-padded chairs around Smith's work desk, and Smith adjusted a gooseneck lamp, making it focus on the center of the workbench. Brayden reached into the satchel and with his finger and thumb removed the large diamond, carefully placing it in the center of the beam of light.

It had been several days since Dennis had seen or handled the stone and he couldn't resist picking it up and rolling it in his fingers. It refracted the lamp's light into the full spectrum of glimmering colors. "This stone should have a name, like the Hope Diamond," Dennis said, placing the stone back on the table.

"Perhaps it already does," said Smith, picking up the stone with a pair of long tweezers. Using a double loupe pair of magnifying glasses, the old man studied the gem from every conceivable angle and at different positions to the light. Then he laid it back on his desk. "Show me what else you have."

Brayden locked eyes with the man. "What makes you think I have anything else?"

"Have you forgotten so soon young man? You told me already that there might be others, therefore there are. I'm old but not a fool. Show me everything you have." He held out his hand.

Just as Dennis gave him the nod to proceed, a tiny bell above the door leading to the showroom began tinkling. All three men looked up at the bell, which was visibly moving. Someone had come into the shop in spite of the door leading to the mall area being closed and an old-fashioned, paper "BE BACK SOON" sign on the door, and Smith had set the clock's hands forward an hour.

"It's probably just my assistant," Smith said, his hand still extended to receive the next stone in Brayden's money belt.

Brayden unzipped the belt's pocket and produced a second satchel—this one with the name "Zales" on the fabric. He laid it on the table. Dennis reached out and covered the satchel with his hand.

"Before we go on, let's hear the price you are willing to pay for the diamond," Dennis said in a firm but friendly tone. "We may not be as old as you, but we aren't fools either."

✦ ✦ ✦

Marie and her physician partner had made it back to the top of the bridge when Andriana looked back toward Caesar's Palace and spotted the yellow taxi cab with its advertising marquee for a jewelry store. The sign was too far away to read the address, but it was enough to spark new resolve in her mind.

"Is there a jewelry store in that hotel?" she blurted out, grabbing Marie by the arm.

"What?"

"Is there a jewelry store in that hotel?" she repeated in a nearly frantic voice.

"Yes. I mean I think yes. Every hotel on the strip has a jewelry store," said Marie.

"Do you have a gun?" Andriana demanded.

"I'm a federal agent. Of course I have a gun."

"Give it to me. I know where they have taken my gemstones. They are going to sell them to a jewelry store."

"Are you nuts? I'm not giving you my gun!" said Marie in a loud enough voice that passersby had stopped to eavesdrop.

Andriana started back down the steps, taking them two at a time, leaving Marie no reasonable alternative but to follow. Within minutes they were in Caesar's Galleria Bar, rushing from shop to shop looking for a jewelry store. Near the far end they thought they had found the small business. Foot traffic in the mall was still busy … thus the small paper sign on the door seemed curious. Why be temporarily closed during a busy time of the evening when potential buyers were out for dinner and the late shows?

They stopped in an alcove across from the store

and watched. The interior seemed empty; however, the interior lights were burning brightly. Soon a twentyish-appearing woman in spiked platform heels—thought of wearing the shoes made Marie's feet hurt—came to the door and went in without giving the sign a glance. They could hear her call out someone's name as she propped the door in an open position.

Where were Ballard and his buddy Cannon? And where was the diamond?

"They have got to be in there," said Andriana. "Look, there is one of their basketball hats lying on the counter."

The woman who was now behind one of the showcases began polishing the glass with a rag and blue spray bottle. She picked up the cap and tossed it like a Frisbee toward a wastepaper basket in the corner.

"It's called a baseball cap, but you are probably right. It does look like the one Cannon was wearing. Let's find out."

"May I help you?" said the foxy-looking clerk as the two women entered the store.

From the back room the men heard and immediately recognized the voice in the showroom on the other side of the door. Brayden snatched the diamond and the unopened Ganem satchel from the workbench and turned away from Smith. He quickly placed the stones inside his wide, fabric belt, zipped it closed and fastened it around his waist, and then pulled his shirt down over it. He adjusted his jacket and then looked toward the rear door. For fire safety, every store in the mall required a fire exit door.

"What are you doing?" Smith asked. "That door has an alarm on it. I don't know who you are afraid of, but if you open the door the alarm will sound and both police and fire protection people will automatically be summoned. If you feel the need to hide, you could step into the vault. They will never find you in there," Smith said with a little chuckle—finding their nervousness somewhat amusing. These two amateurs were acting like frightened children. Now that he had seen the diamond for the second time, he wanted it and was determined to get it at any cost.

It was Dennis who kept a level head and pulled Brayden back into his chair and put his finger to his lips in a "be silent" motion.

Smith studied the two men and then held out his hand, indicating that they should remain still and that he would handle the situation. He arose and went to the door. Before opening it he flipped off the light switch— casting the workroom into darkness. The door opened and then quickly closed.

"Good evening, ladies. Is Kathryn taking good care of you?" asked Smith, nodding toward the attractive clerk.

Marie and Andriana look at the kindly, old, white-haired man with his gold, wire-frame glasses and the quaint, starched apron covering his white shirt and striped tie. He didn't act like he expected an answer and so they didn't give one.

"We are looking for two men, late fifties, medium builds. They were here in the mall just a few minutes ago," Marie said in an official-like tone.

"There hasn't been anyone in the shop for the last half an hour," the clerk said, glancing at Smith for confirmation.

"There were a couple of rather rough looking men here just before you returned from dinner, Kathryn. They were looking for a pawn shop. They must have had a bad day at the tables," Smith said with a nod of sympathy. "I told them they were in the wrong part of town and directed them toward the monorail and the downtown area. There are lots of legitimate pawn dealers there."

Kathryn picked up her bottle of glass cleaner and proceeded to polish the glass, deferring to her boss for any further questions.

"What about in the back of your store?" insisted Marie. "I'm a federal agent and we need to talk to the two men."

"I assure you, madam, that the two men in question left the store and were walking toward the exit to the street when I saw them last. As you can see, the back room is just for storage." As he said this he walked to the door and swung it open revealing a darkened room. He let the door swing back closed on its own.

Andriana was half-out the door when she called to Marie, "Come."

"So you are criminals?" said Smith, a tone of disgust in his voice, closing the door behind him. His assistant was still in the showroom seemingly unaware of the men's presence.

Dennis and Brayden were standing with their backs flat against the wall behind the door to the showroom. Both looked like they had seen ghosts. When they didn't answer the jeweler turned on the bright overhead lights and asked again. "Are you criminals? Did you steal the diamond? I can't deal in stolen merchandise. You need to leave."

Brayden finally took a deep breath and turned to the old man. "We found the jewels—quite by mistake. We didn't steal them from anyone. No one has shown us any proof that they belong to anyone but us. That woman who claims to be some type of a federal agent has never shown us any identification. The other woman is a partner with a bunch of Polish Mafia thugs who have tried to kill us. We have the diamond and they don't. If you want to buy it, give us a fair price and we'll be out of here, otherwise we'll find some other buyer and it will be your loss."

"You said 'jewels.' What about the rest of the gems?" coaxed Smith.

"Until we get an offer on the diamond, we don't have anything," Dennis interjected.

Smith gave both men long, appraising looks and then picked up a pad and wrote down a six figure number. He handed it to Brayden who looked at it and showed it to Dennis.

"You can't be serious?" said Dennis. "We know for a fact that the stone is worth twice that on the wholesale market and five times that retail."

"How do I know that the stone isn't stolen, just like the woman said? I will do a bank transfer of funds right now for the money and then you show me the rest of what you have. If they are of equal or better value I will buy them and give you an extra $100 thousand for the diamond. Take it or leave it."

It was a whole different world than either of the

friends had ever been exposed to. Shady, spur-of-the-moment deals, bank transfers of hundreds of thousands, offshore accounts, and threats by federal authorities.

"Four hundred thousand isn't enough, regardless of what else we have. We need five hundred thousand and we need it in cash. You take it or leave it," Brayden said, glancing at Dennis who gave him an approving nod.

"What? You think that I keep that kind of money in my vault? You must be nuts. If I would agree to such a transaction, it would take me at least until afternoon tomorrow to get the money together. Maybe I just call the lady back here and turn you both in. There is probably a reward that is more money than I would make if I pay you what you want."

Dennis was getting upset with Brayden, who was getting more nervous by the minute. There was a good chance that the two women would be outside waiting for them regardless. Walking out the door with a briefcase full of hundred dollar bills suddenly sounded like a really stupid idea.

"If we were to tell you that there are several stones as big and as good as the diamond—I'm talking rubies, sapphires, emeralds, and more diamonds—could you handle the purchase?"

The old man's eyes lit up and he took a deep breath of his own.

Dennis would later say that he felt as though they were in a showdown at high noon on a dusty, Tombstone-like street. The only thing missing was background music. Brayden looked at Dennis for approval and only got raised eyebrows for an answer. He turned his back on the jeweler and unzipped the money belt. Groping around in the tight pocket he got his fingers on the flimsy Zales satchel and tugged it out. He laid it on the workbench and twisted the switch on the gooseneck lamp.

He untied the drawstring and shook out three almond-size stones: one red, one blue, and one a brilliant green.

Smith walked up to the bench and sat down in his worn chair. He put on his loupe glasses and slowly began the appraisal. Several times he paused and glanced up at the men. Once he looked at the clock. Their 7:00 p.m. meeting already was well into its second hour. Occasionally, voices could be heard from the showroom. Finally, Brayden felt a wave of exhaustion roll over him and found the nearest chair. Dennis paced the room, never taking his eyes off of the hands of the jeweler. He had heard stories of merchandise being switched right in front of the customer's eyes and he wasn't about to let that happen.

Smith, apparently satisfied with his study of the stones, booted up his computer and looked at a screen full of numbers that meant nothing to Dennis or Brayden. At last he pulled a notepad into the focus of the lamp and wrote down four numbers: 5, 4, 3, and 2. He drew a line under the numbers and wrote a bold number 14. He then placed a comma between the one and the four. Still remaining silent, he wrote two zeroes, another comma and three more zeroes. He looked up and slid the paper toward Dennis.

"I will not pay you in cash. I can give you the name

of a bank in Grand Cayman that will open an account over the phone. They open at 6:00 a.m. Las Vegas time. Be here at 8:00 a.m. and bring these exact stones with you. Trust me when I say that I will know if you have switched the stones."

Smith got up from the workbench and turned off the gooseneck lamp. He opened the door into the showroom as Brayden quickly replaced the three stones in their sack and stuffed them next to the diamond. He was barely able to pull down his shirt as Smith turned off the light to the back room.

"Come along now," he said as he led the two men to the rear exit door flipping a switch to disarm it. "By the way, I expect to do more business with you in the future when I come to your town to evaluate the other merchandise."

Brayden didn't say a word but accepted a second piece of paper with the name of a private bank and its phone number. They could hear the door being locked behind them. Looking nervously around for any sign of the two women they silently made their way back in the direction of the hotel's lobby and casino.

"Now what we do?" Andriana asked in a disgusted voice. The two women were sitting on a bench in the Bellagio's long arcade. She had been wearing heels the entire day and her feet were killing her. Any trace of sunlight was long since gone, and even with the brilliance of the Las Vegas Strips' electric light display, recognizing anyone from a distance had become difficult. The women had waited in the gardens outside Caesar's Palace in hope of spotting Ballard and Cannon, but it had turned cold.

Marie finished her phone conversation and let out a hopeless sigh. "He told me to keep looking for them and not to come back until I have them in custody. I think he believes I'm an idiot. We had them in sight and now we have nothing. They've probably sold everything by now and are on their way back to Denver."

"I cannot believe that catching these thieves isn't a highest priority. Why has he not sent you more people to help you?"

"The whole thing looked like it would be an easy case of confronting these men, getting them to confess, and bargaining with them to turn over the diamond for a lighter jail sentence," Marie explained, wondering at the same time why she was confiding anything to this woman.

"The diamond? The diamond! You think that's just it? One diamond? These men have stolen a whole treasury worth of gemstones and you keep worrying about one diamond?" Andriana jumped up off of the bench and walked gingerly across the arcade to a balcony where she could see the famous synchronized fountains and hear the loud accompanying music. This time it was that Italian Mafia guy, Franco Sinatra—something about being "a part of it." Why they were playing a song about New York in Las Vegas, she couldn't understand.

Marie was listening to the song as well and actually felt a little moisture well up in her eyes as she thought about New York, her family, and her friends—few that there were. Andriana was right. They should have had more people working on this bust the whole time, at least a backup person to help her. If this diamond, and the supposed other stones were so important, they could have at least sent someone along with her if for nothing else to keep her company. At first she though these country seniors weren't dangerous. That was before the car chases, the Polish police's arrests, the home break-ins, and the bullets flying around the Cannon's house. And now she was basically alone in the heartland of the American's criminal mecca where even the city's motto was suspicious, hinting that one could do whatever and the facts of it would stay in Las Vegas. She felt discouraged, put upon—basically babysitting this Polish woman to keep her from screwing up everything—and now, she was unable to find her suspects.

Suddenly Andriana shouted, "There they are!" pointing out the window toward the fountain and jumping up and down like a seven year old at the circus.

People passing by stopped to look as Marie dashed to her side. "Who are they—movie stars?" asked one nosy woman, nudging Andriana to the side to get a look.

"They are our dates," snorted Marie, quite tired of interfering strangers.

"What?" said the woman. "You two don't look like the type. Surely those older gentlemen could do better just by asking at the front desk."

Marie turned, ready to belt the woman, but was nearly yanked off of her feet by Andriana—who wasn't going to let the men out of her sight again.

Brayden was starving. All the stress of the day had left him with an acidic stomachache, which he had tried to drown with Tums. That hadn't helped.

"There is a wonderful French bistro at the base of that mini-Eiffel Tower," Dennis said. "Julie and I ate there a couple years ago. They have the best French onion soup with melted cheese, and their bread is fantastic."

"Lead the way," Brayden said, glancing for the hundredth time over his shoulder. It was dark, cold, and a little breezy, enough so that his cap had blown off once so he tucked it into his jacket.

The head waiter showed them to a small, round table in the corner of the room where in better weather the glass doors would have been open to the sidewalk. They could see the Bellagio fountains performing their spectacle, but couldn't hear the music. Their waiter brought them water, fresh baguettes, and salted butter. Their drinks and soups were ordered, and before the last splash of the fountain settled the scalding bowls were placed in front of the men.

"Ouch, ouch, ouch!" exclaimed Brayden, snatching his ice water glass and gulping a mouthful to put out the fire. "Why don't I ever learn? Onion soup always burns my tongue."

Dennis laughed as he blew on his spoon to cool the savory liquid with its string of melted cheese trailing off the edge of the spoon. "Eat some of the bread and butter. It might take away the pain."

The focus on the meal was enough to let the men forget for just a few minutes all of the travails of the day. Both were exhausted. Both were confused about the decisions they had made that day, and both were feeling guilty that they had abandoned their wives with Christmas just days away. Brayden leaned back in his chair, having put away a whole loaf of the bread, the soup, a small Caesar salad, and a shrimp cocktail. "I'm stuffed. Now, I need a soft bed and eight hours of sleep."

"Do we dare go back to your room at the Bellagio?"

"Maybe we should just get a room right here at the Paris. It's almost ten. I need to call Paula. I'll have her make a flight reservation for us for around noon. We can drop off the stones at Smith's in the morning, get the money wired to the bank in the Caymans and be home in Denver by late afternoon."

"I like your plan, just as soon as I have a piece of the cheesecake."

Marie and Andriana had walked up and down the sidewalk on both sides of the Strip for several blocks, but hadn't seen so much as a glimpse of the two men since the sighting from the arcade. The air temperature had dropped and the wind had picked up. Cold and angry, Marie had insisted that they return to the Bellagio lobby.

"I'm an agent with the DEA," Marie said, flashing her badge in front of the desk clerk. "Has a mister Brayden Ballard checked out? His room was on the seventh floor."

To her surprise the clerk insisted on studying the identification badge and writing down the ID number. Only then did she turn to her computer and tap in some letters.

"Mr. Ballard is still registered at our property. He has requested an absolute *do not disturb* notice on the account and on the door," the clerk said in a protective voice. "I'm afraid that unless you have some type of search warrant or a court order, we are instructed not to allow you to disturb the patron."

"Patrons? Is that what you call criminals that are holing up in your hotel?" Marie said. Any semblance of patience in her voice was long gone.

"It doesn't matter," Andriana said tugging on Marie's sleeve until they were three or four paces from the desk. "We know what the room number is. They are still here. We just missed them. Let's go knock on the door and maybe we'll get lucky and they will open the door. If not, I know how to get in without a key."

Marie gave her a look like she was nuts, but was too tired to argue with the woman anymore. The combination of Andriana's stubbornness and her irritating accent—along with her misuse of so many English idioms—was wearing on her.

"Fine, we'll try it your way. If it doesn't work, I'm calling for backup first thing in the morning and we'll just arrest them, take the diamond and be done with it."

"Oh no you won't! I'm not letting my country's priceless jewels sit like prisoners in one of your evidence cages where some dishonest policeman will steal them for himself."

Marie threw up her hands in surrender. "Okay. Let's try it your way."

The women made their way through the casino toward the elevators that led to the guestrooms. Once again Marie had to show her credentials to get past the security guard at the elevators. There was a lot of traffic at the moment so the guy didn't have time to call the desk as he should have. Two other couples got off the elevator at seven making that part unobtrusive. The women walked as casually as possible to the hotel door they remembered from the morning. They knocked.

The sharp knock on the door startled Paula Ballard enough that she dropped the channel changer for her Dish satellite. She was sitting in her favorite chair wearing her flannel nightgown and fuzzy slippers. She was in the middle of the Christmas special of *Blue Bloods*—her favorite cop show—and was feeling sad that Brayden wasn't there to scoff at the ridiculous comments some of the characters made. She tied the sash on her robe and turned hall lights on as she went to the door. She peeked through the front door's little birdhouse window and saw two rather distinguished-looking men standing in the reflection of the numerous Christmas lights surrounding the porch. Dense puffs of steam extruded from their mouths with each breath. Sensing a level of security with the men, she opened the door.

"May I help you?" she asked in a pleasant voice, feeling the blast of freezing air hit her face and bare legs.

"Sorry to bother you so late Mrs. Ballard. I'm Preston Rosen with the Denver Police—special crimes division.

This gentleman says you have met Captain Akardiski of the Krakow, Poland police department."

Paula was so shocked that she didn't answer, nor did she take the extended hand of the handsome Polish policeman. A sudden panic swept over her, but she stepped away from the stoop anyway and allowed the men to come in out of the cold.

She guided them into the living room, a long, narrow room with an upright piano at one end and a large Christmas tree taking up a large portion of the space in front of the picture window. Its lights were twinkling cheerfully in spite of the tension in the room.

"I didn't ask at the door," said Rosen, "does your husband happen to be home?"

"No. He's out of town on business," she said, feeling her voice break a little. She had left the TV on and the muted voices coming from the family room sounded like they could be real people sitting just around the corner wall.

"I won't waste your time with a lot of chit chat," Rosen said. "Captain Akardiski is here in pursuit of a gang of murders and jewel thieves. Records indicate that the two of you and your husband's friends, the Cannons, were in Poland and encountered the men believed to be the thieves. The captain believes you and your husband could be helpful in capturing the men. In addition, there are a large number of antique jewels that were stolen years ago. We think the thieves have brought them into the United States hoping to sell them."

In spite of the panic she felt, Paula maintained her poker face and didn't twitch a muscle when she heard the words "jewels that were stolen." Her heart however, began skipping beats, giving her the sensation that she needed to cough and she could feel a bead of sweat begin to trickle down between her breasts. She was nodding slowly indicating that she was listening, but she didn't utter a word.

"It is very nice to see you again, Mrs. Ballard," Captain Akardiski said, giving her a "trust-me" smile. "I have been told about the trouble at your friend's house apparently caused by my corrupt countrymen. It seems every country has as they say … a few bad peaches in the bucket."

Paula couldn't help but chuckle at his convoluted idiom, causing her to take a deep breath and relax a bit. "I don't understand how I can be of help."

"We have just a few easy questions. Do you mind if we sit?" he asked, moving toward a long, blue-and-white chintz couch. "Have you or your husband been offered any gemstones, either to buy or to bring into this country … perhaps by a stranger?"

Paula took a seat on the piano bench across from the lawmen. She had no intention of lying to the men so thought the question through and then said, "No."

"Have either of you seen any of these people?" Akardiski then laid out three five-by-seven, glossy photos on the coffee table. There, plain as day, were the nasty-looking men who had been pursuing them for what seemed like months. The third picture was a picture taken from a distance of a woman with long, blond hair. Paula knew instantly that it was the woman doctor from Poland. He then produced a fourth photo. It was of another woman, this one with dark hair and brown squinty eyes. Paula had seen the woman many times: at the hotel breakfast buffet, behind the wheel of the funny little car in Poland, and then again just two days ago, hiding behind a cement column at the mall in Parker.

"My eyes aren't as good as they used to be," she said, again not lying, but not exactly being forthright. "I think they are the men who attacked us in Poland, but I can't be positive. They all look so much alike."

The captain cleared his throat at the tangential insult then asked, "What about this women?"

"The picture isn't very clear. I would hate to make a mistake and get someone in trouble. Who is the woman with dark hair?"

"We were hoping you could tell us. She isn't from Poland, yet we think she was there at the same time you were. She isn't a policewoman and she isn't known to be part of any criminal organization. She just keeps showing up on cameras, often at places where you or your husband or the Cannons are."

Inspector Rosen's statement made Paula turn her face away from the man and gaze at the Christmas tree. She didn't want to lie and yet even more she didn't want to have Brayden arrested and put in jail. She just wanted everything to be back to normal. The money would be nice, but they already had a nice life and a wonderful family. Maybe she could just come clean with these men and they would help her and Brayden. Then the phone rang.

She excused herself and went into Brayden's office and closed the door behind her. She spoke to her husband in hushed tones, which was the way he was speaking also. He caught her up to date, mentioning that they had essentially sold four of the gems and would be home in the afternoon. She asked lots of questions about the events of the day. When he told her about being followed by the two women whose pictures she had just been shown, her mind started to race. When she told Brayden about the visitors in the next room, the conversation went still.

"Please don't tell them a thing," he said. "We are in too deep to get out now. Tomorrow we will be millionaires and still have most of the gems left over. Maybe we can return the remainder of the gems and keep what money we get tomorrow. Would that ease your conscience? In the meantime, just put them off until we get back tomorrow. You'll be fine."

Paula didn't answer his question, but told him she loved him and that she had to go. They said goodnight and she hung up the phone. Lying on the desk in front of her during the conversation was a Post-it note with the name "Hakes," and a phone number scrawled in Brayden's writing. She knew who Hakes was. Like a revelation from the heavens, an idea came into her mind. She would need a lot of trust and cooperation. Maybe in the end she would need a good lawyer or two. Maybe even a divorce lawyer.

She stuck her head out the door and yelled that she would be just a minute, and then she picked up the phone and called Julie.

"I need you at my house—yes, right now. Bring that little tape recorder and plan on being up late."

35

The men accepted the offer of coffee and some fruit nut bread and moved into the family room where Paula threw a couple more logs on the fire in the stone fireplace. When she told them she had just thought of something and had to wait for her friend to come they hesitated, but the change in her attitude was curious enough to hold their attention.

Julie came in through the side door without knocking. She stopped suddenly when she saw the men, but then took off her overcoat and joined the others in the living room. Introductions were made although she remembered the Polish captain all too well.

Paula took the mini-cassette recorder and rewound the tape to its beginning and then placed it on the table in front of her. "I am going to tell you a story you won't believe. Maybe it is true and maybe it isn't. When I'm done I'm going to ask for your help. Those parts that I am not clear about, Mrs. Cannon will help me with."

She nodded toward Julie who seemed to be reading her mind. Julie smiled and nodded back. She began with the first travel brochure her husband had received at his office—"Travel adventures for the well-traveled." It included: photo safaris on motorcycles into the back country of Kenya and Tanzania, kayak trips down the Nile, treks on donkeys into the forbidden mountains of Nepal, and, of course, the description of intimate visits to the former Soviet cities few ever experience.

Paula told how the trip the four of them took was not what they had expected and how both Brayden and Dennis had been nearly out of their minds with boredom. Dennis, having a military background had filled the downtime, which was most of the time not on the bus—with war history; while Brayden had become interested in the architecture of the palaces and churches. She told of their climb into the dome of the small church in the town of Chelm and of finding the guano-encrusted bag full of old, colored rocks and a modern fraternity ring.

"Brayden and Dennis became obsessed with the incongruity of an American fraternity ring being in the same container with what eventually were judged to be some type of antique jewels. Then they found the body of what they were sure was an American."

Agent Rosen, who was acting bored with the whole story suddenly sat up straight in his chair. "You never told me about a body," he said to the Polish investigator.

"It was when our husbands returned to the church to see what else was there, that they found the body. That's when they were attacked by the Polish Mafia men and nearly killed. Then the American woman ... that woman there," she said, pointing at the photo on the table, "crashed her car into those gangsters' BMW and saved our lives—that was the same day as the kidnapping."

Rosen reached across the table and pressed the off button on the recorder. "It isn't going to do anyone any good to make up a string of lies, Mrs. Ballard. You need to just tell us about the stolen jewels and what your husband is going to do with them. He is in a lot of trouble, as are all of you. You seem like a very nice person and we would like to help you, but you have got to tell us the truth."

"Where are your husbands and where are the Russian jewels?" demanded the Polish police officer.

That's when a loud bell rang in Paula's brain and the whole story became suddenly clear. This man sitting across from her wasn't here to do any of them any favors.

"I am telling you the truth," said Paula. "May I please speak to you alone?" she asked Rosen.

She stood and walked straight into Brayden's office and waited until Rosen hesitantly followed. Once inside she closed the door and looked him in the eyes. "The man with you is part of them!" she whispered.

"Part of whom?" Rosen asked, confused and irritated.

"Part of the Polish Mafia. In the first place, how does he even know that we have any jewels and that they are Russian, and not Polish? He had Julie arrested when we were in Krakow and thrown in jail just to leverage her arrest against our husbands so he could get the jewels. They aren't just a bag of rocks or cut glass. They are gemstones worth millions. Do you actually believe that he is going to take a fortune in gemstones and turn them back over to a bunch of corrupt Polish politicians? He is using you, probably because his sidekicks were chased out of the US by our husbands."

There was a sharp knock on the office door. "What is going on in there?"

Paula pressed the lock on the door and whispered, "Our husband's lives are in danger. If you don't stop listening to that man and get some real help for us, Mr. Polish policeman in there is going to kill them and take the jewels, just like he killed the American college student Wilson Arbon."

"Open the door!" shouted Akardiski.

"Paula, open the door. This man has a gun pointed at me," said Julie.

Rosen put his hand on the door knob, nudging Paula away from the door. "Who is Wilson Arbon? And why would they kill him?"

"Because, he found the Russian crown jewels. He probably found them at the site where Tsar Nicholas and his family were murdered. He was probably trying to escape into Hungary when he was trapped in the onion dome and murdered. He was smart enough to hide the jewels and leave a clue—his Sigma Chi ring—for some future person to find."

Agent Rosen shook his head to clear his thinking. "You have got to tell me and my bosses this whole story, but not right now."

Then Rosen pulled his Glock out of his shoulder holster, switched off the light in the room, and yelled out the door. "Step away from the door. We are coming out."

He nudged Paula away from the entrance and ducked to a full squat as he swung the door open. The blasts from the Pole's Makarov nearly deafened Paula and Rosen as three bullets crossed the room inches above Rosen's head. A single shot from the agent's automatic struck Akardiski in the mid-thigh, dropping the man to the ground with a scream of agony as the bullet fractured the man's femur, tearing muscle, nerve, and blood vessels as it fragmented. Paula had picked up a Polish pottery vase she had bought at Boleslawiec, and as the Pole tried to raise his gun hand she smashed the vase down on the crown of his head. She suddenly had no more interest in Polish pottery.

Paula and Julie refused every offer of medical help and refused to leave the Ballards' home, agreeing to be interviewed the following morning at the county attorney's office. Before the paramedics had loaded Akardiski on the gurney—leg cuffs in place—there were what seemed like dozens of police and federal agents in the house. It was when the regional federal attorney entered—dressed in a crisp, white shirt, striped club tie, and three-thousand-dollar suit—that the din settled to a quiet hum. It was readily apparent that he was taking over the case.

By nine o'clock Tuesday morning, Paula and Julie were settled around a worn, walnut table in Denver's federal building. They were sitting on hard, metal chairs facing a cluster of men and women in gray and black suits. Two voice recorders and a video camera were recording as the two women began giving full disclosure of the activities of the last four months. Before Paula or Julie uttered a single word, documents were signed and witnessed, giving the women and their husbands full immunity from any prosecution—both federal and state—for their cooperation in the retrieval of the missing jewels and the arrest of the conspirators involved. The stories then proceeded. While the two women spoke and were recorded, their husbands had just awakened from a good night's sleep in the comfortable beds of the Paris.

36

With all the wonders of the electronic age, cyberspace, and the Ethernet, knowledge of the events at the Ballard home remained unknown to the four adults in Las Vegas—who had played cat and mouse for nearly twenty-four hours. Brayden had unplugged the room phone when they went to sleep, and by the time they awoke at seven thirty, both men's cell phones—chargers left back at home—were dead. Brayden plugged the hotel phone back into the wall and called Paula. There was no answer.

"She must be off on a last minute Christmas errand," he muttered to Dennis who was headed for the shower.

Twenty minutes later Dennis had the same bad luck trying to reach Julie.

Room service breakfast arrived and was nearly inhaled by the men. They were to meet Smith at nine and planned to go straight from his shop to the airport.

"I just wish I had brought all of the gemstones with me, then we could conclude this entire fiasco this morning," said Brayden.

As they were leaving the room the porter knocked on the door to pick up the food tray.

"Excuse me … Jim," Brayden said, having read the boy's name off his tag and handing him a ten dollar bill. "Do you happen to have a cell phone on you? Mine is dead and I left my charger at home. I just need to send my wife a quick text message."

"Sure," the young man said handing Brayden the latest model of Apple's miracle machine.

Brayden turned away and quickly typed a message to Paula, indicating where he was and that all was well. They would be home later in the day bearing a very special Christmas gift. He touched the send icon and heard a quick hum as the message flew away.

Ten minutes later, the two men, looking a bit scruffy with their twenty-four hour beards and wrinkled clothes, walked out the back door of the hotel, through the parking garage and onto Tropicana Avenue. Even at that hour there was lots of traffic to contend with while jaywalking to the back entrance of Caesar's Palace. Once in the building they made their way past the sea of mostly empty slot machines and gaming tables to the Galleria.

Brayden gripped Dennis's arm as they approached Smith's shop. "Stop for a second," he said.

"What?" Dennis said, sensing the uneasiness in Brayden's voice.

"Think I recognize that man standing by the door of the jeweler's. Oh my gosh! That guy is the gemologist from Denver, Hakes. What is he doing here?"

The two men ducked into a service alcove and stood with their backs flat against the doors as they watched

Hakes knock on the door of the jewelry store. Seconds later they saw the graying figure of Smith open the door and without even a nod, he let the Denver gemologist into the store.

"Will you look at that? There was no hesitation at all. Those two know each other," said Brayden.

"Now what?" Dennis mumbled.

No sooner had he asked the question when they heard a noisy commotion at the street entrance of the arcade. They watched in amazement as four policemen—wearing chest-protection vests, helmets with visors, and carrying automatic rifles—hustled toward the jewelry store.

Brayden, who had started to walk toward the jeweler turned abruptly and shoved Dennis back into the service nook. Instantly, their heads poked around the corner like a couple of prairie dogs peeking out of their tunnels. They watched as the glass door was hammered with the butt of a gun—the sound echoing up and down the wide, empty shopping arcade. Moments later, Smith appeared and tried to wave the police away, as though they were annoying pests at a picnic, pointing to the closed sign hanging on the door.

The policemen would have none of his hesitation, screaming for him to open the door or face it being shattered. Smith finally relented and reached up to twist the locking knob. Immediately, two of the police were on Smith forcing him to the ground. The others rushed toward the back door of the shop and soon returned with Hakes in their grasp. Both men were led out of the store and forced to stand against a concrete wall—hands cuffed behind them—while the store was searched inch by inch.

The officer apparently in charge spoke into a communication device attached to his shoulder and listened as the answer was received. He then returned to his questioning of Smith and Hakes. Several minutes later, the automatic doors at the mall's street entrance slid open and in rushed the DEA Agent Marie Felstein and Doctor Andriana.

"Get back," urged Dennis. "It's those women from yesterday, the DEA agent and your friendly Polish doctor."

Brayden's hands were trembling as he reached down and felt for the four gemstones in his money belt. They were still there.

"What should we do?" he asked Dennis, not really expecting an answer.

"I have no idea, but staying out of sight is working for now."

They watched as more men came out of the store than had entered through the front door. It was obvious that some had been watching the back door leading to the alley. A short conference was held—the two women having an animated disagreement with the policeman in charge. There was a great deal of head shaking and finger pointing. Finally, the DEA woman threw her hands up in a gesture of defeat and turned toward the door. The officer giving the orders then allowed Smith to lock the front door, leaving the small, closed sign dangling from its chain beside the door. The jeweler and the gemologist were then led toward the mall entrance. No one had investigated the small, dark nook ninety feet away—where the two other men of interest were concealed.

"They've gone. Let's get out of here," Brayden said, starting to move into the light.

He was tugged back into the shadow just in time to miss the return of one of the policemen. The man was carrying yellow plastic tape which he attached to the jewelry store door, and then he turned and left.

"Finally," said Dennis and led the way in the opposite direction. Brayden waited a few seconds so that the men were not walking side by side. They cleared the mall stores and then followed their previous path through the luxurious casino—pausing a couple of times to look back. Brayden led the way into one of the men's restrooms. They waited while the only other occupant finished washing his hands and left, then Brayden turned to Dennis and asked, "What was all that about?"

"Obviously somebody tipped them off that we were coming."

"But how in the world did Hakes get involved?"

"Beats me," Dennis said, splashing cold water on his face then letting it drip because there were only hand blow-dryers in the room. "Somebody must be tapping phones. Probably ours at home as well. Now, what do we do?"

"Going home sounds pretty good to me," said Brayden.

"But then what? Are we just going to tuck the jewels into our home safes and have a gathering around the Christmas tree every year to fondle them?"

Brayden ignored the sarcasm. He had to think. "You

said that the blond woman, the doctor, claimed that we had stolen the jewels from her family and that they could be part of some royal Russian treasure, right?"

"That's what she claimed," Dennis said.

"Then who killed Wilson and how did the gems get to Poland? There are too many unanswered questions to stop now."

"But the police are involved—the real police. The two women are obviously working with the police. It won't take long before Smith and Hakes tell the cops about us and then the real hunt will be on," said Dennis.

"We haven't broken any laws here in Las Vegas. Let's just leave town. We probably can't get on an airplane. They'll be looking for us. We need to get a car. We can drive to Salt Lake City and then fly home from there," Brayden said—more brainstorming than thinking clearly.

They proceeded to the car rental desk in Caesar's massive lobby where they were told that getting a car was no problem. Brayden gave the woman his credit card and they were told to wait. A valet would bring the car around in about twenty minutes—it was just being washed.

Thirty minutes later, the men were sitting in a generic, silver Toyota fastening their seat belts when a buff-looking woman wearing a black, Kevlar vest stepped in front of the car and pointed a large black gun at the driver's side windshield. Brayden already had put the car in gear and inadvertently touched the gas pedal. The Ford's bumper nudged the woman's legs as he slammed down on the brake. She screamed something they couldn't hear because the car's radio had come on at full volume, belting out a Mexican song. By the time Dennis could find the correct radio dial to shut off the noise, there was a loud tapping on the driver's side window. Three feet away from the glass, stood the petite DEA agent. She kept showing up at the most inconvenient times.

"Open the door," she mouthed through the closed window. "We need to talk." She wasn't smiling.

The Las Vegas federal building was in a glass-and-stone eyesore in the city center. The air had turned warm and the sun was glaring as the doors of the black Suburban were opened for the two men in casual dress. Brayden and Dennis stepped out onto the sidewalk and followed a serious-looking man in a suit and sunglasses into the building. The uniformed driver hadn't mentioned Brayden trying to run over her, but did keep reaching down to rub her shin. Marie remained in the SUV and as soon as the doors were closed, it drove away.

To their surprise, no handcuffs had been placed on either man. They were, of course, searched for weapons, but their wallets—and strangely enough the lumpy money belt, still secured around Brayden's waist—was either overlooked or ignored. They were taken to an upper floor of the building and led down a hallway into a windowless room with thick, brown carpeting, tan walls, and bright, fluorescent lights. The men were seated on comfortable, padded chairs on one side of a long, wooden conference table. They were offered bottles of water, which both accepted. Then they waited.

All of the gun-toting police officers and even the plainclothes DEA agents had vanished, leaving the men to sit alone. Fearing that the room sounds would be recorded, neither spoke out loud, but instead sat and pondered their fate. Would they face months of court proceedings and then fines and prison? What would they tell their kids and grandkids about why they were going to jail?

Nearly an hour later there was a knock on the door, followed by the entrance of Marie Felstein and an unknown man in an ill-fitting, black suit. Then, to their mixed feelings of surprise, Paula and Julie entered. Both looked tired and annoyed. The blond, Polish doctor wasn't with them.

"What in the world are you doing here?" said Brayden, jumping to his feet and rushing into his wife's arms.

Dennis embraced Julie then the four clutched one another and the question was repeated over and over with no good answer being given. Finally, the man in the black suit spoke in an insistent voice. "Will you all please take a chair? My name is Gerald Dearing. I am the East Coast regional director of the DEA. I am in charge of protecting our country from the smuggling of arms, weapons of mass destruction, and anything else it takes to keep our country free from the bad guys. The guys who would love to see us all dead. It is my understanding that you have met a few of these bad guys." He paused and looked into the eyes of each of the Denver residents.

"Ms. Felstein has been working for several months trying to intercept illegal diamonds and other gemstones that have been coming into the country to fund radical terrorist cells. One such group of gems appeared to have been discovered by a Denver gemologist." Dearing glanced at a notepad in his hand and then continued. "This man—a Mr. Hakes—in a novice rush to make a handsome profit, called the wrong people—people we happen to have had phone taps on for several months."

"Mr. Hakes? Is he okay?" Brayden said out loud, wishing he had kept quiet.

Agent Dearing looked at Brayden with a judgmental side glance and then continued. "Following his trail led us to the four of you. I have been told by Ms. Felstein about you and your many adventures in Eastern Europe, Michigan, Denver, and more recently right here in Las Vegas. Did I miss any other locations of intrigue? I'm truly impressed with your ability to stay alive. I'm more impressed with your stupidity at persisting to risk your lives for a handful of colored rocks."

Paula wasn't about to sit there and take the insults and threats she and Julie already had heard for the last several hours. She abruptly stood and did something she wished she had done earlier. She walked around the table and grabbed the senior agent by his silk neck tie, tugging his chin upward and tightening her grip as she moved her face close to his. Dearing was too surprised to react.

"The four of us don't care about the jewels, we have been searching for the identity of a murder victim," Paula said in a near whisper.

This brought a jerk of Dearing's head toward her. "What are you talking about? We've never been advised of any murder," he said.

"You don't know a tenth of our story," she hissed, releasing his tie. "You are only interested in finding some diamonds and punishing anyone who has them or tries to sell them, even though you haven't a clue whom they really belong to. We, on the other hand, have been shot at, beaten up, our homes have been invaded, and our personal safety has been at risk a dozen times. Now, you come along and have the nerve to sit there with your smug look and tell us we are stupid? Where were you and your minions when our lives were in danger?"

"This lady here … Marie," Paula continued, pointing a finger, but never taking her glaring eyes off of Dearing, "was the only one who lifted a finger to help us when she crashed her car into those Polish Mafia idiots. On the ride here from the airport she admitted that she has kept you informed all along, but you have used us like pawns in your pathetic chess game. Our lives were in danger and you knew it and you did nothing. You are the ones who should be put in jail."

There was a deathly silence in the room following her outburst. No one made an effort to disagree with her summary.

"We want a lawyer!" said Dennis.

"So do we!" said Brayden.

"Just a minute here," Dearing said. "No one said anything about you needing a lawyer. We just need to get to the bottom of this investigation and find—"

"She didn't mean to be quite so abrupt," said Marie,

cutting her boss off in mid-sentence. "We need their help if we are going to stop the Polish gangsters from hurting anyone else."

"You arrested us and brought us all the way here from Denver and now you just want us to help you find a diamond? Get real. We're not saying another word without a lawyer present," Julie said. Her tone of voice was so pleasant that the words she spoke surprised everyone.

"I apologize if I insulted you. You are not under arrest," said Dearing. "I'll tell you what. Why don't we start all over again? I'll tell you what we suspect and how we think you are involved and then you can tell us how we can go about finding what we need to find and how we can stop the problem from escalating. Is that okay with the four of you?"

The four looked at each other with questioning glances. Then Brayden said, "I don't think any of us have a clue what you just said. But like we said, no more questions or answers until we have legal representation. All of us are hungry and thirsty."

Dearing nodded toward the door and he and Marie got up and left the room.

Four hours later, there was a knock the door of the Paris hotel VIP suite. Dennis took a peak through the lens on the door and saw a bellman standing beside a large, rolling table covered with a bright, white tablecloth. The two couples had been returned to the Paris in the black Suburban after Marie had returned to the conference room. She explained that something very important had come up and their "interview" would have to continue the following morning. Until then, they were requested to stay at the hotel—at the government's expense—until everything could be sorted out.

The two-bedroom suite was on the twelfth floor overlooking the musical fountains and was furnished with the finest of everything. The bellman rolled the table into the living area and transferred the place settings and the pre-ordered dinners to a large glass table. "Is there anything else, sir?" he asked Brayden. "Please call the kitchen if you think of anything. The direct number is on the card beside your plate."

"I don't get it," said Dennis as he held Julie's chair out for her to sit. "This morning we are being hunted like escaped murders and now we are sitting in the lap of luxury."

"Maybe it's our last meal before the execution," said Brayden.

"Or our transfer to Guantanamo," said Julie. "Didn't that agent mention the 'T' word?"

"Whatever their game is, I'm still famished. I should have ordered that turf and surf," Paula said switching the plate of lasagna in front of her with Brayden's steaming plate. "You don't mind, do you sweetheart?"

He rolled his eyes and smiled at his wife. He knew that she, like all of them, had experienced a very stressful day. *Maybe she'll share a couple of bites.* Moving his chair closer to the table he needed to shift the lumpy money belt to his side to make room. He still couldn't believe that none of the authorities had asked him where he had hidden the gemstones.

38

The phone rang in the hotel suite at eight the next morning. The caller informed the Cannons and the Ballards that they were to be dressed and ready for a visit in their suite at nine o'clock sharp. Right on the hour there was a sharp knock on the door and in strode Agent Dearing, Marie Felstein, and Andriana Vlonovitski. Standing outside the room, should their assistance be needed, was the female agent Brayden had nearly run over with the rental car, and a handsome male agent who wore no name tag and carried a very visible 357 magnum revolver on his hip.

"Good mornings" were exchanged, but no one was smiling.

Their room service breakfast table had already been moved into the hallway and chairs had been placed in a semicircle across from the couch. Everyone sat down and Agent Dearing began.

"Ladies and gentlemen, during the last sixteen hours, a great deal of research has been done to tie together this incredibly bizarre story. Dr. Vlonovitski has shared some documents with us, which our experts in Washington have cross-checked with the Hermitage museum in Saint Petersburg, Russia. They have discovered photos of the Russian royal family—Tsar Nicholas, his wife and the children—taken in 1914 while at a performance of the Bolshoi ballet company. These photos clearly show a necklace, broach, and earrings made up of enormous diamonds, and numerous colored gems. Unfortunately, the photo is in black and white so the precise identity of the colored stones is not clear without computer color enhancement. None of these gems have ever been seen since that photo was taken—until the early nineties that is."

"What does that have to do with us?" Brayden interrupted.

It was the blond doctor, Andriana, who continued the story. "In the summer of 1992, a young male, an American, was seen in a restaurant in northern Poland carrying a leather satchel. He was disheveled and unshaven when he arrived. He talked the restaurant owner into giving him a meal in exchange for his hat, which had a Detroit Tiger name. That is a logo right? As the man ate the meal, the satchel was accidently dropped on the floor and a portion of the contents spilled out. It caused an uproar in the small restaurant due to the presence at the adjacent table of an elderly woman. The regal woman saw the scattered stones near her feet on the floor and began shouting in her feeble voice that the colored gemstones belonged to her mother. The woman grasped the man's shirt collar as he bent to pick them up and when he pulled away she refused to let go of him. She was pulled out of her chair onto the floor. The frightened man shoved the woman out of the way and quickly gathered the jewels into his leather pouch," Andriana paused to dab at tears in her eyes with a tissue.

Agent Dearing picked up the story. "The American apparently paused long enough to say something in English which was later interpreted to be an apology to the woman and a declaration that he had found the treasure somewhere in a forest and was not going to give it up to anyone. He left before he had a chance to eat, but he did leave his hat that contained the name 'Arbon' written in ink inside the hat brim."

"The woman was my grandmother," Dr. Vlonovitski said. "The fall from the chair broke her hip. She never recovered completely and died two months later from pneumonia. My father swore an oath to find the man and the jewels, which grandmother claimed were given to Russian nobility by one of the rulers of the Ottoman Empire in the seventeenth century.

"My grandmother died shortly after calling her family to her bedside and admitting that since the Communist régime had come to an end, it was safe for the rest of us—her family—to know that she was in fact, the daughter of Tsar Nicholas II and that I was his great-granddaughter."

There was a silence in the hotel room as the Ballards and Cannons glanced at one another. Although this story sounded too bizarre to be true, all eyes in the room turned toward them. The ball was apparently now in their court. They could buy into the story and come to the rescue of the desperate woman sitting in front of them. Or they

386 STEVEN I. DAHL, M.D.

could claim total innocence and hope to get out of the room without being arrested for theft, smuggling, and a grocery list of lesser charges.

It was Paula who broke the silence. "This story is very interesting and possibly true. But, quite frankly, I still don't understand why you have confined us here. I have children and grandchildren who are expecting Christmas Eve dinner at my home in three days. Unless you can give us a reason not to walk out that door, my husband and I are catching the next airplane back to Denver. If, in fact, your story is true, Ms. Vlonovitski, the jewels you describe are the product of a string of crimes against humanity. The list of tortured and dead associated with your supposed family jewels most likely has dozens of names on it, the most recent of which is the Mr. Arbon, and could well have included some of us here in this room. How can a bag of colored rocks be so important that people must be imprisoned or die in order that you and your so-called people can file by a glass case in a state-run museum and snicker at the possibility that your jewels are bigger and shinier than the Queen of England's or the Pope's? The whole idea that rocks are more important than people is against everything I believe in. I hope you find your family jewels and have a very Merry Christmas."

With that said, Paula, ignoring the others, stood and walked past Agent Dearing toward the bedroom. The others looked at her with puzzled frowns, and then Brayden, Julie, and Dennis stood and followed. Agent Dearing mumbled something to Marie, but it wasn't understood because Andriana had started yelling at all of them in Polish.

Five minutes later the two couples paraded out the suite's door, past the armed agents in the hallway and boarded the elevator.

"Hold on there just one minute. Where do you ..." Dearing said, but the elevator's door opened. The door chimed and the two couples joined a cluster of Japanese tourists for the ride to the lobby floor. Brayden took the handle of Paula's carry-on and worked his way to the back of the car. When everyone piled out, Dennis noticed Brayden leaning over the lower zipper compartment of the carry-on.

"Well, what should we do now?" Julie said in a cheerful voice.

"How about a cab ride to the airport and the next flight to Denver," Dennis said. "I still have my Christmas shopping to do."

"Don't worry," said Brayden. "There will be plenty of time for that. You can shop online from the holding cell." He nodded toward the entrance where the two armed DEA agents had suddenly appeared and positioned themselves by the revolving door. The adjacent elevator opened and Marie stepped out and quickly caught up with the foursome. She grasped Brayden's arm, pulling him toward the porter's alcove.

"We need to talk for just one minute more," Marie said. "Quite honestly, I agree with your wife. I don't see how the Russians or the Poles have any more right to look at the jewels—if there are in fact any such things— than the American public. We did free the Poles from the Germans and bring down the Berlin Wall. Maybe we should get something for it. And as to the long list of those who have died and suffered for the preservation of a bag of colored rocks, I think that list should come to an end with Mr. Arbon. Agent Dearing is on the phone with the attorney general as we speak. I think we can work out some sort of a deal that will make everyone happy—maybe even your previous doctor. The agents at the door will drive you to the airport where a plane is waiting to take you home. I will try to set up a meeting for tomorrow at the office in Denver if you don't mind, so we can do any necessary paperwork. Then you can be done with everything before Christmas Eve. I promise that I will do everything possible to make it a very Merry Christmas for all of you."

Although some kind of trick could have been suspected, Brayden and Dennis felt a sense of trust in Marie—the woman already had saved their life once. As promised, an unmarked, ten passenger jet was waiting for the couples at the general aviation terminal in the shadow of the Tropicana Hotel. They settled in for the ride and were treated to a nice catered lunch during the flight. Dennis looked at his companions and shook his head in disbelief. "You know that this could just as well have been a ride in the back of a police van to a federal processing center and a green bologna sandwich for lunch."

Four hours later, Paula was filling her tub and Brayden was finishing a badly needed shower. The flight home on the government jet had been efficient. No one had talked of anything serious and certainly the gems hadn't been mentioned. It wasn't until the water in the tub was near the brim and Paula had slipped into the steamy froth of fragrant bubbles that Brayden leaned over the edge of the tub. Paula heard a clatter as the thirty-some gems were scattered around her feet and legs.

"Brayden are you insane?" she said when she realized what had just happened.

"Why? The stopper is in isn't it?

Her hand instantly reached deep into the bubbles for the drain and with a shudder of relief she felt the closed drain cap surrounded by the dull-edged stones. Looking up at him with a faux expression of disgust, she gathered up a handful of the stones bringing them to the surface. As the bubbles popped and floated away from her cupped hands, the diamonds, rubies, emeralds and sapphires burst into a rainbow of reflected light.

Brayden smiled at her and said, "It occurred to me that it may have been over a century since such an elegant woman was bathed in the beauty of those magnificent gemstones." He leaned down and kissed the lips of his astonished wife, ignoring the flecks of dirt now floating on the sea of bubbles. He hoped Paula didn't notice them.

It was the third shortest day of the year as the sun broke over the horizon illuminating the snow-covered spruce and bare aspen trees in the Ballards' backyard. The couple had been up early hoping to get a head start on the long list of must-do items before their family would all arrive for Christmas Eve dinner. Julie had called to check on what Paula was going to wear to the 11:00 a.m. meeting at the federal building in downtown Denver. There had been several anxious hours the previous day when it looked like they all might be wearing bright-orange jumpsuits for Christmas Eve. A little after four, Agent Felstein and Agent Dearing rang the doorbell and were greeted by the Ballards and the Cannons.

They refused to come in, but had come by to deliver the news that a deal had in fact been worked out with Washington—approved by none other than the US Attorney General himself. The minutiae of the agreement were still in the planning, but the basics were outlined regarding what they were expected to sign the following day. At first Brayden and Dennis had felt it best that the meeting be held at Brayden's attorney's office—a retired FBI agent—but reassurance from Marie alleviated their fear if not the unlikely possibility of a double-cross and subsequent arrest.

The couples rode together in the Ballards' Tahoe, the men in front as was their custom—long legs trumped short ones. The women liked to visit where they could hear each word spoken and the men wouldn't interrupt. Brayden was trying to conjure up some reassurance from Dennis that they were doing the correct thing. Dennis, on the other hand, was still feeling that they were abandoning Wilson Arbon's memory and perhaps his ghost.

"I'm just not good with us letting the guy's murderers off the hook. Somebody still needs to pursue the case," Dennis said for the third or fourth time—Brayden had lost count.

"Agent Dearing insisted that only the local Polish police have any jurisdiction in the case and with all the evidence of a murder gone, there is nothing there that will prove anything," said Brayden. "We need to take whatever deal they are offering and go back home to our families and our normal lives."

The ladies in the backseat already were busy going through lists of presents they had purchased for the grandkids and were oblivious to the conversation in front. Just to be sure, Dennis leaned closer to Brayden's ear. "I don't care who has jurisdiction. I still have friends in high places ... in NATO and the army's intelligence service. If we get anything out of this deal today except a jail sentence, my new full-time hobby is going to be finding everything I can about the Arbon boy's murderers. And when I do, those responsible are going to be held accountable."

Marie dashed out of the front door of the glass-and-granite stone building, having to slow her pace to keep from slipping on the icy walkway in her heels. In spite of the cold she wasn't wearing a coat and looked terrific in her stylish, gray wool knit dress. She had picked it out that morning at Nordstrom's after her boss told her to dress up for the meeting—a press conference was likely to follow. She waved the Tahoe into a parking spot marked "official business only" and pulled the passenger side door open.

"Did you bring them?" she asked—out of breath from the rush.

Brayden nodded in the affirmative as he put the Tahoe in park and shut off the ignition. "Sorry we're a few minutes late. There's a lot of last-minute Christmas traffic. Is the doctor going to join us?"

"Everyone's waiting inside for you. I started to worry that you had changed your minds and weren't coming," said Marie. Having finally caught her breath, she smiled at Brayden and then at Dennis. She opened the curbside door for the ladies and reached out a hand to assist Julie and then Paula who had scooted across the seat.

Dennis was out on the curb stomping snow off of his shoes from the pile of freshly scraped snow when he noticed the high revving sound of a car engine. He looked toward the three women who were hustling out of the cold toward the office building's entrance. He then turned and saw two cars speeding toward him from opposite directions. His reaction was to jump away from the side of the Tahoe's open passenger door. His feet slipped and he fell into a plowed snow bank.

Brayden had just released his seat belt and was fussing with a small shoulder bag that he had worn since they left home. He had the driver's door half-open when a silver, Ford Taurus crashed head-on into the grill of the Tahoe, slamming Brayden's face into the steering wheel. Within the blink of an eye, a second car, this one a black, Buick SUV, came from behind—screeching to a halt beside the Tahoe, clipping the open driver's door, tearing it from its hinges and barely missing Brayden's extended leg. The airbags on the SUV's dash and steering wheel had inflated with a horrendous explosive force, jamming Brayden's body back into the seat and headrest.

The driver of the first car abandoned it through the passenger side and limped toward Brayden's open door. Though he wore a blue-and-white ski hat pulled down over his ears and forehead, and wide-rim sunglasses, he was easily recognized by Dennis from their multiple previous encounters. It had to be the taller of the two Polish mobsters. He produced a small pistol and crammed it into the side of Brayden's neck.

"Give to me the jewels," he demanded in his heavily-accented English as he pushed the deflating airbags away from Brayden's face.

"Go to hell!" said Brayden, turning to face the assailant and then abruptly butting his head as hard as he could into the hoodlum's nose. The gunshot rang out, resonating off the glass and stone buildings.

The driver of the Buick moved around the car to join his brother, whose nose was flattened and bleeding profusely through the open holes in the knitted mask. The two men dragged Brayden out of the car, onto the slushy surface of the street, ripping the shoulder bag up over his head—wrenching his shoulder in the process. Before anyone in the federal building could react, the two gangsters were back in the black SUV and headed down the street, the car fishtailing on the slippery, wet asphalt.

Although Dennis had spent a substantial portion of his early career training combat soldiers to react reflexively in emergencies, his immediate reaction was one of shock, freezing him in his tracks. The sound of the gunshot may have given him second pause. It wasn't until the gangster brothers were entering their car that Dennis ran toward Brayden.

Marie heard the explosive crash of the two cars and then the Tahoe door crunch from the Buick. Thinking correctly, she pushed Paula and Julie into the foyer of the building and then screamed for security to join her. She turned toward the cars, reaching for her gun, but was hesitant to pull it from the holster.

She and Dennis arrived beside Brayden at the same time, pausing in a state of shock as they looked at the injured architect lying in a pile of blood-stained slush. Seconds later, a well-armed security guard nudged them both out of the way. He spoke into his shoulder microphone, calling for paramedics and backup.

Paula and Julie were restrained by security personnel from leaving the glassed-in foyer, thus they had to watch, not knowing what was really going on as Brayden was attended to out of their view. They had heard the sound of the gunshot echo off of the stone walls, but didn't know the severity of his wound. Paula stood in frozen fear.

An ambulance arrived ten minutes later to find security guards, Marie, and Dennis already had straightened out Brayden's contorted body on a blanket found in the back of the Tahoe and covered him with Dennis's overcoat. His face was a plaster of blood, mucus, and airbag powder and he was shivering. Marie searched, but couldn't find a distinct entrance wound from the bullet. "With all this blood it must have hit an artery," she said.

Dennis felt for a pulse in his friend's wrist but couldn't confirm one. Suddenly he was rewarded with a strong reflex reaction and a complaint. As he moved his fingers he had scraped the jagged scar on Brayden's forearm.

"Watch it!" Brayden said. "That thing really hurts."

Dennis smiled as he was pushed aside, this time by a female paramedic who looked more like a tattooed cage fighter. His friend was going to be okay.

The paramedic called for her partner to start an IV while she completed examining the patient. Brayden, now mumbling curses, was loaded into the ambulance and within fifteen minutes he was on his way toward Denver Health Medical Center. Left behind was the wreckage of the cars, a blood-covered roadway, and a score of astonished bystanders including his panic-stricken wife.

It was only because of Dennis's screaming at the paramedics that they allowed him to crawl into the back of the ambulance. As they sped through the busy traffic, Dennis leaned down to Brayden's ear and whispered, "Did they get all of the gemstones?"

Brayden opened his eyes and with a little blood-stained smirk said, "Not even one of them. Just before leaving the house, I stashed the leather satchel into the Tahoe's console in a paper grocery sack. The shoulder bag was a ruse. Forget about me. You've got to get back there and see that someone doesn't get their hands on them."

At the first gridlocked intersection, the ambulance had to come to a full stop. Dennis patted Brayden on the shoulder and said, "I'll see you at the hospital in a few minutes." He stood and climbed over the lap of the tattooed female paramedic. Before she could snarl at him he had opened the back door of the vehicle and was out on the street.

Agent Felstein was on her phone, still standing in the glassed-in foyer, trying to find out to which hospital they were taking Brayden. A number of black-and-white city police cars had arrived, and two of them had immediately left in hot pursuit of the shooter in the Buick. Agent Dearing had come down from the conference room and was shouting orders to the guilty-looking security guards. "How could you let someone be shot right here in front of the federal building?"

The entire time Paula and Julie were wedged into a corner of the glass foyer, staring out through the windows with tear-stained faces at the two severely-wrecked cars, the bloody street littered with first aid packaging, and unconsciously watching the twinkling Christmas lights and falling snowflakes.

Suddenly, Paula gripped Julie's arm and said, "Look down the street to our right."

There, about two hundred yards away, a man without an overcoat was jogging in their direction.

"Oh my gosh!" said Julie. "It's Dennis! Is someone chasing him? I haven't seen him run that fast in years."

Julie and Paula both broke away from the remaining security man guarding the door to the street and dashed outside to meet Dennis who ignored their yells and headed straight for the Ballards' wrecked Tahoe.

"Hey you," screamed one of the policemen who was leaning on the hood of his squad car writing notes on a clipboard. "Get away from that car you idiot. It's a crime scene."

Before he could react further, Dennis had opened the passenger door of the Tahoe, grabbed the paper bag from the console and stuffed it into the inside of his shirt. He turned toward the policeman who was now running toward him and yelled, "Sorry, officer, I forgot my wallet."

Julie cut in front of the officer and threw herself into her husband's arms. Paula joined the group hug and immediately felt the odd bulge above Dennis's waistline.

"Reach in my shirt and take the leather bag," he whispered to the two women.

Before Julie caught his meaning, Paula slid her hand under his blue-and-yellow striped, silk tie and through the unbuttoned opening in his shirt. Her hand slipped over the paper sack with its crusted, leather bag contents, dragging it into the folds of her overcoat.

"Ladies, step away from this man immediately," the officer shouted. "What did you take from the crime scene mister?"

"Like I already said, I just needed to get my wallet." He reached into his hip pocket and retrieved a black bi-fold wallet and held it out in front of the officer. The three of them then turned away from the policeman and the Tahoe, heading for the building's door.

Marie was totally confused about what had just happened and why, but let it go without question and directed the three toward a gray Ford sedan that had just emerged from the federal building's underground parking lot. "Let's get in that car and go find your poor husband," she said to Paula.

There is nothing like a potential gunshot wound to stir up the emotions of emergency room staff. With all the police and medical chatter on the radios, the ER doctor in charge of Denver's biggest hospital trauma center had heard only rumors as to why the patient was coming through the automatic double doors. "There has been a shooting at the federal building," someone yelled over the sound of the vibrating wheels of the gurney. There was a lot of blood splatter on the EMT, who now looked like she was costumed for Halloween. The patient however, looked alert and even smiled at Doctor Bent when she pulled back the blanket covering the man. He was dressed in an expensive suit, white shirt, silk tie, and wore shiny, black oxfords just like her father wore to church. "He must be someone very important," she thought as she searched for the gunshot wound.

"Where did they shoot you?" she asked in a soft, controlled voice, stepping back so the orderly could begin undressing the patient. "Ballard male mid-fifties vital signs stable," called out the freaky-looking EMT, as though she were giving a breakfast order to a cook at the local diner.

"In my car," said Brayden, looking into the doctor's big, blue eyes.

"No, sir. I meant where are you wounded?"

"Just my head—where all the blood is coming from," he said.

"They shot you in your head?" she questioned as she focused her attention on the clotted mass in the hairline and under his nose.

"No dear. They shot me in the car, but I don't think they hit anything but the car seat, maybe the dashboard. Can you do something about the blood dripping in my eyes?"

The attractive doctor rolled her eyes at the orderly and turned to a male nurse who had just entered the room. "Would you please search his entire body for a bullet entrance wound and then send him for a CT. I think he has had a concussion. He thinks he was shot in his car."

"He's going to be just fine," the pleasant Dr. Bent told Paula an hour later. "His X-rays, CT scan, and neurological exam were all normal, but he definitely sustained a concussion. We sutured up a nasty laceration on his scalp and he has some bruising on his arms and chest. Most of the injury is likely from the explosion of the airbags. There is a laceration on his left forearm, but it looks like an old wound that has been reinjured. I was told that there had been gunshots and he admitted being shot, but we couldn't find a gunshot wound."

Paula just nodded her head and listened as the woman spoke and then asked, "Would you possibly keep him overnight for observation? If he is released I'm afraid he will have to go back to the federal building. We are witnesses to some unknown international crime."

Doctor Bent wrinkled her forehead and shrugged her shoulders. "That's what I was going to recommend since he is still confused about what actually happened to him." She laughed and then in a muffled voice said to Paula, "He keeps insisting that he was shot in his car."

"But he was shot in his car," Paula said, turning away from the doctor to find her friends and the DEA agents.

Brayden spent the night in a fitful sleep. The plastic-covered mattress creaked every time he moved and the pillow was like a sack of shredded tractor tires. The retired drill-sergeant nurse refused to give him anything to sleep. "You've had a head injury, deary," she kept repeating over the intercom every time he pressed his call button, seldom bothering to come in to see him. Paula had taken his cell phone.

Agent Felstein arrived at eight in the morning with good news. The police had captured the Polish gangsters at the airport. The doctor at the nursing station said Brayden was fine and could be released to the care of his private doctor. The best news of all was that all charges by the federal authorities against the two couples were being dropped, as long as Brayden, Paula, and the Cannons were willing to sign away any right to sue the government for injuries, damages, and stress caused by the federal agents and the gangsters while on federal government property.

Brayden listened to her explanation and then made

her repeat it twenty minutes later when Paula, Julie, and Dennis arrived to take him home.

"The papers can all be signed early this afternoon—I'll come by your house. Or we can do it next week. After all, Christmas Eve is tomorrow," Marie said.

"No time like the present," said Paula, getting everyone's agreeing nods.

Brayden spent the rest of the morning sleeping in his own bed. He was awakened by the doorbell and heard Dennis's voice in the hallway. A short while later Agent Felstein, Agent Dearing, a generic-looking male court recorder named Earl, and Dennis's attorney brother-in-law all arrived. Brayden's face was swollen and was black and blue around both eyes. His forehead laceration was throbbing where he had crashed his head into the gangster's nose. A new pain had surfaced in his right hip where he supposed he had strained it getting out of the damaged Tahoe, but later was told that the speeding car had actually grazed his leg.

"Small talk is out," Paula said, interrupting the group's polite introductions and comments about the falling snow. "Just give us the papers to read and sign."

It took nearly an hour before everyone was convinced that things were written correctly. The attorney and court recorder were then excused. Paula offered those remaining something warm to drink and then Marie dropped the proverbial second shoe.

"There is still one problem," she said, addressing both couples. "Now that you have been removed from any charges of stealing, smuggling, tax evasion, and any number of other crimes you may or may not have committed, we need to talk about the actual gemstones. I presume you still have them?"

She was answered with four cold stares.

"Don't forget that the immunity from prosecution was for agreeing to cooperate in prosecuting everyone else and because you and your buddies put our lives in danger," Brayden said. "It said nothing about giving you the stones."

"But your Polish doctor, Dr. Vlonovitski, is here in town. She still claims that the gems you found belong to her family, or at least to her country. She wants them back. My bosses all agree that the situation could be turned from a nasty criminal fiasco into a further bonding of friendship between countries."

"Well," said Brayden. "She may want the gems, but I want the last few weeks of my life back, as well as the pain and fear erased from my memory that several people, including Dr. Vlonovitski and her countrymen, caused."

"And, we want to know who killed an American in the onion dome of a Polish church twenty years ago," said Dennis. "When we find out who he is and why he was killed, then we might remember what happened to the gemstones that the doctor desires so much to have returned—if they ever belonged to her family in the first place."

Marie gathered up her stack of the paperwork and asked for her coat. She didn't respond to Brayden or Dennis until she pushed away from the table and stood up. She turned to Dennis and said, "Perhaps you should return to Michigan after the holidays and speak to a certain alumni secretary—I think her name is Wild, or at least it is now. My sources say that she is more involved in your little affair than you might imagine. At one time she was quoted in a local newspaper claiming that her grandmother's name was Anastasia. As in the daughter of the Tsar of Russia who disappeared with the royal family and later appeared claiming she was of that same royal blood."

Dennis responded with a non-committal, "I'll look up her phone number and give her a call, though I doubt she'll remember me."

"So, what about the lady doctor and her claim to the jewels?" Marie again asked Brayden, having played her Anastasia card with little response.

"As far as we are concerned, she will just have to be patient. We're going to celebrate Christmas and the holidays with our families. There are lots of presents to unwrap, snowman out there to be built, and new powder to be skied. What happens next year will just have to happen." With that he limped down the hallway toward his bedroom.

It was a strange feeling for Paula when she awoke in the dark, unfamiliar surroundings of the hotel in Lansing. The first clue that she wasn't in her own bed was the firm pillow. She heard a faint clattering sound coming from the bathroom, so she threw off the heavy quilt, immediately feeling the chill of the room. She rubbed her stiff neck, then stood, stretched, and opened the bathroom door, squinting from the brightness of the light.

"What in the world are you doing? You've already washed those things a dozen times," said Paula.

Brayden was on his knees in front of the tub, elbow deep in bubbly, steaming water.

"If these jewels really do belong to some royal family, the heirs should at least be allowed to see a perfectly cleansed version." He smiled at his wife and continued to pick out individual stones and rub them with a wash cloth. "Sorry for the noise. Why don't you go back to sleep? Our meeting isn't until ten."

"Just fill the tub for me after you're done playing. I can't seem to get warm," she said.

"Want me to leave the pretty rocks in here with you? It might be your last chance bathing with diamonds and rubies."

"No thanks. I didn't like it that much the first time. Please rinse the tub out before you fill it for me. And add some of the bubble bath on the counter."

With Dennis giving driving directions, they navigated the rental car through the snow-lined streets of the Michigan State campus until he spotted the modest sign on the alumni office. The sun had yet to make an appearance, but lights inside the building burned brightly.

The door of the old, restored house gave a tinkle as it was opened and the four friends entered. There was still a hint of pine bough fragrance, and one string of twinkling Christmas lights were still dangling from a couple of nails, out of reach without a tall ladder.

"Please come in," the woman said as she struggled to rise from behind her desk. "I'm Ms. Wild, but then you remember me don't you?" she said, smiling at Dennis.

"How could I forget such a lovely lady?" he said, pouring on charm that raised Julie's eyebrows.

"Why don't we settle around the conference table?" Wild said, motioning toward the far corner of the room. "The others will be here any moment."

"Others?" Paula said.

"Don't you fret now, deary," said Wild, patting Paula's hand. "Everything will soon be as clear as crystal. Would anyone like tea?"

Before they could respond the tiny brass bell on the

front door tinkled again. A cold draft filled the room as two men in expensive, charcoal-gray overcoats entered the room. The last one held the door for a shapely woman wearing a long, tan coat with a red, fox-lined hood. Her hair was worn in long, spiraling waves and her makeup was flawless. It wasn't until she removed her pumpkin colored scarf that the Ballards and Cannons recognized Dr. Andriana Vlonovitski. She smiled at the couples and nodded at Ms. Wild. In her hand she carried a large soft leather purse.

"These men are from the Hermitage Museum," she said to the Ballards and Cannons in a soft, almost seductive voice.

"Good morning to you too," Paula said, trying not to glare at the woman who had brought so much stress into their lives.

Extra chairs were pulled up around the table and all were seated. The older of the two men retrieved a manila folder from his briefcase and set it on the table in front of Brayden and Dennis. He opened it, revealing a glossy, eight-by-ten inch photo of what appeared to be the formal portrait of an Eastern European family. Next, he removed a magnified version of the same photo— zoomed in on the woman's upper torso. She was beautiful, with a smooth complexion, high cheekbones, and a figure even the elaborate beaded dress couldn't hide. She wore a stunning necklace with intricate filigreed gold work holding a large number of precious stones. Even in the black-and-white mode they sparkled brightly and appeared to be of various types—some being darker in color than others. All were at least the size of the stones

Brayden had been toting around for more than four months.

The older man cleared his throat and spoke in a precise English but with a definite Russian accent. "My name is Professor Nike Kruzloff. The woman in the photograph is the wife of the Tsar Nicholas II of Russia, Tsarina Alexandra. Perhaps you recognize her? She was originally from the area of Darmstadt/Hesson, Germany. The necklace she is wearing disappeared shortly after the recovery of her son's life-threatening bleeding episode—as history notes he was a hemophiliac. There was such a panic because his mother thought he was dying. Alexandra's personal advisor—some thought lover—Gregori Rasputin—was thought to have saved the boy's life by demanding that she refuse the doctors' antiquated care. The necklace was never seen again after that emotional week. Many felt that she gave it to Rasputin as a reward or that she made a pact with God not to flaunt her wealth. Who knows? In any event the necklace was the property of the royal family, not her personally. In all photographs of her thereafter, she wore only pearl necklaces."

"You mean before they were abducted and murdered by her fellow Russians," Julie said, surprising everyone else in the room. "So how did the necklace end up in Poland?"

"Of course, no one knows for sure, but keep in mind that one of the titles of the Tsar was the King of Poland. He loved to travel and often made hunting excursions to Poland."

The man smiled at Julie, sending a shiver down her

spine, and then went on explaining each of the stones in detail and how even though the photo was not in color, the type of stones and their size and cut was well known. He then stopped talking and nodded toward Andriana.

She then turned to Brayden. "We know that you have our jewels, Mr. Ballard, I saw you with them in Poland, and others have seen representative, single stones. Mr. Hakes saw them in Colorado. It is now time to return what is rightfully ours."

"If I were to have the gemstones you're talking about, I would probably have no trouble giving them to the proper authorities. But, first I would need to know who they really belonged to and who you really are. Do you have some identification?" he asked.

"Do you have the stones?" Ms. Wild asked, surprising everyone. "As a child, my mother often spoke about the necklace that her mother wore before the revolution. She would cry, saying how she wished that she had at least one of the rubies to remember her mother by."

This revelation startled everyone in the room except Andriana.

"Are you saying that you are the granddaughter of the last Tsar of Russia?" Paula demanded.

Ms. Wild's eyes grew moist as she brought a crocheted hankie from her sleeve and dabbed at her nose and eyes. "I told my nephew to forget trying to find the necklace, but he had his master's degree in Eastern European history. He was fascinated with his genealogy and the history of his ancestors. He kept finding more evidence that the necklace existed. Before my mother died she told him the stories of the family's arrest and of her escape from the Bolshevik monsters. Once he was done with school, he sold his car and much to my disagreement, booked a flight to Berlin. I never heard directly from him again."

The air in the room was stifling hot and yet the atmosphere was ice cold as Brayden, Paula, Dennis, and Julie did the math in their heads trying to remember the dates and stories and rumors about the world famous couple and their demise. Each tried to remember the facts and the fairytale regarding the escape and survival of the Tsar's daughter Anastasia. Of the Tsar's five children, Anastasia had been the only one to have possibly escaped.

"When exactly did your nephew go to Berlin?" Brayden asked.

"It was in the spring of 1989. He sent postcards from Krakow in June and July to his girlfriend. She passed them along to me before she died of cystic fibrosis. He mentioned that he had met the son of a family who he thought had helped his grandmother hide during the first World War. On the edge of the last postcard he made a little drawing of a cluster of jewels—thirty of them in red, white, blue, and green. We had never heard from or about him since then until Mr. Cannon here showed up at my door last fall."

By now the tears were flowing freely, not just from Ms. Wild, but from Andriana as well.

Then she began to speak. "I was fifteen the first time I saw Wilson Arbon. That's the name he gave everyone," Andriana said.

"Arbon was my first husband's name. Wilson was his brother's son," said Wild.

"I was working at a bakery and he liked the pastries we had there. He was a handsome American, dressed in clothes I had only seen in movies and fashion magazines. I had an immediate infatuation for him. He left for a couple of weeks. When he returned he was excited to talk to someone and picked me to talk to. He said he had found out where his orphaned grandmother had lived. I didn't speak good English and he spoke just enough Polish to order food and flirt. Then one day he came to the bakery and talked to me. He was very excited. He said he had found something valuable that belonged to his grandmother. He opened his backpack and showed me a brown leather pouch. He acted like he was afraid, but I didn't know what he was afraid of. Then I saw a man was sitting at the table behind us. I knew he was a member of a local criminal family—you call them Mafia."

"Did he show you what was in the leather pouch or tell you anything else?" Dennis asked.

"Just where he lived in America—in Michigan. I never saw Wilson again after that night. I soon forgot about him and heard nothing until the night I went to the hotel to treat Mr. Ballard. He said he had cut his arm in the attic of the church. That was when I saw the leather pouch on the bathroom floor."

"Excuse me for interrupting," said the man from the museum. "But this conversation is getting us nowhere. We came here to see the gemstones and to make you an offer for them. Let us get on with our business."

"Just relax," Paula said to the man. "Doctor, I have a question for you. There is something here that I don't get.

Ms. Wild and her nephew are descendants of Russians; how are you related and how is it that you now feel your present country, Poland, has a right to the jewels, if in fact they exist? And if you claim that they are Polish property, why in the world did you bring these men from the Russian museum to see the stones?"

At that moment, the second man had had enough talk. He pulled a small revolver from his jacket pocket and pointed it at Paula. He looked at Brayden and spoke for the first time. "This negotiation is very simple. You give to me the jewels or I shoot your wife." His accent was so strong they could barely understand him.

The shock on the face of Ms. Wild was obvious, but Andriana appeared oblivious to the change in tone of the meeting as well as the appearance of a gun. "You Americans just don't get it do you?" she said. "Even that foolish federal agent, Felstein, believed everything you told her and even more lies that I told her. All of those lies and she believed every one of them just like some child dreaming about your Easter rabbit. The truth is, I don't care about Russia or Poland or the Hermitage Museum and I certainly don't care about the five of you. My friends here work for me, just like my two idiot colleagues you met earlier in Poland and in Colorado. I want the jewels for the money. It is all about the money. Maybe that you can understand since that is all it was about for you also."

"But you are a doctor—" Julie started to say.

"Just shut up your mouth. Ever since I was a young girl it was about the money. I led my American lover Wilson to the onion dome of the church and tried to talk him into sharing some of the stones with me, but he said he had sent them home to his mother in America. When I told my colleagues about the jewels they met me and lover boy in the dome and tried to get him to give them back, but he wanted to fight. Unfortunately, he lost and we couldn't find the pouch or the jewels."

"You will never get them out of the country," Brayden warned.

Andriana laughed at his comment and said, "You are a stupid man. You watch too much American television, Mr. Ballard. You think that the good people always win?"

"I don't even have any jewels here," said Brayden.

"That is probably a lie, but is okay. Here is the truth. My friend Misha here is going to shoot Mr. Cannon and Ms. Wild. Then you can go to your hotel or wherever you hid the jewels and bring them back in one hour or he will shoot Mrs. Cannon. If you still haven't produced all of the jewels in another half hour he will shoot your wife."

A gun appeared in the second Russian's hand and then a third one in the hand of the lady doctor.

"Take these two into the storeroom and shoot them," she said.

Brayden's head was spinning. He couldn't imagine how the whole thing had gone so wrong, but was now very glad he had left his iPhone on and connected to the number he had dialed just before the meeting began. He was searching the room for any kind of a weapon and saw Dennis's eyes darting around doing the same thing. They would have to act at the same moment and they would have to do it soon.

Suddenly, the lights in the room went dark followed

by a startling flash of light and a mind-numbing burst of air pressure and noise. The outside door was broken open and the room was instantly filled with armed men in full assault gear. The two Russian men were slammed to the floor and Andriana was grabbed and forced face-first against the wall. The lights came back on as quickly as they had gone off. Through the thinning smoke, Brayden could see Marie Felstein rush into the room wearing a bulletproof vest with the letters "D E A" in bright yellow. With a magician's speed she snapped a pair of handcuffs on the wrists of the blond doctor. A policeman in full combat gear led her from the room as her two partners were dragged outside into the cold January night air.

The flash grenade had left a shattered lamp in the middle of the floor and some broken shards of glass from a trophy case against the far wall. Otherwise the room was in fairly good condition considering it was stampeded by six policemen in riot gear. As the air cleared and conversations slowed, bottles of water were handed out by Ms. Wild. She was once again the gracious hostess.

"Don't you think it's time that you give up on this stupid game you four are playing?" Agent Felstein said as the last of the uniformed policemen and DEA agents left the alumni office. The closed doors finally were letting the room heat up again. Those in the room settled back into the scattered chairs. Marie re-introduced her boss, Mr. Dearing, who had accompanied her on the raid, but he said little, taking a passive role in the debriefing.

As always, the husbands glanced at their wives before answering Marie's question. Dennis was the first to speak. "The reason we pursued this matter in the first place was to find out about the dead man, Wilson Arbon. We now have a confession of sorts as to his demise. Why he was killed instead of just beaten and robbed, leaves a lot of room for speculation."

"I will get in contact with the Polish police and the US attaché to the Embassy, and give them the information we now have about the murder. That leaves just one remaining piece of business."

Brayden shrugged his shoulders. "And what would that be?"

It was all Paula and Julie could do to suppress their nervous laughs.

Dennis stood up from behind the table, interrupting the conversation. "I need to get something to eat and a good night's sleep," he said, taking his wife's arm and helping her out of her chair. Brayden nodded in agreement and stood, followed by Paula.

"What about the jewels!" Marie said, almost screaming. "The Russian government wants them back."

Agent Dearing then took center stage in the conversation. "I don't think there are any jewels that belong to Russia's royal family. I spent a good deal of yesterday doing some research on my own. I have discovered that the photograph of Princess Alexandra wearing a gem-studded necklace was most likely a photoshopped fraud. In every authenticated photo of her during the years of the royal couples' reign, she wore only pearls. There was however, a major jewel theft the same year that Mr. Wilson disappeared. It was in Istanbul, Turkey. Someone broke into the treasury at the Topkapi Palace. A handful of loose stones—actually thirty in number—was stolen from a glass case in broad daylight. There were also two polished and cut pieces of lapis lazuli missing. It was felt that the origin of the stones dated back to the time of Suleiman the Magnificent. I became overly curious about the theft, so I spoke with the curator of the Turkish State Treasury this morning. He was very kind and excited. After a long discussion he admitted that he is willing to offer a reward for the return of the stolen jewels, if in fact they are the same stones. Agent Felstein can assist you folks in looking into that possibility. A word to the wise however, don't you go to Turkey to make the exchange. It's a very volatile place right now. I suppose it has always been that way."

Negotiations took place over the telephone and through the Internet. Using Dearing's original contact in Istanbul, Agent Felstein assisted Brayden and Dennis in setting up a meeting with the Turks. The Topkapi people had insisted on having each stone evaluated, photographed, and a high-quality color image taken from four angles. Strangely enough, the person they commissioned for the task was none other than the now infamous Glade Hakes who was out of jail on bond awaiting a hearing for interfering with a federal investigation.

There was no way Brayden was going to meet with the man again, so by default, the task fell on Paula and Julie to deliver the stones and then sit there for what seemed like hours while he painstakingly polished, weighed, scanned, and photographed each of the stones. When he was finally finished he made a comment to the women. "If your husbands hadn't of been so pig-headed and let me buy the stones three months ago we all could have been filthy rich."

Neither Paula nor Julie made a comment. Hakes

handed the velvet-lined case to Paula and a stack of paperwork to Julie. "I'll send the information to Mr. Abdul in Istanbul just as soon as his bank transfers my commission money to my bank." With that, he opened the locked door and ushered the women into the hallway.

None of the four friends ever had visited the Middle East before. Their expectations were biased by travel shows and *National Geographic*. They were not ready for what awaited them in Qatar. It was a futuristic-appearing city plopped down in the middle of a vast sand dune bordered on one side by a clear, blue sea. From the airport, the skyline of the city was spectacular with its steel-and-glass skyscrapers in every imaginable shape—and yet plodding along the city streets were men on camels.

They were delivered to their hotel in a pearl-white Rolls Royce and shown to their three-room suite by a beautiful woman in an elegant, silk dress. Much to Paula's surprise, the handcuff-like bracelet on Brayden's left wrist had drawn little attention from anyone on the Emirates flight or at the airports. It had been annoying to Brayden and he had switched with Dennis for part of the journey. All four of the Coloradoans had been happy to see the metal case locked in the room safe and to then strip off their travel clothes and relax in the luxury of their private swimming pool. The pool had a fantastic view overlooking the sea and the surrounding city. Six hours later, after a long nap and a light lunch, they received the expected knock at their door.

To their surprise the representative of the Topkapi

was not a swarthy-looking man with a black mustache and darting eyes, but a tall, regal-appearing woman in her mid-forties with blond, highlighted hair. She introduced herself as Ms. Akoury. She wore a tailored, gray suit over a dark-yellow blouse with a plunging neckline, spiked heels, and a matching oversized, banana-colored, leather purse. Her neck, ears, fingers, and wrists were adorned with an abundance of tasteful jewelry.

As they all took chairs around a marble-top dining table, the lady handed Brayden an official looking paper— multiple hand stamps and all—verifying her identity and authorizing her to negotiate an exchange of the Americans' precious gems for an as-yet-to-be-determined reward. Dennis thought the whole arrangement was weird. He had suggested meeting at a bank in New York or London, but the idea of an expense-paid, first-class trip to the Middle East had won out in the minds of Julie and Paula. As for Brayden, he just wanted the whole affair over with.

"My I see the gemstones now?" the woman asked in a kind, but firm voice.

Paula held out her hand in a "hold it right there" motion. "Before we show you anything we would like to know what it is you are offering in exchange."

The woman poured herself a glass of water from a crystal decanter on the dining table. "We have been told that you are in possession of a number of precious stones which were stolen from our National Museum many years ago. They are far more than just precious stones. Each had a province and a legend to accompany it. Some of the missing stones date back to the time of

Constantine the Great, while others are from a more modern era, such as the Great Crusades. Trust me when I say that they are irreplaceable."

"You still haven't answered my friend's question," said Julie, leaning forward in her chair.

"Fine!" Ms. Akoury said, sounding slightly frustrated. "A reward is what you seek after and if the gems are as purported, a reward it shall be. We are willing to have you attend a very special program at the museum at which you will hand over the gems to the President of Turkey. It will be very special. You will be national heroes in my country and of course you will be our guests for your stay in Istanbul."

"That's it?" said Paula, her mouth agape. She leaned back into her chair and rolled her eyes upward in disbelief.

"Oh yes," said the woman. "You also wanted a more tangible reward. The company that insured the gems at the time of the theft should be repaid for their previous remittance. At the time of the theft they offered a reward of about $500 thousand for the return of the gems. Unfortunately, that company is no longer in business—the European Union recession—I'm sure you are familiar."

"That's ridiculous," said Julie. "Just one of the stones is worth ten times that much. We should just keep them!" She looked at Paula and then at her husband. Before they could react, the woman spoke up.

"That is exactly what I would do if it were me—keep them—and that is what I told my superior. Therefore, after much consideration it has been decided that in exchange for the thirty authentic gemstones you should receive the money the now defunct insurance company paid to the museum."

"And that amount is?" Paula asked.

All eyes and ears were on Ms. Akoury.

"Fifteen million British pounds."

After several seconds of silence, Dennis asked, "Would you repeat that number again so I can write it down."

"Fifteen million British pounds," she repeated. "I'm not sure of the exact exchange rate into American dollars, but £15 million is approximately $22 million—plus or minus depending on the day you exchange the funds from pounds to dollars."

Again there was a long silence. Water was poured into the remaining four glasses and sipped.

Brayden stood up and walked into the bedroom. Moments later he returned with the metal briefcase and laid it on the table. He dialed the combination, flipped open the latches, and opened the velvet folder where each stone sat in a small depression. The crystal chandelier above their heads lit up the stones sending their reflections dashing around the room like a rainbow of strobe lights.

Ms. Akoury let out a small gasp of delight.

It took what seemed like hours to verify the authenticity of each gemstone. Paula and Julie couldn't stand the waiting, so they went to an adjacent mall and browsed through shops containing merchandise that they had never imagined being able to afford. They looked at purses and shoes costing thousands and watches costing more than their homes. Back at the hotel room, a second representative from the Turkish museum arrived to double check the findings of Ms. Akoury and to carry out the banking transactions. When the officials finally left the hotel, Ms. Akoury carried the precious stones in the briefcase, which was securely handcuffed to her wrist.

By the time their wives returned, Brayden and Dennis both had accessed their personal bank accounts. They greeted the women and motioned toward the printed copies of their new balance sheets lying on the dining room table. Their poker faces gave no clue as to their present emotions as Julie and Paula crossed the room and picked up their respective papers.

Paula gave the document a thirty-second study and then in a cheerful tone said, "I don't know about the three of you, but I'm starved. Since the room and the food is on the government of Turkey, may I suggest that we dine downstairs in that fancy French restaurant we have all been avoiding. I would like a rare steak, a fat lobster tail with lots of melted butter, and a raspberry crème brulee."

An excerpt from Steven Dahl's latest adventure,
"Missing Mercy"

1

USNS *MERCY* ANCHORED OFF THE COAST OF CAMBODIA

From the shoreline she looked like a thousand other mega-ships that passed through the nearby sea lanes each month—with one exception. She wore a giant, red cross painted on her main stack and on the stern of the 988-foot-long, converted oil tanker. Inside her thick, double-walled hull there lived and worked nearly a thousand men and women trained in a myriad of medical-related skills—ranging from the operating room cleaning specialist, to the navy crew who maintained and navigated the massive ship, to the brilliant and very arrogant neurosurgeon. The USNS *Mercy* hospital ship was capable of saving the lives of her patients, but could she save herself?

Lights had been officially "out" for nearly thirty minutes when Dr. Ian Sorenson awoke to the sound of boots pounding on the metal stairs that descended to the *Mercy's* sleeping quarters. Normally, the droning sound of the hospital ship's diesel engines, along with the constant motion of the ship, would have kept the volunteer plastic surgeon in a deep sleep. Tonight however, the anchors had been lowered and the engines slowed to just enough speed to keep the generators running, and thus, the lights burning. Outside, the glassy water of the surrounding bay offered only a gentle rocking motion. "It's probably just the footsteps of the duty officer rushing to get back to his video game or his late-night coffee," thought Ian, but the sound was nonetheless disturbing.

Sorenson sat upright in his bunk when he heard the next sound, which seemed to be a muted scream followed by more pounding of feet on the stairs. Then there was a heavy clunk. Sitting up quickly while he was in the middle of the three-tier, metal bunk bed was a big mistake. He instantly regretted the reflex reaction when his forehead smacked against the metal frame of the bunk above him, driving him back into his pillow. By the time he rolled out of the bunk and caught his balance, the sounds were gone. He leaned against the metal bulkhead and pressed his ear against the cold steel trying to hear more, but there was nothing. Ian crawled back into his bunk and held up his smart phone to check the time. It was well past twenty three hundred hours. *I'll never get enough sleep now to make it up awake and alert before I'm due in the operating room at zero seven hundred.*

He thought about going to the small TV room at the end of the enlisted men's quarters and hiding out. ESPN and Fox News ran a continuous loop on the ship's internal TV network, but the quartermaster who gave the volunteer medical staff orientation was very specific about the regulations, especially the "lights out" rule. No one was to be roaming about without a valid reason and that included the NGO (non-governmental organization) doctors and nurses. This was after all, a floating United States naval hospital, currently at sea on a mission of compassion, but in a part of the world that was never completely safe. She was fully stocked, staffed, and outfitted with a crew trained to support US military at war and to do so on a moment's notice. The *Mercy* wasn't, however, armed for combat—either offensive or defensive.

For Ian there would be no chance of getting more sleep. Less than five minutes after he crawled back into his rack, he heard the blasting sound of the ships klaxon horn and then the blinding lights in the bunking area came on. The eighty sleepy-eyed men were on their feet trying to wake up enough to figure out what was happening. The active duty navy men began to quickly dress, while the volunteers stood in a cluster, questioning if anyone knew what was happening. The answer was simple: No one had a clue. However, clarification came moments later when an angry female voice was heard over the ship's public address speaker. The accent was unfamiliar to Ian, but the woman's mood was quite clear.

"Attention all crew and patients of the hospital ship *Mercy*. My name is Ruby. I am now in command of your ship. Your captain is standing beside me to verify my orders. I wish no harm to any of you, especially to any of the patients on board. As long as you obey my orders, you will be safe. We will be lifting anchor and cruising for the next few days. Until you are notified differently, you are to go about your normal duties. Do not ... I repeat do not attempt to overpower me or any of my colleagues. We will take this ship to the destination of our choice and you will then be free to continue on your mission. Any sign of resistance or interference will be met with a most severe punishment."

As the woman stopped speaking there was a cacophony of murmuring heard by everyone on board, then another—more familiar—voice came over the intercom. "This is the captain. Please listen carefully. Let me reiterate the importance of staying calm and obeying orders."

The voice Ian heard was in fact the ship's captain, Captain Larry Trent, a handsome, distinguished gentleman in his mid-fifties with tan, leathery skin, salt-and-pepper hair and a matching beard that surrounded his face like the silver fox collar of a Mt. Everest Sherpa's parka. Ian had met the captain that very evening in the ship's dining room and had been favorably impressed with him.

The captain's voice continued, "We have been boarded by pirates from an unknown country. They are heavily armed, but are adamant that they are not here to harm us. They only want our ship's medical equipment and the medicines on board. They say that if we obey their orders and do not try to interfere with their course of travel, they will let us go about our activities while we sail toward the port they have in mind. Once there, they promise to release us and *Mercy*. In the meantime I need all staff both naval and NGO to do what we do best—care for the Cambodian patients already on board. This will include proceeding with the surgeries we have on the schedule for the next two days. This is not a time for individual heroism, but a time to be patient and obedient."

Ian stood frozen on the warm, metal floor of the enlisted men's quarters. His head was swimming in confusion, and his stomach felt as though he had just been kicked. With no warning, he felt the ship lurch forward. The eighty other men in the enlisted quarters were likewise thrown off balance as the ship moved off her anchor. Brandon, a young pharmacist mate from the bunking isle across from Ian's apparently lost his footing completely, falling backward and hitting his head on the metal bunk frame. When Ian bent over to help the man, he felt a boot kick him in the ribs, dropping him to the ground. Looking up he saw the face of a tall, muscular black man whom he had never seen before. He wore a dark red t-shirt and baggy blue jeans. His feet were clad in Nike running shoes.

"Leave him be," the black man's husky voice bellowed. "Let it be a warning to all of you to follow orders. We will not tolerate any resistance."

Ian grabbed hold of the bunk's railing as he looked into the meanest face he had ever seen. The man was holding a long, flashlight-looking weapon, which Ian recognized from his days visiting his uncle's ranch as an electric cattle prod. In his other hand the man held a long, matte-finish dive knife. The pharmacist groaned and rolled over. There was a two-inch gash on his cheek from hitting his face on the bunk railing.

Ian pulled himself to his feet and began assessing Brandon's wound from eight feet away. He knew exactly which suture to close the wound with and where to find it should he be allowed to do so. The rest of the men in the quarters drifted away and continued getting dressed. The pirate yelled a last warning and left for the stairwell leaving the place in a silent state of shock. And then the room lights went black.

On the *Mercy's* bridge things were far from quiet. The previous hour had begun placidly enough, with the watch officer, Lieutenant Jacob Allen, sitting in the helmsman's padded chair, glancing alternatively at the instrument panel showing the various readings of the massive ship's generator. All was running well. Unlike when they were at sea, things were easy to manage. His iPad was propped against the radar screen displaying a slideshow of pictures from his family's previous Christmas activities. His first hint of trouble was when he heard a motion detector warning bell indicating intrusion on the ship's port side. He turned to the twelve video surveillance cameras and saw what looked like a large animal lurking in the shadows near the side of the ship below the lifeboats.

The ship was at anchor several miles off the shore, not in a dock area where a delivery truck or harbor security car might have triggered the alarm. Jacob was alert now, but not inordinately worried. The last time this had happened on his watch, it had been caused by a young bull Humpback whale who had apparently thought he had found a mate as big as his ego. Tonight unfortunately, it was no whale. When he focused the port cameras and hit the floodlight buttons, he saw a black, ten-meter Zodiac boat hiding against the ships waterline and four or five rope lines extending up the side of the ten-story ship. Squinting, he thought he could make out a person halfway up each of the lines. Immediately, he picked up the phone to the captain's stateroom. He was too late.

ABOUT THE AUTHOR

After thirty years of medical practice—delivering more than seven thousand babies—and raising five children with his wife, Paula, Doctor Dahl now splits his time between their homes in the Arizona desert and the mountain peaks of Utah.

Their most recent travels took them to central Europe, where for over a year they managed the medical care of the Latter-day Saints missionaries and researched the health care systems in such fascinating countries as Poland, Romania, Moldova, and Serbia.

These European adventures added to Dr. Dahl's experiences of living on the tiny islands of the Pacific his Vietnam experience on a navy hospital ship, and time spent in a struggling Liberian hospital.

His previous fascination with ranching, flying, scuba diving, sailing, and serving his country as a major in the US Army all add credence and a realistic twist to his stories.

The best days of his life are those spent with his wife and family, especially with their children and grandchildren. With his sixth novel penned, and another taking shape, he and Paula will stay put in the United States for a while to watch the grandkids grow.

ONION DOME
Steven I. Dahl, M.D.
www.authorstevendahl.com

Publisher: SDP Publishing

Also available in ebook format

Available at all major bookstores.

Other books by Steven I. Dahl, M.D.

Chicken Fried Steak, Action-Adventure
HOA Gold, Action-Adventure
Picasso's Zipline, Adventure/Medical Mystery
Onion Dome, Murder-Mystery
Rattlesnake, Murder-Mystery

SDP Publishing
www.SDPPublishing.com
Contact us at: info@SDPPublishing.com

www.ingramcontent.com/pod-product-compliance
Lightning Source LLC
Chambersburg PA
CBHW020321180626
46812CB00001B/3

* 9 7 8 0 9 9 6 8 4 2 6 1 7 *